The Lady and the Lawman

Published by Barbour Books, an imprint of Barbour Publishing, Inc., 1810 Barbour Drive, Uhrichsville, Ohio 44683, www.barbourbooks.com

Our mission is to inspire the world with the life-changing message of the Bible.

 Member of the
Evangelical Christian
Publishers Association

Printed in Canada.

The Lady and the Lawman

4 Historical Stories of Lawmen and the Ladies Who Love Them

Crystal L. Barnes
Vickie McDonough
Annette O'Hare
Kathleen Y'Barbo

BARBOUR BOOKS

An Imprint of Barbour Publishing, Inc.

On Track for Love

by Vickie McDonough

❧ *Chapter 1* ❧

May 20, 1875

The steady, repetitive thrum of the train's wheels, combined with the large meal served at the last stopover, lulled Cara Dixon into a stupor. The trip to Chicago to attend a fashion trade show and visit her sister had ended in disaster, leaving Cara exhausted and her heart aching. She closed her eyes, giving in to the need to rest.

The train's ear-splitting whistle sounded, jerking her awake. She glanced at the terrain outside. Nothing much had changed. How long had she slept? She covered her mouth as a yawn escaped, then managed a ladylike stretch when no one was looking.

She glanced outside again, in hopes of staying awake. The scenery blurred past so quickly it made it hard to focus on anything. She shouldn't have stayed up so late last night talking with her sister.

But she didn't get to see Ellen much these days, and El needed her after the sudden loss of her daughter.

Glancing down, she lifted up the sapphire necklace Ellen had given her. The beautiful blue oval surrounded by diamonds reminded her of a glistening drop of ocean water. The necklace had first been a gift from their great-grandfather to his future wife. She had worn it at her wedding, as had Cara's grandmother, mother, and Ellen. It would have gone to Allison, her niece, when she married, but sadly, that day would never happen now.

Bittersweet as it was, Cara felt grateful to be entrusted with such a beloved family heirloom. One day she would wear it at her wedding. Blowing out a loud sigh, she stared out the window again, thinking about Davis. The only man who'd ever wanted to tie himself to her had up and died a month before their wedding. After nearly three years, the stinging ache accompanied by thoughts of Davis had faded to wishful memories. He had been a kind man and would have been a faithful husband, but Cara had never been certain he was the right man for her. She had agreed to marry him at her father's insistence. Davis made her laugh quite often with his goofy antics, but he never made her heart sing.

Pa told her to quit reading silly romance stories and hunting for another man. Ellen had told her to be patient and that the right man would come along, but none had. Yes, she was only twenty-one—no, twenty-two now that another birthday had passed. Her special day had come and gone without celebration in the sad aftermath of Allison's sudden death.

Cara wasn't quite an old maid yet. Men had been attracted to her auburn hair—so they'd said—but none so far had been able to withstand her stubborn willfulness. Maybe if she had been raised in Chicago or New York instead of the wilds of Texas, she might have grown up into a more refined young woman.

So much for attending finishing school. The only good thing to come of that was meeting Dinah Stewart and her family.

At the far end of the car, the door opened and a shabbily dressed man stepped in. The hairs on her arms instantly lifted. His hat was pulled down low, and he wore a week's worth of scruffy whiskers. He slowly scanned the railcar, and as his gaze drew near, Cara ducked her head. She'd dealt with his type many times at the store. She bent down as if to pick up something off the floor, quickly unbuttoned the top of her shirtwaist, and tried to cram the necklace inside, but her top was too tight.

She sat up and patted her hair as if nothing was wrong, hoping she was mistaken. But the man yanked his gun from his holster, and his gaze turned hard. He pulled a bag from his pocket. "Listen up, folks! This is a robbery. Get your valuables out, and no one will get hurt."

Cara's gut tightened. She couldn't be the one to lose her family's precious heirloom. She had a short while before the man got to her, but she doubted she could remove it without him noticing. That left her one option, and she prayed it worked.

She reached for her reticule and pulled out her pearl-handled Remington double derringer.

Railroad Agent Landry Lomax entered the third passenger car of the train bound for St. Louis. So far things had gone smoothly, but he'd noticed a ruffian eyeing the train at the last stop. He'd been searching for the man but hadn't yet located him. Perhaps the ruffian hadn't boarded the train, but his gut said he had. Was the man merely curious, or was he looking for someone? Or did he have nefarious plans?

He passed an elderly couple that slept head to head. His gut ached at the sight. He had hoped he and Ada would live to be as old as this couple, but his plans for a long marriage had been robbed of him when his wife was shot and died shortly after.

Though that was ten months ago, his heart still ached at the thought of his lovely wife lying dead. Landry drew in a steadying breath and refocused on his job. He was responsible to see that this train arrived in St. Louis without incident, and he aimed to see that happened.

He gave a brief nod to a young woman who stared at him with obvious interest. She lifted her hand and giggled to her friend or sister sitting next to her. Landry nearly rolled his eyes but managed to stop just in time. The last thing he needed was another woman in his life. He had his job and his daughter—and that was enough.

As he approached the door at the end of the car, he noticed a man standing in the aisle in the next car. The man turned, and Landry recognized his shabby clothing. Landry's gut tightened when his eyes landed on a gun in the man's hand. He shook a bag, and a frightened woman dropped something into it. Then he waved the gun toward something, and the woman shook her head. He pointed the gun in the woman's face, her eyes widened, and after a moment, she dropped what looked like a wedding ring in the bag.

Suddenly Landry mentally calculated the cars again, and his chest tightened. His daughter was in the car with the gunman!

He counted the seats on the right to the sixth row but didn't see Lacy. Had she gone to the dining car? He hadn't noticed her there when he passed through, but he prayed that was the case.

He stepped out onto the windy platform, pulled his gun, and waited for the man to get past where his daughter should be sitting.

Allowing the man to get farther down the length of the car might also enable him to slip in without being noticed. His heart pounded. He couldn't let anything happen to Lacy or the other passengers.

When the man moved past Lacy's seat, Landry reached for the door handle. A woman jumped up and said something to the bandit, and then Landry saw her lift a tiny derringer. Was she crazy? She was likely to get people shot, including herself. At least she had distracted the thief. Landry turned the knob and quickly stepped inside.

He moved to the right side of the aisle, hoping the thief wouldn't notice him since he was still arguing with the crazy woman. As he reached midway, he glanced in Lacy's seat. Asleep. His heart slowed a smidgeon. At least with her lying on the seat, she was somewhat out of the way if bullets were fired.

"I'm not giving you my great-grandmother's necklace, and that's final. So get on along before I shoot you."

The thief chuckled. "That bee stinger wouldn't take down a mosquito."

The woman lifted her chin. "Perhaps not, but it could take out an eye."

The bandit actually backed up a step. Landry hunkered down and moved forward.

The woman glanced at Landry, and her eyes widened. He shook his head, hoping she wouldn't alert the robber to his presence. At least she had the smarts to look away.

"So, we have a standoff. I suggest you go before someone catches you. And while you're going, leave that bag behind so I can return those items to their rightful owners."

This time the man laughed out loud. "Lady, I think I'll take *you* so we can have some fun."

Panic shot through her eyes before she steeled them. "I don't think so."

Landry took a final step, flipped his revolver around, and clobbered the man on the back of the head. The thief turned, his eyes rolled up, and he fell backward against the woman. She yelped and pushed at the thief. Then she hiked her skirts, climbed onto the seat, stepped over him, and jumped down into the aisle. Not at all the behavior he expected from such a lovely dressed lady. She shook out her forest-green skirt, still holding the peashooter in one hand, while the car erupted in cheers and applause.

Ignoring everyone, he kicked the bandit's boots then holstered his gun when the man didn't move. Landry handcuffed him and lifted the man over his shoulder. Again, cheers rang out.

The woman behind him cleared her throat. "Here's the bag of loot he collected."

Loot? The woman's speech held a twang more likely found in someone from the southern parts of the country than around here.

He took the bag from her. With the thief apprehended, he moved to Lacy's seat. She sat up and rubbed her eyes, which suddenly widened as she noticed the man slung over his shoulder. "What happened? Who is that lady with the gun? Aw, shoot. What did I miss?"

"Just a robbery. And don't say *shoot*." He leaned closer to her. "Are you all right?"

His nine-year-old daughter flopped back in her seat and crossed her arms, pouting. "I missed all the fun. I can't believe I slept through the only exciting thing to happen on this dumb trip."

Yeah. She was all right. Grumpy as usual. "I need to take this man to the stock car, then I'll be back. Are you hungry?"

"No, but I'm thirsty."

"I'll bring you something when I return. Stay here."

She rolled her eyes. "Where is there to go?"

"Just don't leave this car, and stay off the platforms. They're dangerous."

"I will, Papa. But stop treating me like a child."

He gave her a quick squeeze on her shoulder. "Be right back."

He hiked the man up higher. "Folks, I'm Special Agent Landry Lomax, and I work for the Missouri Pacific. Once I get this man confined, I'll return your goods."

Another round of shouts rang out.

As Landry walked to the rear of the car, his gaze landed on the feisty woman's. Her green eyes locked with his, and his gut twisted. She was quite lovely with her auburn hair and lightly tanned skin, especially dressed in that beautiful green gown.

He narrowed his eyes, shoving away the interest he felt rising within. "You and I are having a talk when I return."

Cara dropped into the seat, her whole body shaking. She didn't think it was her encounter with the robber, because she'd faced them down before, albeit usually with a shotgun instead of a derringer. It was the handsome man's promise of a talk that had rattled her. What would he need to discuss with her? Would he congratulate her for stopping the robbery?

Somehow his cold blue eyes didn't hold that promise.

A throat cleared, and Cara looked up to see a half-grown girl standing beside her seat. Her heart clenched. The girl was only a few years younger than her niece who'd died.

"Could I talk to you? Please, ma'am?"

She imagined the pretty child had gotten her way more than once with those pleading blue eyes and slight pout of her lip. Cara wasn't inclined to reward such actions, but she would like something to take her mind off of all that had happened.

"Of course." She pulled her skirts over, making room on the seat. "Sit down, if you'd like."

The girl's eyes danced. "Can I see your pistol?"

Cara had yet to return her weapon to her handbag. "I was just putting it away." She lifted it for the girl to see then reached for her bag.

"Could I hold it?"

"Oh no. It's loaded. It's not a toy to play with."

The child sat back and pouted again. Did such a thing actually work in getting her parents to do what she wanted?

"I'm Cara Dixon. What's your name?"

"Lacy Lomax. A pleasure to meet you."

"Where are your mother and father?"

Lacy ducked her head, her expression more serious. "My mama died ten months ago."

Cara reached out to comfort the girl. "I'm so sorry. I lost my mama several years back, so I know how much it hurts."

"Papa is moving us to St. Louis. I didn't want to go, but he got a new job and will be stationed there."

Cara studied the other passengers but didn't see anyone looking their direction, as if searching for Lacy. "Where is he?"

"He took the bad man away and will be back soon."

Cara's heart bucked. "The man who apprehended the robber is your father?"

Lacy nodded. "He's a railroad agent now. He used to be a Deputy U.S. Marshal, but he took the job as a railroad agent so he can be home with me more. Only now we don't have a home."

"I'm sorry, but you'll find a new one, and I'm sure in time you'll grow to like it."

"But I don't know anyone in St. Louis. And I won't have any friends."

Cara's heart went out to the child. She'd experienced a similar situation when her father bought the ranch outside of Dallas and moved the family there. "You'll know me."

"I don't really. And I probably won't see you again after we leave the train."

The passenger car shuddered as it slowed to round a curve. Cara brushed back a strand of pecan-colored hair from Lacy's face and tucked it behind her ear. Would her hair darken to the shade her father's was as she grew older? "Did I understand you correctly that you don't have a place to stay?"

Lacy nodded.

"I live at a lovely boardinghouse, and I happen to know there's a top-floor suite with several rooms available for rent. My best friend's mother owns it, and the food is wonderful. The place is called Aunt Pearl's Boardinghouse. Maybe you could mention it to your father."

Lacy's eyes lit up, and Cara realized they were the same shade as Mr. Lomax's—almost identical to the color of the sapphire stone in her necklace.

The door opened, and Lacy's father stepped inside. He shut it and looked down the aisle. Cara wondered if he was checking on Lacy.

Then the man looked at her, and surprise flickered in his gaze for the briefest of seconds before he schooled his features—a thing he probably did quite often as a lawman.

"Lacy, what are you doing here?"

"You said I had to stay in the car, not in my seat."

"I suppose that is true, but I would like you to return to your seat now."

"But I'm talking with Cara."

He cleared his throat. "We do not refer to people we don't know by their Christian names."

Cara wondered if the man was always so stuffy. "We introduced ourselves and have become fast friends, so I don't mind."

He lifted one eyebrow, obviously not used to having people disagree with him. "Nevertheless, return to your seat. The lady and I need to have a chat."

"Aww. . .fine."

"Lacy. . ."

"I mean, yes, sir." She rose and shuffled her way down the aisle, clearly unhappy.

"Would you care to join me on the platform, Mrs.—?"

"It's Miss Dixon. And I'm afraid if I were to venture out to the platform in that wind, my skirts would fill with air, and I'd sail away."

His eyebrow cocked again, but this time he had a humorous glint in his incredibly blue eyes. "I will see to it that you don't blow away."

She wondered how her hair would handle the wind and why he wanted to talk with her out there anyway. "Can't we talk here?"

He glanced at several people nearby—people who were watching them. "I don't believe you want everyone to hear what I have to say."

"Very well." She slid to the edge of the seat and accepted the hand he offered. Her fingers tingled as they touched his, making her frown. She stood, and he walked past her, opening the door. She held down her skirts as best she could and stepped out onto the breezy platform. She pressed back against the guardrail and smashed one hand against her skirts while the other clamped down on her hat. "What did you need to talk to me about?"

His eyes darkened. "Do you realize how dangerous that stunt of yours was? You could have gotten shot or caused other passengers to be harmed. You should have given that man what he wanted. Nothing is worth risking my daughter's life."

Ah. . .so that was what upset him. But how could she blame him when he'd so recently lost his wife? "I'm sorry, but this necklace belonged to my great-grandmother, and I wasn't about to put it in his grubby paws."

"It's not worth risking your life."

"It is to me."

"Was it worth endangering others? Do you even know how to shoot that peashooter?"

She hiked up her chin. "Of course I do. I'm a Texan, and my pa taught me how to shoot when I was younger than Lacy."

"Well, you need to learn to let lawmen deal with thieves." His eyes turned stormy.

"It's my experience that lawmen are not usually around when a man is bent on stealing. I don't aim to let them steal from me."

He muttered something she couldn't quite understand in the noise of the breeze.

"If we're finished here, I'd like to go inside before I become totally disheveled."

"Go. I can see our conversation is a waste of time anyway."

Cara puckered her lips. "Wouldn't you rather your daughter know how to defend herself when danger comes?"

"We're not talking about Lacy."

"Aren't we? I wonder if you'd be so upset if she hadn't been in that car?"

Cara pushed away from the rail, took a step toward the door, and the train shuddered as it turned. She fell sideways, right into Mr. Lomax's arms. Heat rushed to her cheeks, and her hand pressed against his muscled chest. She looked up and caught him staring down.

Suddenly the wind lifted her hat and carried it away. The pins flew from her hair. Strands of auburn whipped around her face, making it hard to see.

Mr. Lomax grabbed her arm and helped her to the door. They stepped inside, and several people turned their way.

Wonderful. Just wonderful. What must they think? She walked outside a lady and returned a hoyden.

❧ Chapter 2 ❧

Cara stepped down from the train and into the crowd at the St. Louis Union Depot. She tightened her grip on her satchel handle, unwilling to lose it to one of the sticky-fingered men or boys who hung around the depot, looking for easy prey.

The odor of the big city swarmed her. Though the stockyards were several hundred yards from the depot platform, the brisk wind blew the scent toward the crowd. She squeezed through several groups of people and hurried to the stairs leading down to the street. She didn't miss the pungent smells of the big city whenever she returned home to Texas to visit her pa and brothers.

As she waited for a carriage to take her to Dinah's store, she glanced back toward the stairs. Her heart leapt. The overbearing man and his sweet daughter were descending. The girl must surely take after her mother.

Cara supposed she could see his point. He had no idea how good a shot she was and that she wasn't afraid to use her weapon when necessary. Most of the girls she grew up with in Texas knew how to shoot at least a little bit.

She turned back to watch for a cab. As usual, the streets were filled with people, buggies, and all types of wagons. Vendors hawked their wares or food in hopes of making a sale to hungry passengers. An elderly woman with a cart lifted a bouquet of flowers for her to smell. "They're lovely, but I'm not in the market for flowers today."

The woman moved on to the next person.

"Look, Papa! There's Miss Dixon."

Cara heard the child but pretended she didn't. After the trauma of her niece's death and burial, added to the long hours of travel, she wasn't up to another battle with the girl's father. Although, in all fairness, the man had probably been upset for his daughter's sake.

She smoothed back a loose tendril of hair. He had caused her to lose her new hat and most of the pins that had held her tresses in place, and now she looked half-dressed with her hair hanging loose. At least she could buy more hatpins at the store. Dinah must be exhausted, having run the place alone for a week.

She lifted her face to allow the warm sunshine to touch her skin. The days she'd spent comforting Ellen over the loss of her eldest child and only daughter had been difficult. The cut Allison had gotten while slicing a ham had festered, and in just a few days, the fever that had forced her niece to bed also took the fourteen-year-old's life. Why did God allow such a sweet, innocent girl to die? She missed her vivacious niece and ached for Timothy and Ellen. Cara wiped the tears that pooled at the corner of her eyes.

Behind her, a man cleared his throat. Cara ignored him, not wanting to risk losing her spot as first in line.

"Miss Dixon."

Him again. She supposed she had to be neighborly even if she didn't feel like it.

"Yes?" She glanced over her shoulder. "Don't you have a prisoner to see to?"

"I passed him on to another agent since my daughter is with me." He studied her for a moment then stepped to her side. "I'd like to apologize for my behavior earlier. I hope I didn't overly upset you, and I'd like to replace your bonnet."

If he thought her damp eyes were his fault, he was sorely mistaken. Perhaps she should let him replace her hat. She had bought the straw touring hat with hand-dyed silk flowers on top, surrounded by a pouf of fabric in hopes Dinah could replicate it for their store. Losing it had hurt, especially since she probably shouldn't have spent the money to purchase it in the first place. But there was no point holding on to what was gone. "There's no need to do that. Besides, I doubt I could find another one exactly like it here anyway."

He frowned. "Well, what about something different?"

She shook her head. "Thank you, but no. I don't need a replacement. I have several at home."

"Very well. I do apologize for its loss."

"Apology accepted." She smiled at Lacy.

"I told Papa about the boardinghouse where you live."

"Oh?" She looked at Mr. Lomax.

"She did, but I assure you that I can find a suitable place for us to stay."

Lacy tugged on her father's sleeve. "But Papa, I want to stay at the one where Miss Dixon lives. She's my only friend in all of St. Louis."

Mr. Lomax gave his daughter a brief glance. Then he sighed. "I suppose it wouldn't hurt to check it out."

Lacy squealed and clapped her hands.

Mr. Lomax held up his palm. "I didn't say we'd stay there, just that we'd look at it."

Lacy's grin didn't disappear. Apparently she knew her father well and expected they would find Aunt Pearl's suitable.

Cara lifted her hand as the horse and carriage drew near. She wasn't sure how she'd feel having the handsome but disturbing Mr. Lomax around all the time. But at least it wouldn't hurt to share the cab. "Would you care to join me in the carriage? I'd planned to go to the store where I work, but I probably should go home and drop my satchel off first. That way I can introduce you to Aunt Pearl."

The man actually smiled, sending her stomach into spasms at how different he looked. "We'd be happy to share your cab. Thank you." He opened the door once the carriage had stopped, took her satchel and set it inside, then handed Cara up into the carriage. Next he assisted his daughter and placed their bags inside.

Lacy had plopped down beside Cara, so now she'd be forced to sit face-to-face with Mr. Lomax. Her stomach swirled. What was it about this man that made her insides flutter?

The next day, Cara followed Dinah Stewart into Stewart's Fashions, the ladies' clothing store that her dear friend owned. Originally it had been a general store, run by her father, but after Mr. Stewart died, Cara had helped Dinah sell off the inventory, buy a boatload of women's clothing and accessories, and set up shop. She had planned to return to Texas, but it seemed Dinah still needed her, and if she left, she'd dearly miss her closest friend.

After shutting and locking the door, Dinah spun around, eyes sparkling. "I've been dying to get you alone. Isn't that Mr. Lomax the dreamiest man ever?"

Cara supposed she'd be lying if she disagreed that Landry Lomax was good-looking, but Dinah didn't understand how overbearing the man could be. Then again, he had apologized and offered to replace her hat.

Dinah set her lunch pail on the counter. "All right. What are you not telling me? I know something is going on inside that head of yours. Did something happen between you two? Something to do with the train robbery that Lacy started to talk about last night at supper before her father shushed her?"

Stalling, Cara took her friend's lunch bucket along with her own to the back room and stored them in the small icebox. Dinah wouldn't be put off for long.

"Oh! I see."

Cara walked into the store area again, glad to be back, even though she hated leaving her sister during her time of grieving. "You see what?"

"You've set your bonnet for him." Dinah smirked and waggled her eyebrows.

Shaking her head, Cara grabbed the duster from behind the checkout counter. "I most certainly have not. He's far too austere and bossy for me."

"Methinks the lady doth protest too much."

"Be serious, Di. I only met the man yesterday."

"If you're not interested, maybe I'll try to catch his eye." Dinah pulled a child's dress from the front window and returned it to the rack. She looked through their stock and selected another one and placed it in the display area. Dinah glanced at Cara. "Umm. . .you're scowling. I guess you *are* enamored with him."

"Not true. And like I said, we just met."

"Haven't you heard of love at first sight?"

"I am not in love."

Dinah strode over and removed the duster from her hand. "Don't move a hair until you tell me exactly what happened between you and him that has you all defensive."

Cara knew her friend was like a starving dog with a meaty bone. She'd never turn loose of the subject unless Cara explained. "Fine. It's quite simple. A man tried to rob the train, and I pulled my derringer on him because I wasn't going to let him steal my great-grandmother's necklace. While the thief was, um. . .laughing at me, Mr. Lomax snuck up behind him and walloped him. That's it."

Dinah's eyes had grown wider with each sentence. "You pulled your gun on a train robber? You could have been killed."

Cara sighed and rolled her eyes. "You know good and well it's not the first time I've stopped a robbery with a weapon."

"Well yes, but that time you had your shotgun, and it was only a half-grown boy who tried to rob us. God must have been watching over you. What would you have done if Mr. Landry hadn't shown up?"

"Fortunately, I didn't have to find out. Are you satisfied now? Can we get back to work?"

"Not quite. If Mr. Lomax came to your rescue, why are you so upset with him?"

"Who said I'm upset?"

Dinah lifted her brows. "I know you well enough to know when someone has riled you. What did he do?"

"Fine. He yelled at me for endangering the other passengers."

Her friend crossed her arms, the smirk returning. "Ah. . .now I see things clearly. You're upset that he fussed at you instead of congratulating you for apprehending the thief."

"Am not."

"Are too."

Cara lips twitched then broke into a smile. "Perhaps you're right."

"You know I am." Dinah bumped elbows with her.

"He also caused me to lose the new hat I wanted you to make."

"No wonder you're angry with him."

Cara reclaimed the duster. "In his defense, he did offer to replace it, but I refused since I wouldn't be able to get the exact same one."

Dinah rolled up the shades on the front windows and the door. "At least he was enough of a gentleman to offer. You should have said yes and replaced that old straw hat you're so fond of."

Cara gasped and feigned hurt. "Get rid of ol' Bessie? Never!"

Dinah laughed. "Sounds more like a milk cow than a hat."

Chuckling, Cara rushed through her dusting. She and Dinah were as close as sisters. Cara's real sister was twelve years older and had always acted more like a mother to her, even years before their mother had died. Cara hadn't known what it was like to have a close sister relationship until she'd left Texas and gone to finishing school, where she met Dinah Stewart on her first day. Though their upbringings had been vastly different, they discovered they were kindred spirits and had been best friends ever since.

"Mark my words, I predict the two of you will be married before the end of the year."

"Dinah. Have you lost your senses?"

"Nope. I think you're smitten."

"Am not."

"Are too."

Cara held up the dirty duster. "Keep that up, and I'm going to shake this all over you."

Dinah hiked her chin. "I'm right about this, and you can't convince me otherwise."

Cara blew out a loud breath. "I do like his daughter, and that's all I like about him." Well. . .there were his lovely eyes and thick dark hair, and his tall height and that muscular chest she'd collided with. And, oh my, when he smiled. . . She spun away from her watching friend, searching for something else that needed dusting. When had she taken time to evaluate Landry Lomax so thoroughly? They'd only spent a few minutes at most together.

She remembered how her stomach had reacted to his nearness. It had never done such a thing when Davis was around. She'd better be careful of her actions around Mr. Lomax, or Dinah would have them married before the month was out.

❧ Chapter 3 ☙

*L*andry sorted papers at his desk in his new office, but his mind drifted. He had enjoyed a leisurely day yesterday, escorting his daughter around St. Louis, eating in what Lacy called a "fancy place," and driving past her new school, even though it wouldn't open for several months. He couldn't help wondering how his daughter was faring with Aunt Pearl today. The elderly woman had been quite kind in offering to keep Lacy while he worked. Still, he'd only been acquainted with the woman a few days and hated leaving his daughter with someone he didn't know well.

His only other choices had been to bring her to work— definitely not ideal—or to allow her to go to the store with Miss Dixon and Miss Stewart, who also offered to keep her. But he had no idea where their store was, so that was out, even if he could entrust the gun-wielding Miss Dixon with Lacy, which he couldn't.

He'd sure be glad when school started.

He looked down at the list of men he would be supervising, trying to see if he could put names with faces. Earlier he'd met two of them as they were on their way to ride the southbound train. After lunch he read over the manual filled with rules that special agents of the railroad were to follow. Most of them seemed reasonable and fairly straightforward.

He glanced out the window at the busy city. This job would be vastly different from riding across the Great Plains and the mountains of the Rockies, searching for outlaws. His new job had some mighty nice benefits, namely, being with Lacy more and sleeping in a real bed at night instead of a seedy western hotel, barn, or under the stars.

As he stared out the window at the people hurrying to and fro, he couldn't help wondering how long it would be before he missed the quiet of the wilderness. Perhaps he already did.

A knock sounded, and he looked up to see a silver-haired man standing at his door. The short man wore a gray-striped suit with the jacket open, revealing a brocade vest. He reminded Landry of the gamblers he'd seen out west. "I see you're settling in."

Landry grunted, wondering who the man was. "You have me at a disadvantage." Not something he experienced often—and something he definitely didn't like.

"Pete Miller. Welcome to the Missouri Pacific." The man strode forward and stuck out his palm.

Landry rose and shook his boss's hand. "Nice to meet you, sir."

Mr. Miller motioned to the chair. "Mind if I sit? My knees give me fits if I stand overly long."

"Of course not. Please sit." Once his boss was seated, Landry lowered his body into his chair.

"I have to admit I had some doubts when our owner, Mr. Gould, told me he was hiring a former U.S. Marshal, but you've already impressed most of the men here, me included, by apprehending a train robber on your way to St. Louis." Mr. Miller nodded. "Good work."

"Thank you."

The man's lips quirked, and he looked to be fighting back a grin. He cleared his throat. "Word has it that you had an assistant."

Landry frowned, unsure who Mr. Miller was referring to.

A smile broke forth on his boss's face. "A pretty redheaded assistant toting a derringer."

Landry grunted again and leaned back in his seat. Did the people here actually think Miss Dixon was responsible for his catching the thief? He rubbed his jaw. "I suppose, in all fairness, I do have her to thank for distracting the robber while I sneaked up on him. But if I hadn't arrived just when I did, no telling what might have happened. Miss Dixon would surely have gotten hurt—or worse. I heard the thief say he was going to take her with him."

Mr. Miller's eyebrows lifted. "Good thing you caught the man. I'd sure hate for a woman on one of our trains to get kidnapped. Stealing watches and money is one thing, but kidnapping someone is far worse. So, the lady was unharmed?"

Landry thought of Miss Dixon on the windy platform with her beautiful mane of auburn hair flying wild, and he nodded. Ever since that moment, he couldn't get the image to leave his mind for very long before it returned, taunting him. He shoved the unwanted thought back again. "Could you tell me what types of problems you've had with the Missouri Pacific trains?"

"A few robbers stealing from passengers, and an occasional gang thinking they can steal gold, but most of our problems are with people stealing livestock and cargo, and pickpockets."

"You ever work with the Pinkertons?"

Mr. Miller rubbed his left knee. "From time to time. Awhile back, there was a rumor that the James-Younger gang might hit the Missouri Pacific, so we had a couple of Pinkertons riding back and forth from here to Kansas City, but nothing happened, so they left."

"I ran into a couple at different times as a Deputy U.S. Marshal. Most were rather hard men."

"That's been my experience too. When we can, we prefer to head things off ourselves before they happen. You'll meet a few men who feed us information in exchange for some coins from time to time. We've been able to prevent several robberies thanks to their help."

"Smart way of doing things, as long as you can trust them."

"So far they've been accurate."

"What exactly do you expect of me?"

"Oversee the four men under you. Assign them duties and train them if you feel they need it. You can be as involved as you want, as long as you get all the reports written up and turned in."

Paperwork. He nearly groaned out loud. He'd much prefer being on the hunt, but that would take him away from his daughter—and being with her was the whole reason for taking this job.

"If you're up for a walk, I'd like to give you a tour of the place."

Landry stood, eager for a reason to leave his office. How was he going to endure weeks and months inside these walls?

Cara laughed as she stepped onto the boardinghouse porch. "Wouldn't you like to be there when petite Mrs. Abernathy walks into the house with that big poufy hat on?"

Dinah giggled. "Oh my. Yes, I'd love to see Mr. Abernathy's expression."

"At least you tried your best to get her to buy something that better fit her small size." Cara shook her head.

"The woman had her mind made up on that frilly bonnet with feathers and birds, and there was no changing it."

"So true. Remember when you ordered that monstrosity, and I assured you we'd never sell it?"

"I was beginning to think you were right. I have to say, I'm glad to be rid of it." Dinah closed the front door. "I suppose you're going riding since it's my day to help in the kitchen?"

Cara nodded. "But I'd like to see how Lacy and your mother got along first."

"Me too. And I could use a snack." Dinah headed through the dining room to the kitchen on the left side of the big house.

Cara followed, lifting her head and catching a whiff of something sweet Aunt Pearl was baking. Dinah's mother made the best desserts she'd ever tasted. Even Cara's own mother hadn't been as accomplished a cook as Aunt Pearl.

They crowded into the kitchen where Aunt Pearl and Lacy were sitting, eating cookies and drinking milk.

"You two are just in time, although you'll not find a seat in here." Pearl pushed up and retrieved a pair of saucers from the big floor-to-ceiling shelves that held the yellow-rose-patterned dishes used at the boardinghouse.

"I don't need a plate since I'm going riding. I'll take two cookies along with me."

Aunt Pearl handed her daughter a saucer. "I baked your favorite, Cara. Jumbles."

"I see. My mouth is watering." She loved the sugary cookies

with a hint of nutmeg and cinnamon.

"What are you riding?" Lacy lifted her half-filled glass to her mouth and drank.

Cara took two jumbles from the plate. "I have a horse."

Lacy's blue eyes widened. "Truly? Where is it?"

"In the pasture behind the house."

"Can I see it? I love horses." The girl glanced from Cara to Aunt Pearl.

"Do you still need Lacy to help you?" Cara asked.

Aunt Pearl swatted her hand in the air. "No, dear. Lacy has worked hard today and deserves to do something fun."

"Yippee!" Lacy clapped her hands.

"Finish your snack, and I'll run upstairs and change clothes. Then we'll go visit Honey."

"That's your horse's name?"

Cara nodded as she bit into a cookie.

"She's a dun—that's a golden-colored horse—with a black mane and tail," Dinah offered as she placed three cookies on her plate. "I'll go upstairs and change too, then I'll come back down to help you with supper, Mama."

"All right, sweetheart. The water for the chicken is boiling, so I'll go ahead and get it cooking. You can help me make the dumplings and the side dishes."

Cara hurried up the stairs with Dinah following at a slower pace.

"What are you going to do if Lacy wants to ride Honey?" Dinah called up to her.

"I hadn't thought of that, but what could it hurt to let her ride?"

"Lacy's father seems rather protective of her. He didn't even want her going to the shop with us."

That had stung. But considering how upset Mr. Lomax had been after the train incident, perhaps she had cause to be concerned. Cara paused at the landing and faced her friend. "Do you really think he'd mind? Of course, I wouldn't allow Lacy to ride alone, and I'd have control of the reins."

Dinah shrugged as she passed her. "It's your life."

While Cara changed clothes, she pondered her friend's comment about Landry Lomax being protective. But wasn't that a father's duty? Her own pa nearly had an apoplectic fit when she'd told him she wanted to return to St. Louis after completing finishing school to help Dinah when her father had the stroke. Pa's plan had been for her to help out at the ranch until she got married.

She stepped into her split skirt and then tucked in her blouse. Pa had approved of her attending finishing school because it had been her mother's deepest wish for her. She glanced at the image of her parents on the dresser. Mama had been a true southern belle, born and raised in Georgia. "All young ladies attend finishing school," she had said.

Pa allowed it because Cara had been well supervised at the school. Even though several years had passed since she'd completed her time there, he still didn't like her out of reach. She knew it was because he loved her, not because he wanted to keep her corralled. He simply didn't like her being in such a large town without him to watch over her. But she was a grown woman now—twenty-two years old. She smiled as she left her room and closed the door.

Lacy must have been listening for her, because she was waiting in the entryway, bouncing and smiling. "I'm so excited. Papa lets me ride with him once in a while, but it's never for very long. How old is your horse? How long have you owned her? Does she have a baby?"

Cara smiled at the enthusiastic child. "Which of those would you like me to answer first?"

"I'm sorry. Papa teases me that I should have been a squirrel because I hop around and chatter so much."

Cara draped her arm around the girl's thin shoulders and turned her toward the rear of the house. "I, for one, am glad you aren't a squirrel. You couldn't go riding with me if you were."

Lacy giggled. "You're right. I couldn't."

They walked through the house then out the back door and across the porch. The backyard was covered in wildflowers of all colors. Aunt Pearl loved her flowers and used them in small amounts to make pretty bouquets that dotted the downstairs area.

Cara pointed to her right. "That's the carriage house, and the pasture is behind it."

"Does Honey stay out all day?"

"Usually she does when the weather is nice. When it's cold, I put her in a stall with Aunt Pearl's two horses."

Lacy flipped her braid over her shoulder. "Why does Aunt Pearl have two horses?"

"To pull the buggy. Sometimes we need to take our guests to the train depot or somewhere else."

"Oh, I see. How come she didn't pick you up the other day?"

"I told her I'd find my own way home." Cara smiled and reached for the pasture gate. "You sure are inquisitive."

"I know. Papa tells me that too."

"You stay here until I get ahold of Honey. She won't hurt you, but horses can spook easily, by something as common as a skirt blowing in the wind."

"All right." Lacy bounced on her toes. "I'm so excited."

"Try not to move too much when you're around horses."

"Oh. All right."

Cara shut the gate, put two fingers in her mouth, and whistled, but Honey was already trotting toward her. She loved the mare so much. For years Honey had been her closest friend.

"You've got to teach me how to do that. Papa used to whistle songs before Mama died, but he hasn't in a long time."

"I'm sorry, Lacy. It takes a man a long time to grieve over the loss of his wife. My pa still misses my ma, and she's been gone nearly five years now."

"Sometimes I wonder if he'll ever stop missing her. That's why we moved. He wanted to get away from the house where we lived in Denver because it had too many memories."

Cara took hold of Honey's halter and patted the mare. She understood how getting away could help a person heal. She hadn't wanted to leave her family's ranch, but once she got to finishing school and made some friends, she found it easier to heal because she didn't see her ma's touch in everything around her.

"So, this is Honey. To answer your questions from earlier, she's fourteen, and I've owned her for twelve years. She has had three foals—a colt and two fillies."

"What are those?"

"A colt is a male baby horse, and a filly is a female. Foal can refer to either one."

"Wow. Where are the babies?"

"One of them is back at the ranch, and we sold two of them to other ranchers."

"Didn't it make Honey sad when you sold her babies?"

"They were mostly grown-up by then, but it may have made her a little sad to say goodbye."

Cara opened the gate and led Honey to the carriage house.

"Before you ride a horse, you should groom her to make sure she doesn't have any burrs or stickers that could hurt her once the saddle is on. Would you like to help?"

Lacy eyed the mare. "She's awfully big."

"As long as you're quiet and don't make sudden moves, she's as gentle as a kitten. But you don't have to help if you don't want to. Although, if you ever get your own horse, you'll need to be able to care for it."

"I guess I could try. Papa let me brush his horse's mane a few times."

"Well, there you go. You can be in charge of Honey's mane today."

They made quick work of grooming and saddling Honey, and then Cara led the mare outside. "I'll get on first then ride her over to the chopping block. Do you think you can get up on it?"

"Sure." Lacy started to clap her hands then stopped. "I remember what you said about sudden movements."

Cara's plan worked perfectly as she helped Lacy onto Honey's back. "Wrap your arms around my waist and hold on. We'll go slow at first." She clucked to Honey, and the mare started walking alongside the house.

"Oh boy! This is fun. We're up so high."

Cara guided Honey down the quiet residential street. She would miss the longer ride she normally took, but today she'd keep it short because of Lacy. She didn't want the child to get sore muscles from riding too long.

About fifteen minutes into the ride, Lacy leaned forward. "Can we go faster?"

"You'll have to hold on tight."

"I will."

"We'll give it a try, but you be sure to holler if you feel like you're slipping."

"All right."

Cara turned her mare around and nudged her to trot.

Lacy giggled. "This is bouncy."

"Hold on. We're going faster." She softly kicked Honey again, and the horse broke into a gentle lope. She never rode her any faster in town because there were too many things that could happen, like a child running out into the street. Honey had been a cow pony back at the ranch and could stop on a dime if need be, but Cara didn't want to take any chances with Lacy.

As they neared the boardinghouse, Cara slowed Honey to a walk. Mr. Lomax strode off the porch where he'd been sitting, and he didn't look happy.

❧ Chapter 4 ❧

Landry slammed the front gate open and stood there with his arms crossed and a scowl on his face. "Just what do you think you're doing?"

Miss Dixon tugged back on the reins, and her horse stopped. "We merely went for a short ride."

"Get off, Lacy." Landry assisted his daughter down. "Run along inside, sweetie, and get cleaned up for supper. I'll be there in a few minutes."

"I had fun, Papa. Please be nice to Miss Dixon."

Landry narrowed his gaze and flicked his head toward the house. He held the gate open to the short picket fence that surrounded the front yard. "In with you."

"Yes, sir."

Lacy passed through the gate and walked slowly toward the

house. Suddenly she spun around. "Thank you, Miss Dixon. I had a delightful time."

"You're welcome," the vixen called out as she dismounted. As soon as the door shut, she strode around the horse. "Why don't you want Lacy to have some fun? She worked hard today helping Aunt Pearl and deserved to get outside and do something she enjoys."

Landry closed his eyes and took a deep breath as she finished her assault. Eyes open again, he stared at her. "I lost Lacy's mother. I don't want to lose her too."

"I'm very sorry about your wife. I lost my mother, but you don't see my father trying to keep me corralled in a snow globe."

Landry huffed a sharp laugh at the thought. "I'm not trying to keep Lacy locked up that tight."

"Aren't you?"

"She's my daughter, and it's up to me to keep her safe."

"But if you don't give her some freedom, she'll end up resenting you. We merely went on a one-mile ride. I've been riding almost my whole life. What do you think could have happened?"

"For one, we only recently met, so I know next to nothing about you or what your experience is. Two, you didn't even ask me if I minded."

Miss Dixon stepped closer and lifted a finger. "One—it just sort of happened, because Lacy overheard me talking to Dinah about riding. Two—you weren't here to ask, and I only had a short time I could ride before supper." She hiked her chin, her pert nose tilting up.

The thought that he'd like to kiss those puckered lips shot through him as fast as a bullet. He took a step backward.

She blinked and looked away, as if she'd read his mind. "I'm sorry for upsetting you—again. It wasn't my intention. I probably should have asked you if you minded, but like I said, you weren't here."

"Well, I'm here now. What other things do you have planned for my daughter that I need to know about?"

She blinked again, looking confused. "Um. . .nothing at the moment." Her horse stamped its hoof, as if bored with their conversation.

"In the future, please consult me when you do."

"Fine." She spun around and leapt up on her horse, faster than most men could, reined the creature around, and galloped down the street. He couldn't help but watch her go. She did sit the horse well.

Why on earth had that thought about kissing her flashed through his mind? She was far too young for him—and too impetuous and argumentative.

The image of her hair flailing around her reminded him of a wild mustang he'd once seen in Wyoming. Beautiful, exactly as Miss Dixon was. He shook his head to rid it of the thought. There was no denying Miss Dixon was lovely, especially with those green eyes flashing, but he didn't like feisty, troublesome women. Ada had been sweet and quiet. If he were looking for another wife—which he wasn't—he'd search for one like Ada. Dinah Stewart seemed more similar, but it wasn't Dinah who had haunted his dreams the past couple of nights.

Two days after the horse-riding incident, thoughts of Mr. Lomax still pestered Cara. She pricked her finger with a pin and jerked it away from the dress she was pinning together. She stuck the finger in her mouth to suck away the blood. Good thing Dinah wasn't around, or she'd be running out back to upchuck.

Blood was a common thing when you lived on a ranch, but she sure didn't want to stain the fabric. She walked away from the piecing table to stare out the window for a few moments until her finger stopped bleeding.

She bristled as she remembered the tongue-lashing she'd gotten from Mr. Lomax. The gall of that man to lecture her when all she'd done was give a little girl a chance to have some fun.

She blew out a loud breath. Thinking about how Mr. Lomax had lost his wife took the starch out of her. Lacy was all he had now, and it was understandable that he was afraid to lose her. Perhaps she could help him find a balance in protecting his daughter and allowing her to be a normal child.

If only he'd been nice about the whole thing instead of lambasting her. She longed to befriend Lacy, but she didn't want to keep having run-ins with her father. Supper that night had sure been awkward. At least he had tried to be more cordial the past few evenings.

With the blood dried, she returned to altering a dress for Mrs. Whitlow, one of their regular customers. She almost had it done when the bell jingled.

She straightened and looked right into the face of Mr. Lomax. What in the world was he doing here? She hoped he hadn't come to chew her out again. She smiled, even though it took effort. Although she did have to admit he looked mighty fine in that black gunfighter coat, which was shorter than the popular frock coat, with matching pants and waistcoat. The western hat he wore suited him much better than the derby most men in town wore. "Welcome to our shop. What brings you here today?"

He plucked off his hat and glanced around, looking a bit uncomfortable among all the ladies' fashions and unmentionables.

He cleared his throat. "I wanted to see your store. Lacy is needing some new things for when school starts. I also noticed some of her dresses are getting short. Do you sell clothing for girls or only women?"

"We mostly sell ladies' clothing. We do have a few girls' dresses, but I don't think we have anything in Lacy's size. However, we can always make a dress. We'd love to sew some frocks for Lacy. Do you know what style and color of fabric she would like?"

She walked over to where a pattern book lay on the counter and opened it to the girls' sizes. "This pinafore would look darling on her. And there are some new popular colors for girls' dresses like plum, navy, and plaid."

Cara looked up to find Mr. Lomax pinching the bridge of his nose. She raised a brow. "I don't suppose you've shopped much for Lacy's clothing in the past."

"No. Her mother always saw to that task. But I need to now."

Cara cocked her head, unsure what he would think of her idea. "Would you consider letting Lacy come to work with Dinah and me for a few days? That way we could show her our catalogs with the various styles and let her pick out the patterns and fabric she likes, with our guidance, of course."

He looked around the shop. "Where is Miss Stewart? Do you often work alone?"

"Dinah ran out to get some lunch for us. She overslept, and we didn't have time to fix anything at home. And no, usually both of us are here, except for when we need to run an errand or make a delivery."

"What would you do if a man barged in here and demanded your cashbox?"

She resisted rolling her eyes. He was being overly protective again. "For one, most men wouldn't be seen dead in our shop. And two"—she walked around the counter and picked up her shotgun—"I have Mable here for protection."

His eyes widened. "Do you even know how to use that thing?"

Cara set down the shotgun and placed her hands on her hips. "Haven't you ever been to Texas? Shooting is a way of life down there. I've hunted with my father and brothers, chased down rustlers, and even won several shooting contests at the county fair. So. . .yes, I know how to use this. I tried to explain on the train that I know how to handle weapons." But he wasn't really listening then. She hoped he was now, because she didn't plan on explaining it to him again. "Lacy will be perfectly safe here."

He lifted one eyebrow and pierced her with his beautiful blue gaze. "I'll acquiesce that you can shoot. I'll consider allowing Lacy to come here with you. I know nothing about female fashion, except for noticing how pretty a lady looks in a fine garment."

He stared at her so long, she felt her cheeks burning. Surely he wasn't flirting with her.

"Um. . .very well. How much of a budget do I have to work with?"

"I trust you not to go overboard. Just prepare what she needs for school and the next few months. Start with three or four warm-weather dresses for now, then later we'll get several wool ones." He glanced toward the ladies' undergarments then back quickly. He swatted his hand that direction. "And get whatever unmentionables she needs. She could probably use another nightgown also."

Cara clapped her hands. "This will be fun. I have to admit that I thought Dinah was a bit off her rocker when she wanted to start a fashion shop, but it's worked out well. I would much rather be riding the range, herding cattle than sewing, but I can do it for now."

"Why are you here if it's not where you want to be?"

She walked around to the other side of the counter and leaned against it. "I met Dinah and her mother when I attended finishing school here. Dinah became the sister I never had. Shortly after we graduated and I returned home, I got a telegram saying her father had suffered a stroke. I rushed to her side to offer support as soon as I could. After he passed, Dinah needed help running her father's general store, which she'd decided was too much for her. We clearanced the general store stock, refurbished the inside of the building, restocked it, and opened the dress shop."

"How much longer will you stay?"

She shrugged. "Not sure. Pa wants me to return home and get married."

His eyes widened. "Is there someone waiting for you in Texas?"

She shook her head.

"Don't you want to get married?"

"Sure, but nobody in Texas interests me."

"Nobody in the whole state?"

She flashed him a patronizing look. "You know as well as I do that I don't know every man in all of Texas."

"That's true." He smiled, and her heart jolted.

"Do you plan to live in St. Louis the rest of your life?"

"Probably not." He walked over and leaned his hip against the counter, facing her. "I'd had high hopes for this job, but I'm not cut out to work in an office. There are some freedoms in my work schedule, but that means I'd either have to work nights or ride the trains, watching for outlaws. Neither of those are good options since I have a daughter."

"Maybe it will make things easier to know that we don't mind helping out. We all enjoy Lacy."

He stared at her again, setting her heart beating like a windmill in a storm. "Thank you. I think I may have misjudged you, Miss Dixon."

"We did meet in unusual circumstances."

"True again."

"Since we see each other so often, do you think we could dispense with surnames?"

After a long moment, he nodded. "I'd like that. . .Cara."

"Thank you, Landry." She curtsied, and the door flew open.

Dinah entered the shop and stopped suddenly, gawking at them with her mouth open.

Cheeks blazing, Cara straightened and rushed over to snatch the box of food from her. No telling what Dinah was thinking. "Good, I'm starved."

"Miss Stewart." Landry nodded to Dinah then made his way to the door. He paused and glanced back at Cara. "Shall we tell Lacy at dinner?"

"Yes. That would be fun."

"Good day then, ladies." He replaced his hat and closed the door behind him, jingling the bell.

Dinah hurried toward her and laid her reticule on the counter. "What was *he* doing here? What are you going to tell Lacy at dinner? And why in the world were you curtsying?"

❧ Chapter 5 ❧

*M*onday evening, Landry stood in the shadows of the ticket agent's booth with a clear view of all but the far-left side of the depot platform. With tickets sold for the final train, the last agent working had blown out the lanterns and gone home. Less than a dozen passengers milled about, waiting to board. Because livestock was shipped regularly on the late run, most passengers preferred to travel during the day.

The sun had set over an hour ago, and although late spring, the evening was still warm, especially in the small office with the doors and windows shut. A bead of sweat ran down his temple. Landry moved to the south window that faced the darker side of the depot. With the stairs leading to the street on the north side, few people ventured to this area after dark, which made it the perfect spot for a thief to lie in wait. He watched the dozen passengers waiting for the train.

In the past few weeks, pickpockets had stolen from a number of people waiting on trains and those disembarking. From eyewitness reports, the thieves were mostly kids. Fast kids. His heart went out to the homeless children who roamed the streets of St. Louis, but he couldn't let them prey on passengers. It was his job to protect the railroad's clientele.

He wondered if Lacy or the ladies of the boardinghouse were upset that he wasn't home. He should have sent a note that he'd be working later this evening, but he hadn't thought the train would be nearly an hour overdue. He prayed Lacy wasn't too worried.

Sweat ran down the sides of his face. Although not exactly proper protocol based on the Missouri Pacific guidelines, he removed his jacket. Immediately, he felt cooler.

A scuffling sound drew him to the south window. Someone whispered. He needed to be on the other side of the window to see, but he didn't want to risk them hearing him moving about. He couldn't quite make out what they were saying.

He tiptoed back to the door, which he'd left unlocked. His heart pounded at the thrill of the chase—something he hadn't felt since hunting down the robber on the train ride to St. Louis, where he'd met Cara. Instantly the image of her on the platform rose up, taunting him. He scowled, forcing the thought into the recesses of his mind. Thinking about the lovely vixen at a time like this could get him shot—or worse.

He thought about rushing out and surprising the pickpockets. It would be a simple thing to sneak out and grab one of them, but he needed to catch them in the act. He had to have evidence of the crime.

One of the pickpockets passed in front of the door in full view of the window. Landry hugged the shadows in the corner of the office. If he edged forward, he could see nearly all of the depot. He waited for the second person to pass, but no one did. Perhaps the kid had merely been talking to himself, trying to build up his nerve.

Landry watched the boy dressed in shabby clothing stroll over and sit on the bench. Leaning hard against the wall, he could just barely see the kid's legs. He hadn't looked much taller than Lacy as he passed by. What was he waiting for? For more passengers to arrive? Or was he sizing up those waiting, deciding on his prey?

Studying the passengers, Landry attempted to figure out who the kid would go after. A woman whose handbag dangled from her wrist was probably the easiest prey, but women didn't generally carry as much money as men. Although women also rarely gave pursuit once they'd been attacked. An elderly man standing next to a white-haired woman in a brown dress looked like easy pickings too.

A loud whistle indicated the train was finally arriving. Landry eased toward the door and slowly pressed down the latch. It made a soft click, but he doubted the kid could hear it over the noise of the train's brakes. He eased the door open an inch, ready to rush out the second the kid made his attack. He silently urged him to make his move before more people flooded the depot.

The boy rose. He eased to the right, which gave him a clear path to the woman holding the handbag. The lady lowered her arm, and the kid charged forward.

Landry bolted out of the office, partially hidden by a large man who had just moved from the other side of the platform.

The boy snatched the handbag from the woman. She screeched as the kid raced straight toward Landry. He reached out to grab him. The boy darted to his right. So did Landry. Panic filled the child's eyes.

Suddenly the kid slowed. Landry reached for him, but the boy spun around in a fast circle, causing him to miss. Landry adjusted and chased the boy around the dark corner.

He reached for the kid's tattered shirt. Snagged it and heard a rip. Then, without warning, pain radiated across the back of his head. He stumbled and turned, reaching for his gun as he tried to get his eyes to work right. A shadow flew in his direction. More intense pain. Landry felt himself falling into a fog.

Cara slapped her book shut and glanced at the mantel clock in the Lomax's parlor for the twentieth time, at least. Where was Landry? Supper had come and gone. She'd managed to get Lacy, who'd been more than a little concerned about her papa, into bed. Cara had to read to the child to get her to fall asleep. That was over an hour ago, and still no Landry. She hoped no harm had come to him.

She yawned, more than ready for her own bed. Morning was sure to come before she was ready. Rising, she ambled around the large third-floor parlor in hopes of staying awake. The suite, with its two bedrooms, a small washroom, and large parlor, was perfect for Landry and Lacy.

The room looked much as it had before the pair moved in. A modest fireplace lined the back wall, with a pair of blue-and-cream brocade chairs facing it. A darker blue sofa sat on the right side of the room with a drum table beside it, holding a lamp. On the left was a table with four chairs, where a boarder could eat or write letters.

Most of Landry's and Lacy's personal belongings were probably in the bedrooms. While in Lacy's room, she'd glanced at the picture sitting on the dresser of Landry and his wife. She'd been surprised, because Ada had looked a bit homely, when in her mind she'd seen Landry married to a beautiful woman with sable hair and dark eyes. How she'd formed that particular image, she had no idea. Ada must have been very kindhearted and sweet. Cara suspected Lacy took after her mother in many ways.

Not that Landry wasn't kind; he was just businesslike. He had, however, softened a bit, especially the day he visited her at the store. He hadn't yet said Lacy could join her and Dinah, but she felt like he would soon.

She heard a noise downstairs and rushed through the open door to the third-floor landing. The front door opened, and two men entered. Her heart lurched. Then she recognized one man as Landry—and he was being helped by the other person.

She gasped. Had Landry been injured? Cara hurried down the stairs, stopping at Landry's side. She took a quick moment to search for a wound and to catch her breath. Then she asked, "What happened?"

The man assisting Landry touched the brim of his hat. "Now I can see why you wanted to get home instead of going to the doctor."

Landry grunted and pushed away from the man. "Don't need a doctor."

Cara wasn't so sure of that. "Thank you for bringing him home, Mr.—?"

"Holmes, ma'am. Ebb Holmes."

"We're in your debt for assisting Mr. Lomax."

"It was worth it to see your pretty face."

Landry straightened and narrowed his eyes at the man. "I

appreciate your assistance, Holmes. See you tomorrow."

There was no mistaking the dismissal in Landry's tone. The man took the hint and backed toward the door.

"Wait!" Both men turned toward Cara. "Would you be so kind as to inform Landry's superior that he may not be in tomorrow?"

Landry lifted a brow, then winced. Cara noticed a trickle of blood oozing down his forehead from beneath his hat. "I'll be fine in the morning."

She hiked her chin. "I'll be the judge of that."

Landry shook his head while the other man chuckled.

"I'd be happy to tell the boss that Mr. Lomax has taken to his bed."

Landry grunted again, although it almost sounded like a growl. Was there some kind of tension between the two men?

Cara let go of Landry and made her way to the door. "Thank you again, Mr. Holmes."

He nodded and turned toward the porch stairs. Cara wasn't certain, but she thought he said something about "meeting his match."

She shut and locked the door, then hurried to Landry's side. "Can you make it to the kitchen?"

"I'm not dead, you know."

"Thank the good Lord for that." Cara took his arm and guided him through the dining room into the kitchen. She pulled out a chair, and he dropped down a bit harder than she'd expected. Exactly how badly was he injured?

"Pie. I smell pie."

She smiled. Evidently he wasn't too bad off if he had food on his mind. "If you'll be so kind as to remove your hat, I'll gather the medical supplies."

51

"It's nothing. If I could have a cup of coffee and something to eat, I'll be fine."

Cara set the basket of medical supplies on the table then hurried to the stove and poured him a cup of coffee. "We kept a plate on the warmer for you, but since it's been there so long, I don't know how good it will be."

"Boot leather would taste good right about now."

Cara smiled. At least he could joke, so he mustn't be hurt too badly. She got a clean cloth and dipped it in the bowl she'd prepared, then walked over to Landry. He laid his hat on the table and glanced up, and she froze. She'd never been quite this close, staring him in the face before. She swallowed the knot in her throat and reached out to wipe the stream of blood off his face. "What happened?"

While she rinsed the cloth, he took a slow drink of coffee. "I got bushwhacked."

"More details, please." She needed to keep him talking so he wouldn't notice how her hand shook at being so close to him and touching him. She gently parted his hair and found a raised bump the size of a pecan along his hairline. "How did you get this?"

"I was chasing a pickpocket, and someone clobbered me on the back of the head. I think I got the bump on my forehead when I fell down."

"There's another wound?" She moved around behind him, taking the lantern with her so she could see. She set it on the stove. "Lean your head down."

Blood had run down his neck and onto his shirt. Quite a bit of it. She ran her hands through his hair and found a knot the size of a hen's egg. "Oh my! Who would do such a thing?"

"Someone who had no qualms about robbing our passengers. The pickpocket was a kid about Lacy's age. Thought he was alone, but I was wrong. Someone clobbered me just as I got ahold of the kid."

Cara's heart went out to the many orphans that roamed the streets. But she knew better than to try to help them on her own, lest she become their prey. She, Dinah, and Aunt Pearl had spent many an evening stitching clothes for the parentless children, which they donated to an organization that saw to the distribution. Pulling her thoughts away from the orphans, she focused on Landry. "Does it hurt much?"

He grunted. Apparently he was a man of few words when he was in pain. That was better than a whiner, as far as she was concerned.

She dropped the cloth in the basin again and lifted up the lantern to study the wound. "This looks like it should be stitched."

"No doctor. I just want to eat and go to bed."

"Be sensible, Landry."

"It's late. I'm not about to let you go out after dark to hunt down a doctor."

The independent streak in her bristled, but another part of her warmed at his concern. "Thank you for worrying about me, but I would only go as far as the neighbor across the street. The Windhams have offered on more than one occasion to help if we ever needed it. They have a liveryman who can fetch a doctor."

"Is it really that bad?"

"I believe so. It's still oozing blood, and the gap is nearly a half inch wide."

He groaned and lay his head on his arm. "I don't want to be any trouble, but if you honestly think I need a doctor, then let's go to the neighbor's house."

"You don't need to go."

"You're not going alone. Look what happened to me."

"As you know, I won't go without a weapon."

Sighing, he pushed up. He stood with his hands on the table, as if he were dizzy. Then he straightened and headed to the doorway, reaching out to steady himself on the frame.

"I don't think you should be up. Why don't you sit back down and eat while I run over to the Wyndhams'?"

"I don't feel right doing that."

"Fine. I'll help you to the porch, but that's as far as you're going. You can see me all the way. It's the house across the road."

"All right."

With Landry seated on the porch, she grabbed the rifle from the cabinet near the door, then hurried out the gate and across the street to the Windham house. Thankfully, they hadn't yet extinguished the porch lanterns. She completed her task quickly then rushed back to the boardinghouse.

Landry pushed up from the chair far slower than he should. She went to his side in case he needed help, but he managed on his own by holding on to the doorframes and furniture. Cara nibbled her lip as she put the rifle away. He must be injured worse than she first thought to have trouble walking without assistance.

Once he was seated in the kitchen, she refilled his coffee then placed his supper before him. "I'm sorry it's not warmer."

"That's all right. I don't think I can eat much anyway." He picked at his potatoes, putting a bite in his mouth while leaning on his hand, eyes shut.

Cara fixed a small slice of the peach pie she'd baked earlier so that Landry wouldn't feel like she was sitting there watching him eat. "Does your head hurt very bad?"

"Some. It's not as sharp a pain as it was though."

"That's good." She reached out and touched his arm. "I'm so

sorry this happened to you."

He looked up, squinting at her. "Hazards of the job. I was shot twice and stabbed once as a marshal."

Cara sucked in a breath. "You need to become a rancher. It's far less hazardous."

His lips flicked upward on one side for a moment. "I have actually thought quite often about that very thing."

"Truly?" Cara's heart fluttered.

"Yes. But other than being able to ride and shoot well, I know nothing about ranching."

"You could learn. My father and brothers would be happy to teach you."

He peeked at her again. "They would? Why?"

"Because we're friends."

"They don't even know me."

"But I do. And think how much fun it would be for Lacy. She could learn to ride on her own." *And shoot.* But she refrained from bringing up that topic since she figured she knew what he would say.

"I can't do anything for now. I have a three-month contract."

"That's not a very long one. I'm surprised you gave up your marshal job for that."

"I did it for Lacy." He took a bite from a dinner roll.

Cara rose to check his head again. "Could you bow your head for a moment, please?"

He did, and she rinsed the wound again. "Your shirt will need to be soaked in cold water to get the blood out."

"Well, I'm not taking it off right now."

Cara smiled. Was the man shy? "That's fine. You can give it to me after I help you up the stairs."

"Don't need help."

She patted his shoulder. "We'll see about that."

A knock sounded. "That's probably the doctor. I'll be right back."

She hurried to the door and opened it. "Thank you so much for coming, Dr. Rigsby. The patient is in the kitchen."

She led the way then stood back while the doctor introduced himself and inspected Landry's wounds. This wasn't Dr. Rigsby's first visit to the boardinghouse, and she doubted it would be his last. The doctor's silvery hair was tinged with a darker shade. She guessed him to be around Aunt Pearl's age—early fifties.

"Were you knocked insensible, young man?"

"If you mean did I pass out, then yes."

Cara nibbled the inside of her cheek. Landry hadn't mentioned being knocked out. He must be injured worse than he let on.

"For how long?"

"I have no idea. One of the railroad workers discovered me lying on the platform and assisted me home."

"Hmm. . . I will need to stitch the wound in the back of your head but not the one in front. It would be best if you were lying down so we don't risk you passing out and falling."

"I won't pass out. Just do it."

"I'm afraid I don't have enough light in here, plus there isn't enough room for me to move around."

Cara stepped closer. "Why don't we help Mr. Lomax up to his room. Then he can lie down while you stitch his head, and he won't have to move after that."

Dr. Rigsby nodded. "Yes, I think that is best, as long as I have sufficient light."

"There are several lanterns in the suite upstairs, and if those aren't enough, I can get another one."

"Very well, let's get this man upstairs."

Landry pushed back his meal, which was mostly uneaten. He groaned when he stood.

"If you wouldn't mind carrying my bag, Miss Dixon, then my hands will be free to help our patient."

"Of course." Cara took the doctor's bag and allowed Dr. Rigsby to assist Landry. She figured it would embarrass him less that way. As she slowly followed them up the stairs, Cara knew it wasn't likely she'd be going to bed anytime soon.

⋇ Chapter 6 ⋇

I'm so excited to be going to the store with you." Lacy bounced in her seat at the dining table. "And I get to pick out my own dress patterns and fabric. How fun!"

Cara smiled at the enthusiastic child. "I know we'll have a grand time, but you must finish your breakfast first."

Dinah spread strawberry-rhubarb jam on her biscuit. "I've been scouring the books for the most stylish girls' frocks and am anxious to show you the ones I've found."

Mrs. Phillips, a boarder who had stayed with them several times the past year while visiting her sister, looked at Dinah. "I should have you make me a dress for the Independence Day celebration back home. That way it would be different from what the other ladies will be wearing."

"I'd be happy to, although we have several one-of-a-kind dresses in patriotic colors in stock. We also recently received some new summer-weight fabrics in several shades of blue and red. They're quite lovely."

"I plan to visit Annabelle while her young'uns are napping, which means I'm free this morning."

Cara could tell by Dinah's expression that she was hoping to help with Lacy's clothing, but her friend wouldn't turn away a paying customer.

Dinah smiled at the woman. "Please come in at your leisure. We'd love to design something special for you."

Aunt Pearl entered the dining room carrying a tray with Landry's breakfast. "I prepared Mr. Lomax's meal, but one of you youngsters needs to run it upstairs."

"That won't be necessary."

All eyes turned to Landry. He entered the dining room, relieved Aunt Pearl of the tray, and sat next to his daughter.

Cara longed to ask him how he was feeling, but she didn't want to embarrass him. She well knew how prideful men could be when it came to injuries. No matter how bad off any of her brothers had been, they somehow managed to joke about their wounds and admire them as if they were a badge of honor. Landry had allowed her to assist him the night of the attack and yesterday morning, but it was obvious that special time with him was over.

Lacy looked at her father with concern. "Are you going back to work already, Papa? I thought the doctor said you should wait several days."

"I'll be fine. Finish your breakfast. You have an adventure awaiting."

"I know! I'm so excited."

Cara took a bite of bacon. She didn't miss how quickly Landry deflected Lacy's conversation off of himself. That was probably a skill that came in handy as a lawman.

She'd been glad to sleep in her own bed last night after spending the night of the attack in a chair in Landry's parlor. At least the cricks in her back and neck were easing.

Both Dinah and Aunt Pearl had been shocked to learn that Landry had been injured, but both women had also given her a piece of their minds about staying overnight in the third-floor parlor. She tried to explain how she didn't want to leave Landry alone in case he needed help, but Aunt Pearl insisted it wasn't proper.

Cara stirred her eggs around with her fork. If only they knew how many improper things she'd done when living in Texas. They'd be scandalized to know that she often wore her youngest brother's outgrown pants to herd cattle, especially at branding time. And the numerous birthings she'd attended and helped with. Most women thought an unmarried female had no business assisting with such things. Cara's mother had been more liberal in that she allowed her to learn the same things her brothers did, although there were also boring times in the house spent learning more cultured tasks.

Landry cleared his throat.

Cara glanced up to see him staring, and she realized everyone else had left the table. "Oh, sorry. I was lost in thought."

"Where were you? In your thoughts, that is."

"Back home. I was thinking about some of the things I did there."

"Do you miss it?"

"I do, actually. And I miss my family."

"So why don't you go home?"

Cara placed her silverware on her plate and pushed it back. "I will before long. I promised Dinah I'd help her get her store up and running, and she's almost at the point where I can go. I'll miss her and Aunt Pearl, but it will be good to be home." And she wouldn't stitch another thing for months, if she had her way.

"Are you certain you don't mind taking Lacy to work today? It's a long time to keep her occupied."

Cara rose and picked up her plate and his. "Of course I don't mind. It will be fun, and if Lacy gets bored, we'll go visit some of the other shops in the area."

Landry rose and put his hand in his pocket. He pulled out several bills and handed them to her.

"What's that for?"

"Down payment on Lacy's dresses and a little extra for her to spend today if she sees something she loves. Just don't let her go overboard—or bring home something living."

Cara smiled and tapped her index finger against her lips. "Tempting, but Aunt Pearl doesn't allow animals in the house."

Instead of smiling, Landry stared intensely at her lips. Cara's heartbeat tripled its pace. Landry glanced up, capturing her gaze, and held it for a long moment.

She couldn't help wondering if the table hadn't been between them if he would have sneaked a quick kiss. She blinked. Why would she think such a thing?

Dinah rushed into the room. "Oh good. You're done. We need to leave soon."

"Um. . .right." Cara glanced around. "Where's Lacy?"

Landry cleared his throat. "I sent her upstairs to wash her hands and face and get the book she's reading. I figured it would help entertain her if she gets tired of picking out dresses."

"I'll run upstairs and let her know it's time to leave." Dinah rushed through the room, and then her footsteps sounded on the stairs.

"Good idea." Cara called out as she grabbed the remaining silverware and hurried into the kitchen, still flustered over her thoughts about kissing Landry. When she returned to the dining room, he stood by the window, staring out.

Cara reached for the meat platter and remaining bowl and carried them to the kitchen.

"Thank you, dear." Aunt Pearl smiled. "Have a nice time at work."

"Will you be driving Mrs. Phillips to the shop?"

"No. She mentioned walking over to her sister's to see if she'd like to go with her."

Cara grimaced. "I sure hope she doesn't bring all six of her children."

"That would not be good with all the pins and things you have for sale." Aunt Pearl handed Cara three pails. "Here are your lunches. As you can see, I made one for Lacy."

Cara kissed the kind woman on the cheek. "Don't work too hard."

Aunt Pearl giggled. "I probably will."

"You always do." Cara smiled as she left the kitchen. It was nigh on impossible to get Dinah's mother to slow down. An evening of sitting and stitching was her idea of relaxing. Cara much preferred a long ride in the country or reading an exciting novel on colder days.

As she reached the entryway, she found Landry waiting, hat in hand. She set the pails on the hall table and turned to face him. "Are you sure you feel well enough to go to work?"

"I'll be fine. My head's still tender in back, but otherwise I'm good."

"Just be careful. No more chasing thieves until your head is healed."

He lifted one eyebrow and looked to be fighting a smile. "Yes, Dr. Dixon."

Cara's cheeks warmed as she realized she sounded more like a wife than a doctor. "Lacy needs you."

He sobered. "I know. But there's a part of me that hopes you'd miss me too if something happened."

Cara reached out to touch his sleeve. "Of course we'd miss you."

"We?"

"Well, me. I would miss you." And she knew she would. He already filled her dreams.

He glanced around and then placed his hand over hers. "It does my heart good to hear that. Thank you for taking such good care of me."

"It was my pleasure."

"I'm ready!" Lacy hollered as she raced down the stairs to the second floor.

"I'm coming," Dinah called.

Cara yanked her hand away at the same time Landry stepped back.

He glanced upstairs again and then leaned forward. "Would you have dinner with me sometime as a thank-you?"

Cara's heart bucked. "I'd love to."

He smiled then placed his hat very gingerly on his head. "Saturday evening?"

She didn't miss his tiny grimace when the hat touched his head. "Saturday is perfect. I'll be looking forward to it."

Friday afternoon, Landry rode his horse across the vast railroad yard. He was grateful for Jonesy, his steady, well-trained mount, a veteran of the War between the States. The noises of the busy rail yard didn't faze him.

Landry had ridden around the outskirts of the railroad property, checking where fences needed to be repaired—and there were quite a few. Fixing them would help with the freeloader traffic and might also keep out thieves who weren't bold enough to use the main entrances.

He stopped to chat with the yardmaster and instructed him to schedule a crew to repair the fences. As the man returned to his work, Landry checked his pocket watch and then reined Jonesy back to the depot. The 4:15 was due in anytime. He wanted to observe the removal of the freight and passengers' bags. There had been numerous reports of missing luggage. He wasn't sure if a railroad employee was doing the stealing or someone else.

He rode across a half dozen sets of tracks, found a secure place to leave Jonesy, then climbed up onto an empty buckboard to survey the operations. The warm sun heated his shoulders, and he wiped the sweat trickling down his temples. He understood the draw of living in Denver, where'd they'd been for the past four years. The summers had been nice, but he hadn't liked the months and months of cold, snowy winters one bit.

He studied several groups of railroad workers clustered in twos and threes, waiting for the arrival of the train. One man—the baggage clerk—laughed and punched another worker in the shoulder. Landry stiffened, but the man took his playful attack without offense and laughed also. Landry allowed the tension to flow out

of him. It wasn't good business for railroad employees to be rough-
housing in full view of the passengers waiting to board.

Landry jumped off the buckboard and sought out a shady area.
For some reason he'd yet to figure out, he felt hotter in the city than
when he was riding in the country. Perhaps it was the three-piece
suit he wore. He checked his watch again. The train was late.

He returned his watch to his pocket. He was anxious to learn if
Rolly Herman had been successful in his task. He'd assigned Herman, a newer employee, to ride the route and covertly count the
number of passengers in each car after every stop from here to St.
Claire and back. Pete had informed him that the ticket numbers
and money collected by the conductors weren't always adding up.
He hoped there was another reason for the missing funds other
than the conductor pilfering them.

Landry removed his hat and fanned himself with it. He reached
behind his head and gently probed the area where he'd been hit.
Wincing, he decided that was a pretty dumb thing to do. It ate at
him that he'd let down his guard and been jumped. What if the
man had shot him instead of clubbing him? He might have died—
and then what would happen to Lacy?

Cara's suggestion about him trying ranching had been circling
around in his mind. Other than working in an office or a store all
day, which he already knew wasn't something he cared to do, most
jobs contained a degree of danger. Ranching would too, but it surely
wouldn't be as hazardous as a lawman's job. He'd be confronting
cattle—or horses—instead of armed outlaws bent on killing him.

And Cara was right. Lacy would love it. She'd always had a passion for animals of any kind and often brought home little critters
she'd found. He smiled at the memory of Lacy, then five, trying
to convince Ada to let her keep the frog she'd caught. Ada could

hardly stand to look at the creature and had ordered it out of the house. He'd let Lacy keep the poor thing in a crate for a couple of days, and then he'd set it free while she was napping.

Those memories were precious. He missed Ada, even though things had been rough between them the last few years. She didn't like him being gone so much, but when he was home, she had fussed at him to the point he wanted to leave. If he'd gotten a job in town, would things have been better between them?

One thing was for certain, until he settled down to a permanent job, which he didn't feel he could do just yet, he had no business thinking of marrying again. But then the image of Cara holding that derringer in her small hand with that determined look on her face or the image of her on the windy platform invaded his thoughts.

He forked his hand through his hair, reminding him of when she'd run her fingers through his hair while inspecting his wound. Although he'd been in horrible pain, his senses had gone on alert, and he realized he enjoyed her touch. He sure hadn't expected to meet a woman like her. Furthermore, he hadn't ever thought he'd be attracted to one who was so independent. But there was no denying that he was.

And now he had committed to take her to dinner, but he had no idea where to go. Perhaps Pete could offer a suggestion. He probably should bring Lacy along as an escort, although he wouldn't mind spending time alone with Cara.

The train's whistle drew him back to the job at hand. He hopped onto the buckboard again and watched the train pull into the depot. There was no sign of the pickpocket he'd seen the other day. The only children on the platform were a baby that a man held and a toddler girl grasping the hand of a woman in a blue dress.

He studied the baggage clerk and his assistant then glanced

down the track to the warehouse where all manner of freight was stored. A crew already had a large stack of crates on the loading dock, waiting to be carried on board.

Everything looked normal. The train belched smoke and screeched as it slowed to a stop. The brakes whooshed. The awaiting passengers stood at attention, ready to board. The doors opened, and people began exiting the train and milling about.

The baggage clerk caught the bags being thrown down and set them in a row near the edge of the platform, while his assistant stood at another door, tossing bags up to another man inside the baggage car. It all worked like a well-greased machine. Though none of it was his doing, pride warmed him.

He watched dozens of passengers, some heading for the stairs and others being directed by the porter to where their luggage was being unloaded.

Suddenly a man pushed his way through the crowd, past the porter, to the baggage. He grabbed a plaid bag and took off at a fast walk toward the stairs.

"Hey!" A man chased after him. "That's my bag."

The first man broke into a run. He turned away from the stairs, raced to the edge of the platform, hopped over the railing, and jumped eight feet to the ground. The baggage clerk and porter started after him.

"Stop!" Landry yelled at the workers. He hoped they'd return to their jobs and protect the remaining baggage. He didn't wait to see if they obeyed but jumped off the buckboard and ran for his horse. He leapt on and pulled up the reins. "*Yaw!*" He slapped the end of the reins against Jonesy's flank, and the horse charged forward.

The thief sprinted toward the street. Landry rode at an angle, hoping to intercept him before he disappeared into the crowd. The man saw him, shifted directions, and raced back toward the depot stairs. Landry closed the distance. The man was ten feet from the stairs. Landry pulled Jonesy to a fast halt, leapt off the horse, and grabbed the man around the neck. His forehead hit the thief's shoulder, radiating pain in the same area where he'd bumped it before. But he held on. Jonesy moved forward, blocking the street and the man's escape.

The man rammed his elbow into Landry's side. Landry gasped from the pain. Footsteps hurried their way. A man ran past them, turned, then slammed his fist into the thief's face. The robber went limp in Landry's arms, and he lowered him to the ground.

Clapping and cheers rang out. Landry looked up to see a crowd watching from the platform. He reached into his back pocket, pulled out a length of rope, and secured his prisoner. He hoped they'd get some info about other thieves out of the man.

The passenger who punched the thief reached for the plaid bag.

"You got a baggage claim ticket for that?" Landry asked.

He scowled. "It's in my bag."

"So you say. I'm Special Agent Lomax. If you don't mind, I'd like to see proof of that."

"All right." The man relaxed and stuck his hand in his jacket pocket. Frowning, he searched his pants pockets. Suddenly his gaze lit up, and he reached for his hat. He pulled the claim ticket from his hatband and handed it to Landry. "Here it is."

Landry checked it against the ticket on the bag, then handed the satchel to the man. "Thank you for your assistance, but in the future, it would be better to let the railroad crew capture a thief. We wouldn't want you getting injured."

The man straightened. "I'm a Texan, and we fight our own battles."

He reminded Landry of Cara. What was it with Texans needing to be so independent? Landry watched him walk away. In truth he was glad the man had knocked out the thief. He'd been losing his grip, and his head was throbbing—again. At least he hadn't hit the back of his head where the stitches still remained.

Two crewmen rushed to Landry's side. "You need help?" the taller one asked.

"Yes. Take this man to the nearest police station and tell the officer on duty that I'll be in to make a report soon."

"Yes, sir, Mr. Lomax. Fine job apprehending the robber."

"Thank you."

Landry limped over to where Jonesy was grazing and gathered the reins. By the pain in his knee, he guessed the thief had kicked him. He climbed onto his horse and sat there for a moment, watching the crowd thin out. He rubbed his side where the man had hit him. Ranching was sounding better and better.

⚜ *Chapter 7* ⚜

*C*ara stood in front of the mirror, fastening her necklace. The diamonds encircling the sapphire glistened like stars against a Texas night sky. She missed seeing that. Because of the streetlights, a person had to ride several miles out of the city to see very many stars here.

Dinah leaned against the doorframe. Her honey-gold dress with tiny brown flowers looked good with her blond hair, and the small green leaves enhanced her hazel eyes. "You look amazing in that royal-blue shade. I love how the fabric shimmers."

"Green is a better color for me with this wild red hair, but I wanted to wear my great-grandma's necklace tonight, and this dress matches it."

"Every man in that restaurant will be staring at you." Dinah sighed. "How romantic."

Cara's heart ached for her friend. Dinah was a kindhearted woman who would make a wonderful wife to a good man, but so far no man had shown interest in her. And that surprised Cara. So many men seemed to like blonds. It made no sense that one hadn't snagged Dinah yet. Perhaps God was saving her for someone special.

Landry popped into her mind. Was he the man God meant for *her* to be with? Cara could imagine spending the rest of her life with him, so long as he wasn't fussing at her. Delightful shivers raced through her.

"Are you sure you don't want me to keep Lacy here?" Dinah asked, her voice lowered. She glanced out the door then leaned in again. "I mean, how can you have a romantic night out with a nine-year-old along?"

Cara rolled her eyes. "We're not courting. It's merely a thank-you dinner for me helping Landry when he was injured."

Dinah snorted. "You're delusional if you believe that. Haven't you noticed the way he stares at you during meals?"

Cara feigned adjusting her necklace then pinched her cheeks, hoping Dinah didn't notice the blush warming them. That's one thing she despised about being a redhead.

"I could be wrong, but I think Landry is yours to—how do you say—um. . .lasso, if you don't mind marrying an older man with a child."

"His age isn't that far off from mine." At least one of her four brothers was surely older than Landry. What would Papa think if she showed up with a man nearly thirty years old? Papa was seven years older than Mama, which couldn't be too far off from the difference in her age and Landry's.

"Well, I do hope you have a wonderful time. I've only dreamed of going to one of those fancy theaters like the Olympic."

Cara hurried to her friend's side. "We'll simply have to go together one day."

Dinah gasped and splayed her fingers over her chest in feigned shock. "No escort? Why that's positively scandalous."

Cara smiled.

Quick footsteps rushed up the stairs. "Papa is back, and wait until you see the carriage he brought!" Lacy rushed into the room then stopped suddenly, her eyes wide. "You look like a princess."

The awe in the girl's voice made Cara blush all over again. "So do you."

"My dress isn't as pretty as yours." Lacy brushed her hands down the rose-colored frock.

"Of course it is." Dinah stooped down. "If you look at Cara's, you'll see ruffles at the bottom just like yours. And you have ruffles at the collar and the end of your short sleeves, so I'd say your dress is even fancier than Cara's." She glanced past Lacy and winked.

"See. Yours is the fanciest and prettiest." Cara mouthed, *Thank you*, to her friend. "And we will look lovely next to your handsome papa."

Dinah's eyes widened.

Cara quickly turned and pulled on her gloves, which had been on the bed. She picked up her handbag and her lacy shawl, not that she expected to need it in the heat they'd been experiencing. Her stomach quivered at the thought of the delightful evening ahead. She had accompanied a few young men to group outings that the finishing school had hosted, and she'd danced with many of the young men who lived near her family's ranch when there had been shindigs to celebrate different occasions, but she had never gone out unescorted with a gentleman. Yes, Lacy was going, but it wasn't the same as Dinah or Aunt Pearl joining them. "I'm ready."

"I'll tell Papa!" Lacy bolted toward the stairs.

Dinah sighed. "Someone needs to teach that girl how to behave. If I didn't know better, I'd think she was born in Texas." The twinkle in her eyes indicated she was teasing.

"Well, I'll have you know that I'm a prime example of how a woman can be raised in the wilds of Texas and have impeccable manners." Cara lifted her skirts and skipped out the door.

Dinah erupted in laughter.

At the top of the stairs, Cara halted her antics just in time to see Landry enter the door dressed in a black frock coat, black pants, and a gray brocade waist coat. Her mouth went dry at how handsome he looked, even standing there with his mouth open, staring at her.

He hurried up the stairs. "You look amazing." His gaze ran down her body then back up. "I'll be the envy of every man we pass."

Cara had been thinking almost the same thing. It would be hard for a woman to keep her eyes off him.

"Shall we?" He stuck out his elbow.

The quivers she experienced earlier were close to a full-blown earthquake now. Even her hand shook as she looped her arm through his. How would she get through this whole evening if her nerves were on edge?

He patted her hand. "Relax. This will be an enjoyable time. I've been looking forward to it since we set the date."

"You have?"

He nodded then frowned. "Haven't you?"

"Of course. But I didn't realize that men did the same. My brothers never show much excitement unless they get a new horse or gun."

"I can't speak for all men, only myself." He helped her down the stairs, going slowly so she didn't trip on her full skirt.

At the bottom of the stairs, Aunt Pearl stood there with a big smile on her face. "You two look enchanting."

"Thank you." Cara looked around. "Where's Lacy?"

Aunt Pearl waved her hand toward the door. "In the carriage. She is so excited. Have a wonderful time, but don't stay out too late."

"Yes, ma'am." Landry opened the door. Cara lifted her skirts and stepped outside, her gaze landing on a beautiful cream-colored carriage pulled by a matching pair of white horses that each wore a red-feather headpiece. The driver stood at the open gate, waiting for them.

Lacy leaned out one of the windows and waved. "C'mon. I'm starving."

Landry sighed as they walked down the stairs. "So much for a romantic outing."

Cara giggled, and he smiled. She had a feeling this would be an evening she would never forget.

Landry knew he'd never forget his first evening out with Cara. He sat at his desk, staring out the window, remembering each glorious moment. First, they'd had a fine dinner at Griffin's, an upscale restaurant that Pete had recommended. Cara had eaten a steak, while he had lobster, and Lacy ate chicken.

The play they attended at the Olympic Theater had been outstanding, even though one of the singers had been a bit off-key. Cara had giggled at the man, which had set off Lacy and then Landry. The people sitting nearby had frowned at them, making Cara snicker even more.

The ride home was quite special. Lacy had fallen asleep, so he told the driver to take a scenic route through one of the city's many parks. Cara had chatted mostly about her life in Texas before going to finishing school. He'd been impressed with the long list of tasks she'd participated in, including roping cattle, branding, and helping with birthings—something she'd told him in a whisper.

He smiled at the thought of her embarrassment and not wanting Lacy to hear, even though she was still sleeping. He leaned back in his chair. Now he better understood why Cara was so independent. Life on a ranch never stopped, and when something needed doing, a person did it, whether they were a male or female.

She sure was an intriguing woman. And she'd taken his breath away in that incredible blue dress. He leaned his elbow on his desk, jaw in his hand. He was in trouble.

After Ada died, he hadn't planned to marry again. He'd loved his wife dearly, but theirs had been a young love. They'd married when they were both seventeen, and they grew up together. Things were much different now. He had a whole new perspective on life.

Like how fast things could change. He pressed his fingers to the back of his head. The wound that had been stitched still hurt some, but the pain wasn't as raw as before. He'd be glad when he was able to get the stitches removed.

As they often did lately, his thoughts returned to Cara. She was young, though not as young as Ada when he married her. As much as he liked Cara and was growing to care about her, he had to make sure she would be a good mother to Lacy. After all, she was only thirteen years older than his daughter.

He shook his head, unable to grasp the idea that he was actually thinking of Cara and marriage in the same sentence. He'd only met the woman two weeks ago, when she'd stormed into his life, gun drawn. He'd known Ada for four years before marrying her.

"Looks like you've got something awful heavy on your mind. My guess is it's either a woman or the job."

Landry glanced up to see Pete inclined against the doorway. Whenever the man was standing, he was leaning on something. Or else he was sitting. His knees must give him a lot of trouble. "Come in and have a seat."

Pete nodded. Once he'd dropped into a chair, his expression turned sober. "The early morning train was robbed."

Landry stiffened. "Did they get the payroll shipment?"

"Yes. They nabbed it near Rolla."

Landry slammed his fist on his desk. That's what he got for taking time off to enjoy a night on the town. As soon as the thought entered his head, he knew how ridiculous it was. He couldn't work constantly. "Was it the James-Younger gang?"

Pete shrugged. "From the description the guards gave, I'd say no."

"How did they even know about the payroll? Besides the two of us, only the banker and the guards knew about the gold shipment. Do you think we have a snitch working for us?"

"That seems the only logical answer."

Landry rubbed his jaw. "I know *I* didn't say anything to anyone about the payroll other than to you and the guards, and I'm sure you and the banker didn't. So that leaves the guards."

"I can assure you that my lips were sealed tighter than a lady's corset." Pete smiled. "And that's pretty darn tight. I've had to help Esther with hers many times."

Landry chuckled, grateful for the levity. He had done the same thing for Ada plenty of times. "What do you suggest we do?"

"I was hoping you'd have a few ideas."

Landry thumped his fingers on the desk as several ideas circled in his mind. "We can keep the same guards and wait a week or two then ship a fake payroll, although they won't know it's not real. I can hire extra men as undercover guards to help me in case the outlaws show up. Or we can get rid of the guards we have now and hire new ones, although how we find trustworthy men, I'm not sure."

"I know quite a few men on the police force. Perhaps I can find several who'd like to make some extra money."

"That's as good a place as any to start."

"All right. Sounds like a plan." Pete slapped the arms of the chair. "I'll talk to my contact and see what he has to say."

"One more thing." Landry held up his index finger. "Rolly Herman reported in. His passenger count equaled what the conductor reported. All funds were accounted for on that run."

"That's good. See if you can hire some outsiders to do what Rolly did. It may be the conductor recognized him, or it could be a different conductor that's doing the pilfering."

"It's probably a good idea to keep undercover employees riding the various routes until we catch the thief. It irks me that a man would steal from the very company that's paying his wages."

"You and me both." Pete slowly pushed up, grunting as he straightened. "You're doing good work here, Lomax."

"Thank you, sir." He watched the man limp away, then riffled through the paperwork on his desk. He wondered what Pete would say if he knew Landry wouldn't be signing another contract when it was time to renew.

On Wednesday Lacy twirled around the shop in her new blue dress. "Do you think Papa will like it?"

Cara smiled. The light blue dress with dark blue flowers, trimmed in white lace, looked darling on her. "He will love it because you're the one wearing it."

Lacy stopped and gazed at Cara, nibbling her lower lip. "Do I look like you in your blue dress?"

"Oh sweetie, you are beautiful. I know women who'd do about anything to have pretty blue eyes like yours." Cara ran her hand down the girl's hair. "And you have such lovely, thick hair."

"I do?" Her eyes widened.

"You do," Dinah piped in. "And you don't have to worry about being teased for having wildfire hair like Cara."

"Who teased you?" Lacy frowned.

"Lots of people, my brothers most of all." Cara gathered up the leftover fabric pieces from the dress she'd been cutting out.

"Then I'm glad I don't have a brother. That's mean of them."

Dinah sighed. "I always wished I'd had one, but now I think I'm glad I don't, if they're as bad as you say."

Cara carried the fabric remnants to the scrap bin. "They're not always bad. For one thing, each of them would fight like crazy if anyone or anything threatened me."

"So, it's all right for them to pick on you but not others." Dinah rolled up a new batch of lace that had arrived in the day's shipment.

"Yep, that's the way of things."

The bell above the door jingled. Cara's heart bucked when she saw Landry entering.

"Papa! Look at my new dress." Lacy trotted over to her father, who closed the front door.

"My, my! Don't you look lovely!"

She twirled around again. "Truly?"

He bent down and kissed the top of her head. "Have I ever lied to you?"

"No, Papa. I'm so excited to have some new dresses. Can we go out to the theater again so I can wear one?"

"We'll see. How about if I take all of you to lunch? I'm tired of eating alone."

Cara glanced at Dinah, who waggled her brows in a teasing manner. Thankfully, her back was to Landry so he didn't see. "That would be wonderful. We don't have any upcoming appointments."

Dinah tapped her lips. "I should probably stay here in case someone stops by."

"Nonsense. You need to eat too, especially since we didn't bring anything from home."

"No, I feel I need to keep the shop open. I won't object if you want to bring me something when you return." Dinah swatted her hand in the air, indicating for Cara to go.

Dinah was definitely matchmaking, but this time Cara didn't mind. "If you're certain."

"We'll be happy to bring you whatever you desire," Landry said.

"Thank you. Cara knows what I like." Dinah walked over to Cara and gave her a gentle nudge. "Go on, and take your time."

One of these days, Cara needed to get Dinah to come to Texas. Surely one of her brothers or the hundreds of available men would take an interest in her. Cara smiled as she walked toward Landry. She hadn't expected to see him until this evening, so she was thrilled that he stopped by. What was happening to her? Landry was the only man to make her go all jittery on the inside. Was this the beginning of love? If only her mother were still alive for her to talk to.

"I thought we might pick up something from a street vendor to take to the park. That way Lacy can run around and maybe find some other children to play with for a bit."

"Oh boy!" Lacy grinned and clapped her hands.

"That sounds delightful," Cara said. Especially since the heat wave of the past week had moved on and a cooler north wind made the temperature more pleasant. "I miss being outside."

"I suppose that's where you spent most of your days back in Texas." Landry glanced down at her as they walked along the sidewalk.

"True, at least in warm weather. It's funny how I seemed to get a penchant for more domestic chores once winter set in."

Landry chuckled. "I knew you were smart."

"You did?"

He winked, then reached over and squeezed her hand, letting it go before Lacy could notice.

Her heart fluttered at his touch.

Landry bought three roast beef sandwiches and apples from a vendor near the park, and they found a place where they could sit in the shade. Lacy ate fast then hurried off to play with a group of children who were kicking a ball around.

"I was surprised to see you when you came into the store." Cara took the last bite of her sandwich then wadded up the paper it came in.

"I went with my boss to talk to a man at the police station. Pete headed home afterward to eat with his wife, and since I was in the area, I decided to see if you were free—and Lacy too, of course."

It warmed Cara's heart that he had sought her out and not just his daughter. Was he developing feelings for her, or did he just enjoy her company?

She glanced over and found him frowning. "Is something wrong?"

His gaze captured hers. "Problems at work."

"Is it something you can talk about?"

He was quiet for a moment then nodded. "I think so. You already know we've had issues with pickpockets and outlaws robbing the train. Monday morning, we had a payroll that was stolen. The thing is, only a few people knew about the shipment."

"So you think one of the railroad employees told someone about it?"

"That seems to be what happened, which is a shame. Railroad employees are trusted with quite a bit of responsibility. I hate to think one of them is stealing from the Missouri Pacific."

Cara could tell how much the situation weighed on him. "What are you going to do?"

Landry blew out a loud sigh. "My boss and I have some ideas."

"I'll pray you catch the bandits."

He reached over and took hold of her hand. "Thank you. I appreciate that."

"Is your boss putting pressure on you to capture the thieves?" She tried to ignore the tingles coursing up her arms from his touch. She'd left in such a rush she hadn't thought to grab her gloves. The warmth of his hand on hers made her heart pound faster.

"Not yet. We did catch that man I told you about, who stole a bag off the platform last Friday. He named several other thieves in exchange for a deal. The police located one of those men and apprehended him, but several others are still out there. And then there are the kids who are pickpocketing."

"My heart goes out to those poor children. I wish there was more I could do to help besides stitching clothes for them."

He squeezed her hand. "You have a good heart, Cara."

"It's no more than any honorable person would do."

"You'd be surprised. Many people wouldn't want to sully their fine reputations by aiding street children."

"Well, horse flops. Those folks need to come out of their fancy houses and see what it's like to live hand-to-mouth."

Landry lifted one brow, his mouth quirking. "Horse flops?"

Cara felt her cheeks warm. "Did I say that out loud?"

He chuckled. "Yes, ma'am, you did, and that's just one of the many things I like about you."

"Many?" She hated how her voice quivered, but this man had a way of turning her composure all catawampus, like a roped calf lying on the ground, waiting to be branded.

He stared at her as if he wanted to kiss her, and she couldn't look away. His thumb caressed her wrist, enhancing the delicious chills. The look on his face made her want to fall into his arms and never let go. Was this love?

"Papa, look!"

Landry suddenly released her hand, blinking his eyes. He looked as if he'd been in the same enticing fog she had. If they'd been alone, she felt sure he would have kissed her.

❧ Chapter 8 ❧

*H*ave you decided if you want to attend the Paris fashion trade show in Chicago?" Cara asked Dinah as they walked toward the mercantile where they picked up their mail.

"I don't know." Dinah shrugged. "It's a long way, and I'd have to keep the store closed for nearly a week."

"That's true, but think of the fun we'd have getting to see the latest fashions before almost anyone."

"Good afternoon." Dinah smiled at Helen Avery, the woman who owned the millinery down the street from her dress shop.

Cara waved to the kind woman who swept the sidewalk in front of her hat store. She and Dinah had bartered hats for a dress on several occasions.

Dinah smiled as they passed Mrs. Avery. "I much prefer working in the store than going to big trade shows."

"I know, but as a store owner, you need to keep up with the latest fashions or your customers will go elsewhere."

Dinah sighed. "I suppose you're right. And we need to start looking for someone to replace you soon."

Cara glanced at her friend. Could Dinah tell that she was homesick? That she missed her father and brothers? But when she returned home, she would miss Dinah and visiting Ellen. That would be much harder to do when she was back in Texas. She wondered how her sister was faring after losing her daughter. At least if she and Dinah attended the fashion show, they could stay with Ellen, and then Cara would know better how her sister was doing.

She had promised Dinah she would stay for a year and help get her store established, and that time would be up in less than four weeks. Dinah's business was almost too much for the two of them. It was past time for her friend to hire someone else.

There was another reason Cara hesitated to go. If she left St. Louis, she'd desperately miss Landry and Lacy. Should she extend her stay or go home as planned? Landry seemed interested in her, but she was so naive that she didn't know if he was just being friendly or if there was more to it. She would love to find out, but she wasn't about to chase after the man.

Dinah paused to let a horse-drawn tram pass by. "You're frowning. What are you thinking about?"

"Returning home. I don't like leaving you and your mother, but I can't stay here forever."

"What about Landry?"

Cara shrugged. "I can't answer that."

Dinah looped her arm through Cara's. "But won't you miss him and Lacy if you leave?"

Talking about her feelings had never come easy. Perhaps because

84

she had so many brothers who would tease her if she became emotional. But Dinah was her dearest friend, and they could talk about anything. "I don't know what to think about him."

Dinah nudged her arm. "I'd be willing to bet he's smitten—if I were a betting woman, which I'm not."

She stopped walking to look at her friend. "Why do you think that?"

"Are you really that naive? Weren't you in love with Davis?"

Cara thought about the man she would have been married to if he hadn't up and died a month before their wedding. "I thought so."

Dinah stepped back to allow a couple to pass. "How does what you feel for Landry compare to that?"

As she watched the people milling about, shopping and talking, horses and buggies passing by, she couldn't find the words to compare the two men. Davis was an inexperienced, mostly grown man of only nineteen, whereas Landry was a seasoned man and father who'd been married and lost his first love. Davis was goofy and kept her laughing, while Landry treated her like she was a knowledgeable woman. Davis's tentative touches to her face and arms mostly tickled, while Landry's sent delicious shivers coursing through her body. "Apples to oranges."

Dinah huffed and released her. "Naive, like I said. Come on. We need to open the shop."

All throughout the day, whenever she had time to stop and think, Cara compared the two men, and by the end of the day, she knew there was no comparison. She hated that quirky and fun Davis had died so young, but she realized now that she was relieved they weren't married. She'd been too young to know her own heart—and her heart wanted Landry.

But did he want her?

After work Cara rode Honey around the pasture with Lacy sitting behind her. She didn't think Landry would object to Lacy riding inside the fenced area. The confined space didn't allow a speed any faster than a trot, but Lacy giggled every time they did, and Honey didn't seem to mind not getting her regular run.

Lacy sighed, her warm breath tickling the back of Cara's neck. "I love Honey. I wish I had a horse like her."

"Honey is a nice horse, but you would need to start with one a bit smaller."

"Papa won't ever let me have one. It's not fair since he has Jonesy."

Cara smiled. "Jonesy is his horse?"

"Yes. I think he named him after a friend or maybe the man he bought him from. He's had Jonesy longer than me."

"Most people keep a good horse for many years, which is why you must be sure you really want one. And they are a lot of work and cost money to maintain properly."

Lacy sighed again. "Maybe I should ask for a puppy or a kitten instead."

Cara started to smile at the girl's second choice for a pet, but she recognized the loneliness in Lacy's voice. Though she'd had her sister and brothers, she still felt lonely quite often when she was young. The boys horsed around with one another, and Ellen helped their mother. Then Ma had died, and Ellen took her place, maintaining the house and cooking the meals. She'd pretty much lost both her mother and sister, even though she and Ellen had never been all that close.

Perhaps she should talk to Landry about getting his daughter a pet. But then, Lacy couldn't have one until they had a permanent residence. Would they stay in St. Louis? Or move on?

Cara guided Honey back to the gate. "Our ride is over for today. I need to groom Honey then get inside and help Aunt Pearl with supper."

"Aw, shucks. I thought it was Dinah's day to help."

"It is, but Mrs. Higgins needs a dress altered for her daughter's birthday party, which is tomorrow evening. Dinah wants to complete the alterations tonight."

"So that's why she brought that dress home?" Lacy grabbed hold of Cara's hand and slid to the ground.

Cara dismounted and glanced at the girl who'd had a funny tone when she'd asked that question. "Yes. Why?"

"Whew!" Lacy ran her hand across her forehead as if wiping off some sweat. "I hate orange. I was so afraid that dress was for me and that I'd have to pretend to like it and be grateful."

"To be more accurate, the dress is a peach color, and it's not one of the best colors on you."

"Good. Can I lead Honey to the barn?"

"Sure. Just stay close to me." Cara was sure Honey would behave, but one never knew when a dog might rush through the yard and spook the mare.

Cara secured the gate to the pasture then handed Lacy the reins. The girl's big grin warmed Cara's heart.

As they walked side by side, Lacy glanced at her. "Why haven't you ever married? I mean, surely you're old enough. Papa took you out. Are you going to marry him?" Her eyes lit up. "I would really like that."

Cara's heart bucked. She couldn't talk about marrying Landry with his daughter, especially when nothing had been mentioned about it between him and herself. "I almost got married once."

"Truly?" Lacy's blue eyes widened. "Why didn't you?"

"He got sick about a month before the wedding and died."

Lacy stopped and turned to give Cara a hug. "I'm so sorry. I bet you were really sad like Papa was when my mama died. He's been sad for a long while." She stepped back and led Honey into the barn. "That's why we came here, you know."

Landry had needed a change, she understood that, but now they had no house at all. At least Cara could walk around her family home and remember her mother sewing the curtains in the dining room or spending all winter to make the braided rug that now adorned the parlor floor. Each room held special memories with her mother. Her heart ached that Lacy didn't have that. If only she could mother the girl and give her new memories.

Lacy paused at Honey's stall. "Can I help groom her?"

"Of course. Just let me get the saddle off."

While Lacy ran the curry comb over the part of Honey that she could reach, Cara raked out the soiled hay and added a fresh layer. Then she put clean water into the bucket and feed in the box.

With Honey groomed and happily eating in her stall, Cara and Lacy walked out of the barn. Cara closed the doors.

Lacy tapped her arm. "Before you go in, will you show me how to shoot?"

The girl never ceased to surprise her. She glanced around, glad that they were all alone. "I don't think your father would like that."

"I don't want to shoot it. Just hold it."

This was a bad idea, but when Cara had been curious about weapons, her pa had said it was better she learned about them with him there than sneaking off alone with a gun. So he'd taught her all she knew about handling, cleaning, and firing revolvers, rifles, and shotguns. She was even a fair hand with a bow and arrow, but she wasn't about to tell Lacy that.

With resignation, she nodded. "Let's go back over to the fence."

Cara withdrew her derringer from her pocket and removed the bullets, then dropped them back into her skirt. She handed the gun to Lacy. "This is about as small as a gun comes."

Lacy ran her hand over the pearl handle. "This part is so pretty."

Cara turned the gun in Lacy's hand. "Never point a weapon at anyone unless you intend to shoot them. That includes an unloaded gun. You never know if someone left a bullet in one of the chambers."

"Oh. I'm glad you told me that."

"Go ahead and point it at the tree out in the pasture. Then I need to get cleaned up and help Aunt Pearl."

Lacy did as told, and then she made a firing sound. *"Pkeew! Pkeew!"*

"What in the world is going on here?"

Cara spun at the sound of Landry's voice. He scowled at her.

Uh oh. She was in trouble—again.

"Lacy, go inside and get cleaned up for supper." Landry's heart still pounded at seeing the pistol in his daughter's hand. What was Cara thinking?

"But Papa—"

"Give me that and go." He thrust out his hand, and Lacy passed the derringer to him.

"It was my idea. Don't be mad at Cara."

"Go!" Landry pointed at the house.

Head down, his daughter trudged toward the door. Landry whirled around to face Cara, who stood there with her arms crossed.

"You were teaching my daughter how to shoot? Without my permission? What were you thinking?" He held up his palm toward her. "No, wait. You weren't thinking at all. She's only nine years old."

Cara frowned. "Don't be so tyrannical, Landry. I took all the bullets out, so there was no danger. She'd only been holding it for a minute."

He stepped closer. "Tyrannical? I'm her father."

"And if you don't answer her questions about things like horses and guns, she's liable to go behind your back and try them out on her own. And that could be very dangerous."

She was right, much to his chagrin, but he wasn't ready to admit it. He raised his brow. "I suppose that's what you did."

She hiked her chin. "Are you saying you never did?"

Her evasive response wasn't lost on him. But, once again, she was right. "I probably did." Every chance he got. And he'd paid for his actions by having to do extra chores. Lots of them.

"I might have experimented on my own—some," Cara said in a quiet voice. "But what child hasn't? I figured it was better to satisfy Lacy's curiosity with me here and the derringer unloaded, rather than having her pick up one of your revolvers out of curiosity."

"For your information, I always unload my weapons once I get home." He had a deputy friend he'd ridden with whose seven-year-old son had accidentally shot his ten-year-old brother when he'd picked up one of his father's loaded guns. Fortunately, the wounded boy had lived, but it served as a warning to him.

"That's a wise thing to do. I can assure you, I would never risk Lacy getting injured."

He stood with his hands on his hips, shaking his head. "I know you think that, Cara, but accidents happen."

"Well, they're less likely to occur if Lacy is familiar with weapons enough so that she can respect how dangerous they are."

"I'll admit that is true, but Lacy is *my* daughter, and you shouldn't have let her handle a gun without my permission." It still rankled him that she hadn't asked him first, but he knew Lacy had probably pestered her half to death until she had agreed to let her hold the tiny weapon just so the girl would hush.

"You're right. I'm sorry."

"Apology accepted." He wanted to stay angry, but it was awfully hard, staring into those pretty green eyes. Cara had braided her lovely cinnamon-colored hair, and the long plait hung over one shoulder and down her chest. Intriguing wisps curled around her face, and the white western hat and the boots she wore looked completely out of place with her pretty emerald day dress.

Cara scowled, her brow puckering in a charming manner. "What are you thinking?"

How much he'd like to haul her into his arms and kiss her. He licked his lips. Then he held out the pistol. "Here."

She took the derringer and shoved it into her pocket. Her gaze dropped down. "Are you mad at me?"

He was. Furious. And yet he wasn't. How could a man's emotions be so conflicted? Ada had been steady. Cara was as fiery as her hair. "I'm trying not to be angry."

"I'm really sorry, Landry. I didn't think there was any harm in her holding an unloaded weapon. I was shooting well before her age." She shrugged one shoulder.

It bothered him that he'd upset her. "Cara, I may have been a bit. . .tyrannical."

She glanced up, her eyes dancing and lips quirking in an intriguing way. "A bit?"

He held up his thumb and index finger, holding them about an inch apart. "This much."

"Oh no." Cara opened her arms wide. "This much."

Landry couldn't resist the opportunity presented to him, and he stepped forward, taking hold of her waist and pulling her toward him. "Cara Dixon, you're the most aggravating and interesting woman I've ever met."

Her eyes sparkled in the afternoon light. "So, are you going to kiss me?"

He chuckled. "Is that what you'd like?"

For a moment, she looked as if she would say no, but then she shrugged. "I'm tempted. I've never kissed a tyrant before."

He growled and hauled her closer, his lips colliding with hers. He pulled her against him as she wrapped her arms around his waist. This was probably a horrible idea, but it felt wonderful. Cara was soft, warm, just like her lips, and she returned his kiss with a fervor he wouldn't soon forget.

He seriously needed to consider marrying this amazing woman.

Chapter 9

Cara sat in the parlor, stitching a pair of boy's pants for an orphan. She finished the hem on one leg and glanced up, watching Landry and Lacy leaning over a checkerboard.

Lacy picked up a red disk and hopped it over three of her father's black pieces. The girl giggled and clapped her hands. "I won!"

Landry blew out an exaggerated sigh. "You beat me again. How did you get to be so good at this game?"

"You should know. You're the one who taught me. Can we play another one?"

Landry glanced at the mantel clock. "It's getting late. Let's put this up, and then you need to get ready for bed."

"Yes, sir." Though Lacy responded properly, her tone indicated her disappointment.

"We can play again tomorrow." Landry slid the playing pieces across the board and dropped them into their tin can.

Lacy put the board and can in the cabinet. She walked over to Cara, paused, then leaned down and hugged her. "I hope I didn't get you in too much trouble today," she whispered.

Cara thought back to Landry's amazing kiss. "It worked out just fine. Don't you worry, sweetheart. Sleep well."

"You too." She started for the stairs then turned back to her father. "Are you coming?"

He rose. "In a few minutes. Go ahead and get changed, and I'll be up to pray with you."

"Yes, Papa." Lacy headed up the stairs, and Landry stood watching.

After the door to their suite clicked shut, he moved across the room and sat down next to Cara. "She's growing up so fast."

"My pa used to say that about me." She laid her stitching in her lap and folded her hands over it.

"So, where are Aunt Pearl and Miss Stewart tonight?"

"Aunt Pearl said a good book was calling to her, so she retired to her room a bit early. Dinah is altering a dress for a girl whose birthday is tomorrow evening. Her mother will be picking it up in the morning."

"Good. That means we're alone." He slid his hand across the settee and laid it on top of hers. "That kiss has been driving me nuts."

Cara nibbled her lip. She hadn't been able to forget their wonderful embrace and kiss. It was one of the most exciting things that had ever happened to her. Did he feel differently? "What exactly do you mean?"

He drew her hand away from her lap and rested it on the couch, with his clutching hers. The touch of his warm skin on hers sent chills charging up her arm. "I mean I can't quit thinking about it. I want to do it again."

She turned to face him. "You do?"

He sighed. "Very much. But it isn't wise, given the fact that we are both single."

"Well, it would be worse if we were both married—to other people, I mean."

He chuckled and ran his thumb across her skin. "You are right again. How did you get to be so wise?"

"It just comes naturally," she said in a teasing tone. "Or perhaps it's because I'm a Texan."

He shook his head, but a big smile engulfed his handsome face. "I need to tell you something."

He turned in the seat so that he was facing her better. "And what is that?"

"I originally agreed to help Dinah for a year, and that time ends the first of July. I got a letter from Pa this week, reminding me that he expects me to return on time. He misses me, but I think he also wants me home so that he can set me up with some rancher he knows."

Landry was quiet for a long while. "What if you were to tell him that you'd already met someone who'd taken a fancy to you?"

She opened her mouth, but nothing came out.

He reached out and gently pushed up her jaw, then he ran his finger down her cheek. She closed her eyes, enjoying every second of his touch.

"Cara, look at me."

She opened her eyes and was immediately captured by his intense gaze.

"I realize we haven't known one another long, but I don't want you returning home and spending time with other men. We need to see where these feelings we have are taking us."

Disappointment nibbled at her. She had hoped his kiss meant he felt as strongly as she did. She had wanted him to propose. "We have several weeks yet."

He frowned.

How long did it take a man to know if he loved a woman? Perhaps she should try being less trouble. It was true that they hadn't known one another long, but she knew she'd never felt this way about another man, not even Davis. She dreamed of Landry nearly every moment of the day and night. She'd already set up a home in her mind and longed to be Lacy's mother. The thought of him not being sure of his feelings made her eyes sting—and she never cried.

She needed to change the topic before she embarrassed herself. "Have you had any luck capturing those outlaws?"

"No. But the payroll robbery was the most recent one. I still think someone working for the railroad tipped off the thieves."

"That's awful. Honesty and loyalty are very important in Texas, but I've learned that's not always the case in other places." She tugged her hand away from his and started stitching so he wouldn't grab it again. "I'm not saying St. Louis is bad, because there are vile people everywhere."

"I know what you mean. Out west people seem to value honesty and trustworthiness, and their word is gold."

"Exactly." She threaded her needle and began hemming the other pant leg. "Dinah and I have decided to attend the Paris Fashion Show in Chicago next week. We'll be leaving on Monday."

"So much for our spending time together."

"She and I have been discussing this for a long while."

"But you just got back from there." He crossed his arms,

evidently not pleased.

"I went to visit my sister, and it's a good thing I did. I was able to be with her when her daughter Allison died and to comfort her and Timothy and the children."

"My apologies. I'm sorry about the loss of your niece. I can't imagine how hard it must be to lose a child."

"I certainly hope you never have to find out."

"Me too."

"As I was thinking about our trip, I got an idea how you could capture the robbers."

Landry watched Cara sewing the tiny pair of britches, and a part of him wished she were making them for their child. He'd almost asked her to marry him, but he had to be sure that marrying Cara was the right thing for them both—and for Lacy especially. He was almost certain, but one thing he'd learned as a lawman was not to rush. Be patient. Take time to look at something from all angles. It always paid off in the end.

Still, waiting was hard when all he wanted to do was tug her back into his arms and show her how much he cared. He needed to be careful. Landry realized what she had just said. "What's your idea?"

She dropped her sewing and looked at him, eyes warming again. "I was thinking that since I already plan to go on the trip with Dinah, I could spread the word that I'll be carrying a lot of jewelry. You could covertly help get the word out so that we could lure the outlaws into a trap. What do you think? Good idea, huh?"

Landry bolted off the couch, unable to believe the gall that Cara had to put herself—and Dinah—in harm's way. "That is a horrible idea."

Cara scowled and crossed her arms. "Why? What don't you like about it?"

"For one, you'd be putting yourself in danger, and I can't tolerate that. I won't allow it."

Cara jumped up. "What do you mean, you won't allow it? You're not my boss."

In spite of being upset that she'd be so reckless with her safety, he was attracted by her blazing eyes and fierce expression. "I care for you, Cara. I don't want to see you get hurt."

"I've been in far more dangerous situations than riding a train."

"I won't deny that, because I've spent some time in Texas chasing outlaws, so I know how rough things are there. But that doesn't mean you set yourself up as the bait. It's far too dangerous."

"I disagree." She hiked up her chin, her lips forming an intriguing pout.

He wanted to kiss her despite being upset with her. He turned and walked across the room, putting space between them. "It's my job to oversee the security of the railroad and its passengers. I can't allow you to do such a foolhardy thing."

"Fine." She snagged her sewing and dropped it in the basket at the side of the sofa. Then she made a beeline for the stairs. "Goodnight."

"Cara, wait. Don't storm off mad."

She kept going and shut her door a bit harder than normal.

Landry blew out a frustrated breath and forked his hands through his hair. What an infuriating woman. How was it he could love a woman that stubborn and daring?

Love?

The word made him pause. His love for Ada had come slowly and taken years to cultivate. How was it that Cara had stormed into his life and so handily stolen a huge chunk of his heart?

The little thief.

Landry smiled in spite of his frustration. He turned down the lamp and climbed the stairs. He needed to spend time reading God's Word and praying about his relationship with his little vixen. He needed God's clarity on the situation so that he didn't jump ahead too soon.

His mind drifted back to Cara's crazy plan. He hated to admit that the idea had merit—although he wouldn't risk putting her in danger. But what if he and Pete spread the word that there would be a big shipment of jewels on one of the trains? They could hire extra men and set a trap. It just might work.

Dinah moved across the train seat, closer to Cara. "I sure hope you know what you're doing. I don't want either of us to get shot."

"We'll be fine. You'll see."

"I hope you mentioned your little scheme to Landry."

Oh, she had, and he'd shot it down—more than once. "I told him."

"So, where is he?" Dinah looked at the watch pinned to her bodice. "We left Chicago nearly an hour ago. I thought the reason he met us there was to escort us home."

"It is, but he's also working. He's checking the other cars, and then he'll join us."

"You want me to move across to the backward-riding seat so you two can sit together?" She winked.

"No, silly. You stay right here."

"I sure hope you get married in St. Louis so I don't have to ride the train all the way to Texas."

Cara gasped. "Dinah! What makes you say such a thing?"

"I told you before that Landry is smitten. It's written all over his face."

"Well, he hasn't talked marriage, so you'd better hush."

Dinah snickered and laid her head against the seat. "I'm exhausted, but so glad you made me attend the fashion show. I learned a lot, and knowing more about the latest fashions will help us offer our clients garments that are more stylish." She shifted in her seat, as if trying to get comfortable. "Your sister and her husband were extremely hospitable, considering what they've been through so recently. And their three boys are a handful but delightful."

"Yes, they are." Ellen had been thrilled to see Cara again so soon. Cara was relieved to know they were handling the loss of their daughter as well as could be expected. The fashion show, while not exactly her cup of tea, had been interesting, and some of the outlandish garments had her and Dinah giggling, much to the consternation of others seated nearby.

"So, you think the trip was worth it?"

Dinah nodded. "I do. Having to make most of Lacy's outfits made me realize that I need to expand my selection of girls' clothing. The items we ordered at the show will be a great start. I think the mothers will love them and want to buy the latest fashions for their daughters. I've done some calculations, and if we can sell most of them, it will leave me enough funds to reorder and a tidy profit."

"That's fabulous. Now we need to focus on hiring someone to work with you."

"I've narrowed down the list of applicants to three women. I'll have them come in again when you're there so we can both visit with them. Now I'm going to try to sleep a bit." She popped up and moved across to the bench facing Cara. Dinah winked then laid her head back against the seat. "There's more room over here."

Cara didn't see how her friend could sleep on the noisy, rocking train. She was far too anxious to relax. In spite of Landry's objections, she had covertly spread word that she was carrying a large amount of jewelry that she'd bought at the fashion show. She hoped it wasn't too late to nab the outlaws. They would only know about the jewels if they'd been hanging around the depot and had overheard her.

She pulled her derringer out of her reticule and placed it on the seat under her skirt. At least she'd be ready if they came. She wished Dinah would have agreed to do the same, but her friend had been too frightened to carry a weapon. It was probably for the best. Dinah might shoot herself or another passenger.

Where was Landry? He should have joined them by now. Had he encountered problems in another car? She glanced down the aisle to the door at the far end, then pulled out the dime novel she'd borrowed from Aunt Pearl and started reading.

A short while later, Landry entered the car. His dark gaze immediately landed on hers, making her heart clench. Had he learned what she'd done?

He dropped beside her, glanced at Dinah, then motioned toward the rear door.

She hiked up her chin. "I'm not going out on that platform and losing another hat. I just bought this one."

"Fine. Let everyone in the car hear what I have to say."

"Hear what?" She feigned innocence.

He leaned close, his eyes stormy. "You went behind my back and told people you were carrying a boatload of jewels."

Trainload, but she didn't think it was wise to correct him right now. "I merely wanted to help you capture the thieves."

"By endangering yourself and others?"

"Most things worth doing include some measure of danger."

He leaned over, elbows on his knees, and held his face in his hands. "You're the most exasperating woman I've ever met. You ought to return to Texas. At least on the ranch you'd be safe from outlaws."

It wasn't the right time to mention that there were plenty of outlaws in Texas. She leaned back, knowing she deserved his tongue-lashing. She could only hope he'd forgive her and that this wouldn't ruin their relationship.

Chapter 10

Landry glanced at his pocket watch for what felt like the fiftieth time. Thirty minutes more, and they would arrive in St. Louis. He allowed some of the tension to seep out of him. Surely, if the outlaws were going to attempt a robbery, they would have done it by now. Perhaps they'd dodged a bullet. Or two.

He was so angry with Cara. What a reckless, foolhardy thing to do. Yes, she was trying to help, but he never wanted her to risk her safety to assist him. He loved her—he knew that now—but how could he entrust Lacy's well-being to someone who'd so willingly and recklessly endanger herself?

Would she have done the same thing if Lacy had been along? Somehow he couldn't believe she would. But no matter how he felt, he didn't dare risk his daughter's safety. He needed to think and pray hard before asking Cara to marry him.

He glanced over at her. She'd pretty much kept her face in the dime novel she was reading. Every once in a while, she'd reach up and wipe her eyes. Was the book upsetting her, or was it him? Perhaps she'd finally realized how careless she'd acted.

Landry was anxious to get back and see how Lacy had fared with Aunt Pearl the past two days. She had done fine when he'd escorted Cara and Dinah to Chicago. Making the long trip twice in one week was a bit much, but it had allowed him to watch over the passengers and freight.

He yawned and stretched. Sleeping in his comfortable bed at the boardinghouse would feel good after all the jostling of the train.

The door at the far end of the car opened, and Landry froze. He ducked his head, covertly watching the three men who entered. They strolled down the aisle, looking at each of the passengers—no, just the women. They passed right by a pair of men sitting together and didn't even glance their way.

This was it. They were looking for Cara.

He glanced at her, then tugged his hat lower and slowly pulled out his gun. Cara stiffened beside him, set her novel aside, and slid her hand beneath the folds of her skirt.

"They're here. Try to relax," he whispered.

He'd stationed another agent in the middle of the car. Landry was glad he had the sense not to turn around and look at him once the outlaws had passed him. He blew out a breath when a third agent at the far door of the railcar lifted his hat and scratched his head—a signal that he was aware of the situation. It was three against three, but how could they stop the men without the passengers—or Cara and Dinah—getting hurt?

Landry double-checked that all the chambers in his revolver

were loaded. Cara suddenly jumped up, rushed past him, and fled out the back of the railcar.

The three robbers noticed her and charged toward the rear door. Landry leapt up and raised his gun, stepping between her and the thieves. The other agents slipped up behind the trio. Several passengers gasped and ducked down.

"I'm Special Agent Lomax. I suggest you drop your weapons. There are three of us, and we each have a bead on one of you. Go for your guns, and you're dead."

The two outlaws in back looked behind them then dropped their guns and raised their hands. The ruffian closest to Landry narrowed his eyes, lifted his gun, and fired at the same time Landry did. The bullet whizzed past his temple, and the glass in the door behind Landry shattered.

People screamed, and Dinah jerked awake, looking around, wide-eyed. The bandit Landry shot grabbed his gut and dropped to his knees. Landry hurried forward and kicked the man's gun out of reach. He pulled a length of rope from his pocket and tied the outlaw's hands. Groaning and cursing, the man eyed Landry with hatred.

His men had tied up the other two robbers and were leading them toward the cattle cars, where they would stay until the train arrived in St. Louis. A lacy handkerchief appeared from over his shoulder, and Landry glanced up to see Dinah's concerned expression. "Thank you."

He pressed the handkerchief against the man's wound. The robber moaned. Most men didn't survive a gut shot. Landry hated the thought of killing a man, but he'd deal with those feelings later. He hauled the man to his feet and looked at the back door. Where was Cara? Had she run through the next two passenger cars? Was she hiding somewhere?

His gaze shifted to Dinah. "I need to get this man to the cattle car. Could you please check on Cara?"

"Where did she go?"

He nodded with his chin toward the back door.

Dinah glanced out, the breeze flowing through the broken glass, lifting loose tendrils of her dark hair. "You want me to go out on the platform while the train is moving?"

A man sitting nearby rose. "I'll take this man up front for you."

Landry shook his head. "I'm obliged, but it's my job."

"How about I check on the young lady then, since her friend is hesitant to venture out?"

Landry studied the older man whose hazel eyes held only concern. He nodded. "I'd be grateful, Mr.—?"

"Harold Oswald."

"I shouldn't be long." Landry guided the thief toward the front of the car while Mr. Oswald headed to the rear. At the mail car, he handed the wounded man off to Rolly Herman then started back. Concern for Cara made him anxious to see her, although he had no idea what he would say to the vexing woman.

He entered the passenger car next to the one Cara had been riding in and looked up to see Dinah rushing toward him, fear engulfing her face. He quickened his pace and met her halfway. "What's wrong?"

Dinah's eyes glistened with unshed tears. "Cara has been shot."

Fear grabbed hold of his heart like an attacker choking the breath out of him. He stepped past Dinah and ran to the end of the car, flung the door open, and rushed through the next car. Cara was lying on the same seat where she'd been sitting earlier.

Mr. Oswald sat across from her, looking worried. "I found her on the platform. The bullet that broke the glass hit her in the shoulder. She's a tough little thing. Didn't even moan when I helped her up."

Cara pushed up. "I'm a Texan. We don't moan."

Landry hurried to her side. "Are you all right? How bad is it? Let me see."

"I lost my new hat." She frowned.

"For heaven's sake, Cara. You've been shot. I'm worried about you, not a stupid hat that can be replaced."

"Fine. I was shot through and through. I'll live long enough to torment you another day."

Landry frowned. "That's not funny. You could have been killed. I knew this harebrained idea would get someone hurt."

Cara winced as if he'd slapped her. Landry felt a sharp pain in his gut. He knew his words had hurt her, but what she'd done was more than foolish. The thought that she could have been killed left a hollow ache in his gut.

"Let me see your wound."

She hiked her pert little chin. "Dinah tended to it."

Landry blew out a sigh. "You need a doctor. I'm going to go find one." He shot to his feet, needing to do something for the woman he loved—the woman he was still spitting mad at for endangering herself and the other passengers.

"Anyone here a doctor?" he hollered. When no one responded, he stormed down the aisle. He should have found a doctor for the outlaw, but he'd been so focused on making sure Cara was safe that he hadn't thought about it.

Dinah slipped past him and hurried toward Cara.

Landry stormed toward the door. What irked him most was

that her little plan had worked. He worried that she would willingly put herself in danger again should a similar situation arise.
Yes, they'd caught three outlaws. It was still a drop in the bucket,
but perhaps knowing these men had gotten caught, as well as the
man he'd apprehended the day he and Cara first met, would make
other outlaws hesitant to attack the railroad.

He entered the next car, calling out for a doctor. His relief was
immense when a man rose, grabbed a black bag, and headed his
way. While the doctor tended Cara, Landry stood guard.

What was he going to do? He loved Cara. But he feared she'd
do something foolish again, and this time it might be Lacy who got
hurt. He couldn't risk that. No matter how much it broke his heart
to realize it.

Four days after getting shot, Cara sat next to her father on the
train, headed home to Texas. Her arm ached, but she would live
and should have full use of it once it healed. Her heart was another
issue. She doubted it would ever be whole again.

She stared out the window, watching the last of St. Louis
pass by. For the past four days, Landry had avoided her. She'd
taken her meals in her room the first two days back. Then her
father had arrived, and she'd eaten downstairs with him and
the others, but Landry hadn't said a word to her. Whenever she
caught his eye, he always flicked his gaze away. He hated her,
and it was all her fault.

Saying goodbye to Lacy had been one of the hardest things
she had ever done. The girl had cried and told her she had hoped
Cara would marry her father so she could be her new mama.
Tears burned Cara's eyes. She hated disappointing the little girl

she'd grown to love.

With how things had ended between her and Landry, he probably wouldn't want Cara writing to Lacy. He'd want to cut things off completely so his daughter didn't get hurt further.

The one comfort she had was that Dinah and Aunt Pearl were there to love on Lacy. Perhaps now that she was gone, Landry would turn his eyes on Dinah.

Just the thought made her press her hand to her churning stomach. When had she fallen in love? And how had it happened so quickly?

"Are you all right?" Her father looked at her with worry etched on his leathery face. "Is your arm hurting?"

"Some." It was better he thought that, especially since it was true, than he discover her heart was shattered.

"Are you sure you don't want some of the pain powder the doctor left for you?" He patted his pocket. "Got it right here."

She shook her head. "It makes me sleep too much. I wonder, though, if you'd mind checking on Honey. I'd rest better knowing she was doing all right."

He smiled. "Happy to." He rose and ambled down the aisle, looking every bit the Texan that he was, still dressed in his cowboy garb.

With him gone, it was harder to hold back the tears.

She understood now why her father had wanted her to marry. Love was a wonderful thing, as long as both people felt love for one another. But to care for someone who didn't return your affection was pure misery. Perhaps if she'd tried to be more ladylike or sweet like Dinah, then Landry may have fallen in love with her. But she was too daring for him.

She'd messed up any chance she had with him when she'd gone

ahead with her jewelry plan. It didn't matter that they'd apprehended the outlaws. Landry hadn't even thanked her.

Cara leaned her head against the glass. She hadn't been able to tell him goodbye. Not that it would have mattered. He'd made it clear how he felt by ignoring her. It would be easier for them both with her gone.

She longed to be home. Longed to lope Honey across the plains and feel the wind in her face. She had hoped to one day do that with Landry and Lacy by her side, but that day would never happen now.

How many months—or years—would it take for her aching heart to heal?

Two weeks after her accident, Cara's arm had mostly stopped hurting. If only her heart would do the same. Pa had said that only time could heal such a wound. She wished she could make time fly by, but it had dragged since she returned home.

She brushed Honey, more than ready to take her first ride. Pa had forbidden her to ride until the local doctor had given his approval, which he had done this morning, but she wasn't allowed to lift anything heavy. She pulled a burr from Honey's mane and flicked it to the ground, not even caring that it pricked her skin. She sighed and laid her head against her horse.

Would she ever feel whole again?

Moping wouldn't help a thing—she knew that—but she'd never had a broken heart before. With a deep breath of resolve, she stiffened her spine and took hold of Honey's lead. Together they plodded out of the stall.

"Hey, sis, want me to saddle her. . .you know. . .since you aren't supposed to lift nothin'?" Billy, her youngest brother, walked toward her. At fifteen he was already nearly as tall as their pa.

"Yes, that would be nice. Thank you."

Cara grabbed the saddle blanket and laid it on Honey's back. She ducked her head to hide her grimace, caused by the upward motion, then she stepped aside.

Billy tossed the saddle on and cinched it. Then he turned to Cara. "Need a boost? I don't imagine you're ready to pull yourself up just yet."

"Once we get outside." Normally, her brothers wouldn't offer to help because they knew she was fully capable of doing things herself. Having to let them help was humbling, but she didn't mind in this instance.

As they walked out of the barn, Billy glanced sideways at her. "It's good having you home, sis."

"Good to be here."

"You plan on staying?"

"For now. Dinah hired a woman to work with her, so she doesn't need my help anymore."

"I'd best get back to the house. A man arrived to talk to pa. Probably lookin' to buy a horse, and with everyone else out rounding up strays, I'm the only one that can help if he needs it. You sure you'll be all right on your own?"

Cara nodded. "I'm taking things slowly. Just a nice walk today to see how I do."

"That's smart."

They heard voices at the front door and turned together. Pa exited the door with another man following. Cara's heart bucked. Even from this distance she recognized Landry's build. What was *he* doing here?

"That was fast." Billy swatted a fly. "That man must know just what he wants, to get done so quickly. I best go see what it is." He started to walk away, but Cara grabbed his arm.

"He's here to see me."

"You? How come?" His brown eyes narrowed. "Is he the yahoo that has you so upset? Want me to go slug 'im?"

Cara smiled at his eager willingness to defend her. "Let me talk to him first. If he upsets me again, you can have at 'im."

"All right. Just holler if you need me." He took Honey's reins. "I'll hitch her to the corral. I'll be in the barn."

Pa stayed on the porch as Landry trotted down the steps, hat in hand. Cara's whole body quivered. She could think of only two reasons for Landry to be here. Had he finally forgiven her? Or had he come to lambast her for upsetting Lacy so much?

Cara looked past him, hoping to see the girl, but she wasn't in sight. Standing her ground, Cara let him come to her. His long strides ate up the ground before she had time to regain her composure at seeing him here. He clenched the brim of his hat, his gaze uncertain.

Her heart thundered.

His blue eyes moved from her face to her shoulder and back. "It's good to see you're doing so well."

"Thank you."

He ducked his head. "I owe you an apology."

Cara blinked, surprised by his statement. "For what? I'm the one who's sorry."

He smiled—soft and gentle. "I was overly stubborn. I knew what my heart wanted, but I was upset at you for endangering yourself. I should have told you how I felt sooner."

Cara licked her lips, wondering how he actually felt. If her heart raced any harder, it just might stampede clear out of her chest. Dare she hope he loved her as much as she did him?

He stepped closer. "You stormed into my life and stole my heart before I knew what was what."

She sucked in a gasp.

"You scared me spitless when you got shot, and then I wondered how safe Lacy would be with you. I had to think things through. And then you were gone, without even a goodbye." Pain laced his eyes.

"I would never purposely endanger Lacy, but at the same time, I believe a female needs to know how to defend herself. I'll not back down from that."

"Sticking to your convictions is one of the many reasons that I love you."

Cara sucked in another sharp breath, unable to believe what she was hearing. "You love me?"

"Yes, so much so that I can't let you go." He opened his mouth to continue, then stopped, looking unsure. "That is. . .I mean. . .as long as you feel the same."

Finally, she allowed herself to smile and reached out to touch his arm. "I do. I love you so much, Landry. I've been miserable the past two weeks, thinking I ruined things between us."

"When I got home the day you left, and found Lacy all red-eyed from crying, I felt gut-punched. I knew I'd messed up and that you were gone because I took too long getting over being upset about you risking your neck in that train robbery. I realized I was mad because I loved you so much and was worried about you. Please put me out of my misery and marry me, Cara."

"Yes, oh yes!" She grabbed her hat and threw it into the air. Then she grabbed her shoulder. "Ow."

"Careful, now." Landry gently pulled her into his arms, a wide smile on his handsome face. He leaned down, and their lips met. He pressed her against him, holding her deliciously close, kissing her like there was no tomorrow. Her nervous quivers from moments before turned into delicious shivers.

A loud squeal from the direction of the house broke them apart. Cara turned to see Lacy running toward them. As the girl drew near, Landry stepped in front of her.

"Slow down and be gentle. Cara's wound is still sore."

A big smile engulfed Lacy's face. "Is it true? Are you going to be my new mama?"

"It looks that way, since your papa asked me to marry him."

Lacy squealed again and clapped her hands. Then she slowly stepped forward, into Cara's open arms. Landry wrapped his arms around the two of them.

"I'm so excited that we'll be a family." Lacy leaned her head against Cara's chest.

"I have a question," Cara said. "Where are we going to live?"

Landry released his hold and stepped back. "I turned in my badge to my boss in St. Louis. The job was entirely too dangerous—crazy women and trainloads of outlaws." He smiled and winked at Cara. "I talked to your father, and he's willing to teach me how to be a rancher, so it looks like we'll be living in Texas."

Cara couldn't suppress her grin. "Sounds like life will be perfect, except that Dinah will have to travel here for the wedding."

Landry took her hand. "I think she'll be willing, all things considered."

Cara's father walked toward them, eyes twinkling. It seemed like today everyone was smiling. When she woke up this morning, miserable and lonely, she never could have imagined the day turning out as it had. For two weeks she'd prayed for Landry to come to his senses and to forgive her, and he finally had. God had answered her prayers.

She could hardly wait to become Mrs. Landry Lomax.

Vickie McDonough is an award-winning author of nearly fifty published books and novellas, with more than 1.5 million copies sold. A bestselling author, Vickie grew up wanting to marry a rancher, but instead she married a computer geek who is scared of horses. She now lives out her dreams penning romance stories about ranchers, cowboys, lawmen, and others living in the Old West. Her novels include *End of the Trail*, winner of the OWFI 2013 Booksellers Best Fiction Novel Award. *Whispers on the Prairie* was a *Romantic Times* Recommended Inspirational Book for July 2013. *Song of the Prairie* won the 2015 Inspirational Readers' Choice Award. *Gabriel's Atonement*, book 1 in the Land Rush Dreams series, placed second in the 2016 Will Rogers Medallion Award. Vickie has recently stepped into independent publishing.

Vickie has been married for more than forty years to Robert. They have four grown sons, one daughter-in-law, and a precocious granddaughter. When she's not writing, Vickie enjoys reading, doing stained glass, watching movies, and traveling. To learn more about Vickie's books or to sign up for her newsletter, visit her website at www.vickiemcdonough.com.

Mistaken Marshal

by Crystal L. Barnes

To God be the glory.

Lo, I am with you alway, even unto
the end of the world. Amen.
Matthew 28:20

Trust in the Lord *with all thine heart; and lean not unto*
thine own understanding. In all thy ways
acknowledge him, and he shall direct thy paths.
Proverbs 3:5–6

❧ *Prologue* ❧

"Once upon a time in a land far, far away—"

"No, no, no." Eleven-year-old Andy sat up on his pallet in the middle of the cabin's living room floor. "Not one of those stories, Grampa. One of *your* stories. From the old days. You know, with the outlaws and shootin' and showdowns."

"No." Dalton popped up from his place beside his big brother and added his two cents. "I want to hear a story like Robin Hood."

"A love story, Grampa." Six-year-old Madelyn, the youngest, squeezed her doll tighter and cuddled closer into her grandmother's side on the couch.

Beau Bones sat back in his rocker. "A love story, shootouts, and Robin Hood, huh?" He scratched his jaw. "Gramma, can you think of a story like that?"

"There is one that comes to mind." She shared a conspiratorial grin with him as she stroked their granddaughter's dark curls from her brow.

"You think they're ready for it?"

"Yeah!" Andy said.

"Please, please, please, please," Dalton begged.

Leaning forward in his rocking chair, Beau pitched his voice to a mysterious tone. "The year was 1875."

The boys snuggled back down in their blankets, the firelight from the hearth dancing across their eager faces.

Beau leaned back in his chair and let the years drift away. "The days were hot, and the Wild West was still alive and well in Small Tree, Texas."

Chapter 1

Small Tree, Texas
August 1875

*L*iving the life of Robin Hood wasn't what it was cracked up to be. In fact, Jodie Ross was getting mighty sick of it. Especially when dodging bullets. She knew she should've stayed with the horses like usual.

"Jerry, I oughta skin you alive for pickin' this town. I told ya we had enough, but would you listen to me? No. Now look at us." Another round whizzed by her head, making her duck back beneath the windowsill. She flicked a short strand of dark hair out of her face to glare at him. "We're like fish in a barrel in here."

Her much older brother continued to fire out the broken window of the general store with nary a glance her direction or hint of worry to his tone. "Did ya leave the horses where I told ya?"

"Of course. But I don't see how we're gonna get to 'em with half the county shootin' at us."

Jerry gave Dix and Pat a nod before tugging down his gray bandanna and exposing her to that wild grin she'd learned to fear. "You know I always got a plan, Jo."

A plan? What kinda plan would get them outta such a tight spot? The last time they'd been holed up like this, it'd taken— "No. Oh no. Jerry, you wouldn't. You didn't. You promised."

"Aw, don't be such a stick-in-the-mud, Jo. Live a little." Grinning all the while, Jerry grabbed a barrel of pinto beans and shoved it up next to her other side.

Dix and Pat darted back into the room and crouched their large frames behind the oak counter. A heartbeat later an explosion shook the building and shattered what little glass remained on the windows and shelves.

She was gonna kill him. That's all there was left to it. Because if she didn't, they were all gonna end up dead. With ears ringing and gunpowder stinging her bandanna-covered nose, Jodie socked her brother in the chest, scrambled to her feet, and stepped over the unconscious form of the storekeeper. She darted after the others, leaving Jerry to grab up the remaining loot and supplies.

The short distance between the now gaping back end of the general store and the oak grove behind the small town felt like a country mile as Jodie dashed across the grassy expanse. By the time she entered the trees, flying lead splintered the bark above her head.

She glanced over her shoulder for Jerry.

"Don't stop. Keep goin'." He tossed the bag of foodstuffs into her arms and grabbed her elbow, propelling her forward until they reached the horses she'd staked near a small creek.

Dix and Pat already galloped upstream, heading toward the rendezvous point.

More bullets slammed into trees as she snatched Blossom's reins from a nearby branch. Their pursuers were getting closer.

"Hurry up." Jerry circled his horse in the water.

"Go. I'm right behind you." For once he listened. Loud splashing accompanied Jodie's hurried clamber into the saddle. Dropping the bag's handle around the saddle horn, she sank spur.

Something black and tan bolted through the trees right in front of her. Blossom reared with a squeal. Before Jodie could react, she found herself tumbling heels over head.

Another horse bolted from the trees to Beau's right, making the wild galloping cease and his crazed horse rear, sending him tumbling backward to the ground. He hit the dirt hard, seconds before something slammed into his air-deprived chest. At first he thought it was the beast, until the assault continued. An elbow connected with his stomach. Another with his jaw.

Blinking away stars and gasping for breath, Beau did the first thing that came to mind, a move that'd occasionally worked on his brothers—he pinned the smaller person's arms down with a bear hug.

"Let me go!"

"Easy. I'm not—"

A boot heel connected with his shin. "Jerry!"

With a grunt, Beau tightened his hold and seriously considered granting the kid's request when a shout from his right stopped both their movements.

"Hold it right there." A short man broke through the trees, a shotgun in his hands, both barrels aimed at them.

Another lanky fellow stumbled into the creek-side clearing and halted, straightening. His dishwater brows rose. "He caught one of them?"

"One of who?" Beau glanced at the dark-haired kid in his hold, a kid who wore a bandanna covering all but his wide blue eyes. A bandanna? What on earth had that spawn-of-Satan horse gotten him into?

"See if you can find the others," Shorty ordered.

The troublemaker turned his head, causing the bandanna to slip, revealing smooth cheeks without a hint of stubble.

"Right." With a nod, Lanky hurried toward the water.

Without warning, the kid sank his teeth into Beau's arm and broke from his hold.

"Ouch! Why, you little brat!" Beau snagged the boy's leg, knocking him to the ground, and pinned him in the wet sand. "I ought to turn you over my knee."

"We're going to do worse than that."

At the new voice, fear flickered in the kid's eyes.

Keeping his hands on the young man's shoulders, Beau looked up to find a well-dressed, if winded, older gentleman standing next to Shorty, gun drawn.

"Nice work, mister. You just caught yourself an outlaw."

An outlaw? Beau glanced down at the youngster whose voice hadn't even changed. He couldn't be more than thirteen or fourteen. How could someone so young already be an outlaw? Troublemaker, yes, but outlaw?

"Where are the other three?" the gentleman questioned.

Shorty cocked his head toward the water. "Lawson went to see if he could find their trail."

"Mr. Grimes, perhaps you should lend Mr. Lawson a hand."

With a nod, Shorty took off as another man approached, horses in tow.

"Mr. Hewitt, toss this fella a rope and help them, please, sir." The dapper gentleman took the horses' reins from the balding man Beau had met at the livery earlier that day and turned to Beau. "I believe Mr. . . . ."

"Bones," Beau offered as he accepted the rope from Hewitt and set to binding the outlaw's hands.

"I believe Mr. Bones and I can manage this one on our own." The leader paused, drawing Beau's gaze upward. The bearded man looked from Beau to Satan's Spawn—or Buster as the horse was more commonly known, a name which now made much more sense considering his aching backside—and back again. "Bones? Are you any kin to our late marshal?"

Beau finished securing the knot, one perfected by what his brothers used to use on him through the years, and hauled the youngster to his feet. "Yes, sir. He was my uncle."

"Well, looks like you two were cut from the same cloth."

Beau wished that were true. His namesake had been brave, fierce, afraid of nothing and no one. He was the only one who'd ever believed Beau could amount to something, could do more than struggle in his brothers' shadows. He'd hoped by coming to Small Tree, Texas, he could prove his uncle right. Prove everyone else wrong. Prove that he could be his own man. But on his first day in town, he couldn't even ride his uncle's horse.

"I'm Mayor Arthur Jones." After shaking Beau's hand, the graying gentleman led the way through the trees, the prisoner between them. "I assume you're here to settle your uncle's estate, Mr. Bones. Are you going to be in town long?"

"Well, I, uh. . .I'd thought to stay on awhile, but—"

"Wonderful. We could sure use a man like you around Small Tree. As you can see, trouble has already found us in the short time since your uncle's passing. My condolences, by the way."

"Thank you."

"What would it take to talk you into staying on and being our new town marshal?"

Beau couldn't help laughing at the outlandish thought. "Not much, bu—"

"Stupendous! You're hired."

"Hired? Wait. What?"

"The job comes with a monthly stipend, plus room and board." The mayor kept talking, but Beau's brain couldn't take in any more.

Hired? Him? A marshal? He didn't know anything about being a lawman, only the wild tales his uncle used to spin when he'd come to visit. Tales a little boy with seven older brothers could only imagine experiencing. He couldn't fill his uncle's boots, not in a thousand years, not in ten thousand. The mayor was highly mistaken if he thought Beau could handle such an important job. Sure, he'd always dreamed of such a chance, but he couldn't. . .

He wouldn't. . .

It wasn't right to let the mayor, the town, think him capable—

The outlaw stumbled, breaking Beau's inner argument and his grip on the kid's arm. The boy pivoted toward the trees.

"Oh no, you don't." Beau had tried that move with his brothers too many times to count. Snagging the youngster's waist, he tossed him over his shoulder.

The mayor angled him a grin. "See, I knew you were the right man for the job the minute I laid eyes on you. This way, Marshal.

I'll show you where you can lock up this prisoner. Then we'll send for the judge."

At the praise, Beau couldn't help standing a little straighter. Maybe he could do this job. Maybe this was the exact opportunity he'd prayed for almost all his life. Maybe, just maybe, if he tried real hard, he could prove the mayor hadn't just made the biggest mistake of his life by making Beau Bones the newest marshal of Small Tree, Texas.

Jodie couldn't get off the new marshal's shoulder soon enough, but she could've lived forever without hearing the resounding clank of a latching cell door. The harsh smack of metal upon metal echoed all the way to her core, chilling her to the bone even in the August heat. A simple bunk, a single window, and a host of iron bars surrounded her. How had her life come to this?

"You might as well sit down, sonny." The one called Mayor Jones handed the large key ring to the younger rat with the dark brown eyes, broad shoulders, and way-too-fast reflexes. "You're not going anywhere anytime soon."

"That's what you think," she mumbled.

"What was that?"

Stiffening her spine, she faced the dandy. "Nothin'."

Her brother wouldn't leave her there to rot. He'd get her out.

Marshal Bones settled a hand on the bars, his handsome face coming much too close to a look of compassion. "What's your name, kid?"

"None of your business. And don't call me kid." The man had a lot of nerve calling her a kid. He only had a few years on her at most. Probably couldn't be but twenty-three, surely not old enough to call her "kid."

"You wouldn't want to tell us where the others went, would you?"

Jodie crossed her arms and glared in response.

"That's what I thought." The dark-haired lawman turned to the mayor and shrugged. "It didn't hurt to ask."

"Keep working on him. Maybe you'll find out something." The mayor donned his bowler hat over his pristine silver and brass locks. "I'll let you know as soon as the search party returns, and I'll get that telegram off to the judge for you. You go on and settle in here, and I'll let you know what I find out."

"Much obliged, sir."

"I'll also have Mrs. Lottie send two plates over from the boardinghouse." Mayor Jones stepped to a door just past the left end of the cell and opened it. "Your uncle stayed in here when he had prisoners to watch. Sometimes even when he didn't if the boardinghouse was full."

"Thank you, sir. This'll be just fine." The lawman paused. "If you don't mind, can you ask them to bring my things over from the boardinghouse when they come with the food?"

"Of course. That shouldn't be a problem. Mrs. Lottie's boys are dependable lads."

"Good to hear." Bones fiddled with the keys as the mayor headed toward the exit. "By the way, what did this kid do?"

"He and his gang robbed Haskins General Store before they blew up the backside of it."

The strapping lawman swiveled her direction, eyes wide. "You *what*?"

Offering him a smirk, Jodie strode to the bunk and plopped onto the gray blanket covering the lumpy mattress. She was gonna wring her brother's neck for getting her into this mess. Her gaze strayed to the mesh of bars.

If she ever made it out of here.

Beau stared at the baby-faced whippersnapper sitting on the bed inside the cell. How could someone so young get into so much trouble? Sure, boys got into trouble at all ages, but blowing up a building? He had to see that for himself.

"Mayor Jones." Beau rushed to the door and caught the man stepping off the boardwalk. "Mayor Jones, sir."

The gentleman turned around. "Was there something else?"

"Yes, sir. I, uh. . . Could you point me in the direction of the general store? I just arrived in town today, and I figure I should see for myself—"

"If there are any clues. Great thinking. You'll probably want to talk to Mr. Haskins too. I'll introduce you. Follow me."

Clues? Haskins? Was that the store owner? The mayor knew more about being a marshal than Beau did. He'd better learn fast or everyone would know what a fraud they'd hired. Lengthening his stride, he hurried after Mayor Jones.

❧ Chapter 2 ❧

*I*f that marshal menace didn't step outta the office soon, Jodie was gonna explode. Pacing across the tiny cell once more, she tried to ignore the sounds of trickling tea splashing into a tin cup and the unwelcome urges it evoked.

She wasn't sure how much longer she could maintain her dignity and abstain from using the chipped chamber pot under the bed. She should've taken care of such business while Bones was out doing whatever he'd been doing, but she hadn't needed to go then and she'd had no idea how long he'd be gone.

"Kid, you're driving me crazy with all that pacing. Can I get you a book or something?"

Jodie sprang on the offer. "Yes, please." Anything to have a moment of privacy.

With a nod, Bones set his cup on the desk. "I got just the thing right here." He stepped to the bag two boys had brought over with supper.

Muffling a groan, Jodie sank onto the mattress, her heel bouncing with the urgency coursing through her.

The marshal crossed the short space between them and extended a black leather-bound book through the bars.

"Don't you have a book in your room or something?"

Wrinkles scrunched his forehead. "You don't want this book?"

Jodie sprang from the mattress and snatched it away from him. A Bible? Of all things. "If I read this, will you *please* lock the front door and go to the other room for a minute?"

"Do I look that stupid?" He folded his arms. "I never did search you. Do you have some kind of something to pick the lock on you?"

She did have the fork from supper in her boot, but she wasn't about to tell him that. Besides, she had much bigger concerns than picking locks at the moment.

"You do, don't you?"

Her attention darted to those too-keen eyes of his. If she didn't get better at hiding things, he was gonna discover all her secrets.

Bones extended his hand. "Come on, kid, hand it over."

"*If* I do have something, and *if* I do hand it over, will you do as I asked?"

"*If* you do have something, and *if* you do hand it over. . .I'll. . .think about it."

"Aw, come on. I'm not gonna do nothin'." She shifted her weight from boot to boot. This was taking too long.

"Then why do you want me to leave the room?"

"Because."

"Because why?"

"Because I want some privacy."

"Privacy? What for?"

"That's it! I can't take it anymore. My name is Jodie, not Jo like that possum-playin' storekeep said. I'm a woman, not a man, not a *kid*, and I *need* some privacy, 'cause I ain't about to use a chamber pot with you in here."

Bones's eyes grew larger and larger until she feared they'd pop out of his head and land at her feet. His gaze darted the length of her, lingering in places she'd learned to disguise years ago when Jerry's gang members had started taking more than a passing interest in her shape.

"Y–y–you're a sh–she? H–he's a she? Y–you're a woman? I—" He pointed to his shoulder then to her then back again.

"Yeah, you hauled a woman in here like a sack of meal. Now would ya lock the door and get outta here?"

Tripping over his feet in his haste, the marshal scrambled to the front door, tossed the lock into place, and then darted to the side room, his face beet red and his eyes looking anywhere but at her.

His door barely clicked shut before she rushed to do her business.

He was guarding a woman. He was *guarding* a woman. He was guarding a *woman*! Beau struggled to make his lungs function as he gripped his knees. What on earth was he going to do? He straightened, setting his topsy-turvy world to spinning more. Gripping his hair, he closed his eyes and gulped for air and clarity.

He couldn't guard a woman, could he? Could a woman even stand trial? Why would a woman help rob a general store?

Moreover, why was she dressed like a man? How old was she? How could he have hauled her over his shoulder and not known. . .not felt. . . ?

Opening his eyes, he scrubbed his hands together, trying to rid himself of the burning stain. He couldn't believe he'd treated a woman with so much disrespect. He'd never done such a dishonorable thing in all his born days. Then again, he'd hardly spoken to any woman who wasn't family, and still not much even then. It never turned out well.

How on earth was he going to guard a woman, let alone get more information out of her? His hands grew clammy just thinking about it. Beau stared at the door, knowing he couldn't leave her alone too long. The town had hired him to be their marshal. They were depending on him to make sure they got justice. He couldn't quit and let them down so soon. Not to mention how that'd dishonor his late uncle's memory.

But guarding a woman? What was he going to tell the mayor? Should he tell the mayor? Was this something that would get him fired before he even started the job? Would they want to hire a woman to take his place and guard the prisoner? His brothers would have a heyday with that one.

And what about her gang? Mr. Haskins was depending on him to find out more, to get the stolen money back. If he got fired, he couldn't do that. No, he'd just have to—how had Uncle Beau put it?—bite the bullet and face the situation like a man. Yes, he'd just pretend to be his uncle. Uncle Beau wouldn't care what gender the prisoner was. He'd only care about bringing the wrongdoers to justice, about doing what was right no matter the cost.

Beau straightened. He could do the same. He could guard a

woman. He could learn to be the best—or at least second best—marshal the town of Small Tree had ever seen. Screwing his courage to the sticking place, he threw open the door and marched from the room.

A squeal sent him covering his eyes and scampering behind the desk.

Jodie faced the wall and yanked her last suspender over her shoulder. "Don'tcha know how to warn a body?"

A loud crash jerked her back around in time to see the strapping marshal bouncing on one leg. Gripping his shin, he stumbled into the hat rack beside the desk and tumbled to the floor. The hat tree tumbled with him, smacking the desk then him as a host of papers slipped from the edge and buried him alive.

The pile of pages shifted and groaned, then Bones emerged, covering his eye.

Jodie rushed to the bars. "Are you okay?"

"Swell." Leaning against the side of the desk, he tipped his head back, accidentally bumping his cup of tea and sending the tan brew pouring over his dark locks. The liquid trickled down his cheeks, across his fingers, and dripped off his chin onto the mess surrounding him. "Just swell."

Placing her hand over her mouth, Jodie fought the urge to laugh until his exasperated gaze met hers. Then she lost the battle. Loud guffaws shook her shoulders, and she doubled over with uncontainable laughter. If she hadn't already used the necessary, she would've been in big trouble. Before long, deep chuckles accompanied hers, adding to her mirth.

She wasn't sure how long they laughed, but when their

merriment finally faded, they both sat on the floor, staring at one another.

Jodie smiled. She couldn't remember the last time she'd had such a good laugh. That it should come the same day she got thrown behind bars, with the man who'd done the throwing no less, was ironic to say the least.

"You really oughta get a doctor to look at that." She pointed at his face. "You look like ya got the makin's of quite the shiner." Jodie had to admit that even covered in tea and with the growing color around his eye, the new marshal was a mighty handsome man.

Bones offered her a slanted grin that did funny things to her insides. "It's not the first time. Probably won't be the last."

"Really?"

"I've got seven older brothers."

"Aw. . ." With a nod, she turned her attention to her knitted fingers, a wave of sadness washing over her, removing the humor.

"What about you? You got family?"

Even though she knew she shouldn't, she found herself answering anyway. "One."

"Brother?"

She nodded. "But he's a lot older than me."

Silence met her admission, then. . ."Jerry?"

Her gaze jerked to his. "How'd you know?"

"You yelled for someone by that name before you kicked me in the shin."

"Sorry about that."

"It's all right. I understand."

"You do?"

"Seven older brothers, remember?"

"Right." She examined the dirt caked under her fingernails,

something she'd never allowed to stay long until she'd gone to live with Jerry in one abandoned cabin after another. Her mama had been a stickler for clean hands. Why she thought of Mama now after all these years Jodie didn't know, but something about this man made her think of the past, made her remember better times when she wasn't constantly looking over her shoulder or wondering if she'd be sleeping under the stars or a roof that night.

Sure, it was nice having something to share with the misfortunate folks she ran into, but honestly, she couldn't remember the last time Jerry or one of the others had shared more than a glare with someone down in the dumps. They sure didn't go out of their way to help anyone but themselves.

She might as well face the truth—the only one in the Ross gang who cared about ministering to hurting people was herself. How long had she been fooling herself? How long had she allowed herself to believe Jerry's lie, believe the men were in this for the good they could do? The answer—too long. *Her* motives might've been pure, but she was really little more than a thief, worthy of the hate and scorn the men of this town had shown her.

Jodie dropped her face into her hands. Why had she ever listened to Jerry when she knew deep down what they were doing was wrong, that Mama and Papa wouldn't have approved?

Loud footsteps and voices carried from the boardwalk outside, and the doorknob rattled. "It's locked. Marshal Bones, are you in there?"

Bones scrambled to his feet, and Jodie did the same. She hurried to the bed as he rushed to let the mayor, the general store owner, and the other men from the search party in. That they came in empty-handed brought her a momentary rush of relief—her brother and the gang had gotten away—but on its heels worry, doubt, and the nagging question arose: Would they come back for her, or would she hang for their crimes?

"Sorry about that. Just an added precaution." Beau shut the door behind the handful of men, praying they wouldn't figure out how much of a fool he'd made of himself moments ago and praising God they hadn't been there to witness the event.

"I see." The mayor looked at him oddly.

"Can't have the prisoner getting away, sir." He swiped a hand through his hair, hoping they'd think the wetness was from pomade instead of sweet tea, and discreetly wiped it on his pants.

"No indeed." Mayor Jones glanced around the room. "What happened here?"

"I, uh. . ." Beau stooped and started scooping up the scattered papers. "I'm, uh, working to get things organized, but I can finish this later." He placed the haphazard pile on the desk then scooted it away from the edge when it started to teeter. "Do y'all have news?"

"Yes. . .I. . . That boy must have hit you harder than I realized earlier. Do we need to send the doctor over to look at that?"

Beau touched the tender spot under his left eye and stifled a wince. "Uh, no, sir. I'll be fine. Most every man's nursed a shiner at some point in his life. Right, fellas?" He looked to the others, who grinned their agreement. "So, the news?"

"Yes, I thought you'd like to know I finally got a response to my telegram." The mayor shook off his distraction and focused on Beau, not his eye or the messy room. "Judge Johnson will be here at the end of the month to try the case. That's three and a half weeks. I'd hoped it would be sooner."

"I say we save us all some trouble and hang him now," Mr. Haskins growled, his wiry arms folded over his wide middle, his frown no smaller than it'd been earlier that afternoon when they'd inspected the damage to his store.

The mayor's gaze strayed to Jodie, and for some crazy reason, Beau found himself holding his breath.

Haskins stalked to the bars and gripped the metal. "Where are the others, you thieving skunk?"

Jodie pretended not to hear a word, which only made the proprietor madder.

Beau kept a close eye on him even as he asked, "I take it y'all didn't have any luck finding their trail?"

"As far as we can tell, they went into the water and rode upstream." Hewitt, the livery man, scratched his bearded jaw that held more hair than his head. "We thought we found a couple of places where they came out, but the trail went dry both times. We were hoping the kid might've said something that would help us."

"Not yet."

"However, I'm sure Bones will get to the bottom of things." The mayor clapped Beau on the back. "He is, after all, our late marshal's nephew."

Beau offered a smile that felt weak even to himself. These people were going to see him for the fraud he was before the day was out, he just knew it. He had to get them out of there and fast. "I appreciate y'all coming by to let me know what you found. Maybe we can try again tomorrow."

"No sense in that." The lanky Mr. Lawson shook the hat in his hand, sending water droplets onto the scarred floorboards. "Rain started coming down on us on our way in."

As if on cue, a rumble of thunder echoed above them, and large drops barraged the roof.

Beau felt guilty at the rush of relief that washed over him, knowing they wouldn't witness his nearly nonexistent tracking skills anytime soon.

Short Mr. Grimes joined Haskins at the cell door. "Whether we like it or not, this kid's our only lead on where to find the others."

Which meant finding justice for this small town all came down to Beau's ability to talk to women.

They were doomed.

∾ Chapter 3 ≫

If this young buck was Small Tree's idea of a lawman, they were doomed to be struck by outlaws time and again. Jodie stood on her bunk and stared out the barred window inside her cell, trying to catch a breeze and getting more than a little entertainment as Marshal Bones wasted yet more bullets on a line of tin cans that hadn't budged since he'd placed them on the muddy ground twenty minutes ago.

The way he loaded, fired, and unloaded the Colt Peacemaker left no doubt in her mind that this guy didn't know the first thing about guns—which made him about the most dangerous man in Texas. If her brother tried a jailbreak, the marshal might aim at Jerry and hit her instead.

"You want me to show ya how to do that?"

Bones jumped at her voice, pulling the trigger, and finally sent a tin can flying. He stood still as a statue, then with agonizing slowness, he turned and faced her. "Y—you want *me* to let *you* shoot a gun?"

"It's either that or risk bein' shot myself by one of your wild bullets."

"I'm not *that* bad."

Jodie cocked an eyebrow.

"O—okay, maybe I am that bad." Studying the gun in his hands, the marshal shifted his weight between his large boots, which, now that she looked at them, didn't have a single scuff mark. Mud, yes. Scuffs, no.

This stalwart man might be dressed like a cowboy with his leather vest, navy shirt, and Levi breeches, but he was a dude if she ever saw one. "What city do you hail from?"

His wide, chocolate gaze swung to hers. He opened his mouth as if to speak, then shut it and looked away. "San Antonio."

Well, at least he was from Texas. "Never shot a gun before, have ya?"

He opened his mouth, paused, scanned the meadow, then ducked his head and shook it. Straightening, he met her gaze with a lift of his chin. "I'll figure it out though."

"Hmm. . .maybe, but anybody can shoot a gun. It takes skill to actually hit what you're aimin' at, and with your new job, I'd say that's one skill you can't afford not to have." Jodie rested her chin in her hand. "So what's the verdict?" With a wince at her misguided word choice, she lowered her hand. "You want me to teach you while we wait for the judge to arrive? I ain't got nothin' else better to do."

Except count the days and hours and minutes. Nineteen days. Perchance they were her last on this earth. She'd rather they be spent doing something good.

In the past four days, she'd already read most of the four Gospels. At first she'd read out of sheer boredom, but slowly she'd come to crave the time turning pages. It'd been years since she'd laid eyes on a Bible, and she'd found the hope offered there more comforting than she'd expected, especially the passage about the thief on the cross.

That the Son of God could forgive such a worthless, guilty man as that guy had brought tears to her eyes and a prayer to her lips for the first time in many years. At the peace that had flooded her soul in that moment, she had no doubt that God had forgiven her, just like that undeserving man, but she had no guarantee He'd get her out of this situation of her own making alive. After all, sin had its consequences—the thief had still died on the cross next to Jesus—and she deserved every bit of judgment the courts decided to deal out.

"I can't just give you a gun." Bones shielded his eyes from the glaring sun overhead. "I'll be fired before I can spend my first pay."

"I can teach you a few things without ever touchin' that Peacemaker."

"Yeah? Like what?"

A hard knock rattled the jailhouse door behind her. "I'll tell ya after we eat. Sounds like lunch just arrived."

"What do you mean, 'I don't have to do this outside'?" Beau was beginning to question the wisdom of taking advice from an outlaw and not just because she was a woman. Whoever heard of target practicing inside a building?

"Empty the gun."

"What? How am I supposed to know whether I hit the target?"

"Do ya want me to teach ya or not?"

Pursing his lips, Beau emptied the revolver, the bullets pinging onto the desk. "Okay, now what?"

"You got a dime or a quarter?"

"Uh. . ."

"Don't look at me like I ain't playin' with a full deck. Do ya or don'tcha?"

With a shake of his head, Beau leaned back in the desk chair and dug in his pants pocket. He sure hoped no one walked in during this nonsense. It seemed like this woman had a knack for making him look like an idiot, which really wasn't much different from other females he'd met. Sometimes he wondered if he'd be better at talking to and understanding women if he'd had seven sisters instead of seven brothers, or if he was just doomed to be inept around them regardless.

The dime clicked onto the desktop. "Okay, now what?"

"You see that rear sight notch?"

The what? Beau resisted the urge to swipe a hand across his face.

"The rear sight notch—that divot on the top there."

Knowing he looked like the novice he was, Beau pointed to the groove in the metal near the back of the gun.

"Yeah, that. Balance the dime in that notch. Rest your arms on the desk. . .*but not* the butt of the gun."

Beau lifted the revolver a fraction. Heaven help him. Maybe he should just quit while he was ahead.

"Good." Jodie drew her pointing finger back inside the cell and propped her elbow on the bar. "Now, line up the dime and the front sight—that metal stickin' up there on the end—with some spot on the wall there. Steady your aim, and squeeze the trigger without makin' the dime fall off."

"Okay. . ." That sounded easy enough. Holding his breath, Beau lined everything up and—the dime fell off.

"*Squeeze* the trigger. Don't jerk it. Try again."

Beau did. Again.

And again.

And *again*.

After the umpteenth try, he dropped the gun on the desk beside the contrary dime and raked both hands through his hair. "This is impossible."

"No, it isn't. Hand it here, and I'll show ya."

He might as well.

Jodie accepted the Colt, set the dime in place, and aimed at the wall, and he was that amazed when, after five rapid-fire squeezes, the dime didn't budge. It was probably too scared to move in her presence. At the moment, he felt a little frozen in place himself. Who could do such things?

"See. It is possible. Now here, you try."

He only accepted the revolver because she dropped it in his hands and he didn't want his uncle's prized possession to hit the floor. There was no way he'd ever be as good as her. Why should he even try?

"Go on. Take another whack at it. It took a lot of practice for me to be able to do that. You'll get it."

He didn't know about that. Besides, he doubted time was on his side. There had to be a jailbreak in the works. If he had a sister like Jodie, he wouldn't leave her behind.

Which meant Beau had better learn how to shoot—and fast, if

he wanted to keep his job.

Lifting the Peacemaker to eye level, he lined up his shot and squeezed the trigger.

Jodie watched Bones squeeze off another round, the dime remaining pretty-as-you-please on top of the gun. "Good job. You're pickin' this up faster than I expected. I think it's time we take this outside."

The dime fell off. "Ou—outside?"

"Yeah, you know that place with grass and sunshine and fresh air?"

"I know what you meant." He scratched his chin, moving closer to the cell. "I still can't let you out of there, Jodie, and they've started building in the field behind the jail."

She'd noticed. Her first guess would be a schoolhouse or a church. The building could be used for both. "You're the marshal. I'd say you can do whatever ya want."

Bones stopped walking, stopped scratching, stopped everything, and stared at her like she'd spouted some heresy. Brother, for a man with authority, he sure didn't act like one.

"You *can* take me outta here, ya know. Your job is to guard the prisoner, right? Who says ya have to guard me in here? I promise I'll be on my best behavior, and then we can practice where no one else will see."

Practice where no one else could see. Through the barred window, Beau glimpsed the meadow that any man, woman, or child could view if they rounded one of the buildings on his side of Main Street. He'd love to practice where no one might notice and realize what an amateur they'd hired. Might figure out he was taking lessons from an outlaw. But to actually let Jodie out of her cell—that was out of the question.

Wasn't it?

For well over a week, he'd watched Jodie scour the Bible like a starving man. They'd hardly spoken, save firearm instruction, which was fine with him, but he'd heard every sniffle from her corner of the room, spied every tear that'd trickled down her smooth, sun-bronzed cheeks. The words had touched her, may have even caused a change of heart.

If someone showed an ounce of faith in her, would she be willing to reveal her gang's location now? Isn't that what Uncle Beau had done for him, believed in him when no one else had? Why else would he have mentioned only Beau in his will?

Should he give Jodie a chance? The town was expecting him to learn more about her gang. Not to mention, he definitely could use more lessons if he planned to do this job with any measure of success, and he *really* wanted to succeed this time.

For once, he wanted to be able to hold his head high when he walked down the street, to have a job he felt good about, was actually good at, and could keep all on his own. He wanted to have his folks, his own family, proud of him for a change and stop seeing him as the baby who couldn't do anything without their help or who was a failure because he didn't excel in the family business. He wanted to stand on his own two feet, feel comfortable in his own skin for a change. This job was his ticket to a better life, and he wasn't about to waste that now if he had anything to say about it.

Nevertheless, letting Jodie teach him and digging for secrets meant more talking, more close interaction with a female with high, defined cheekbones, eyes the color of a summer sky, and dark locks with a touch of curl. His tongue turned to sandpaper in his mouth. How had he ever thought her a man?

And just like that, he knew how he'd get her out of town without anyone knowing he was allowing a prisoner to teach him. Holstering his inherited gun, he started for the door.

Chapter 4

*I*n the flickering candlelight, Jodie stared first at the garment dangling from her fingertips, then at the cherry-faced lawman on the other side of the bars. "You want me to wear *this*?"

The calico dress dripped with ribbons and lace. She hadn't worn something so. . .so. . .feminine in a decade. For reasons she couldn't define, tears stung her eyes.

"I—it's too big, isn't it? I'm sorry. I had to guess at your size, and Haskins was asking so many questions. I had to tell him my sweetheart was riding into town and I wanted to have a present for her."

"You have a sweetheart?"

With wide eyes, the marshal shook his head. "I—I don't. . . . That is, I'm not. . . You see, w—women don't really find me attractive."

"Really? I find that hard to believe." Realizing what she'd admitted, Jodie gulped and gathered the gift into a ball. "I'll, uh, be sure to be dressed and ready when ya come out in the mornin'."

'Cause she undoubtedly wouldn't sleep a wink that night. The marshal was gonna let her out of the cell tomorrow. He was gonna let her teach him *outside*. He trusted her, and he'd bought her a lovely dress. She draped the flowered material across the front of her and swallowed an uncharacteristic squeal.

She was getting out of the cell tomorrow!

Beau stepped out of the side room and glanced in the cell—then glanced again.

A stunningly beautiful woman sat on the stained cot, leaning against the brick wall, her head lulled to the side, with dark, long lashes fanned across her smooth cheeks. Soft morning light shone through the barred window, accentuating her delicate face and bringing a touch of red to her dark locks. If he hadn't recognized the blue dress with the yellow flowers as the one he'd purchased the day before, he'd say a stranger had waltzed in during the night and replaced his prisoner with a curvaceous female that would take any man's breath away, including his.

Jodie looked. . .amazing.

Nobody in their right mind would dream of associating her with the dirty-faced kid he'd locked up earlier that month. He could hardly make the connection himself, and he'd instigated the change.

The woman was a miracle worker to make anyone think her a man for a fleeting second. How on earth was he going to spend a day with her and learn a single, blessed thing? And asking questions—that was totally out of the question. His tongue was already tied in so many knots his stomach had given up on the competition.

Footfalls sounded on the boardwalk outside, jerking Beau out of his trance. Breakfast. Someone would bring in breakfast soon. Why hadn't he thought of that before? He had to get Jodie out of that cell before everyone knew that the *he* was a definite *she*.

Beau hurried to the desk, yanked the keys out of a drawer, and ran to the cell door. "Jodie. Jodie, wake up."

She didn't move a muscle as the barred door clanked open, and he rushed to her side.

"Jodie, we've got to get you out of here." He touched her shoulder to shake her awake.

A bony knee drilled under his ribs. His back slammed against the ground. A wiry arm pressed against his throat. Air struggled to get through.

What on earth had he done?

❧ Chapter 5 ❧

*J*odie blinked away the haze of sleep and focused on the idiot foolish enough to touch her. A handsome man with dark hair and wide brown eyes gasped in her hold.

"Bones?" She scrambled to her feet, hauling him up with her. "I–I'm so sorry. I thought you were one of my brother's gang. I—I—I didn't mean to. I'm sorry. Are you okay?"

He took a step away, holding the keys like a dagger between them.

What had she done? How could she have treated him like that? He wouldn't dream of taking her out of the cell now. She'd ruined everything with her unladylike reflexes. Sudden tears stung her eyes, and for once, she didn't stop them. She was a horrible human being.

Melting onto the side of the bed, she buried her face in her hands. *Oh God, I'm so sorry. Why do I have to be this way? Please change me. I don't want to hurt anyone anymore.*

"Do you always wake up like that?"

Jodie jerked at the nearness of the deep voice, sure that the lawman would've gotten as far from her as possible, but he stood in the same spot, rubbing his neck.

"My brother normally kicks my boot to wake me."

"I can see why." After a final rub, he lowered his hand, his gaze steady and much too keen on her. "Other men. . .they've. . ." Bones motioned at her, a pity filling his eyes she couldn't stand.

Folding her arms, she lifted her chin. "Gotten too friendly? Maybe so, but they ain't never tried it twice."

The last one who'd been dumb enough Jerry had beaten to a bloody pulp, and that was *after* she'd deterred him with her Peacemaker pressed into his middle.

"I can understand why. I'm. . .sorry you had to go through that. Just for the tally books, I wasn't. . ."

"I know."

"In my book, women should be treated with respect. I'll, uh, remember the tip about the boot for next time."

"Next time?" Her gaze collided with his. "Ya mean. . .you're still gonna let me teach ya?"

"I can't blame a woman for defending herself against a perceived threat, now can I?"

He could, but the fact that he wouldn't made her want to jump off the bed and kiss him. "I promise ya won't regret it."

"Then we'd better get you out of this cell before they deliver breakfast. We need to make this bed look like someone is still in it."

Jodie hurried to help him tuck her discarded clothes and pillow under the blanket in a convincing manner. She'd just rearranged the "legs" when a knock, which actually sounded more like a kick, rattled the door.

"Marshal, you awake?" A young voice carried through the wood.

"Hurry." Bones grabbed her hand, hauled her from the cell, and shut it behind them.

"Marshal?" Another kick-knock.

Motioning her to a chair in front of the desk, the lawman headed for the door. Their normal morning delivery boy, one of the boardinghouse owner's sons, stood on the other side.

"Why, if it isn't my new friend Arnie? I see your ma nominated you to help with deliveries today."

The freckled-face lad cocked his head. "How'd you know it was me and not Wallie? Everyone else in town gets us confused."

Jodie wasn't sure either. The boys were mirror images of each other. Although now that she thought about it, this Arnie did seem to have more freckles on his cheeks than the boy who'd brought breakfast the day before.

Bones tousled the lad's flame-colored locks. "What kind of lawman would I be if I couldn't tell two brothers apart?"

Arnie thought about it a moment then nodded. "Yeah, I guess that's true."

Carrying the towel-covered tray, the roughly ten-year-old boy took two steps into the room and stopped dead-still at the sight of her. "Woo-ee, Mr. Marshal. I heard your gal was coming into town, but nobody mentioned how purdy she is. She sure is a good-looker."

"Yes, well, I, uh. . ." Bones tugged at his collar.

Jodie felt heat climb into her own cheeks, but she couldn't hold back the smile at the lad's compliment. It'd been so long since she'd worn a dress, and the marshal hadn't said a word about her appearance. Thank the Lord for the honesty of a child. "Why, thank you, kind sir. You're a pretty good-looker yourself.

Where'd you get that red hair from?"

"Thank you, ma'am. My ma says her daddy had red hair, so I guess from him." Arnie set the tray on the desk in front of her. "Sorry I didn't bring you no breakfast. I didn't know you'd be here." He glanced toward the jail cell. "My pa always used to say, 'You snooze you lose,' so I guess you can have his."

"That'd teach him not to be such a slug-a-bed, wouldn't it?"

A toothy grin parted the boy's cheeks. "Yes, ma'am."

"Then I reckon I'll take your pa's advice. Just this once."

Arnie angled his attention to Bones. "I like her." He turned back. "You gonna be here long, ma'am?"

Jodie peered toward the marshal, whose look was as uncertain as she felt. "I'm, uh, I'm not sure, Arnie. For a little while at least."

Where she resided after that would be up to the judge.

Beau felt every eye in town on them as he drove Jodie past the stores on Main Street. He kept waiting for someone to rush out and demand he take the prisoner back to jail, but every man who looked their way doffed his hat with a wide, goofy grin and called out a cheery greeting. Greetings that, for some strange reason, a part of him wanted to shove back down their throats.

Only once the wagon cleared town did he feel safe enough to breathe a normal breath. That is, until he peeked Jodie's way, and that breath lodged in his throat like a chicken bone.

Head tilted back, face angled toward the sun, the much-too-attractive woman sucked in a lungful of air, drawing his gaze to curves that hadn't been apparent the day before.

Forcing his focus toward the heavens, he tried to dispel the image from his mind and the obstruction from his throat. God help him.

"Mmm. Doesn't the air smell wonderful out here?" Jodie stretched out her arms.

He slammed his eyes shut. *She's my prisoner. She's my prisoner. She's my prisoner.*

"I really appreciate you doin' this, Marshal. I know ya didn't have to."

"Yes, well. . ." He tried again to dislodge the airy chicken bone. "I appreciate your willingness to teach me. We'll, uh. . . That is, why don't you call me Beau?"

Her beaming smile shoved the bone firmly back into place.

She's my prisoner. She's my prisoner. Clearing his throat again, he fixed his gaze on the twitching ears of the horses. "By the way, what's. . .*ahem*. . .what's your last name?"

That was a good lawman-type question, one he couldn't believe he hadn't asked in the past week and a half. Although he highly doubted she'd have answered then, and he still wasn't sure she'd answer now.

She turned toward him. "Ross. You sure are coughin' a lot. Do ya need some water?"

Ross, huh. Maybe he'd been right about the outing loosening her tongue. Ross. . .Ross. . . ? Had there been a Wanted poster with that name on it? Whatever answer that might have entered his head went sky-high as Miss Jodie Ross turned and leaned over the back of the seat, offering him a view of, well, her seat.

Heaven help him.

Maybe he should turn the wagon around. There was no way he'd be able to learn how to shoot that day. If he fired a gun in his current state, there's no telling what he'd hit.

"Ah, here it is." Jodie turned and plopped back down beside him, no guile whatsoever in her gaze, and uncorked the water canteen before offering it to him with another of her distracting smiles.

The woman really had no idea of her effect on him. Turning up the container, Beau chugged the contents. Maybe he could drown himself back to sensibility.

When he came up for air, Jodie offered him the cork. "Better?"

He wasn't sure whether to nod or shake his head, so he settled with a simple "Thank you."

"So, how far're we goin'?"

"Not far." He couldn't take a whole day of this torture.

Jerry couldn't take a whole day of this torture. Tossing the twig he'd been skinning with his pocketknife aside, he headed toward the horses.

A twig snapped behind him.

With a sharp pivot, he cleared leather and aimed toward the sound.

"It's me." Pat's voice preceded him moments before his chestnut broke through the thick brush lining the cave entrance.

Jerry lowered the gun. "Where's Dix?"

"Mount up 'n' I'll show you."

Moving toward his gelding, Jerry voiced the question that'd been eating at him for days as they'd waited for sufficient time to pass before scoping out the situation. If that posse'd hurt one hair on his sister's head, he'd kill them all. Pat and Dix had no doubt picked up on his anger. Probably why they'd insisted he guard the stash while they rode to town. They'd said it was because no one would recognize them, but they probably feared he'd do something rash and get them all caught. He did too. That's why he'd gone along with their plan.

"How's Jo?"

"Asleep on a bunk in the jail."

"Did you talk to her?" Jerry made quick work of slapping leather on his mount and making sure the rags tied around his horse's hooves to help disguise the tracks were still snug.

"She's asleep. What do you think?"

Good point. That girl could sleep through a train derailing in a hurricane. Until something touched her, then look out, brother. He swung into the saddle and followed the stocky man from the cave. He'd feel a lot better if he could talk to Jo, let her know everything was gonna be all right, that he'd get her out of there. But the men were right—they had to play this smart. At least they were willing to help spring Jo. Probably 'cause they preferred her cooking to their own tasteless grub.

After traveling a few miles, Pat pulled to a stop and made a twittering whistle. A faint responding call came from a cluster of live oaks and scrub brush farther ahead. With a nod, Pat swung down.

Jerry did the same. Scanning the area, he spied Dix's mustang a distance to his left, munching on the waist-high grasses around a mesquite tree. "What're we doing out here?"

"We followed the marshal and his girl." Pat spoke barely above a whisper.

"You mean Jo's alone in town?" Jerry hissed. "Why didn't you just get the key and sneak her out?"

"The livery man was watching the place like a hawk from across the street. Besides, we need to know what we're up against."

Fighting down the urge to punch something or someone—not to mention, hating to admit that the man was right—Jerry followed Pat into the trees that lined some kind of wash. At any other time, it would've likely been dry, but after the recent rains, the creek bed held an inch or so of running water.

Because Dix was disguised by his brown hair, vest, and broadcloth breeches, they nearly stumbled onto him kneeling between two boulders before they saw him. Without a word, he handed the spyglass to Jerry and pointed through the scrub brush hiding them from view.

A fetching brunette in a bluebonnet-colored dress stood next to a Stetson-wearing man loading a Peacemaker. More than one bullet hit the ground during the process. A star glinted on his chest as he squatted to retrieve them. Jerry followed the man's aim to a line of tin cans. Successive shots splintered the silence but not a single can.

Jerry grinned. This greenhorn was what they were up against? Snatching Jo out of his hold would be easier than a Sunday stroll through the meadow. All they had to do was pick the right time.

Chapter 6

"All right, let's see if we can do better than last time." Under the wide expanse of a shady oak, Jodie moved a safe distance away from Bones, set her attention on the tin cans, and folded her arms.

Their first lesson outdoors hadn't gone well. Not only had the marshal bumbled through setting up the tin cans, knocking them over twice before getting them all standing erect, but then he'd fumbled through loading the chambers and dropped half the bullets on the ground more than once. The man then had proceeded to try her patience with an aim she could outdo with a blindfold, a broken trigger finger, and a half dozen lawmen breathing down her neck. Hopefully, whatever had disturbed him last time wouldn't bother him today.

A shot cracked the silence.

Not a single can teetered.

Swallowing an exasperated sigh, Jodie inspected his stance as another round missed its intended target. What happened to the guy who could keep a dime in place? "Are you sick or somethin'?"

Beau lowered the Colt revolver. "No, why?"

"You're shakin' like a leaf in a hurricane."

"I—I can't help it. You're making me nervous."

"Nervous? Me? How? I didn't make ya nervous at the jail, did I?" A memory of a tumbling marshal covered in tea flashed through her mind. Maybe she did.

"Can't you turn around or something?" His gaze skittered over her for the dozenth time that day before flicking back to the targets.

Well, I'll be... Why, if she didn't know any better, she'd think he found her... Naw...couldn't be. Someone like him couldn't find someone like her...attractive. Could he? For some reason a smile tickled her lips. It sure would be nice to have someone so kind, so handsome, so understanding feel that way about her, but who was she kidding? Men with his charm, connections, and character never fell for gals of her ilk. He'd be an idiot to fall for a girl who might swing before the month was out. The smile slipped away.

Pushing the wishful thoughts aside, she waved his attention back toward the line of tin cans. "Come on. You can't ask the next outlaw who crosses your path to turn around, now can ya? Only a coward shoots a man in the back, and you're no coward. Use that excess energy to hone your focus. Block out the distractions. Breathe, aim, and fire."

"Like it's that easy."

"Give me the gun, and I'll show you it is."

"Fine."

Block out the distractions, she says. Breathe, aim, and fire, she says. It's that easy. Ha! That woman had no idea what a distraction was. Oh, but she was about to.

Beau waited for Jodie to finish reloading the revolver and adjust her hands on the grips. He then stepped up close behind her as she lifted her arms and whispered in her ear, "Don't miss."

The shot went wild.

Unable to squelch his grin, he did manage to swallow the chuckle building in his throat, but all humor died the instant she swiveled toward him, inadvertently brushing his chest with her shoulder. They both froze, mere inches apart.

With a hard swallow, he forced his fingers to stay by his side, even as the air between them became charged with some kind of intensity, like the anticipation felt while a burning fuse ate its way toward a powder keg.

Her lips parted a fraction, drawing his gaze.

What would it be like to kiss her, someone with such vim and vigor? Would what he felt in that moment explode into something altogether wonderful or wound them both irrevocably?

Before he could decide, he found himself leaning toward her. . .until her soft gasp yanked him to his senses. He took a mighty step back, avoiding her gaze and the revulsion he'd no doubt see there. Why, he was no better than the men in her brother's gang. It'd serve him right if she turned that Peacemaker on him.

"I, uh. . . Excuse me." Although there really was no excuse for him or his shameful behavior. Heading toward the targets, he gave her ample opportunity to repay his forwardness with whatever punishment she wanted to mete out.

For the first time in her life, Jodie wanted to run after a man and do something more than pound him. Okay, maybe she wanted to pound Beau a smidgen, but only because she'd really wanted him to kiss her and he hadn't gone through with the desire plastered across his features. No man had ever shown her such respect, which made her want to chase after him all the more and lay her lips against his, a feeling so foreign and wonderful she couldn't tear her eyes from his strapping frame as he picked up the targets.

What was she supposed to do? A sharp longing for her mother and her sage advice gripped Jodie's insides, but on its heels a snippet from one of Mama's favorite hymns. . .

Take it to the Lord in prayer.

More of the song evaded her, but the message came through loud and clear. She latched onto the suggestion.

God, I'm in over my head. Show me what to do, please.

She'd no more said "amen" when a calm washed away her worry, and in its place came the impression to wait. An odd notion, given that her days were numbered, but considering that she hadn't any better ideas, she opted to heed the advice.

After placing the hammer on an empty chamber, she set the gun beside the extra box of bullets on the wagon bed, wandered to the tree trunk, and sat down to do just that.

Leaving a loaded gun with a bandit probably wasn't the wisest thing Beau'd ever done, and not a mistake he planned to repeat, regardless of how beautiful or beguiling she was or how much he'd acted like a cad. Thankfully, Jodie didn't seem of a mind to use the weapon on him, idiot that he was. Because no lawman worth his salt would fall for a prisoner's feminine wiles. He could almost hear Uncle Beau, or at least his father, berating him. He had to do better at this job, and that meant no distractions and definitely no falling for the prisoner he guarded. Why did his first jailbird have to be a woman?

Women were completely and inexcusably nothing but trouble. They never took what he said in the manner it was meant, they always assumed the worst, and they never, ever considered how their laughter affected a guy's confidence. Just once he'd love to find a woman who believed in him and cared enough to look past his faults to see his heart. Surely there was a woman like that out there somewhere. After all, Texas was a mighty big place.

Knowing his luck, she probably didn't live in Texas though. If he couldn't find such a gal in a bustling city like San Antonio, he highly doubted he'd find such a woman in tiny Small Tree.

God, can't You take pity on this man?

Picking up the last tin can, Beau faced the wagon. *Might as well get this over with.*

He wandered back to the wagon, only to find Jodie reclined against the wide base of the spreading oak, her eyes closed in slumber, reminding him of how she'd looked yesterday morning in the cell. On the tails of that memory came the recollection of how she'd reacted to being awakened.

No woman should have that kind of gut reflex, outlaw or no. Why hadn't her brother protected her from such ill treatment? Better still, why had he dragged her into such a life in the first place? Had Jodie actually been a willing participant in his unlawful acts?

Lifting his hat, Beau swiped a sleeve across his brow, then resettled it and rested both palms on the wagon bed, his eyes landing on the revolver. With a sigh, he looked over his shoulder at his sleeping teacher. He'd only known Jodie for a short while, but the longer he knew her the harder it was for him to view her as an outlaw. His near-kiss earlier was a loud testimony to that. The woman was easy on the eyes, well put together, no denying that, but if he was honest, that wasn't all that made her attractive. This woman might've done bad things, might be a little rough around the edges, but there was a goodness in her he couldn't miss.

Would the judge miss it? Would he only see what she, or rather, what her brother's gang had done, or would the judge dig for the heart of the matter, the instigator of the crime? Leaning his back against the wagon, Beau nudged up his Stetson and rubbed at the tension building in his temples.

As marshal, didn't it fall on him to make sure the right person paid the penalty? Yes, Jodie was guilty of being a part of a gang. Yes, she was present at the explosion. Yes, she'd had goods from the mercantile in her possession, but had he ever stopped to ask how she'd come to have those goods? Had he ever asked how she'd come to be a part of that gang or what function she played in it?

He needed to know the truth. After all, the truth set people free.

Chapter 7

"We need to talk."

Jodie tore her attention from the exciting account of David versus Goliath and shifted her gaze to the marshal. The light from the oil lamp accentuated his striking features. Why hadn't he kissed her?

Shoving the better-left-unasked question aside, she marked her spot with her finger and closed the Bible. "We do?"

He'd hardly spoken to her since they'd left their shortened target practice. That he'd had a lot on his mind had been apparent with the way he'd scoured the papers on his desk. Either that or he was making an elaborate show of avoiding her. His current willingness to talk hopefully meant the former.

He looked at the sheet he'd been scribbling on since he'd locked her back in her cell. "We do."

"Okay." Jodie slipped the Bible's ribbon into place and gave him her full attention.

Beau sat in a chair right outside the bars so close she could see the ink smudges on his fingertips. With his leg bouncing, he glanced between her and what had to be his notes, his face a study in seriousness.

"Somethin's wrong. What is it?"

He rubbed the twin lines between his dark brows, leaving an adorable smudge, then dropped his hand to his lap with a sigh. "I'm not good at talking to women."

"You're doin' a pretty good job of it right now."

"Seriously. I—I sometimes stutter or. . .or things don't come out right and I make them mad."

"I won't get upset."

"You say that now."

"I promise. Just pretend I'm a guy and tell me what's on your mind."

His gaze swept over her from baggy shirt to broadcloth breeches before returning to her face. "Th–that's not possible."

Squelching the delight that rose up within her, she tried to think of another solution. "Would it help if I turned around?"

"I thought about that, but I need to see your face." He drew a deep breath and focused on the paper he repeatedly smoothed over his knee. "Let's just get this over with. . . I. . .*ahem*. . . The judge will be here in two weeks. We need to have a plan of how to present your case."

"My case? Wait. Did ya just say *we*?"

His movements stilling, he met her gaze head on. "I want to help you, Jodie, but I need to know the truth. About everything."

She opened her mouth to ask *why* but decided not to look a gift horse in the mouth. He wanted to help her, and she wasn't in any position to refuse. She doubted anyone else in this town would feel so kindly toward her.

"Everything? From the day of the robbery?"

"That's a start, but the more I know the better prepared I'll be to help you."

"You talk like you've done this kinda thing before."

"Not exactly. Let's just say my family has made it their business to know a thing or two about the law."

Which could mean any of a half dozen things.

His hand brushed hers, snatching her breath and her attention. "Trust me. Please. I won't let you down."

After a moment of consideration, she consented with a nod. Pulling away from his touch so she could think, Jodie drew a deep breath and gathered her thoughts.

"I hardly knew my brother before my parents died and I went to live with him. Jerry's fourteen years older than me, so he seemed more of an uncle than a brother. We got along pretty well. He taught me lots of things Mama never would've allowed, like shootin', 'n' trappin', 'n' fishin'—things I really enjoyed. Only after I got good at it, he started takin' trips for work. I hated it. He always left me behind. He said a neighbor would check on me, but they hardly ever did. He'd leave me alone in our cabin for days, then sometimes weeks at a time."

"How old were you?"

"About ten." Her mind went back to that last time he'd left her alone in their shack in the woods. Jerry'd promised to be home for Christmas. He'd already been gone five weeks, his longest absence yet. When Christmas came and went without seeing hide nor hair of him, she'd begun to wonder if something bad had happened, if God had taken him too, leaving her well and truly alone in the world.

Winter had whipped in sudden-like upon her, gripping the world in frost. Her supply of food and firewood dangerously low, she'd had to scrounge for fallen branches and dry brush to keep the hearth burning, divvying up what meager vegetables she'd stored and fishing for more meat. Some days she'd skipped meals to make sure she'd have enough for the next day.

"I'm sorry."

Jodie blinked, her gaze slipping from the past to the man outside the bars. "Yeah, well, finally, after one long absence, I told Jerry I'd had enough. I was through stayin' by myself and was goin' with him whether he liked it or not." Surely them being together was better than being alone. Although right now Jodie wasn't as confident of that.

"You didn't have any other relatives?"

"None that I know of." Jodie pulled her knees up to her chest and leaned against the cool brick wall. "Besides, I liked Jerry. He always made everything excitin'." Avoiding Beau's gaze, she rubbed at a stain on her breeches, much like the one God had scrubbed from her soul.

With sudden urgency, she gripped her knees and stared at Beau. "I swear I had no idea Jerry was hurtin' people. When I finally found out what he did for a livin', he told me they only took from those who could afford it so they could help the less fortunate, like Robin Hood. He convinced me we weren't doin' nothin' wrong, but. . ." She turned her head aside, unable to watch Beau's reaction to the rest. "I realize now the only one I was foolin' was myself. I—I wanted to believe we were helpin' folks, but lookin' back, I. . .I was the only one who ever gave any of our spoils away."

"So you participated in other raids?"

She wasn't sure how he kept the contempt out of his voice. "Not like the men. Before this last time, I only held the horses and kept watch. I just cooked 'n' cleaned 'n' looked after the supplies."

"Why the change?"

"I. . .I'm not sure. Maybe Jerry was afraid I'd do somethin' stupid."

"Like?"

"I don't know. Run away?" She finally looked at Beau, relieved to see his open expression hadn't changed. Why, only Heaven knew, but she leaned forward, eager for him to understand. "I think Jerry sensed my restlessness, that I was tired of livin' in the woods and wanderin' hither and yon, tired of dealin' with the others in the gang. I wanted out. I just hadn't been brave enough to tell him. Besides, it wasn't like I had anywhere else to go."

Leaning back against the wall, she breathed a sigh. If only she'd acted sooner, she wouldn't be in such a mess. Maybe she could've even gotten Jerry to change his ways and come with her. Maybe she could've met a good man like Beau and had a chance at a home, a family—love. Now she'd do well to be put on a chain gang instead of the end of a rope.

Beau scratched his chin and returned his grip to his thighs. "So you never actually stole anything?"

Frowning, Jodie considered his question. "I. . . Only what Jerry gave me. But I knew—"

"And the goods from the store here in town—were you the one to carry them out?"

What was he getting at? "No, Jerry did, but—"

"Did you shoot at anyone?"

"No."

"So, your gun should be clean?"

"Of course." Finally catching his drift, Jodie stared wide-eyed at the man in front of her. "You think you can get me out of this alive."

"I'm no lawyer, but. . .I think so. On the Wanted poster I found, there's not a description of a young boy being in the gang, and definitely no description of a beautiful woman."

He thought her beautiful? Wait. "My brother's wanted?"

"Yes and his gang of *two* men."

"But I just told you—"

"That you cooked and cleaned and suffered the advances of such men."

"But I—"

"I'm not discounting what you've done, Jodie. Yes, you knew better, but you said yourself you wanted out. Not to mention, I highly doubt anyone would begrudge a child not wanting to be left alone. If you'll tell the judge all that and where to find your brother, I'm sure he'll go lenient on you."

Her rising hope plummeted. "You want me to rat out my own brother?"

Feeling a bit like a rat himself, Beau leaned forward, gentling his voice. "I know I'm asking a lot, but I don't see any other alternative." The woman in front of him looked away, making it slightly easier to say how he truly felt. "Please, Jodie. I. . .I want to see you get a second chance."

"I do too, but I. . .I'm not sure I can do that." She turned her head, allowing him to see the anguish in her blue-eyed gaze. "You have brothers. Would ya throw one of them to the wolves to save your own hide?"

As much as he disliked his brothers at times, the answer came easy. "No. . .I wouldn't."

"Then please don't ask me to do that. There's got to be another way. Wouldn't my testimony be enough? You said the judge wouldn't hold my choices as a child against me."

"I believe most wouldn't, but without some show of good faith, some proof that you truly desire to change, it's all dependent on your word. I can't guarantee that'll be enough for the judge."

"A show of good faith?" Jodie scooted forward and put her boots back on the floor. "What if I helped repair the damage at the mercantile, worked off the debt?"

Scratching his chin, Beau leaned against the chair back. "That, uh, that might actually help. Do you know anything about carpentry?"

"Well, not really, but I'm a quick learner, and if that doesn't work, maybe I could help restock the shelves or somethin'." She straightened, her countenance brightening. "And you could take me to church on Sundays. That'd surely say somethin'."

"I, uh, that's not a bad idea. Let me talk to a few people in the morning, and I'll see what I can arrange."

Jodie offered him a grateful smile, making him feel ten feet tall and bulletproof. He sure hoped this worked.

Jodie worked to hold the length of wood steady while Beau nailed the shelf's support on the other end. "You didn't have to do this."

"Do what?"

"Help."

The marshal withdrew another nail from his back pocket and positioned it against the two-inch strip of wood. "I promised

Haskins I'd keep an eye on you. I might as well make myself useful."

"I know, but this isn't your debt to pay."

Lowering the hammer, his gaze connected with hers. "I want to help you."

The way he said those words sent warmth spreading through her middle. "Thank you."

With a nod, he finished sinking the nail in place, then moved to her end. Grasping the brace near her hand, he held it against the wall. "Set that marble on the middle of the board, please."

Jodie did as requested and watched him nudge the wood up and down until the glass ball quit rolling and the board was level. "Hey, that's pretty smart. Where'd ya learn that trick?"

"I did some work once with an elderly carpenter who was going blind. He taught me." Beau tossed her a grin and held out his palm. "Now you're sworn to secrecy."

"My lips are sealed." Grinning back, she handed him a nail. "Why aren't you still workin' for him? You didn't want to be a carpenter?"

"I don't know." He tapped the nail into place and scooted down the board. "Mr. White died shortly thereafter."

Enjoying the easy way he talked to her while his mind was occupied with something else, Jodie handed him another nail. "Did you find another carpenter to work with?"

The nail disappeared into the wood. "No, a bricklayer."

"Oh." The marshal was beginning to sound like a jack-of-all-trades. "So why aren't you buildin' houses?"

"The man and his family decided to move to Colorado."

"And you didn't want to move."

"My folks wanted me to finish my schooling." Grabbing more nails, he continued down the narrow strip, anchoring it to the wall.

"Oh. So what else have you done?"

He took a few more nails in hand. "Umm. . . I've worked for an attorney"—*bam, bam*—"a house mover"—*bam, bam*—"a mercantile owner"—*bam, bam*—"even a flag maker." He motioned to the foot-wide board on the floor.

She grabbed the other end, helping him lift it into place on the anchored strip of wood.

"Do you have that while I nail this down?"

"I've got it." Making sure the wood plank stayed balanced on the oak strip and pressed against the wall while he nailed, Jodie commented on his recent job choice. "So, now you figured you'd try your hand at bein' a marshal?"

"I didn't plan on this job, didn't even ask for it, but it's growing on me." He drove a nail through the plank into the strip on the wall. "I enjoy helping folks."

Which somewhat explained his desire to help her.

Reaching over her shoulder, he readied another nail against the board and lifted the hammer.

Finding it hard to breathe, to think, with him so close, Jodie said the first thing to reach her lips. "I'm glad."

Warm air tickled her neck, raising gooseflesh on her arms. "I am too."

"Really?" She turned her head to read the truth in his coffee-colored gaze, only to find his face mere inches away.

"Really." His gaze traveled over her face, ending on her lips.

Would he kiss her this time?

He leaned forward.

"How's it going back here?"

At Haskins's voice, Beau's head whipped toward the curtain-covered doorway, and Jodie's face flamed. Tucking her cheek against her shoulder, she pretended to be engrossed in holding the board, which could probably hold itself now.

"Uh, just fine." Beau smacked the nail into the wood, grunting as he nicked his thumb, and quickly stepped away. "Almost done with our second shelf." He tucked his injured thumb inside his fist and stashed it behind his back. "How are you liking the looks of things?"

"Are you sure it's gonna hold the weight of my merchandise? Looks kinda flimsy to me."

"It'll hold *me* when we get done."

"See that it does." With a frown, Haskins shifted his glare to her. "And see that none of my stuff goes missing while he's in here."

"I promise you, sir, you've nothing to worry about."

"Yeah, well—" The tinkling of the bell above the front door stopped the shopkeeper's next scathing remark. "I'll be back."

Jodie breathed a sigh when the crotchety man left the room, and sent Beau a concerned look. Would this show of good faith really be enough?

"We're gonna try somethin' different this time."

Beau sent Jodie a concerned glance, wondering what kind of creative lesson she had for him that day. The last two target practice sessions hadn't gone well. In fact, they'd been nothing more than a waste of time. He'd begun to wonder if it was possible to be a good lawman and not be able to hit the broad side of a barn.

"We're gonna take turns," Jodie continued. "While I shoot, you're gonna tell me a story, and while you shoot, I'll tell you one."

"A story?" He didn't see how storytelling was going to help his aim.

"Yes. Any kind of story ya want. About your childhood, your family, former jobs—you name it. Oh, and here, don't forget this." She flicked a dime his way.

He caught the coin in midair. "How is this supposed to help?"

"Remember, you balance the dime as you shoot to help steady your aim."

"I know about the dime. I meant the storytelling."

"I know." Grinning, she snapped the loaded cylinder closed and spun it. "Humor me. I want to see somethin'."

"Fine. Uh, who goes first?"

"Your choice."

Curious about what story she'd come up with, he lifted the pistol from her palm. "I guess I will."

"Okay." Jodie trailed behind him until they were a short distance from the wagon and stood opposite the targets. "Let's see. Oh, I know. There was this one time when I was a kid. I think I was about five or six. Papa was out workin' and I was helpin' Mama in the garden. She sent me to fetch water from the creek, and I found a stray dog hidin' in the bushes."

"It didn't attack you, did it?"

"Oh no. He was real friendly, but he was about the size of a small horse. Or at least he seemed so to me, and I could tell he was hungry. So I decided to do somethin' about it. I led him back to the house, and while Mama was busy outside, I took him to the kitchen."

Grinning, Beau put the dime in place. He could see where this was going.

"I've never been very tall, so I couldn't reach much in the kitchen. But I could reach the egg basket on the table. I wasn't allowed to help at the stove without Mama, so I cracked some eggs in a bowl and scrambled them. I didn't know dogs shouldn't eat at the table, so I coaxed the critter up onto a chair."

Beau shook his head as he took aim.

"Needless to say, Mama came in about the time the dog had its dirty paws perched on the tabletop and was lickin' the last of the egg off her clean table. You'd think the roof'd caved in she put up such a racket. She took up a broom and went to squealin' and shoutin' at that dog so much Daddy came a runnin' in from the field to see what was wrong. He burst through the door, and the dog was in such a fever to get out of there, he knocked Daddy down in his haste. Mama ended up whackin' Daddy on the head, swattin' one last time at the dog."

Beau joined in Jodie's laughter, then steadied his aim and fired. The tin can spiraled into the air.

With a shout, he turned to Jodie. "I did it!"

Her grin widened. "I figured you would once you stopped thinkin' so much."

"Huh?"

"Yesterday, when we were workin' on the shelves, I noticed you relaxed more when your hands and mind were busy. You didn't become self-conscious or hit your thumb until Haskins interrupted. I figured the same might work out here." She tapped the brim of his hat. "Sometimes, Beau Bones, you think too much." Jabbing a thumb in the direction of the remaining cans, she ordered, "Try it again."

He resumed his stance. Three of the remaining four cans toppled off the log.

With a whoop, Beau snatched Jodie around the waist and spun her around. Laughing, he staggered to a halt, only then realizing the line he'd crossed in his excitement. Jodie stood inches away, her arms braced against his, blue eyes sparkling, inviting.

An acorn pinged off his hat.

Blinking back to his senses, he looked upward and gave God a silent thanks. Beau gave Jodie a final squeeze and released her. "Thanks for your help."

She ducked her head, tucking a strand back into her bonnet. "Glad to do it."

"It's, uh, your turn, right?"

"Um. . .yeah." Taking the gun, Jodie moved away, heading to the wagon, undoubtedly to reload the Peacemaker.

With a sigh, he lifted his hat and raked a hand through his hair. *God, what am I doing here? She's my prisoner.* He had to get this attraction under control. Jodie had enough on her plate without romance muddying the waters, and who was to say she even returned the feelings? No, he had to keep his distance. He would be her friend, her advocate. Nothing more.

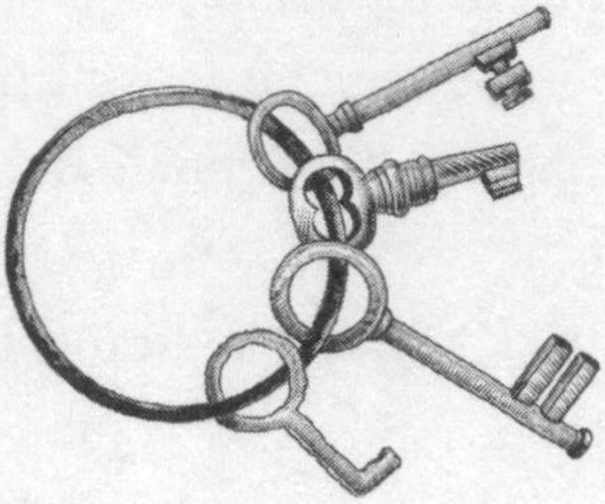

Chapter 8

Dipping his hat against the setting sun, Beau continued his meandering trek around town. As with the times he'd done this before, he kept his eyes peeled for anything suspicious, anyone watching or paying too much attention to the jail or happenings around town. He still couldn't shake the itch that a jailbreak was in the works.

No one in their right minds would leave someone like Jodie behind, sister or no. Her gang had to be planning something.

Two men he didn't recognize dismounted and slipped into the saloon down the street.

It looked like a good time for Beau's nightly visit to remind Mr. Shirley to keep the uproar to a minimum. He'd already had to settle three minor fights in the two weeks since he'd become marshal. If it hadn't meant Jodie sharing a cell, he might've locked up a few of the troublemakers to sleep off their inebriated condition and perhaps rethink their misconduct. Instead, he'd settled for a stern warning that must've done some good, because the rabble-rousers had changed faces each time.

Beau wasn't kidding himself. He knew some of these men probably respected his name more than his person, and one day they would surely test him. For now he was thankful that day hadn't come.

As he stepped up onto the boardwalk in front of the establishment, Beau ducked his head and peered through a window's plate glass. The place had a good turnout, not surprising for a Saturday evening. Most appeared to be the normal cowboys from neighboring ranches who sought to spend their week's pay on the world's vain pursuits.

Beau edged to the doorway and, from the shadows, peered over the batwing doors. He finally spotted the pair sitting belly-up to the bar talking to the rotund proprietor. Both were sturdy, one with black hair and garb, the other with overly long brown locks that curled from beneath his battered Stetson. Although they donned an air of nonchalance, their eyes were much too watchful.

Taking a steadying breath, Beau pushed inside. Most paid him no heed. A few glanced his direction. Carlos Shirley frowned. Beau tried not to let their reactions faze him and continued his meandering walk to the bar.

"Evening, Mr. Shirley." He nodded to the dusty pair. "Gentlemen." Turning, he leaned his elbow against the scarred wood. "I see y'all are gearing up for a banner night."

Boisterous laughter erupted from the back corner as one greenhorn patron spit and sputtered at the crowded table, earning many sound pats and slaps on the back.

"Don't worry, Marshal. I'll see things don't get outta hand. I ain't forgot yer warning."

"See that you don't." Beau settled his gaze on the pair. "I haven't seen you two before. Welcome to Small Tree."

The black-haired one lifted his glass in acknowledgment, but neither said a word.

"Are you planning on staying long?"

The "talkative" one of the duo tossed back the last of his drink and donned his battered hat. "Nope."

Beau hid a frown as the two made their exit. Ignoring Shirley's muttering about running off paying customers, he bid the man goodnight and followed the pair outside at a more sedate pace. By the time he slipped out the batwing doors, they'd sunk spur and galloped up the road away from town. Neither of their chestnut horses had a distinguishing mark between them.

Almost like they were doing their best to blend in.

To go unnoticed.

Which made Beau notice them all the more.

His nagging itch turned into all-out hives.

Jerry waited ten minutes from the last chime of the church bell, then nodded to his men. Sneaking from the cover of the trees, they slipped past the handful of horses dozing in the shade of the livery stable and peered down the dusty road dividing the town in two.

Empty. Just as he expected.

He smiled behind his bandanna. They'd silence Small Tree's sorry excuse for a marshal, grab Jo, and be miles away before anyone was the wiser. With nervous energy pulsing through his system, Jerry darted across the street, Dix and Pat on his tail. Guns drawn, bandannas in place, they barged inside the jail.

And stopped short.

Empty?

Not what he expected at all. An itch settled between Jerry's shoulder blades as he scanned the barren office.

"Where's the marshal?" Pat questioned as Jerry strode to the cell.

Empty as well.

Things weren't going according to plan. He hated when things didn't go according to plan. "Jo's not here either. He must've moved her somewhere."

Was the numbskull guarding his sister not as stupid as he looked? Had he suspected a jailbreak? Were they being watched even as they spoke? "We gotta get outta here."

The men didn't have to be told twice. They made a beeline for the trees. When they were well enough away with no one following, Jerry brought them to a halt.

"Now what?" The irritation in Dix's voice was unmistakable. That the mostly silent man spoke at all touted his growing impatience with the situation. They'd never hung around one place for so long, and the lack of movement was eating at all of them. This setback didn't help.

"Let me think." Jerry paced across the small clearing and stared at the minnows darting around in the shallows of the creek. Where would they have taken Jo? Pat had said the trial was set for next Tuesday. Had they moved it to another town?

"I ain't gonna stick around here forever and get my neck stretched for some female." Untying his horse from a branch, Pat tugged the bandanna from his face. "What if she decides to rat us out?"

"Jo wouldn't do that."

"Maybe not to you—you're her brother. But there ain't nuthin' keeping her from squealing on us." Pat shared a glance with Dix, whose grave expression sounded his agreement. "That marshal's up to something. I could see it in his eyes last night."

"Then all the more reason for us to get her outta there." Jerry closed the distance between them. "We need to find where they moved her. Check the saloon. Keep your ears to the ground and see what you can find out. I'll keep an eye on the jail. We'll meet back at the camp at sundown."

Maybe by then the pair would have cooled off, and they'd have more answers and could form a new plan.

Jodie shifted on the split-log bench in the crowded new church. One would think for a new building they'd've made it big enough to hold everyone with a little extra space. As it was, Beau's thigh was pressed against hers, adding to the heat and increasing her awareness of his presence, if that was even possible. If she thought the man was a good-looker in Levis and a vest, he was downright gorgeous in a three-piece suit and tie. God had surely outdone Himself on Beau Bones. And not just with his looks. She'd never met a man more trustworthy and respectable since her father had died.

A hush fell over the room, drawing her attention to the front, where Reverend Miller, with his lanky stature and large nose, was taking his place behind the podium. Poor man put her in mind of an eel she'd once caught while fishing for supper. Thankfully, he didn't have the temperament to match, definitely wasn't as slippery, and for a preacher, he sure was soft-spoken. Jodie had to strain to hear him from the back of the room.

"Today's reading is from Proverbs chapter 3, verses 27 through 31." He lifted his Bible higher. "Read along with me. 'Withhold not good from them to whom it is due, when it is in the power of thine hand to do it.'"

Jodie shifted in her seat, wincing at the splinter that jabbed her backside almost as sharply as the verse stabbed her conscience.

" 'Say not unto thy neighbour, Go, and come again, and to morrow I will give; when thou hast it by thee. Devise not evil against thy neighbour, seeing he dwelleth securely by thee. Strive not with a man without cause, if he have done thee no harm.'"

Clutching her hands together, she resisted the urge to hide her face. How many times had she been a part of her brother's scheming to do people wrong? Maybe not directly, but every time she didn't open her mouth, every time she turned a blind eye to his actions, she'd contributed to his plans to harm others without cause.

" 'Envy thou not the oppressor, and choose none of his ways.'" The preacher closed his Bible, placing it back on the podium. "In this life, we all have choices. Some are easy. Some are hard. Sometimes we think making no choice will save us from the consequences, but making no choice is a choice in and of itself. We either choose to follow God and His ways or we don't. There is no middle ground."

Jodie shifted again and avoided Beau's gaze when he glanced her direction.

"When we have the opportunity to do good," the preacher continued, "we shouldn't wait for someone else to do it or for a better time. We should follow God's leading and do as Jesus would.

You may ask, 'How do I know what Jesus would do?' Ask yourself, 'What would love do?' in the situation. If it was your child asking for help and not a stranger, would you lend a hand? If it was you stuck on the side of the road in the rain with a broken axle, what would you want a passerby to do?

"Sometimes love requires getting messy. Sometimes it requires our time. Sometimes our goods or money. But when something is done from a heart of love, it will make a much bigger impact for the kingdom of God than something done out of compulsion. As we leave this place today, consider those around you. Look for opportunities to make a difference. Is there good you are withholding?"

The preacher bowed his head in prayer, but Jodie didn't move. She couldn't move as his final question echoed in her soul, eating at her calm. *God, are You trying to tell me to give up my brother's location?*

"So, what did you think of church?" Beau questioned as he slid tin cans on the top shelves in the mercantile storage room. Jodie had been quiet ever since they'd left the service two days ago, and her continued silence was making him nervous.

She paused in piling bolts of fabric on another shelf. "Huh? Oh, it was fine. I enjoyed the singin'."

So it must've been something in the sermon that was bothering her. "Reverend Miller delivered quite a message, didn't he?"

"Mmm."

He finished emptying his hands and turned to study her. "If you want to talk about it, I'll try to help."

She continued stacking items and emptying crates onto the

shelves. As her silence lengthened, he resumed his work along-side her.

After some time, a sigh turned his head.

Jodie stood, head bowed, her hands gripping the edge of a shelf. "Do you think he's right?"

"Pardon?"

Rotating around, she leaned her back against the shelf and folded her arms. "Do you think the preacher was right?"

"About which part?" He shoved a barrel against the wall near her.

"The part about not withholding good."

"You mean the verse out of Proverbs 3? 'Withhold not good from them to whom it is due, when it is in the power of thine hand to do it'?"

"Yeah." Her head hung lower. "That part."

Scratching his neck, he leaned against the shelf beside her. "You're wondering if withholding the information about your brother's whereabouts is withholding good from the townsfolk, aren't you?" He hadn't realized until now that's where her mind had been, but he could see that being quite a dilemma.

Jodie rubbed at the creases in her brow. "If I tell y'all where he is, it'll do y'all good, but not him."

"Are you sure about that?"

"What?" She sought his gaze.

"Think about it. Has it done you good to get caught?"

"I. . .I suppose it has, but Jerry won't see it that way."

"If memory serves me correctly, you didn't see it that way at first either. In fact, I seem to recall some kicking and biting and *yelling*."

A hint of a smile curved her mouth for a brief moment then fell prey to the worry in her pale eyes. "But what if there's a shootout? I can't be responsible for my brother's death. He's the only family I got left."

Unable to resist the cry for help in her gaze, Beau slipped a supportive arm around her shoulders and squeezed. He wished he could shoulder this burden for her, make this easier, but some things only God could help with.

"I know it's not an easy decision to make, Jodie, but God will show you what's right. Why don't we pray for His help right now?" Relishing the feel of her at his side even though he knew he shouldn't, Beau bowed his head.

Jodie relished the feel of Beau's arm around her. No one had comforted her in such a way since her parents died. Jerry sure wasn't the demonstrative type. Bowing her head, she couldn't help leaning into the strong man beside her and wondering what it would be like to have his support all the time. Someone to pray with, talk to, and share her troubles. Someone who knew her faults but didn't shun her. But as her mama would say, if wishes were horses, everyone would ride.

"Father God. . ."

Jodie reined in her wandering thoughts and focused on Beau's prayer.

"You see Jodie's situation, her dilemma. This isn't an easy decision, but she wants to do what's right. I know that makes You proud. Show her, Lord, the way in which to go. Give her wisdom and the strength to do what You want her to do. Help everything to go well next week, better than we could imagine. In Jesus' name, amen."

With a final squeeze, he slowly removed his arm.

She missed it immediately. "Thank you."

"Anytime."

The sincerity in his dark eyes tugged at her insides.

He touched her hand, as if he too longed to keep the connection alive between them. "You might try reading all of Proverbs 3, especially verses 5 and 6. They've helped me many times when I haven't known what to do."

"Okay."

"And if you ever want to talk. . ."

She squeezed his hand. "Thanks, Beau."

❧ *Chapter 9* ❧

*S*oft daylight crept through the bars above Jodie's head, marking the passing of another sleepless night. Another night without a peep from her brother. Another night without a single notion of how to deal with the verses from Proverbs 3. Another night of pondering more and more questions than answers. With a yawn, she rubbed at the tension between her eyes, then rested her cheek against her bent knees.

She'd been so certain Jerry would come for her, but it was becoming apparent she was guarding a man who didn't care to risk his neck for hers. She might as well accept the fact she was in this alone.

"I am with you always."

Too exhausted to be startled by God's whisper in her heart, she lifted her eyes to the window. *God, I'm a mess. Why do You* waste time on me?

"*I have loved you with an everlasting love.*"

Hugging her knees, she closed her eyes and welcomed the comfort. *God, what do I do about Jerry? He's not ready to face You or a judge, but I don't want to die. I don't want to go to prison. I want a second chance to do things right.*

Wasn't that what her quandary all boiled down to? She wanted to do what was right but wasn't sure what *right* was. Was that turning in her only kin or showing him mercy? Betraying her brother or allowing him to go on hurting folks, to go on taking from those who'd done nothing to deserve such treatment? What was right? What was good?

She knew what Beau wanted. She knew what the town wanted. But what did God want? Opening the Bible on the blanket at her feet, she angled the pages toward the meager sunlight and reread the verses in Proverbs 3, starting at the beginning.

"*My son, forget not my law; but let thine heart keep my commandments: for length of days, and long life, and peace, shall they add to thee.*"

Long life. Peace. She surely wanted both of those.

"*Let not mercy and truth forsake thee: bind them about thy neck; write them upon the table of thine heart: so shalt thou find favour and good understanding in the sight of God and man.*"

She could definitely use some favor, but if she showed her brother mercy, would she be forsaking telling the truth?

"*Trust in the Lord with all thine heart; and lean not unto thine own understanding. In all thy ways acknowledge him, and he shall direct thy paths. Be not wise in thine own eyes: fear the Lord, and depart from evil.*"

With a sigh, Jodie bowed her head. Did she trust God? Really trust God? Enough to let go of what she wanted to happen and allow God to direct her? Maybe that's why direction seemed so fuzzy—she was too busy trying to make things go her way.

God, I give up. You know what's best for Jerry, and You know what's best for me. I trust that You'll do right by us both. If I need to speak with Beau about the rendezvous point, then give me the opportunity. If I need to remain silent, then help me to know that and to do so with a peace that comes only from You. Show me what I need to do, and give me the strength to follow Your lead. . .whatever that may be.

From his seat behind his uncle's desk, Beau gazed at the woman sleeping peacefully in the jail cell. After listening to her restlessness the past few nights, a part of him was relieved to see her finally resting. He could only hope that meant she'd come to a decision. What that decision was he had no idea. Would she finally reveal her brother's location, or had she decided to face the judge's verdict without that admission in her favor? He honestly couldn't blame her either way. He'd be hard-pressed to betray one of his brothers, no matter how much they'd teased and tortured him in the past. Family protected family.

A bird twittered outside the window, and the ticking clock on the opposite wall filled the silence of the late morning. Time was running out. If only he could think of something else to do to help Jodie, to guarantee her freedom. He couldn't stand to think of what would happen if he failed. Jodie didn't deserve to pay for her brother's crimes, for her decisions as a starving, lonely child. She deserved to have a second chance, to have a real life. A life with love and laughter and. . . Oh, he might as well admit it—he wanted her to have a life with him.

Jodie was a special woman. She had character, and he could see her growing in God and integrity every day. How could he get that across to the judge? He didn't know anything about Judge Johnson. If only he did. Maybe he should send a message to one of his brothers, see what he could find out. As soon as he considered the thought, he dismissed it. No, he needed to do this on his own. Well, not completely on his own.

God, please help us.

Jodie's fate would be decided in a matter of days, and in a way, so would his. Life wouldn't be the same without her. Not only that, but if he couldn't get her to give up her gang, would the town force him to give up his new job? A job he'd actually come to enjoy and wouldn't mind keeping. When they heard him fighting for her freedom in court, would they consider hiring him a mistake and send him packing? He didn't want to return home a failure again, but what else could he do? Jodie's brother was the true guilty party.

God, please don't let the wrong person be punished here.

Jodie shifted on her bunk, drawing his attention. Striped sunlight angled across her features, highlighting the delicate turn of her nose and chin, the soft curve of her cheek. Even in her patched, baggy clothes, her beauty shined. He couldn't believe how blind he'd been upon their first meeting. That just proved people normally saw what they wanted to see.

The words, "*Help them see,*" whispered across his heart.

Beau propped his head in his hands. *How, God?*

He already planned to reveal she was a woman, to have her share her story of the past, and to show the work she'd done toward restitution. Without the true guilty parties present, what more could he do?

An odd case his oldest brother had related to him awhile back surfaced in his mind.

God, is that You?

The idea was outlandish. Crazy. Completely unlike him. Just crazy enough it might be God—and it might work. If the judge went for it. And Jodie.

He stared at the woman in the cell, the idea growing on him until a smile tugged on his lips.

Yes, it just might work.

"Jodie, I, uh, wondered if we could talk?"

Jodie stilled at Beau's question. So that's the way it was to be. Dawn barely even hinted outside her window, and God was already supplying her with an answer. With a nod, she set aside the towel she'd been drying her face on and moved to take a seat on the bunk.

"No, out here." Beau unlocked the cell.

Surprised, Jodie changed course and followed him to the chairs in front of the desk. Warm lantern light pushed back the predawn darkness but did nothing to settle the swirl of nervous grasshoppers that took to hopping in her gut.

She perched on the edge of her seat and gripped the sides. "I have something I want to talk to you about too, but you first."

"All right." He settled on the chair in front of her and rubbed his legs. "Look, I know you've been struggling over what to do about your brother."

She nodded. Peace had alluded her until she'd surrendered to God early yesterday morning. She was acutely aware that they were less than three days from the trial. Unfortunately, her brother might not even be in the area anymore.

"Well, I, uh. . .I, uh. . ."

Clearly she wasn't the only one unsettled by this conversation. Swallowing a smile, she stilled Beau's sliding hand with a touch.

"It's me, Beau. Just tell me whatever it is you're thinkin'."

He turned his hand to grip hers. "Look, I, uh. . .I had an idea come to mind yesterday while I was watching you sleep. I—I mean, while you were sleeping. I—I mean I was watching you, but that is. . .I mean. . .not like. . ." Ducking his head, he used his free hand to rake through his already tousled hair.

Her smile broke free at how completely adorable he was when he got flustered. "What was your idea?"

"We're friends, right? I mean, you like me? I'm not completely abhorrent to you?"

"Of course you're not. What kind of question is that? You're the best friend I've ever had."

"Good." With a deep exhale, a wave of his nervousness seemed to wash away. "Good. Because I thought of this old ca—"

The door slammed open, wood splintering from the frame.

With a hard yank, Jodie carried Beau to the floor between the chairs.

Two men stepped into the room, their hard soles thudding against the planks.

"We've c— What's goin' on here?"

At the familiar voice, Jodie jerked her gaze up to find her brother standing not three feet away.

With his gun barrel aimed at Beau's head.

❧ Chapter 10 ❧

*B*eau's blood ran cold at the sight of the six-shooter aimed their direction, but instead of freezing him, the chill cleared his head. Snapping upright, he shoved Jodie behind him and darted a glance at his gun belt hanging on the hat rack behind the desk.

"I wouldn't try it, mister." The second man, stout like the "talkative" one from the saloon with eyes as black as sin above a dark bandanna, leveled a second gun on him.

"Come on, Jo." The first man barked the order, his dark hair and pale eyes a testament of his identity. The light blue color that was fetching on Jodie looked more like frigid ice on this fellow.

Jodie didn't move, except to tighten her grip on Beau's arm. "You don't have to do this, Jerry. I'm okay. If you'd just give these people back—"

"Quit wastin' time 'n' come on."

The pressure on his arm shifted, and Beau felt Jodie rise.

"I–I'm not goin' with you."

"*What?*" the second man exclaimed.

Jerry's eyes widened then narrowed. "Quit your foolin', Jo, 'n' get over here. We ain't got time for your nonsense."

"It's not nonsense. What you're doin' is wrong, and I don't want to be part of it no more. Do ya think Mama and Papa would be proud of what you're doin'? That God is pl—"

"Enough!" Jerry raised a fist, clearly clinging to his calm by a thread. "Get over here. I ain't lettin' you hang for my crimes. Now come on."

Beau felt Jodie's gaze on him, but he didn't dare tear his focus away from that pistol. *God, help us.*

After a heartbeat of silence, a delicate hand slid onto his shoulder. "No, I'm stayin' with Beau."

Even as his chest expanded with pride and another emotion he couldn't name, Beau's heart skipped a beat as Jerry's countenance darkened.

"Beau, is it?" Her brother cocked a brow. "Well, I ain't leavin' here without you, and if he's the only thing standin' in your way. . ." His thumb pulled the cock back the full distance.

Beau's breathing ceased.

Jodie glanced back over her shoulder for one last peek of the marshal lying unconscious behind the bars a heartbeat before her brother dragged her the rest of the way out of the jail and tossed her into a saddle. "You didn't have to hit him."

Jerry swung onto his own mount. "He put his hands on you."

"He was only protectin' me."

"So am I." Jerry kicked his horse into a gallop behind Dix and Pat.

When her horse quickly followed suit, Jodie realized her brother'd dropped a rope around her saddle horn.

As much as she wanted to slip the rope and turn around, she knew she couldn't, at least not yet. She had the sickening feeling if she tried to go back, if she fought her brother, he'd keep his threat to shoot the marshal. Something she couldn't let happen.

Seeing that gun aimed at Beau, she knew without a doubt that somewhere in the past month she'd fallen in love with him. It was ridiculous, a prisoner falling in love with the prison keeper, but she couldn't deny it. And that's why she'd had no other choice than to leave with her brother, even though every fiber of her being had wanted to stay. Beau knew that, and the look in his eyes before Jerry'd laid him flat said he wouldn't let her go without a fight. Or at least she hoped that's what that look meant.

God, what do I do?

Something banged against her leg. A bag. She pulled one of the straps off the saddle horn and squinted at the inside in the growing dawn. A money bag? Grinning, Jodie grabbed a handful of bills, then hesitated. Her brother would notice the missing bills quicker. She dug to the bottom of the bag and found a jumble of coins.

Leaning over the saddle, she draped her arm against her leg and dropped a coin…then another…then another, praying all the while Beau would find her trail and come to her rescue.

Before Jerry realized what she was doing.

With a groan, Beau sat up and rubbed his aching jaw. Opening his eyes, he took in his surroundings and scrambled to his feet. He gripped the bars on the door and yanked with all his might.

The metal only clanked together.

He had to get out of here. Jodie needed him. Shouting at the top of his lungs, he rattled the cell door. When that didn't summon anyone, he moved to the window that revealed the sun cresting the horizon. How long had he been out? "Help!"

He glanced around. The key, the key. Where was the key?

There. On the desk. On the corner closest to him.

Surveying the cell, he tried to find something long enough to help him reach it. The bed frame was metal. That wouldn't work. Wait. He yanked the lumpy mattress onto the floor.

"Hallelujah." It was a rope bed, just as he'd hoped. Finding one end, he quickly untied the knot and began untangling the lattice work. Maybe all that time dealing with his brothers' shenanigans had been a good thing after all. Maybe God had been preparing him for this work all his life and he just hadn't known it. Maybe he'd finally found his place in this world. Now he just had to get back his woman.

The last of the rope slid free. Now to make a lasso. *Thank you, Austin.* Quickly forming a honda knot, he praised God his next-to-oldest brother had rebelled and gone through a cowboy phase he'd never grown out of. In no time at all, he had the lariat made and swinging on the outside of the bars.

Lord, guide my aim.

His first toss overshot the key ring, but as he reeled it in, the rope caught and dropped the ring to the floor. He just had to get it closer. He swung again, missed, and tried again. This time the loop surrounded the keys. *Yes!*

Beau gingerly drew the prize his way. When he could finally reach it, he snatched up the key and crammed it into the lock. He darted out, grabbing up his gun belt and some extra bullets before racing across the street where the livery man was just opening his door.

"Hewitt!"

The balding man swiveled his direction. "Marshal, what's wrong?"

"Saddle some horses. My prisoner's been kidnapped."

"A jailbreak?"

Beau didn't stop to explain. He continued down the street, shouting over his shoulder, "I'll be back shortly with more men."

"What is it, Lawson?" Beau watched the lanky man pick up something small and shiny from the dirt. Their posse of about a dozen men had split up, covering multiple directions, trying to find the gang's path on the hard, trampled ground. Beau had made sure to keep Lawson, the best tracker in the area, with him. Cyrus, a quiet crack shot, rounded out their small group.

"I'm not sure." The tanner stood, surveyed the area again, took a handful of steps down the road, and stooped once more. "If I didn't know any better, Marshal, I'd say we've got ourselves a money trail."

Beau swung down from the saddle and approached. "A money trail?"

Midday sunlight glinted off a penny and five-cent piece in the man's outstretched hand.

Cyrus meandered past them a short ways, glanced around, took a few more steps, knelt, and held up a half-dollar.

Jodie.

Hope sprang to life in Beau's chest. He hadn't lost her. "Where does this road lead?"

Lawson shoved the money into Beau's hand and reached for his saddle. "It splits not too far from here, going in multiple directions."

Which explained why the gang had chosen this path. Beau and Cyrus followed suit, remounting. "Any of those directions lead to a possible hideout?"

"More than one." Lawson kneed his horse, his attention on the ground. "Good thing your prisoner is showing us the way."

Keep it up, Jodie. I'm coming.

✦ Chapter 11 ✦

Jodie breathed a sigh of relief when her brother called them to a stop. As if it too were exhausted, the sun propped itself on the horizon, lengthening the shadows and lessening its scalding touch. Moving gingerly, she climbed from the saddle and locked her knees to keep from sinking all the way to the ground. She hadn't ridden so long or so hard in many a day. They'd only stopped long enough to water or trade out horses, putting them miles from Small Tree and the marshal.

Needless to say, her backside hurt like nobody's business and she couldn't wait to fall into a bedroll. Slipping the few coins in her grip into her pocket, Jodie arched her back and twisted away some of the kinks.

"Get some supper goin'." Jerry tossed a saddlebag her direction.

She didn't even try to catch it. The flap popped open as it hit the dirt, sending potatoes spilling out onto her boots. Not ready to try her brother's temper in her current state, Jodie forced her limbs to move, scooped up the bag, and shuffled over to a gigantic boulder. Welcome blood returned to her extremities as she gathered sticks, built a campfire, and took stock of her supplies.

When she knelt to start slicing spuds, her knife froze over the first potato as a sudden thought struck—these were stolen potatoes, as were the ham and salt. She couldn't cook these. She glanced at her brother where he worked with the others rubbing down their horses. He'd be furious if she refused, but the only one around for him to threaten now was her, and he'd never hurt her. Maybe if he realized she'd changed, that she wasn't gonna go back to the way things were, maybe he'd let her go.

God, give me strength.

Emptying her hands, Jodie rose on unsteady legs. How did she tell the one who'd taken care of her for almost a decade that she didn't want to stay with him? *Thanks for all you've done for me, but I don't need you anymore.* Yeah, that would sit well.

God, what do I say? She rubbed her hands on her thighs and tried to summon up the words and the courage to move.

Jerry must've felt her gaze, because he looked her way before she was ready. "What's the matter?"

Stiffening her spine, she clenched her hands together. "Can we talk?"

"After supper." He turned away as the men led the other horses toward the creek trickling a short distance away.

"No." She held her breath, swallowing a gulp when he looked back. "Before."

With a huff, he tossed the burlap bag by his saddle and stalked her direction. "What?"

"Jerry, I. . ." She glanced off, her focus falling on the food. Sighing, she looked back into eyes much like her own. "Jerry, while I was in jail, I. . ." She lifted her hands in a shrug. "I changed."

"You forgot how to cook?"

"No, I. . .I remembered." Shoving her hands in her pockets, her fingers collided with the last few coins. Was Beau nearby? Had he found her trail? Or was she in this alone?

"Lo, I am with you always."

That's right; she was never alone. God had promised never to leave her. Even if Beau never showed up, she could face the future, get a fresh start. . .with God. She straightened, relying on His strength to get her through this and all the days ahead.

"I remembered what it was like to be in one place for more than a week. I—I remembered the fun I used to have working alongside Mama and Papa. I remembered what it was like not havin' to constantly look over my shoulder. I remembered. . ." She reached out and touched her brother's arm. "I remembered God."

Jerry yanked away, but she had to give him credit for not stomping off.

"Or should I say He showed me that He hadn't forgotten about me. Jerry, we don't have to live like this."

"Oh, what am I supposed to do? Go traipsin' back to town and turn myself in to your beau?"

"Would that be so bad?"

With a shake of his head, Jerry walked a few steps away and then stalked back. "They'll hang me. Is that what you want? Those people back there. . .they don't care one whit about folks changin'. They won't care if you've turned over a new leaf. All they'll see is what you've done, what I've done. They spout off a bunch of religious claptrap, but in the end all they want is your hide. Don't you see. . ." He gripped her arms. "There ain't no goin' back. They ain't gonna forget. They ain't gonna accept you. There ain't no happily-ever-afters in this life. Face it, Jo, there's no such thing as a second chance."

No such thing. . . Was what he said true? Would they not care about the good she'd done, the restitution she'd tried to make? Was it just wishful thinking to believe she could have a future? Would all her striving be for naught? Was there really no such thing as a second chance?

She paused, considering, then straightened, her resolve strengthening. "No. No, I refuse to believe that. God took me back. He'll take you back too."

"Ha. Even if He did, they ain't gonna forget what we've done. I ain't goin' back, Jo." Jerry turned and began walking away.

Swallowing the Texas-size lump in her throat, Jodie forced out the words, "And I ain't stayin'."

He stopped. After a moment, his shoulders lifted then sagged. "So be it." With a sad shake of his head, he continued walking toward the other men.

A twig snapped. A shotgun cocked.

Before Jodie could spot the source, Jerry took off running for his horse.

Bedlam erupted. Three men emerged from behind trees. Beau! Shouts. Scrambling. Whinnying. Pat vaulted onto a horse bareback. Beau landed a lasso around him, yanking him onto the creek bank. A shot went off.

Jodie dropped to the dirt.

Beau peered about and spotted Jodie lying in the dirt near a saddlebag. His heart stopped. Shoving the rope into Cyrus's grip, Beau sprinted toward the woman he loved. In that moment, he couldn't deny it. He loved her. And if he'd found her only to lose her again, he didn't know what he'd do.

Please, God, no.

He dropped to his knees and grabbed her shoulder. "Jodie?" Rolling her over, he found tears streaking her cheeks. "Where are you hurt? Are you shot?" He scanned her form. No blood.

"I'm fine."

Thank God.

Swiping a hand over her face, she sat up. "Jerry left."

Beau surveyed the area in the waning twilight. Sure enough, her brother was missing. He didn't know whether to be relieved or upset.

"He wouldn't listen, Beau. I tried to get him to turn hisself in."

Pulling her into his arms, Beau tucked her head beneath his chin. "I know. I heard part of what you said. Don't worry. We'll find him." Although, for the sake of the woman in his hold, he wasn't sure how hard he'd look. With the other two gang members in custody, Jerry Ross would have to start from scratch, and hopefully the town would be satisfied enough with the other two to let Beau keep his job.

Leaning back, Jodie stared up at him. "Do you think he'll ever change?"

"If God can stop Paul and turn his heart around, He can get ahold of your brother. No doubt. We'll pray for him."

With a nod, Jodie leaned back into Beau's chest about the same time a throat cleared behind them.

"Uh, Marshal?" Lawson peered down at them with an odd expression.

"Oh." Beau pushed to his feet and helped Jodie to hers. "Mr. Lawson, I'd like you to meet *Miss* Jodie Ross, the *lady* who left you a shining trail."

"Lady?" After scanning the length of the dirt-coated woman, Lawson focused on her face. "Well, I'll be. . ." He glanced over his shoulder to where Cyrus held a gun on the pair of outlaws tied to a sturdy oak. "Hey, Cy. Come get a load of this. He's a she." Lawson's attention shifted back around. "You've been guarding a woman all this time? And the work at the mercantile. . . The missus is gonna hit the floor when she hears this one. Ma'am, that was a mighty brave thing you did, leaving us that trail. Made my job tracking y'all a whole lot easier."

"You'll be sure to tell that to the judge?" Beau questioned.

"Oh, yes, sir."

"Thank you, Mr. Lawson." Jodie smiled then peered up at Beau. "What now?"

Indeed, what now? Beau scanned the growing darkness. "I guess we'll camp here for the night and head back to town in the morning."

"What about Jerry?"

"I, uh. . ." Beau scratched his chin and glanced at Lawson. "You think you could find his trail in the dark?"

Lawson cocked his head in thought as he surveyed the area. "With us being so close to a creek, I've a feeling he pulled the same stunt he did back at Small Tree and traveled upstream a ways. Without a full moon, it'd be nigh unto impossible to find his exit point by lantern light, not to mention the risk to the horses."

The man had a very good point. "What about in the morning? We've got to get these men and Jodie back to town before the judge arrives."

"We can look, but I'd guess he'll be long gone by then."

Beau would be too if he were in Jerry's shoes. "Might be wiser to wire the sheriffs in the surrounding counties with his description and get these two behind bars."

"What you gonna do with Miss Ross here?"

Jodie shared an uncertain glance with him.

"I guess we'll figure that out when we get back to town."

After another day and a half on horseback, at a much slower pace, Jodie caught a glimpse of Small Tree in the distance. She shifted in her saddle. Did she really want to go through with this? Did she really want to risk facing a judge and whatever verdict he might render? Would it be better just to knee her horse and make a run for it? She glanced about and found Beau's gaze on her. For some reason, her insides calmed.

Beau nudged his mount and closed the gap between them at the front of their pack. "Having second thoughts?"

"No, I'm through with runnin'. Just a little worried about tomorrow." She turned her focus back on the town. "You think the judge has arrived yet?"

Peering upward, Beau took in the position of the sun. "Possibly. Depends on if the stage is running late or not." He cleared his throat. "Jodie, before we were interrupted back at the jail, there was, uh, something I wanted to discuss with you."

"Yes?"

"I, uh . . ."

A shout and jangle of harnesses yanked their attention to the road behind them. The stage barreled their direction, the hooves of the six-horse team thundering against the hard-packed earth. Their group broke apart, moving to the grassy sides of the narrow road. As the red-and-yellow Wells Fargo coach hurried past, a man with a handlebar mustache and salt-and-pepper hair stuck his head out the window. His dark eyes widened, his focus fixed on them as he continued down the road.

Jodie glanced at Beau to find him wide-eyed, his mouth gaped slightly open. "Do you know who that was?"

Beau jerked at Jodie's question. Tearing his gaze away from the stagecoach's passenger, he looked across the road. "Lawson, I thought they said Judge Johnson was presiding over this case?"

"They did."

"Well that's not who was on that stage." He kneed his horse into a gallop. This wasn't happening. He'd rather deal with a stranger presiding over Jodie's case. There's no telling what would happen now.

Then again, maybe he was wrong. Maybe his mother was just checking up on him. Maybe Judge Johnson really was on that stage. Maybe, just maybe, his eyes were deceiving him and that wasn't—

"Beau, what's wrong?" Jodie rode up beside him. "Who was that?"

Beau watched the stage rein to a stop in the middle of town. A heartbeat later, a well-dressed, well-groomed older gentleman disembarked and turned their direction, sending Beau's stomach plummeting. Even from this distance, there was no denying who'd come to town.

"My father."

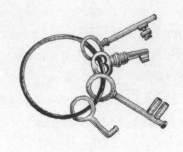

⊱ Chapter 12 ⊰

$\mathcal{J}$odie glanced between Beau and the distinguished-looking man across from him on the boardwalk and couldn't help but see the family resemblance. Both had strong cheekbones, a defined chin, straight nose, and dark eyes. However, the older gentleman had a presence that she could only describe as overpowering.

The men shook hands, Beau's normally congenial manner subdued. "Father, I didn't realize you were coming."

"Did not."

"I apologize. I *did not* realize you were coming. Did Mother send you?"

"No, Judge Johnson called upon me for my assistance since he is currently detained with another case and I was free for a few days. Your mother sends her regards though and wonders why you have not returned home yet."

"I see." Beau's Adam's apple bobbed. "I have, uh, taken a job here."

"Then it is not your uncle's affairs that have delayed your return?"

"Uh. . .not exactly." Beau shifted in his boots.

"Then what, *exactly*?"

"Hey, Marshal!" Lawson stopped his horse at the hitching rail across the street, the other three coming to a halt beside him. "You want us to take these two inside and lock them up for you?"

After a long blink, Beau turned to face Lawson. "Yeah, if you don't mind. I have some business to handle out here. Keep an eye on them for me until I get through, will you?"

"Sure. What you gonna do with her?"

Beau glanced Jodie's way, uncertainty covering his handsome features.

Before he could voice a word, she touched his arm and gave a small smile. "Don't worry. I don't mind waitin' with him."

She took a step toward the jail, but Beau's hand on hers stopped her progress. "Outside the cell. I don't want you in there with those two."

With a nod, she squeezed his fingers. "Okay."

"Marshal? Your job is the town *marshal*?"

Beau tried not to wince at his father's tone as Jodie slipped inside the jail. This might be the hardest conversation he'd ever had with his father, and he'd had quite a few. And tomorrow they'd meet each other in court. Wonderful. Why couldn't his life ever be easy?

Gathering his courage, Beau faced his father. "Yes, I'm the marshal. I have been for nearly a month now."

Father came as close to a public display of emotion as Beau

had ever seen as he snagged Beau's arm and dragged him into the alley between the livery and feedstore. "Are you out of your mind? I wanted you to show interest in the law, but this. . . Your mother is going to have a fit of the vapors when she hears what you have been up to." He swiped his handkerchief across his face and began to pace. "And that woman, if you can even call her a woman in that outfit. . . ."

His temperature spiking, Beau stiffened. "Mind what you say about Jodie, sir."

Father stopped midpace and stared at him, his graying brows winging upward then slamming low. "What did you say to me?"

"I don't want to fight with you, sir, but I won't have you speaking ill of Jodie. She just risked everything to bring those two outlaws you saw to justice."

His father looked at him askance, then gave a nod of acquiescence. "Fine, but you will give your resignation as marshal and return home with me as soon as this trial is over. Your position is still avail—"

"I'm not resigning." Beau wasn't sure where he got the courage to interrupt his father, but as long as he was being stupid, he might as well spit it all out. "I enjoy being the town marshal. Furthermore, I'm good at it."

"But you have never even fired a gun."

"Yes, I have, sir. Jodie taught me, and I've been practicing."

Father planted his hands on his hips and lowered his head. After mumbling something under his breath, he gave a huff and met Beau's gaze. "I do not have time for this nonsense. I have accommodations to find and a trial for which to prepare."

"So do I. And I have wires to send."

"Fine. We will finish this discussion after the trial. Agreed?"

Beau wouldn't change his mind, but he nodded anyway. He dreaded tomorrow more than ever before.

Jodie smoothed a hand down the bluebonnet-colored dress she hadn't worn since the last time she and Beau had gone target practicing. Sitting in the middle of the wooden pew at the front of the schoolhouse, she felt about as conspicuous and perilous as one of those tin cans. Whispers surrounded her and she could feel every stare centered on her. Why had she let Beau talk her into wearing this getup? She'd just have to change when his father sent her to the state prison.

Beau touched her hand, making her start. "It's going to be okay."

That's what he thought. She tossed a backward glance at the lanky man beside Dix and Pat, then whispered to Beau. "Lawson said Judge Bones is one of the hardest judges around."

"He is."

"Then how are you so calm?"

"Because the two truly guilty parties are sitting behind you."

Jodie peeked again at Dix and Pat, handcuffed and stuffed in the pew next to Lawson. Their hardened glares made her glad Beau had insisted on giving her his room last night and staying at his desk to keep an eye on things.

A door beside the chalkboard at the front of the building opened, and Judge Bones stepped inside. Dread pooled in her stomach as a hush fell over the building and everyone rose to their feet until Beau's father took his seat.

The somber man set a gavel on the teacher's desk then took in the crowd gathered. When his focus landed on Jodie, clad in ribbons and lace, his gaze shot to his son.

"Who is the defendant? I was told the individual on trial was a"—he glanced at the paper in front of him—"Joe Ross."

Beau rose. "She's the defendant, Your Honor. Her name is Miss Jodie Ross."

"Jodie?" The judge's gaze flickered between the two of them, then leveled on his son.

"Yes, sir. Jodie. Jo for short. We believed her a man when she was arrested."

"Then you men need to get some spectacles. Young lady, are you telling me you were a part of the gang that robbed and blew up the general store?"

Jodie peered up at Beau, who gave her an encouraging nod, so she rose to stand beside him. "Yes, sir." She rotated slightly and gestured to the two men behind her. "Dix and Pat were the other two members in my brother's gang."

Murmuring ensued, quieted only by the judge's gavel.

"Am I also to believe you were instrumental in capturing these two men?"

"Yes, Your Honor." Jodie glanced at Beau, wondering if she should say more. At his nod, she added. "When my brother's gang broke me out of jail and forced me to go with them, I left a trail for the marshal and his men to follow."

Judge Bones sat back in his chair, his expression revealing little. "What kind of trail?"

"Coins, sir."

"Is this true?" The question was directed at Beau.

"Yes, Your Honor. With your permission, I would like Miss Ross to share her story with the court. I believe you will see she is a prime candidate for rehabilitation."

"We shall see. Continue, young lady."

After another encouraging nod from Beau, Jodie gathered her nerve, ignored the stares, and forced herself to tell everyone of her past—from her childhood to that day.

With as stoic a face as she'd ever seen, Judge Bones listened as she told of her part in her brother's gang, about the day of the general store robbery, and the day her brother kidnapped her from the jailhouse. He then shifted his attention to Beau. "Is there anything else you would like to add, Marshal?"

"Yes, Your Honor." Beau returned to his feet and shared about the times he'd found her reading the Bible, the work she'd done at the mercantile, and her request to attend services at the church. He then shared his account of the jailbreak and subsequent capture.

"I see, and you believe Miss Ross should be excused from serving time in prison for her crimes?"

Beau stiffened beside her. "I believe Miss Ross has demonstrated her desire to become a productive part of society, rather than to continue in her brother's unlawful footsteps, Your Honor."

"And you would have me simply release her on her own recognizance? That is not permissible. She must have a place of residence, a job in the community, and a guardian willing to take responsibility for her and her actions and to teach her to live within the bounds of society. Does she have these things?"

Jodie locked her knees to keep from wilting to her seat. She didn't have any of those. Prison. She was bound for prison. *God, give me strength.* Drawing a shaky breath, she forced herself to meet the judge's gaze. As she began to shake her head, Beau cleared his throat beside her.

"Actually, Your Honor, she does."

Jodie's gaze collided with Beau's. "I do?"

"She does?" The judge seemed equally shocked.

"Yes, sir." Beau drew a deep breath and straightened to his full height. "If Miss Ross is agreeable, she has a job waiting for her that also includes accommodations."

"And what job is that?"

Turning his focus on her, Beau offered a tentative smile. "The job of being my wife."

Jodie's gasp was echoed by the others present.

"*What?*" The judge's voice boomed to the rafters, the crowd joining in the uproar, but Jodie couldn't tear her gaze away from the man staring at her with an intensity that sent her pulse thrumming through her veins like a freight train. Was this really happening?

"Your wife? You want to marry me? You'd marry me just to keep me out of prison?"

Beau took a step toward her, closing the gap between them. "No."

Her thrumming freight train crashed. "But you just said. . ."

"I said I want to marry you, but it's not just to keep you out of prison."

"It's not?"

"No." Shaking his head, he lifted a thumb and traced her jawline, setting the fire from the crash spiriting through her veins. "It's because I don't want to let you out of my sight. I want to wake up with this beautiful face looking at me every morning and go to sleep with you resting beside me every night. I want to know you're safe and taken care of and to help all your dreams come true. I want *you*, Jodie Ross. I want you as my wife, because imagining a day without you is torture, and there's no one else I'd rather spend my life with. I. . .I love you."

❧ Chapter 13 ❧

A ringing gavel and a shouting judge interrupted Jodie's response and sent silence pouring through the room as Judge Bones's threatening glare traveled the expanse, coming to rest on his son.

"Marshal Bones, a word. . ."

Before Beau could move, a throat cleared behind them, drawing everyone's attention to the center aisle where Mr. Haskins stood rotating his flat-brim straw hat in his hands.

"Your Honor, if I may, I have something to say."

"Who are you?"

"My name is Robert Haskins. I own the general store that was robbed." The bald man glanced Jodie's way with an indiscernible expression before looking back at the judge.

"Make it quick."

Haskins tugged at his vest and straightened. "Your Honor, I. . .I would like to drop the charges against Miss Ross."

A wave of shock rippled through Jodie and flowed through the crowd.

The judge silenced their murmurs with a bang of his gavel.

With another glance in her direction, Haskins continued. "Miss Ross isn't responsible for blowing up my store. Those other two men are. In fact. . ." Peering at his hat, Haskins rotated it in his wrinkled hands. "When I was coming to, I heard Miss Ross trying to talk her brother out of it."

The uproar and banging ensued again.

Ignoring the chaos, Jodie stared at the man offering her freedom. Why was he doing this?

As if in answer to her question, the crotchety old man continued, "Miss Ross paid for whatever part she played in her brother's crimes by helping rebuild and restock my shelves." He lifted his chin. "She deserves a second chance."

Jodie sat. Hard. Tears pricked her eyes. She knew Jerry'd been wrong.

The judge regained order, and with a final bang of his gavel, declared, "Case dismissed. Miss Ross, you are free to go. As for these other two men, we will deal with them this afternoon. Marshal Bones. . .a word."

Everything continued around Jodie in a haze. Free? Case dismissed? She wasn't going to prison? Her nightmare was over?

Beau gave her arm a parting squeeze. Why didn't he look happy? He said something to Lawson, pointing to Dix and Pat, then headed toward his father.

Jodie's gaze landed on Mr. Haskins, who was already making tracks for the door. "Mr. Haskins." She stood and moved out of the pew, her voice growing in strength as the stunned haze lifted. "Mr. Haskins!"

Halfway across the schoolyard she caught up to him. "Mr. Haskins. . ." She caught his arm, forcing him to stop and face her. The same hard expression was firmly back in place, but this time she saw beneath the veneer. "Why?"

"Why what?"

"Why'd you do it? Why'd you stand up for me? I thought you hated me."

"You paid your time. Now don't make me regret it."

"I—I won't, but. . ."

Haskins's gaze lazily roamed over her face. After a moment, his veneer cracked, and he cupped her cheek. "You remind me so much of my daughter."

"I do?"

"If only I'd. . ." With a cough, he dropped his hand. "Yes, well. . .if you need a job, you come see me. Don't you let that marshal force you into marrying him if you don't want to."

"I, um. . .I won't. Thank you."

"Don't mention it. Ever." A quick pivot and the old codger stalked away, leaving Jodie staring after him.

A shout behind her drew her attention.

Beau.

She smiled. Then his words in the courtroom came slamming back through her. Beau? What on earth was she going to say to him?

Beau hurried to close the distance between himself and Jodie. Curious eyes followed his progress, but for once, he didn't care. He had to know how Jodie was faring. What had Haskins said to her? Had she given any thought to his proposal?

"Jodie. . ." He cupped her arms. "Are you okay? I saw you talking to Haskins."

"I'm, uh, I'm fine. He, uh. . .he offered me a job." Avoiding his gaze, she stared at his hand on her arm.

Did she want him to let go? Had he acted too rashly and lost her? Messed up like he had with every other woman he'd taken a chance to get to know? "Wh—what did you tell him?"

"I. . .thanked him." She still wouldn't look at him.

It was true; he'd lost her. He dropped his arms to his sides, releasing her. Why did he always mess these things up? What was wrong with him? He thought he'd finally found the one gal who looked past his faults, who understood him. He raked a hand through his hair. Was there any way to salvage this mess? If only she'd look at him, maybe he could gauge his chances.

"Beau. . ."

"Yeah?"

She lifted a hand to the side of her face. "Can we go somewhere else to talk? Everybody's starin' at us."

Jodie was ashamed of him, didn't even want to be seen with him. What was the use of talking? "It's okay. You don't have to say it. I—I understand."

She caught his arm as he turned to leave. "Understand what?"

"I get it. You have a choice now. I'm not your only pass to freedom. You don't have to tell me you don't return my feelings; you don't have to try to let me down nicely. I get it." He'd told his father he'd meant what he'd said, and he had. Looks like he'd made a laughingstock of himself again. Only this time the pain was worse—he didn't think he'd recover.

"But I do."

He looked at her in confusion. "You do? You do what?"

"I do return your feelin's." A small smile curved her mouth, raising his hopes. "I love you, Beau. I just don't understand how someone as amazin' as you could love me."

"You don't. . ." He couldn't believe what he was hearing. Apparently his speech earlier hadn't said enough. "Oh hang it all." Snatching her to him, he pressed his lips to hers and tried to get his point across another way, another oh-so-much b—

"Ahem."

Beau jerked back at the familiar throat clearing. He didn't have to look to know his father stood right behind him.

Jodie stared up at him with dreamy eyes that made him want to pull her closer again.

Father must've read his mind, because he cleared his throat again. Loudly. *"Ahem.* Do I take it that she has accepted your proposal?"

If the way she kissed him back said anything, she had, but he needed to hear more. "Jodie. . .what do you say? Will you. . .will you do me the honor of being my wife?"

Licking her lips, she leaned near and whispered, "Will you kiss me like that every day?"

With a barely restrained smile, he pressed a kiss to her ear and whispered back, "Gladly."

"I still don't understand how you could love me."

"I'll gladly show you how the rest of my life. You're one of a kind, Jodie Ross, and only a fool would miss that." He pulled back to see those sky-blue eyes he loved. "What do you say, sweetheart?"

"Yes. . .I'll marry you."

His wide grin matched hers as he leaned back in.

"Not until you introduce her to your mother."

Beau stopped a hairsbreadth from Jodie's lips. His father really knew how to ruin a moment. Jodie was right; they should've gone off somewhere else to talk.

Knowing his father would stick around until he got an answer, Beau stared at his bride-to-be. "Are you all right with that?"

"I haven't had a mama for years. I'd love that. Do you think she'll like me?"

"She'll love you." Beau dropped a kiss on her nose. "Father, do you think Mother would be opposed to traveling to Small Tree? I have a job to see to and a house to build—"

"A house?" Jodie's wide eyes searched his face.

"Yes, a house. My woman deserves a place to call her own."

Her smile grew, if that was even possible. "With a picket fence?"

"With a picket fence."

"And a puppy to play with in the yard?"

Beau suppressed a laugh. "I'm fine with a good guard dog."

"Oh Beau." She threw her arms around his neck. "I love you." She jerked away. "I'm gonna go tell Haskins I'm gonna work for him."

"Why?"

"The sooner we can buy all the materials, the sooner we can get the house built, and the sooner we can get married."

Beau's laugh broke free at her eagerness. "Whatever you want, darlin'."

"No daughter of mine is going to work if I have anything to say about it."

"Father!"

"Daughter?"

Beau took in the wonder on Jodie's face then looked at his father, only just realizing the significance of his word choice. Was he actually giving them his blessing? Earlier he'd questioned Beau's sanity.

Folding his arms, Father inclined his head. "You heard what I said." He relaxed his stance and gave Jodie a hint of a smile. "Young lady, you are a remarkable woman. It is quite an accomplishment, winning over a town and getting my son comfortable talking to the feminine sort, not to mention making him willing to stand up for you in front of a crowd *and* his father. She brings out the good in you, lad. Like a good wife should."

His chest swelling with pride, Beau slid an arm around Jodie's waist and tugged her a little closer.

"Consider the house a wedding present."

"But—"

"No *buts*, my boy."

Knowing it was senseless to argue, Beau nodded. "Thank you, sir."

"Very good. I will see you two at dinner." With that, his father strode toward town.

"I take it that was his way of invitin' us to dinner?"

"Yep."

Jodie cocked her head to the side. "I like him."

"The feeling seems to be mutual."

"But I'm still gonna work for Mr. Haskins."

"Or you could work with me. . .at least until the babies come."

"Beau!"

"What? You don't want to be my deputy?"

She pitched her voice to a whisper. "We can't talk about babies, can we?"

"Why not?" Surveying the area, he noted the schoolyard had emptied and pulled Jodie close. "We're alone, and we're engaged to be married. I think it's pretty natural to talk about babies. We'll need to know how many rooms to build on that house."

Jodie leaned her head against his chest. "I can't believe all this is happenin'. Only this mornin' I was a prisoner wonderin' how many years I'd be stuck behind bars, my only family miles away. Now I'm a free woman, engaged to a wonderful man who wants to have a family with me. How did I get so blessed?"

"I've been wondering the same thing." Tilting up her chin, Beau touched his lips to hers, marveling at how what he'd thought had been a mistake—getting roped into a job he'd never asked for—had turned into one of the greatest blessings of his life.

❧ Epilogue ❧

Beau scooped up his sleeping granddaughter and placed her on the pallet next to her snoring brothers. Taking her place on the couch, he pulled his wife into his side and welcomed her head on his shoulder.

"I love that story." Jodie tucked her stocking feet onto the couch and leaned more fully into him. "Especially the ending."

"Do you still feel the same now as you did then?"

"Oh no."

"What?" He tilted to see her face.

She grinned. "I love you even more now than I did then."

"That's better."

Her quiet laugh warmed him, and he wrapped his other arm around her.

"You know, I still wonder the same thing I did then."

"What's that?"

He brushed a curl away from eyes still as blue and as beautiful as they were forty years ago. "How I got so blessed to have you."

"As do I, love." Lifting her face to his, Jodie met him with a kiss so sweet, so right, that it reinforced one thing he'd learned over the years—with God, there are no mistakes.

Award-winning, bestselling Christian western author **Crystal L. Barnes** is a member of American Christian Fiction Writers (ACFW). Accused of being quite the character at times, Crystal has performed in several plays, loves to sing southern gospel music, and contributes to her church's worship team on a regular basis. When she's not writing, reading, or singing, Crystal enjoys spending time with family, exploring on road trips, and watching old movies and sitcoms. *I Love Lucy* and *Little House on the Prairie* are two of her favorites. Find out more and connect with Crystal at www.crystal-barnes.com.

Rocky Mountain Regrets

by Kathleen Y'Barbo

If a man say, I love God, and hateth his brother, he is a liar:
for he that loveth not his brother whom he hath seen,
how can he love God whom he hath not seen?

1 JOHN 4:20

Chapter 1

Benton Springs, Colorado
June 1889

The little girl looked like a ray of sunshine on a cloudy day. Her mama, not so much.

Oh, the lady whose hand the girl clutched was pretty enough—if you liked the pale, fragile type, which he did not—but she hadn't spared a single smile the entire time she'd been standing in the doorway of the Benton Springs Inn.

Zeke Potter kept his thoughts to himself as the dark-haired woman finally took a step inside. She met his stare and refused to look away. Maybe she wasn't as fragile as he assumed.

"Morning," he said as he shifted his attention to her golden-haired child and then swept off his hat in a cowboy's version of a formal greeting.

"Good morning, sir," the girl responded solemnly. "Are there beds for sleeping here? The train was not at all what we expected, and we are quite exhausted."

Her mama quickly shushed the girl. "Are you the innkeeper?" she asked in the same accent that marked her as not being from around here.

He knew that accent. Zeke gave the pair another head-to-toe perusal. These travelers had indeed come a long way from England to land here in Benton Springs, though they didn't appear too worse for wear, despite the little one's claim.

"I am not," he told her. "Though I'd not advise you to wait until he returns to take up a key and find a room."

She lifted one dark brow in an expression that had him wondering if she had experience in questioning suspects. "And why is that?"

Zeke lifted the corner of his mouth in the beginning of a grin— the best he had to offer in the way of showing amusement in that moment. "He's down at the jail sleeping off last night's high living and low entertainment."

"Not in front of the child, please," she snapped as she covered the little one's ears.

"Forgive me," Zeke said, and found he actually meant it. "I didn't mean anything improper by it. It's just that on nights when there's a full moon, Bud—he's the innkeeper—likes to hike up to the peak and set up his paints. So when I say high living and low entertainment"—he paused to look down at the girl and then back up at the lady—"well, that's just a joke between him and me."

Her expression told Zeke she found no humor in it. Or him.

Well, fine. He hadn't tried this hard to be nice to anyone in years. Time to quit. He opened his mouth to say something to that effect, but the little one beat him to it.

"We came in on the train from Fort Worth," she announced. "I'm not sure I like this city as much as I liked Fort Worth. I haven't decided yet."

"That is not polite," her mama said.

"But it is true," she insisted. "I liked Fort Worth even more than England."

As it appeared a debate was about to happen, Zeke took their distraction as his cue to leave.

He situated his hat back on his head and turned away, aiming for the exit that would take him out into the alley. "Wait," she called to his retreating back. "Where are you going? We need some help here."

"I can't help you, ma'am. Wait until Bud has caught up on his sleep or pick a key and find a room." He turned the knob and let himself out into the alley.

"Surely it isn't proper to merely help oneself to a key," she called.

"You're right. Not proper at all, but that's how things work around here. Be sure to sign the book. That'll make it proper," echoed behind him as the door slammed shut.

He stepped out into the alley and right in front of Mack Swenson. "Morning, Sheriff," he said as he stepped around the tall Swede whose bunkhouse Zeke was currently calling home.

"Zeke," his old friend said, "missed you at the breakfast table this morning. Where are you off to in such a hurry?"

"Sure is a popular question this morning," he responded as the sheriff fell into step beside him.

"Is it now? Who else has been asking?"

"Didn't catch her name, but she sure was prettier than you," he said with a sideways look and a laugh.

"You must mean Miss Broderick."

Zeke halted his steps and turned to look at Mack. "So you've met her."

"Not yet, but I hope to." Before Zeke could ask, he clarified. "Pinkerton man out of Fort Worth sent a letter of introduction and asked a favor. He wanted me to talk to you, actually, but I hadn't got around to it. Now that she's here. . ."

His pause could mean only one thing. "No."

"No to what? I haven't asked yet. Unless you've already turned her down."

He took off walking again, leaving Mack to hurry to catch up. "It is true, you haven't, but when you do, the answer is going to be no. And no, I haven't turned anyone down but you. Just now."

Mack stepped in front of him. "Then I'll tell you what she will ask when the time comes. She wants to find the little one's papa, and she believes he is here in Benton Springs. Or has been here in the recent past."

"Oh."

"Oh?" The sheriff grinned. "I thought the answer was no."

"It is," he said. "Generally when a man comes to these parts, he's looking to get lost and not to be found. Especially not by his womenfolk."

"He's done a good job of it too. The Pinkerton detectives couldn't get any further than our town before the trail went cold."

Zeke recalled that detective coming around asking questions some months back. He'd been too deep in his own grief to care about anyone else's worries. Thus, he'd steered clear of the man.

But then, he steered clear of most folks on general principle.

"Well, there's more," Mack said as he appeared to study Zeke.

"That little girl had a twin brother who died. His daddy has no idea of it."

Pain slammed him, but Zeke refused to let it show. His own loss of his wife and son had come more than a year ago but was still just as fresh as if he'd gotten the news this morning.

"Is the answer still no?"

"I haven't been asked a question," he said as he picked up his pace.

Mack grasped him by the shoulder and hauled him around. Any other man who did that would have been met with fists flying.

But Mack was the closest thing he had to family anymore. So his fists remained by his sides.

"I'm going to help that lady best I can," Mack told him. "The hotel is no place for her and the child, what with the loose way Bud runs things, so if she'll agree to it, I'll be fetching them out to stay with Rose and me until the man she's looking for is found or she gives up and goes back to England."

"That's neighborly of you," he managed, knowing it was Mack's way of forcing him to look at her across the table every day until he gave in. "But the answer is no. I'm busy."

"Busy chasing the man you won't forgive?"

The truth stung, especially since he'd been working on forgiving Simon Benton ever since the preacher helped him understand what it meant to hold a man in unforgiveness. And as much as he wanted to be free of the nightmares that plagued him, Zeke still hadn't managed to figure out how to turn the Englishman who'd failed him over to the God who had never failed him.

"I need to speak to him," Zeke said.

"Talking to Benton isn't going to make any difference. Forgive the man and let it go."

"Easy for you to say," he snapped. "You've still got your family. Thanks to Benton, mine is cold in the ground."

Mack opened his mouth to offer a counterargument, likely some nonsense about the namesake of their town being just a human and thus prone to making poor decisions. Or maybe he was going to say something about how Simon Benton spread his money all over Benton Springs to make life better here—so much better that the townspeople voted to change the name of the place to honor him—and thus he couldn't be as bad as Zeke made him out to be. He'd just run scared when he saw what happened on his watch.

Instead, he closed his mouth once more and released his grip on Zeke's shoulder. "Suit yourself. You're right. I don't have any idea what it's like. No one but you and the Lord can imagine what it's like. But I do know what unforgiveness does to a man, and I don't want that for you. Abigail and Ezekiel wouldn't have wanted it either."

In all the arguments Mack had made against taking revenge on Simon Benton, he'd never once dared invoke the names of Zeke's wife and son. Doing so now seemed more than unfair.

"She told you that," he continued. "Just like she told Rose and me. 'Forgive him' were her last words. We all heard it. In any case, maybe the Lord is giving you a chance to get out of whatever valley you're laid low in by helping someone else. Have you thought of that?"

Anger blinded him, but something more powerful rose up to keep him still. "*Listen to him,*" came the quiet voice that he hadn't heard in far too long.

Special Constable Eloise Broderick of the London Metropolitan

Police allowed her gaze to scan the limits of the primitive but clean and comfortable room. Though she could easily go back down to the lobby and choose another key, the door would likely open to another room just like this.

Despite her claims that the furnishings were not up to par, little Eugenie Broderick had been exhausted enough to settle in the middle of the bed and fall fast asleep. Though she was a very grown-up ten-year-old, blond curls swirled around her, forming a halo of gold. Unlike her fraternal twin, Theodore, who inherited the dark hair and eyes of the Brodericks, Gennie was the image of her late mother. So much loss in her brief life and yet the child slept as if she hadn't a care in the world.

Sighing, Eloise settled onto the chair beside the window, then toyed with the ribbons on her bonnet as she considered what to do next. Someday soon her niece would have to learn that sucking her thumb was not acceptable, but now was not the time to remove yet another comfort from her. She had already lost so very much.

Carefully lifting the notebook from the valise on the floor beside her, Eloise turned to the page where she had left off earlier and continued her reading. In all, there were three notebooks filled with information—costly information from Woodrow Pike of the Pinkerton Detective Agency—gleaned over a period of nearly seven months.

She'd gone over every line of all three notebooks so many times that she'd lost track of the number, and yet each time the trail fell cold right here in this city. Finally, the detective in charge of the case had written to say he'd learned nothing further and would no longer be taking her money to continue to try and find a man who did not want to be found.

Along with his letter, he had sent these three notebooks and a list of four names to contact should she wish to go any further with her search. Name by name, she had eliminated the men recommended by Detective Pike until just one person remained. The note beside his name warned her to contact him only if the others had been eliminated and, even then, not to get her hopes up, because his answer would very likely be no.

Shifting positions, Eloise set the notebook aside. Much as she knew the detective had her best interests in mind when he refused to continue with the case, she also knew she had to be certain whether her brother was still out there somewhere.

A soft knock jolted her. Eloise glanced over at Gennie and then walked swiftly to the door and opened it. A fair-haired lawman removed his hat to offer a nod of greeting.

"Miss Broderick, I'm Sheriff Mack Swenson. May I have a word?"

She nodded and stepped out into the hall, carefully closing the door behind her. "How may I help you?"

"Detective Pike of the Pinkerton Agency wrote to me that you'd be gracing our fair city with your presence. I understand you're looking to inform Mr. Broderick in regards to an unfortunate situation. And I do offer my condolences on your great loss, ma'am."

"Thank you," she said. "I'm pleased that Mr. Pike has written to you, but I understood that it was not the sheriff with whom I would need to speak regarding finding my. . ."

She paused. Her own detective training had taught her that a man was often quick to come to the aid of a woman in distress, quick enough to get the job done when there was no other way to do it. Since the Pinkerton agent had not been successful using what she assumed would be good investigative work, perhaps it was time to assume an alias. Of a sort.

"Forgive me. The loss is still fresh." Which it was.

"I do understand," the sheriff said, his expression kind. "And for that reason, I would like to say that my family wishes to offer any help that we can. My wife and I have a place a few miles outside of town that would make for a much more comfortable base of operations for you and the little one. My Rose is a good cook and a good mama to our son, and she'd be pleased as punch to feed you two and to watch the girl while you went about the business of finding her papa."

"Oh."

Not at all what she had expected he would say. And yet she'd already begun to wonder what she would do with Gennie while she was searching for James. She certainly couldn't take the child along, and yet she would never consider leaving her here in this hotel room alone.

"Are you certain?" she asked. "Given that we're strangers to you, I don't understand why you would make such a generous offer."

"It isn't generous at all," he said with a chuckle. "My Rose is starved for companionship, and she would love nothing better than to talk about her homeland with you. She's English too. Came over with me as a bride and professes not to miss it a bit, but I know better. Our boy is about your niece's age, so she would have a friend there."

"I see. Well," she said as she considered her options. "Yes, perhaps. But will you allow me to pay a visit first to be certain your wife is in agreement with you on this?"

His grin broadened. "You're a wise woman," he said. "I'd say that's a fair request. She's fixing my lunch right now, and my deputy and I are expected to be home to eat it in an hour. Might I invite you and the little one to join us? We'll be taking the wagon."

She matched his smile. "Yes. Thank you, Sheriff."

Rousting Gennie from her sleep proved easier when lunch and an afternoon ride in the country were offered as incentives. A short while later, the trio were seated together on the wagon's bench while the hapless deputy, a fellow named Wilson, struggled to stay upright in the back as it bounced along on the rough-worn trail that led away from the city.

Their host kept up his end of the conversation by answering the barrage of questions posed to him by a curious Gennie. This left Eloise free to take in the breathtaking landscape without having to comment.

This place was so unlike England and the village of their births, and yet Eloise could see why her brother loved Colorado so much. From the mountains in the distance, their colors shifting from purple to blue and their tops dusted in sugary white, to the wide expanses of prairie and lush green copses of shimmering aspen trees, startling beauty abounded.

James had written letters describing this, but his eloquent words paled in comparison to actually seeing it for herself. Only when she looked back at the collection of homes and buildings that made up Benton Springs did she recall that she was very near to civilization.

"Mr. Benton must have been a very nice man to have a whole town named after him," Gennie said as Eloise returned her attention to the conversation going on in the buggy.

"Indeed he was," Sheriff Swenson said. "Or rather, is. He is still very much alive, or at least that's what I think until proven otherwise."

Eloise gave him a sideways look. "You don't know for certain?"

"Well no," he admitted. "It's been awhile since any of us have seen him, but I don't doubt he's around."

"Has he just disappeared, then?" Gennie asked. "That's terribly sad."

"I suppose you could say that," the sheriff said as he slowed the buggy to ease it around a tight turn in the path. "It's certain that no one has seen him in more than a year."

"If he cared about the people enough to give them money for homes and to build businesses, why would he leave?"

Deputy Wilson spoke up. "Most folks think it all started back when he made a promise to keep safe a local wife and child while the menfolk were away."

"That's enough of that," Sheriff Swenson interrupted. "No sense telling tales. None of us here knows what really happened."

"What happened was easy enough to tell," Wilson continued, obviously undeterred by the sheriff's warning. "Biscuits were still warming on Benton's stove, but his place was empty. As to the family he was supposed to be watching, the house caught fire with the wife and child in it. The wife managed to escape and lived a few hours, but the child was—"

"That'll do, Wilson! There is a child present," the sheriff snapped. "Another word and you'll be out on your feet to walk back to town without any hope of lunch or possibly a job."

"Yessir," Wilson mumbled before pulling his hat down tight and focusing his attention out the back of the wagon.

The sheriff slid an apologetic glance over Gennie's head. Eloise returned the gesture with a smile and a nod.

"But I don't understand," Gennie insisted. "If they found the woman and child, where are they and where is Mr. Benton?"

"Eugenie, there will be no further discussion of this topic. Please let me know you understand and intend to comply with this."

She recognized the look of defiance threatening to rise on

Gennie's face. It was a look she knew well. Bracing herself for an argument, Eloise was pleasantly surprised when Gennie offered a polite, "Yes, ma'am."

A few minutes later, the wagon turned off the path and rolled beneath an arch proclaiming SWENSON RANCH. Up ahead a plume of smoke rose from the chimney of a cozy two-story farmhouse, while somewhere off in the distance a dinner bell clanged.

"Right on time," the sheriff said as he pulled the wagon to a halt in front of the house.

The front door flew open, and a dark-haired woman of approximately Eloise's age hurried out onto the front porch. "Welcome, Mrs. Broderick," she called. "I'm so glad you and your daughter are here."

She indeed recognized the woman's accent as that of a kinsman. "Thank you for your hospitality. You are very generous."

Guilt prodded her, but Eloise recovered quickly. The purpose for her visit was to find her brother, a case that must be solved by any means. In her work with the Metropolitan Police, she never would have felt bad about misrepresenting herself while working on a case, and thus she should not in this matter either.

Or at least that is what Eloise tried to convince herself of as she returned the woman's smile. "Please, just call me Eloise. And this is Eugenie, though she prefers to be called Gennie."

"Then Eloise and Gennie you shall be," the woman said with an unmistakable accent. "My name is Rose."

"Would you be from London?" Eloise asked.

"Southwark, just the other side of the river," she responded. "And you?"

"London proper," Eloise said rather than admit the posh address in Knightsbridge the Brodericks called home when in the city. Best not to mention the ancestral home in the country and give away her background completely.

"Oh, I do miss London," Rose said with a shake of her head. "Not that I would give up any of this to go back though."

"I like the sound of that," the sheriff said. He swept his wife up into an embrace that lifted her off her toes. "Because I sure would miss your cooking."

Rose swatted at his swiftly retreating back with the dish towel she'd slung over her shoulder and then turned to look back at Eloise. "That man," she said with a smile. "He does try my patience. Now won't you two come in? I've saved two spots at the table for you. We can take care of your trunks later."

"There are no trunks," Deputy Wilson said as he ambled past. "I reckon they're eating but not staying."

"Wilson," the sheriff called from somewhere inside, "there you go talking again."

The deputy spared the ladies a confused look then hurried past them to disappear inside. Rose paused as if studying Eloise. "So you'll not be staying with us? I do worry about you two alone in town at that hotel." She paused. "Oh, what am I saying? Come on in. You must be famished."

Eloise reached out to touch Rose's sleeve. "So you truly do not mind hosting us?"

"Mind?" She shook her head. "I was looking forward to it. Between the ranch hands, the sheriff and his deputy, and our son, I am surrounded by nothing but men. I was hoping for a little female company."

"I thought perhaps your husband had spoken without seeking your opinion on the matter. I can see now that isn't the case." She bit her lip and then shrugged. "So under the circumstances, if you'll still have us, then we would be honored, wouldn't we, Gennie?"

Silence.

"Gennie, I am talking to you."

The girl ignored her to stare off into the distance. "Eugenie Broderick, mind your manners. I asked a question." Eloise looked in the direction where her niece was intent on focusing, only to see a familiar fellow ambling toward them. "One of the ranch hands?" she casually inquired as her pulse quickened.

"Him?" Rose laughed. "Oh no, though he does more work around here for no pay than our hands do for the wages we give them."

"Hey there, cowboy," she said as he took the steps up to the porch two at a time. "Come and meet the Brodericks."

The man Rose called "cowboy" removed his hat. "We've met," he said, green eyes narrowing.

"We have," Eloise agreed, "though I don't believe I got your name."

"That's because I didn't offer it," he said as he leaned against the porch post.

"Shame on you, Ezekiel Potter. Where are your manners?" Rose turned to Eloise. "Eloise Broderick and Miss Gennie Broderick, allow me to introduce you to Zeke Potter. He boards here in the bunkhouse and takes his meals with us. He also builds and repairs furniture when we have a need for it. I assure you the next time you see him he will be on his best behavior."

The man in question affected a dazzling smile and then a courtly bow. "Pardon my ill manners, Mrs. Broderick, Miss Broderick. Meeting you has been a pleasure." He cast a glance toward Rose. "Have I sufficiently redeemed myself?"

"Go on in," she said with a shake of her head. "But you're

impossible, you know that, don't you?"

"I've been told," echoed behind him as Zeke Potter walked away.

Ezekiel Potter. Surely there was only one in the town of Benton Springs.

Because if that was true, then the last man on the Pinkerton detective's list had just walked past her and tipped his hat. And he was staying right here on the property.

"Mrs. Broderick," Rose said, interrupting her thoughts. "Shall we go in now? I'd hate to think the menfolk would start lunch without us, but I wouldn't put it past them."

"Thank you," she replied with a smile. "After you."

⊱ Chapter 2 ⊰

Zeke watched the lady from the hotel take her seat beside Rose and knew trouble was brewing. Something in the woman's expression told him to watch out for her. And yet as the biscuits were passed around and the conversation began, Mrs. Broderick seemed intent on pretending he wasn't even there.

Despite the fact Rose had seated her directly across the table from him, she spent most of the meal reminiscing with her hostess about their English homeland and never spared him a glance. Apparently bored with the lively discussion going on beside her, the little girl aimed her blue-eyed gaze at Zeke.

"Have you been to England, Mr. Potter?"

"I have not."

"I much prefer your country to mine. If I weren't intended to marry well, I should prefer to stay here."

"Marry well?" he asked as he tried to hide his amusement. "Can you not do that in Colorado? In due time, that is. Unless you're planning a wedding soon?"

"Of course not. I'm only ten." The girl affected a serious expression. "How could I possibly marry well here? I am to marry nobility, and there are none here."

"Well," Zeke managed without allowing laughter, "I do see your problem."

"Yes, but I have plenty of time unless my father decides to give up the title to his cousin. Eight years at least."

"That is good news," he told her. "Eight years of enjoying Colorado before marriage sounds fair."

Mrs. Broderick must have heard him, for her brows rose and her eyes shifted to the girl beside her. "Gennie, what sort of nonsense have you been discussing with Mr. Potter?"

She looked up at her aunt. "No nonsense at all. Since I am the last of the line unless Cousin Emma's papa takes over, my length of stay in Colorado is based on when I must marry."

Confusion showed on Mrs. Broderick's face. "I fail to see what one has to do with the other, but please do not enlighten me." She shifted her position to give him a stern look. "I also fail to see why this is a topic that an adult might discuss with a child."

"It makes perfect sense," Gennie insisted. "The lack of eligible nobility limits my—"

"Eugenie, I asked that you would not enlighten us, so that is quite enough."

"Yes, ma'am," she said.

Zeke took note of the look that passed between them. The child had said too much, but what had she said? That she was of nobility? Surely not, for there was nothing wrong in admitting that. And yet what else of consequence had the little girl said?

Nothing that he could think of.

He braved another glance at Mrs. Broderick. What secrets was this woman hiding? Maybe there was more to the story of her missing husband than anyone had been told.

Old habits died hard, and his life as an investigator caused him to ask questions others might ignore. But he was no longer the sheriff. He had to get out of that habit.

Eventually.

Mack nudged him then leaned in. "Is the answer still no?"

"I haven't been asked," he said as the ladies rose to begin clearing the table. "So that's not a yes or a no."

"Sure it's a yes, but I'm willing to wait until you realize that." Mack pushed back from the table and gave his deputy a nod that sent the fellow scrambling to stand. "Back to work. Can we offer you a ride into town, Zeke?"

He watched the Broderick woman go ahead of Rose to disappear into the kitchen as he pondered the question. "No," he finally said. "I've got some work to do right here."

"Thought so," was Mack's parting response. He stood and put his hat on, then called to Rose. When she appeared in the door, he grasped her in an embrace then kissed her on the cheek before they parted.

For a moment, Zeke envied his friend for the love he'd found. Then he recalled how painful it was to lose such a love. No, he'd had his turn at being a husband, but now he was done.

He turned around to see the child staring up at him. "Why does kissing make you sad, Mr. Potter?"

The question left him momentarily without a response. Finally, he shook his head. "That's not a question I expect a child to ask."

She continued to watch him. "I have been told I am too curious."

"Have you now? Who told you that, your mama?"

She hesitated, but that moment of hesitation meant something. Zeke just didn't know what yet.

"By many," was her answer as she looked back toward the closed kitchen door. "But I saw how sad you looked when Sheriff Swenson kissed Mrs. Swenson. I assume there was a reason." She paused. "Is there?"

It usually wasn't fair to question a child, but she had come to him. And until now she had been the one asking the questions. Now he would ask a few of his own.

"Why don't you tell me about your mama?" he said in an attempt to catch her off guard and change the subject.

A worried expression crossed her face. "What do you mean?"

"Oh, I don't know," he said casually. "The two of you have traveled a long way to get to Colorado. She must want to find your papa very much."

"She does," the girl said. "It is very important that she finds him as soon as possible."

"Why?"

Her eyes darted toward the kitchen again, a sure sign she was not happy with the direction his questions were headed. Finally, she shrugged. "Surely you know my brother has died. It's very sad. My papa, he should know. Because once he knows, he will certainly choose to do the right thing by us and—"

"Eugenie," cut sharply through her story as the kitchen door flew open. "Do stop bothering Mr. Potter and come into the kitchen. I could use your help, and I am certain he has other, more important things to do."

The last part of that statement was made directly to Zeke,

her eyes narrowed and her expression unmistakably hostile. For a woman looking to ask him to help her find someone, she certainly was going about it the wrong way.

Maybe Mack had already told her he wouldn't agree to it. No, he decided as he stepped out into the afternoon sunshine. The stubborn sheriff still thought he would.

Something was up—he knew it. What that something might be was another thing entirely.

He shrugged off the thought. Maybe they'd all come to their senses and decided to leave him alone. That was fine by him. He had other fish to fry. Other men to find.

What he'd do when he found Simon Benton was something he had not yet decided. He'd promised the Lord he would try and forgive the man for allowing an unforgivable loss to happen on his watch. But could he?

There was only one way to know, and that was to stand in front of the man who let his wife and child die and look him in the eyes. Only then could he offer words of forgiveness.

Eloise reluctantly allowed Gennie to follow the Swenson boy out of the kitchen. She watched as the somber old-for-her-age girl turned into a laughing child as the two hurried away.

"They'll be fine," Rose said as she set the last of the washed dishes on the drying rack.

"I suppose," Eloise responded as she hurried to the window to watch Gennie and William spill out onto the front porch where they were joined by two yapping brown dogs.

Her time with the Metropolitan Police told her that there were many factors that were out of a person's control. And though

Gennie was truly not born of her, she was as much her child as if Eloise had given birth to her. While the girl needed a mother, especially now, she also needed a father.

Her father. And that was James.

"Eloise?" She felt Rose's hand on her shoulder. "She will be fine."

"Yes, of course." She gave the children—now taking turns tossing a stick that the dogs retrieved—one last long look and then turned toward her new friend. "I suppose I'm just a little protective of her."

Rose's dark brows lifted briefly in a clear indication she felt that was an understatement. To her credit, she kept her thoughts to herself.

"She's all I have left of my family until James is found," Eloise hurried to explain. "I cannot allow anything to happen to her."

"Which is why you brought her with you instead of leaving her behind to come search for her father," Rose said.

Only partly the truth, though she would never tell Rose or anyone else the real reason. That she was determined to make James look at his child, something he had never done.

"Have you asked him yet?"

Eloise shook her head. "Asked who?" She paused. "Oh, Mr. Potter? Not yet. The Pinkerton detective warned me he would say no. I've been trying to decide how to approach him in order to convince him not to say no."

"Mack told me the same thing," Rose said. "But he also said he doesn't think he'll stick to it."

"I see." She thought a moment. "Did he offer a reason why?"

"No, but I can tell you. Zeke may show a tough side to most people, but he's got a good heart." She paused. "A broken heart, to be sure, but good nonetheless. I don't think it would be gossiping to tell you that he lost his wife and child in a terrible accident a little over a year ago. Their home burned to the ground."

Eloise shook her head as she recalled the story the deputy had tried to tell on the trip here. So the family Simon Benton had been looking after belonged to Mr. Potter.

"Oh no," she said softly. "That's horrible."

"It was. We saw the smoke from the fire, but by the time Mack and the other men got there, it was too late. Little Ezekiel was just seven, and Abigail was expecting a child in a few months." Her expression softened. "Mack won't talk about it, even now, so I have to assume it was an awful thing to see. He brought Abigail back here to meet the doctor, but she was too far gone to save."

"How did Mr. Potter escape?"

"Oh," Rose said. "He was away. He was the sheriff of Benton Springs at the time, and Mack was his deputy. He'd gone to Austin to testify against a gang he'd help catch. It all happened while he was away."

"So he came home to find this terrible tragedy had happened in his absence? I cannot imagine the pain."

She nodded. "Or the guilt."

"Why would he feel guilty?" she asked as the sound of children laughing floated in on a breeze through the open window. "Surely it wasn't Mr. Potter's fault he was away. He was doing his job, which certainly did not end with the arrest."

This Eloise knew from experience. During her employment with the Metropolitan Police, it sometimes seemed that she spent as much time in the courtroom testifying as she did in tracking and arresting culprits.

"Yes, that's true. He did have to make the trip, there is no question about that. Mack offered to go in his place. He wrote to the judge, but his request was denied."

"Because Mr. Potter was the witness and your husband was not?"

"Yes, I can see you know something about the law."

"I do. Before I took on this search, I worked in the law in London."

"As a lawyer?"

"No, nothing nearly as glamorous as all that," Eloise said in a way she hoped would end this line of questioning.

"All right, well, back to the story. You see, Abigail, well. . ." Rose's voice trailed off and she seemed lost in thought. A moment later, she returned her attention to Eloise. "As I said, she was with child. She did not suffer pregnancy well, the poor woman. In fact, after she delivered their son, I told Mack the boy would never have a brother or sister. When she found herself in that situation again, well. . .let's say she took to her bed and ceased to be a proper mama for him."

"I see."

Rose nodded. "Mack and I offered to take them in while he was away, but Abigail wouldn't hear of it. She wanted her home and her bed only. I wish Zeke had ignored her and let the boy stay with us. . . ."

Again her voice trailed off, and this time her eyes shimmered with unshed tears. Eloise reached over to offer a reassuring touch on her shoulder.

"Well, anyway, we all thought that Simon Benton's offer to keep watch over the family was a godsend. He lived nearby and could keep an eye on the family and take care of the ranch too." She paused. "He did so much good here. Helped so many people. Well, it just seemed natural that he would step in and do this too. No one questioned it. It's just how he was."

"What happened to him?"

Rose shook her head. "No one knows. The last time he was seen in town was the day of the fire. No one has seen him since."

"Is it possible he died in the fire?"

Again she shook her head. "No."

Thinking like the investigator she was, Eloise asked the next most obvious question. "Did anyone search his home?"

"Yes, Mack and Zeke did. It was as if he'd just walked out and was expected back any time. He still had a pan of biscuits set out as if he was coming home to eat them. Since then there have been searches for Simon, but none came up with anything. Mack has tried to persuade Zeke to give up searching but hasn't been able to do so."

Silence fell between them. Then, abruptly, Rose walked toward the window and rested her palms on the sill.

"Zeke was never the same after that. He walked into the sheriff's office the next morning and handed Mack his badge. When he wasn't away hunting Simon, Zeke was sleeping in his barn on the property. Mack insisted he stay in our bunkhouse if he wasn't interested in rebuilding his own place, but it was a fight to get him to agree."

"He was bound up in his grief."

Rose turned around to face her. "He still is. Which is why he will say no."

"Yes, I see that."

"But what you don't see is that he needs to help you. For himself. He needs something to focus on that isn't revenge." She paused to give Eloise a sweeping glance. "You're not looking to get revenge on your man, are you? Because if you are, say so now. I won't be responsible for my behavior if I find out that's the case. I'll not see Zeke used that way."

"No, I'm not," she said. "And the truth is, James is not my man." She paused until she was certain she should go forward with telling the truth. "He is my brother, and Gennie's father. Her mother died in childbirth."

Rose's eyes narrowed. "But that detective told Mack he was your husband. Why would he do that?"

"Detective Pike made the assumption on his own. I realized later that my letters might have been vague on the point, although that was not intentional. It seemed prudent to allow him to continue thinking as he wished rather than correct him."

"Prudent how?"

She let out a long breath. "I see it now as a grievous mistake, but at the time I was desperate to have someone take up the cause of finding James. You see, I've had my share of grief as well. The loss of Gennie's brother, well. . ."

She had come to the limits of the truth that she was ready to admit, so Eloise fell silent. Rose studied her but said nothing for what seemed like an eternity.

"You're living with guilt too, aren't you?"

The question struck hard, leaving her only able to nod. After a moment, she found her voice. "James was happy here in Colorado. It is I who forced him to leave the first time. You see, when Father died, he was the heir. The new earl. Had he remained here, the line would have died with him. I insisted he return."

"So he returned," she offered.

"He did, but only because I convinced Father's solicitors to cut off his funds. Until then, James was receiving a nice sum of money each month from the estate. With nothing to live on here, James could only accept a ticket home."

"But life as the new earl didn't agree with him?"

Eloise shook her head. "He did the right thing. James always did, eventually. He married, and in short order the twins were expected. Unfortunately, he took that as his cue that his responsibility to the title was complete and left England again, this time for good. It was some months before a letter arrived asking us not to seek him out. Saying that his children would be better off without him. He hadn't even seen them and he was already walking away."

"Oh," came out as a soft whisper. "That's very sad."

She managed a nod. "He never met his son. I am determined not to allow that to happen with his daughter. So yes, I did allow an untruth to help my search. I regret that."

"That isn't all you regret, is it?" Rose said gently.

"No," Eloise said. "But those regrets are mine alone and not to be shared."

"Yes, all right. Well then, I'm sure you'll want to see your room and get settled. Mack has promised to come home early with your trunks."

"Thank you," she said. She looked past Rose to spy Gennie and her new friend, who were laughing at the antics of the brown dogs. A moment's relief washed over her to see the girl so happy, so unguarded.

"Go on," Rose said. "You look exhausted."

She hadn't slept well in so long that she couldn't remember what that felt like. Still, there were responsibilities, and she would not shirk them.

As if reading her mind, Rose nodded toward the window and the children outside. "I'll watch them." She gestured to a basket on the sideboard. "I've got mending to do, and it's just as easily done out on the porch. I prefer it there, actually. When I call William in for his afternoon studies, I will send Gennie up to you. How's that?"

"Thank you," Eloise said again. "Truly, I cannot possibly make it up to you for all you've done for my niece and me."

"Don't you worry about that," Rose said with a smile. "You just concentrate on finding that little girl's papa. I love happy endings—that is payback enough for me."

Chapter 3

*E*loise intended to close her eyes for just a few minutes. Just a brief respite from the tiredness that chased her, and then she would be up and about.

The room was lovely, its walls a confection of pink trailing roses that swirled down the wallpaper and across curtains of a matching hue. The canopy bed was as soft as it was feminine, and the pillows were every bit as comfortable as the ones in the ancestral home back in England. Had she not known she rested her head in Benton Springs, Colorado, she might have thought she had returned there.

The pillows were soft, the bedcoverings softer. And her eyes were oh so tired.

So when she opened her eyes and peered at the tiny silver clock on the bedside table, Eloise immediately assumed the timepiece hadn't been wound properly. Surely it was not late afternoon. That was impossible.

She rose and padded to the window where the lengthy shadows confirmed her greatest fear. It was indeed that late, and Gennie was nowhere to be seen.

Lacing up her boots with shaking hands, she gave her mussed hair a brief moment's repair and then hurried downstairs. A trio of voices in animated conversation lured her down the hall to where an open door revealed a well-appointed library and what appeared to be a schoolroom lesson going on.

Seated at the end of a wooden table, Rose read from a book she held in front of her. William and Gennie listed in rapt silence. When she paused to ask a question, both children raised their hands. Each was allowed to offer an answer before Rose moved on to reading again. From where Eloise stood, the children could not see her, so she remained very still and quiet.

Finally, Rose noticed her standing in the doorway and stood. "All right, children. I want you to continue your reading until I return."

Boy and girl both dipped their heads and did as Rose asked. Eloise smiled at the studious look on Gennie's face. While she was extremely intelligent, the girl had never been formally educated. Rather, her tutors had handled her brother's lessons and, presumably, allowed her to join in.

It irked Eloise that she did not know that for sure.

"I hope you don't mind," Rose said as she joined Eloise in the hallway. "Gennie was keen to join William in his studies. She told me you were sleeping, or I would have had her get permission. Do you mind terribly?"

"No, but I wonder if you do. Taking on the education of one

child is difficult enough. The last thing I wish is for Gennie to become a bother."

"She is anything but, Eloise," Rose said. "In fact, I have never seen William take to his studies with as much enthusiasm as he has today. I think perhaps there is a little friendly competition between the two." She paused. "So would it be all right if she stayed, at least until the end of this lesson? I would hate to try and keep William's mind on his studies if he is wondering where Gennie went off to."

Eloise considered the question for just a moment and then nodded. "If you're certain."

"I am," she said. "Thank you."

"No," Eloise said. "Thank *you*. Would you mind terribly if I spoke with her for a moment?"

"Of course not." Rose called Gennie over to the door, then left them to go back and join William at the table.

"Sweetheart," Eloise said, "are you enjoying yourself this afternoon?"

"Very much so," she said, her eyes shining. "It has been ever so long, and I miss it terribly. Mrs. Rose doesn't mind me learning at the same table with William, unlike my brother's tutors. They were terribly particular about it all. I had to hide and listen from behind the curtains in the nursery. Here I can sit at the table." Her face turned somber. "I can sit at the table, can't I? I will be very good and do as Mrs. Rose says."

Eloise hugged her niece and smiled. "Of course you can. As long as Rose doesn't mind, I am certainly not going to either. So please just do one thing for me."

"What is that?" she asked.

"Do your best work and do not be a problem to your hostess.

We are guests here, Gennie, and as such we are not to be a burden."

She matched Eloise's smile. "I will, Auntie. . . I mean, Mama."

Eloise shook her head. "About that. I was wrong to ask you to carry on with an untruth about our relationship. I have explained to Mrs. Rose that you are my niece and will clarify that with anyone else who assumes otherwise. Will you forgive me for asking you to lie?"

Gennie fell into Eloise's arms with a giggle. "I love you so, Auntie Eloise. I truly didn't mind pretending you were my mama, so it did not feel like a lie. In fact, I wish it were so."

"Oh sweetheart, as do I." She held the girl at arm's length. "Now off you go before your teacher wonders why I have taken you away from your studies for so long."

The girl hugged her again and then skipped off to return to her chair and her book. Rose stood and joined Eloise at the door. "She seems very happy to be allowed to stay. I wish William was as pleased when I tell him it is time for his books."

"I credit the teacher for her interest," Eloise said. "She really does enjoy spending time with you and William."

"And we enjoy her. She's a lovely child."

"I agree." Eloise paused. "Now, perhaps you might be able to help me with something. I wonder if you might know where Mr. Potter generally is this time of day."

Rose's smile broadened. "I know exactly where he is because I sent him there. He's gathering wood for a repair on my rocker and possibly more chairs for the schoolroom. Do you have a plan, or are you just going to ask him outright then argue with him when he tells you no?"

"A little of both," Eloise said with a smile.

Zeke looked up from his work to see the Broderick woman heading his way. Rose must have told her where to find him, for otherwise he'd never have been spied this far away from the farmhouse.

He might have ignored her had his eyes not refused to move from her image. Tall but not overly so, Eloise Broderick walked with a certainty that put him in mind of a person set on a goal.

Which she was. This he knew.

She hadn't asked him her question at the table earlier because she intended to ask him now. Here. Where she wouldn't be denied in front of strangers.

Zeke shifted the ax to his shoulder and continued to watch her. The terrain was steeper here, the land populated with aspens and pines that climbed the mountain and disappeared up into the lands that were covered in snow.

Her footing was sure on paths that might have been difficult for a woman of her background. Whoever Eloise Broderick was, she apparently was not as delicate as he had assumed.

He turned away from the sight of the woman to study his progress. He'd managed to find enough wood to fill the cart, enough to begin another project that would keep him busy for a few weeks. Rose had asked for more chairs to place around the library table, and he'd noticed that there were a few missing slats in the porch rocker where she did her mending. He easily had sufficient wood to tackle these jobs.

And yet he went back to chopping as she drew nearer, as if the physical activity would somehow keep Eloise Broderick and her request for his help at bay. It did not, of course.

In due time, she stepped into the clearing to quietly watch him fell another tree and then begin the process of chopping it into usable pieces. She might have continued to watch in silence had Zeke not finally tired of it.

He lowered the ax and leaned his arms on the upended handle before looking in her direction. Her dark eyes watched him though her expression gave away nothing of what she was thinking. He knew, all the same. Still, he would make her tell him.

"Is there something you wanted, Mrs. Broderick?"

"A moment of your time will suffice for now."

Zeke nodded. "All right. Where's your shadow?"

"Gennie?" At his nod, she continued. "She and William are having a lesson with Rose. She was intent on staying rather than joining me on my walk."

"Likes her schoolwork then," he said as he straightened his back to stretch out the ache that had formed over the last hour. "That doesn't surprise me. She's a smart one."

"She is, but now that I've found you, that's not why I'm here. I did promise this would only take a moment."

"You did, so go on and take your moment before I go back to chopping wood." The English lady appeared to be looking for the right words, so he decided to help her. "You want to ask for my help to find your husband," he supplied.

"No."

Not at all what he expected. "No?"

She shook her head. "First, James is not my husband. He is my brother. Any reports to the contrary are my own fault for allowing a misunderstanding to continue."

"I see. Well, that really doesn't make any difference, I suppose."

"It does to me," she quickly responded. "I was unwise in believing that a lie, whether outright or of omission, would be

261

justified. It is not."

"I do agree."

Before he could say anything more, Miss Broderick continued. "I'm glad to hear it, because should I have need of your advice, I would very much like you to spare me any concerns you have about me being a woman alone and answer with the truth."

Miss Broderick did have a curious way of speaking. Part of it was the fact she wasn't from around here. The rest, he suspected, was just to confuse him.

So far it was working.

She was looking at him as if he should give her an answer, so he did. "I always speak the truth, Miss Broderick, but I appreciate your permission to do so." He shook his head. She didn't deserve the sarcasm. "Look, I'm sorry. I'm not good at talking around things, and I'm in the middle of something here, so let's just get right to the point. I know you're here to ask me to find someone for you, but the answer is no."

"I've made no such request," she said, her face devoid of expression. "In fact, I had another purpose altogether in mind."

He gave her a sideways look. Again she had surprised him. "And what would that be?"

"I thought I might be able to help you." She paused only a second. "In exchange for the advice I mentioned. I also have skills that may help you."

"Is that right?" He shrugged and reached for the ax. "Well, I don't know what you've been told, but I don't need your help with anything other than possibly taking up the other ax and helping me finish off this tree."

She moved closer, her gaze flitting from him to the cart and then back to him again. "I'm sure you're being sarcastic again, but I see issues that I might mention."

"Do mention them then," he said as he lifted the ax and brought it down on the tree. "I'll just get back to work while you talk."

"Fine," she said. "I could easily help you, as I have more strength than it might appear. I have been known to fell a tree and cut firewood without complaint. It is quite chilly in the English countryside, and I do like a warm fire."

He spared her a look that told him she was now beginning to irritate him, then went back to his work. She slipped out of his view and returned a moment later with the ax.

Before Zeke could gather his thoughts and warn her about the foolishness of proving a point in such a manner, the Englishwoman lifted the smaller ax and brought it down on the mark he'd made at the end of the tree, cutting a decent notch in the wood.

"Put that down," he demanded. "You're going to hurt yourself."

Of course the stubborn woman ignored him. Three more blows, and the tree limb was severed clean.

She straightened and gave him a direct look. "I don't see a mark for the next cut. Where would you like it to be?"

He set his ax aside and walked over to her. "Give me the ax, please."

Her dark brows rose. "Whatever for? I can help you while we chat."

Zeke seized the opportunity to remove the tool from her hand. "I make it a habit never to chat with a woman armed with an ax."

She smiled, and her face lit up. "I suppose that is fair. So now that I am unarmed, perhaps you and I should start at the beginning. What do you say?"

He set the ax aside and then returned his attention to the

woman. "I'd say it's a waste of time. I'm not going to help you find anyone."

"And I'd say I haven't asked." She shook her head. "Look, we got off on the wrong foot. Let me remedy that. I am Eloise Broderick, former special constable for the London Metropolitan Police, now exclusively guardian to my niece Eugenie Broderick, and yes, I am indeed in search of my brother James Broderick, her father." She paused. "Please, just call me Eloise."

Chapter 4

*E*loise tried not to show her pleasure at her companion's confusion. Surely Zeke Potter had never suspected he was not the only former law enforcement officer in the town of Benton Springs.

But then that was exactly why she had been hired as a special constable. Rarely did anyone suspect she was in the employ of the Metropolitan Police until her job had already been done. Unfortunately, her job here was only just beginning.

"You don't believe me?" she asked with a tone she hoped would be innocent enough. "I thought a man of your experience would have guessed."

Mr. Potter remained silent, though he did finally shake his head. "I wondered how you were going to get around to coercing me to help you. Did Mack put you up to this?"

"Excuse me? What does the sheriff have to do with my past employment history?"

He walked over to the cart and tossed the ax inside, then retrieved the larger implement to do the same. Finally, he spared her a backward glance. "The sheriff will do just about anything to divert my attention. Using a pretty lady with an unlikely story would be exactly something he would think up to try and get me to change my answer."

With that statement still hanging in the fresh mountain air between them, he maneuvered the cart around toward the path leading to the ranch and set off walking. So aversion was his intended tactic. It most certainly would not work.

Eloise easily caught up and fell in step beside him. "Thank you," she said cheerily. "I don't generally think of myself as pretty, but I am not averse to a compliment."

As she expected, Mr. Potter ignored her. No matter. It was a lovely afternoon, and the terrain was not so steep here that she found it difficult to keep up.

"For the record, I have not yet asked any question. Have you not noticed that?"

He stopped short and looked over at her. While he was taller by a bit, she did not feel intimidated by him.

Mr. Potter swiped at his forehead with the back of his hand. "You will, and when you do, the answer is no."

"Very well. Then I shall have to phrase my question carefully so as to make fullest use of this no of yours. Thank you for the warning."

The former lawman opened his mouth as if to respond then clamped his lips shut in a tight line and resumed his pace. The cart groaned behind him as he tackled a sharp incline, but the wood he had stacked there remained in place, as did the axes.

Marching along beside him, Eloise kept a wary eye on the path. She knew the dangers that lurked in deep woods, and they were not always human. A rustling sound to her right caused her to cringe, though she hoped her companion did not notice.

"Are you afraid of the woods, Special Constable Broderick?"

"Former Special Constable Broderick," she corrected. "Temporarily, I hope, but former nonetheless. My current responsibility is to my niece, so there is no room for anything that would keep me tied to London. My commanding officer has promised to do his best to hold my place, although he cannot guarantee it will be there when I return. That is why I intend to pay a substantial sum to find my brother so that they will be reunited and I can return to my job. And no, I am not afraid of the woods. Rather, I am familiar enough with the woods to be wary and listen or watch for any unusual signs."

She caught Mr. Potter looking in her direction. At least she had his attention.

Then he froze. She did the same. "What?"

There. The sound again.

Before Eloise could turn and look, Mr. Potter grasped her wrist. "Behind me, please," he said softly. "Hide low behind the cart. And this would be an exceptionally bad time to argue."

She recognized that tone as one that she should heed and did as he asked.

A moment later, he retrieved the gun from its holster on his hip and aimed over the pile of wood. A shot rang out. Then a roar shook the trees. Finally, silence echoed around her as Mr. Potter lowered his weapon and disappeared around the other side of the cart.

Slowly Eloise rose to find her companion hurrying away. "Stay with the cart," he commanded when he noticed her following. "Use the ax if it circles around and comes after you."

"If *what* comes after me?" she called.

"The bear," trailed behind him as Mr. Potter disappeared into the thicket.

"Bear? Wonderful." Of all the perils in the forests of the Broderick country home, bears were not one of them.

She crept back to the spot she'd been assigned and waited. Around her the chirping of birds and the whispers of wind through the trees belied the fact that danger lurked nearby.

When she could take it no more, Eloise snatched up the ax and took off in the direction of the man and the animal he pursued. Here there was no clear path through the forest. Instead, she made her way carefully through shrubbery, trees, and rocks. She paused only once to listen for any sounds. Hearing nothing, she continued.

Only after another shot rang out up ahead did she consider she might be moving in the wrong direction. Turning east, she twisted through similar rugged terrain to follow the sound. The ax was getting heavy and the slope was steep, but she continued moving toward the place where she expected to find Mr. Potter.

A roar went up just a few yards ahead, but the brush was so thick she could not tell if it was man or beast. Moving carefully forward, she stumbled onto a clearing and saw that it was both.

The wounded bear was circling something. Closer inspection told her that something was the prone form of Zeke Potter. His arm moved, letting her know he was still alive. But for how long, especially with the animal sniffing him as if he was its long-awaited next meal?

Her police training kicked in. Eloise scanned the clearing and spied Mr. Potter's gun. She'd only counted two shots, so it was possible there were still bullets in the chamber. However, the bear was dangerously close to the weapon and might catch her before she could reach it.

Mr. Potter moved his head, swiveling until he spied her. He managed only one word: "Run."

Unfortunately, the animal saw her too. With a roar, the beast rose up on his back legs and took three steps toward her.

Wielding the ax, she stood her ground. "I won't leave you here," Eloise told Mr. Potter.

The bear took another step. She swung the ax, knowing the effort was futile and glad the animal was not yet close enough to strike. But it was something, and doing nothing was not an option.

The animal's front paws rose up in the air as if to strike at her. Its roar was so loud her ears hurt, but she held tight to the ax. Closing her eyes, she swung the ax in the direction of the angry animal. Then, without warning, a shot rang out. She opened her eyes to find the bear crumpled at her feet and silent.

Without the animal obstructing her view, she could see Mr. Potter seated next to the spot where the gun had been. Now the weapon was in his hand, a pale plume of smoke showing it had just been fired.

She dropped the ax and hurried to him, crouching down to evaluate his injuries. Blood cascaded from what was surely a nasty scalp wound, but he otherwise looked unharmed. She tore off a strip from her underskirt and bound his head while ignoring his protests.

When she was done, Eloise glanced around at the bear and

then back at Mr. Potter. "What happened?"

"I thought he was down." Mr. Potter rose to his knees and then sat back again. "He wasn't." This time he managed to climb to his feet. Eloise did the same. "Now I'd say he is."

Voices rose up behind them. "Over here," Eloise called, though she wasn't certain to whom she was speaking.

Their identities became clear when the sheriff, his deputy, and a few others she recalled from the lunch table tumbled into the clearing. The deputy reached them first.

"That English lady is here with Zeke and a dead bear," he called to the others. "Are you all right, ma'am?"

"Yes," she said as she willed her voice not to shake. "I'm fine, but Mr. Potter may need further examination by a doctor. I did the best I could, but I'm not sure the bleeding will stop on its own."

"I'm fine," Mr. Potter protested. "Just a little cut."

Sheriff Swenson arrived to survey the scene as the deputy relayed the information to him. "You sure you're fine?" At her nod, he turned to Zeke. "You look like you're going to have a nasty headache."

"At least I'm still standing," he said as he nodded toward the bear. "Long as I've lived here I haven't seen one be so aggressive. I shot in the air to frighten it off, and it still kept coming at me. I tried to chase it off. Couldn't let it stay so close to the ranch, not with children there."

A cold chill ran down Eloise's spine. What if the beast had appeared while the children were playing? She pressed that thought far away. As her mother had often advised, she would not borrow trouble.

"Do you think this is the animal I've been getting complaints about?" the sheriff asked Zeke. "I've heard from a half dozen folks that they've either been chased by it or had their livestock threatened. Laird Anderson claimed the thing wandered through his house and made a mess of his kitchen while he was working at the post office. At the time, I thought maybe he'd had vagrants come through, but now I wonder."

"I'd say it was the same one." Zeke dusted off his trousers and turned his attention to the bear. "I hate to take an animal like this down. But there was no choice. It went after both of us."

"If it behaved that way to you, then I'd agree it's probably the one that's been aggressive to others. Good that we've ended that before someone was seriously hurt."

While Mack barked orders to the cowboys to haul the bear's carcass down the mountain, Zeke turned his attention to Mrs. Broderick, who was now holding on to the trunk of an aspen as if she depended on it to remain upright.

Miss Broderick, he corrected. Or, if he believed her claims, Special Constable Broderick of the London Metropolitan Police.

She caught him studying her and, he decided, looked like she was about to jump out of her skin. Zeke took that as his cue to close the distance between them. Before he could speak, she did.

"Mr. Potter, you saved my life." She paused and glanced down at the ground before returning her attention to him. "Thank you seems quite insufficient, but I will say it all the same. Thank you."

"I owe you a debt of thanks as well," he said. "If you hadn't interrupted that bear, I wouldn't have been able to get to my gun. Given the mood it was in, I doubt I would have survived."

The woman's smile was shaky at best. "Yes, well, then we are even, I suppose. If you'll excuse me, I would very much like to go back to the ranch and hug my niece now."

"You sure you're ready to try that?" He gave her an appraising glance. "You look like I ought to put you in the cart and haul you down."

Her laughter was a welcome sound. "And you look like you'd fall down first."

Zeke shrugged. His head was pounding, but he'd never let on to her or to Mack.

"Come on. It's just a scratch." He offered her his hand, and she took it. "We will help each other."

She looked up at him. "Exactly what I was thinking."

He paused. "Why do I suspect you and I are talking about two different things, Miss Broderick?"

"Eloise, please," she corrected.

"Since we've fought a bear together, I suppose you ought to call me Zeke." He paused to negotiate a turn in the path. "As to my previous statement, you haven't put up any argument, Eloise," he said as he helped her down the path while praying he didn't embarrass himself and take a tumble.

Rather than respond, she merely smiled. Her wish to hug her niece was quickly granted, as Rose and the children came hurrying up the path.

Eloise released her grip on him to kneel and take the little girl into her arms. Meanwhile, Rose gave him an appraising look. "For a man whose only intent this afternoon was to gather wood to repair my chair, you certainly do know how to find trouble, Zeke Potter."

Though Mack's wife continued to scold him as they set off toward the ranch house, Zeke's attention was on the special constable from the London Metropolitan Police. The girl was more than half her size, yet Eloise had hauled Gennie into her arms and was carrying the child down the mountain ahead of them as if it were the easiest thing in the world.

The woman's dark hair had come unbound from its pins and swung freely in the breeze, mingling with the fair hair of the child. Gennie rested her head against Eloise's cheek, her arm wrapped around her aunt's back as if she would never let go.

Zeke's heart caught. Anyone who didn't know better would believe these two were mother and child. If the little one's father wasn't found, that just might be the case. Either way, without a mama, Eloise was all Gennie had in the way of female family.

He felt his resolve slipping. Maybe he could help her. Just a little.

Mack's boy called to Gennie, causing her to wriggle free and hurry away down the trail. Eloise caught the escaping pair and linked arms with the children, all the while laughing at their antics.

Rose hung back to allow him to catch up. She had that look on her face, the one where she was about to tell him something he ought to hear but wouldn't like. So he saved her the trouble.

"Save your speech," he said. "I'll help her."

"Well, how about that? It took a Rocky Mountain grizzly bear to knock some sense into you." She shook her head. "I'll have to remember that next time. Too bad your shirt is ruined."

He looked down at the blood that covered him and shrugged. "Looks like I'll be making a side of biscuits for breakfast tomorrow to go with the bacon and eggs."

"Do you think you can bribe me to wash the blood out of your shirt with a pan of biscuits?"

Zeke grinned. "I do."

Rose laughed, and Eloise glanced back at them, her face radiant.

Then she smiled, and Zeke knew for certain he had found bigger trouble than an angry grizzly or a friend's wife who was irritated with extra washing. Instead of his life being threatened, this was worse. It was his heart.

Chapter 5

*E*loise released the children's hands, and they ran the short distance to the porch where a man she presumed was the doctor was waiting. "Is Zeke the only one who needs doctoring?"

"Dr. Ross, meet Eloise Broderick and her little girl, Gennie. She had a fright, but she's not harmed, and oh, goodness, that was fast," Rose called. "You must have been driving by when they went to fetch you."

"Pleased to meet you, Mrs. Broderick," the rail-thin man said as he stood. "And Rose, indeed I was just passing by. I'm glad I was too. Zeke, if the blood on your clothes is any indication of what's underneath that bandage, you might have to have some stitching."

"I'm fine," Zeke grumbled, and yet he allowed the doctor to lead him away. He returned to the ranch house a short while later with a fresh bandage and a frown. Though he waved to Eloise, who was keeping a close eye on the children as they played, Zeke made his way to join the men who were processing the remains of the bear.

The thought of that beast, its teeth and that awful growl, made her shiver. Still, she was a Special Constable and not the type to frighten easily. Unfortunately, how to handle oversized angry bears was not part of her training.

That evening after the meal, Rose proclaimed they would have an evening of games. "Might I stay downstairs?" Gennie asked, her excitement evident.

Eloise caught Rose watching them. "Are you not the least bit tired?" Eloise asked, hoping the girl was as tired as she.

"Go on and get some rest," Rose said to Eloise as she set up the checkerboard. "You've had an exhausting day. I will send them both to bed at a reasonable hour, I promise."

"Yes, please," Gennie added. "May I?"

William and Rose joined in until saying anything but yes was impossible. Eloise barely recalled anything after that until Gennie climbed under the quilt bubbling with the news that she had bested William at both checkers and charades but had lost at chess. "Will you teach me chess?" she asked.

"Perhaps another time," Eloise managed as she roused herself sufficiently to be certain the girl had combed her hair and brushed her teeth. "Now sleep."

"But I'm not tired," she protested with a yawn.

"Perhaps not, but I do believe your eyes are. So only rest them. The remainder of you may remain awake."

Gennie gave her a skeptical look then finally nodded. "Yes, all right. That sounds fair."

"I'm very glad you think so. Now good night, little blue eyes, and would the rest of you please remain still so that your eyes may get their rest?" Eloise turned her head so the child would not see her smile.

Eloise opened her eyes to find Gennie sound asleep with one arm flung across her pillow and one leg hanging out of the quilts. Rising, she tucked the girl back under the covers, then dressed quietly and went downstairs to find the most delicious smell coming from the kitchen. To her surprise, instead of seeing Rose at the stove, Zeke stood there.

"Good morning," he called over his shoulder. "You're up early. Help yourself to coffee."

"Not as early as you." She filled a mug with the dark brew. "Are you always the breakfast cook?"

"Always." He gave her a sideways look as he dodged the pops of the meat sizzling in the big iron skillet. "The biscuits are under the towel, and the bacon is nearly ready."

She took note of the bandage wrapped around his forehead. "How are you feeling this morning?"

"I'll live," he said. "Have a seat."

Eloise took a seat at the small table tucked in beside the window and sipped her coffee while Zeke finished his work at the stove. The sight of a man cooking was a rare thing for her, but seeing *this* man bustling about the kitchen was something altogether different.

"Almost done," he said as he tossed the last of the bacon onto the platter. A moment later, he set down two plates and took a seat across from her.

Somehow he'd added scrambled eggs to the menu without her even noticing. Apparently she'd not exactly been attentive.

No, that was wrong. She'd been too attentive to the man to notice what he was putting on the stove. Eloise sighed as she took a mouthful of the deliciousness that was Zeke Potter's breakfast offering.

"Good?"

She nodded. "Excellent."

"Thank you," he said. He reached out to place his hand over hers. "For saving me yesterday."

The warmth of his hand atop hers caused Eloise's breath to catch. She looked up into his eyes, and her heart lurched. Oh, this was most unfortunate.

Before she could respond, Sheriff Swenson came in. Eloise snatched her hand away. Heat once again climbed into her cheeks as she looked toward the lawman.

"Good morning," he said with a grin that was far too broad. "What did I miss?"

"Probably not a thing," Zeke grumbled.

"You're right about that," Mack said as he joined them at the table. "Anybody going bear hunting this morning?"

"Not funny, Mack," he said. "My plan is to help process that beast. I figure there'll be enough to make jerky and some decent hide on it that your wife will want to use for chairs or some such thing."

"You'd have to ask her." His attention went from Mack to Eloise. "How'd this fellow end up being the only one who got marked by that critter?"

She smiled. "That fellow saved my life, so he earned that mark."

"The hard way," Mack commented before his expression softened. "Glad it wasn't worse, and I am relieved that bear found you instead of one of the children. No offense," he quickly added.

"None taken," Zeke said.

When she'd finished her breakfast, Eloise left the men to their conversation. By the time she returned with Gennie, the kitchen was occupied by Rose and William.

Eloise poured herself another mug of coffee while the children chattered away about the games they'd played the night before. She returned to the table to find Rose watching her.

"I understand you've already had your breakfast," she said with the beginnings of a grin.

Eloise matched her smile. "I did. Is it true that Zeke always cooks breakfast?"

"Zeke, is it?"

She felt the heat rise in her cheeks. "Yes," was all she would admit.

"He does," Rose said. "It was the deal he made when he came to stay in the bunkhouse. He'd help Mack by keeping things running smoothly around the ranch, and he'd help me by making breakfast. Mind you, that was him putting the restrictions on our hospitality, not us." She paused. "I don't mind a bit that I do not have to wake up two hours before daybreak to feed Mack and the crew."

"I would guess not." They lapsed into a companionable silence while the children continued to laugh and talk amid bites of breakfast.

"I'm grateful you're here," Rose finally said. "William has been starved for companionship, and the Lord never did see fit to give him a brother or sister."

"I am grateful, but I feel as though I'm not earning my keep," Eloise said.

"Now you sound like Zeke. You are two of a kind for sure."

Eloise smiled. "I doubt that seriously."

"Go ahead and doubt, but that doesn't make it not true." She paused. "So I need a favor. If you want to earn your keep, maybe I have a solution."

"Anything," Eloise said. "You've been more than kind."

"All right." She cast a covert glance at the children then returned her attention to Eloise. "Let Gennie learn alongside William as long as you're here." She held up her hand as if to stop Eloise's protests. "Please, let me tell you why. That child of mine is as stubborn as his father. He would rather be out on a horse or doing whatever the cowboys are doing than staying inside learning his letters and numbers, but I am determined he will be educated like his father and me and not run wild. Until Gennie came into our lives, it was torture just to get him to pay attention for a few hours in the afternoon. Would you believe this morning he asked if we could have school in the morning and the afternoon because he wanted to show Gennie that he was just as smart as her with his subtraction?"

Eloise smiled. "That's wonderful, but—"

"Look," Rose interrupted. "I know you love your niece and don't want to be parted from her, but you've got a case to solve. With her here, you can go about the business of finding your brother without worrying about a little one tagging along."

She gave the idea a moment of thought. "That is true. But I had hoped to solve two cases, actually. So perhaps I do need some help with Gennie."

"No, you would be helping me, remember?"

"Yes, all right, but I need some help from you," Eloise said. "Tell me everything you know about Simon Benton."

Her brows rose. "What are you up to, Eloise?"

She shrugged. "As long as I'm looking for one missing Englishman, I can just as easily look for the other one."

"Absolutely," Rose said. "What do you want to know?"

She held up her hand. "Give me just a minute to go and get my notebook. I want to write everything down."

An hour later, with several pages of her notebook filled with information on the elusive Simon Benton, Eloise aimed the borrowed buggy toward Benton Springs. Her first stop was the post office, where she took her place at the end of the line. When it was her turn, she greeted the postmaster, a man named Laird Anderson, according to the sign above his head, with a smile.

Before she could speak, Zeke Potter took his place by her side. "You two together?" the postmaster asked.

"Yes," Zeke said.

"No," she corrected. For as much as a friendship had begun between them, no business deal had been struck.

He leaned close. "Before we were interrupted by that bear, you made mention of a substantial sum of money."

She turned to face him, his nearness jolting. Still, she refused to flinch or step back. "That was yesterday."

"Glad you shot that bear, Zeke," Mr. Anderson said as he scratched his bald head. "That thing made a mess out of my kitchen not a week ago and would've torn the rest of the house up too if me and the dogs hadn't managed to turn him toward the door and send him outside. The wife won't so much as open a window for fear he's going to crawl in it."

"Tell your wife it is safe to open the windows," Zeke said with a grin. "The closest that bear is getting to a kitchen is on the seat of Rose Swenson's chairs."

"Well, good riddance," Mr. Anderson said with a nod. "Now what can I do for you?"

This was usually the point in a conversation where Eloise would pull out her badge and commence the interrogation. However, a badge from the London Metropolitan Police meant nothing here.

"I have some questions," Eloise and Zeke said at the same time.

"Well, all right," Mr. Anderson said. "But I don't have answers unless you ask them. You aiming to mail something or wondering if you've got a delivery?"

"Neither," they said in unison.

"Stop that," she told him.

Zeke responded with a grin. "I accept your proposal."

"Well, ain't that nice. Zeke Potter's getting hitched," Mr. Anderson said to those waiting behind them. "He just accepted her proposal." He shook his head and looked back at them. "Since when does a woman do the proposing?"

"She doesn't," Eloise snapped, retrieving her badge and showing it to the postmaster. "I am Eloise Broderick, special constable assigned to the London Metropolitan Police, and I have some questions for you in regard to a man who has received letters from England at this post office."

The postmaster's thin brows rose. "Well, all right then, but congratulations all the same."

"We're not—"

"Thank you," Zeke said, turning his attention to Mr. Anderson.

Eloise felt a tap on her shoulder, and she turned to see a sweet elderly lady with snow-white hair piled into a tight knot on the top of her head. "Yes?" she asked her.

"Congratulations. We do love Mr. Potter here in Benton Springs."

"Truly, we are not—"

"Well, whether you are or you are not, would you mind terribly moving along? Some of us are in a bit of a hurry."

Eloise looked beyond the lady to the steadily growing line behind them. "Oh yes, of course. I'm so sorry. I'll just be a minute." She returned her attention to the postmaster, who was now deep in conversation with Zeke. "I believe I was before you," she told the annoying former lawman.

"You were, at that," Mr. Anderson said. "As I was telling Zeke, I never did hear of anyone by the name of James Broderick picking up mail here in Benton Springs. Him being an Englishman, I would've remembered. Simon Benton, he was the only one like that."

"Tell me about Simon," she interjected.

The request seemed to confuse him. "Well now, I guess he was a nice enough fellow, seeing as how we all voted to rename the town for him. He did a lot of good around here." Mr. Anderson cast a quick glance at Zeke. "Well, mostly."

"Mostly?" She shook her head. "What do you mean?"

"Eloise," Zeke said firmly, "we've taken too much of the postmaster's time. Let's go."

"Listen to him, honey," the lady behind her said. "After all, he's going to be your husband, and you'll have to learn to obey him."

"I will do no such thing," she snapped, then instantly regretted her reaction. "I do apologize, ma'am, but you see, he and I are not being married. It's all a misunderstanding."

"Come on, dear," he said as he led her away from the line.

"Zeke Potter, you are incorrigible," she said, making sure everyone in the post office heard. "I am not your dear."

"Oh honey, he saved your life," the elderly lady said. "I heard it myself from my husband when he came home from doctoring poor Zeke. One swipe of that awful bear's paw and that poor woman would have been dead is what I was told. Our former sheriff is a hero, and he shall bear the scars of his bravery for all time."

Zeke beamed. "Well, thank you, Mrs. Ross."

Of all the nerve. While she didn't want to take credit for creating a distraction so that Zeke could shoot the creature, the fact is that it happened just that way.

"Actually the truth of the matter is a bit different, Mrs. Ross," Eloise said as Zeke led her out the door.

"Oh honey, my husband would know, now wouldn't he? Congratulations on your engagement to such a heroic man," echoed behind as the door to the post office slammed behind them.

Eloise yanked her arm away from Zeke. She had learned early on that she was much more effective as an investigator when she could remain focused no matter what was happening around her.

Failing that, she could at least turn some of her irritation on the source. "What just happened in there?"

Zeke grinned. "According to the doctor's wife, we just got engaged. Oh, and Mrs. Ross will probably be shouting my praises for a while. Apparently I am a hero. I don't mind that at all."

"No," she managed. "I can see that you'd be fine with that. However, we did not get engaged, and I did not get the information I came for."

"Maybe not, but I did." He nodded to the buggy. "I can't help but recognize that as belonging to the Swensons. I'm guessing that's how you got to town?"

"You should know, since you followed me," she said. "And hitched your horse to the back of it, I see."

If that was his attempt at an innocent look, Zeke failed miserably. "Have you considered that finding you at the post office might have just been a coincidence?"

She looked up into a face that was anything but innocent.

"No." Then she realized what he said. "Wait. What information did you get?"

Dr. Ross's wife stepped out of the post office and eyed them curiously. "Still arguing? My dear, you're just going to have to learn to let your future husband win."

"He is not my future husband, or my fiancé." She turned to Zeke. "Will you please confirm this? This is exactly how rumors get started."

❧ Chapter 6 ❧

The last thing Zeke intended to do was to get in the middle of two women squabbling, even if he did have a hand in causing it. So he adjusted his hat and walked over to the Swensons' buggy then climbed in. It didn't take but a second for Eloise to catch on and climb aboard.

"Give my thanks to your husband, Mrs. Ross. He did a fine job stitching me back together."

He guided the buggy away from the post office and gave his companion a sideways glance. "I'm sorry about all that. I figured this was the best way to save us both. And if it makes any difference, Mrs. Ross is a little hard of hearing."

"She heard the part about a proposal just fine, and you did nothing to correct that," Eloise said. "I will admit to miscalculating on my choice to question the postmaster when the post office was open. Next time we speak, I will not make that mistake."

"What else can you ask him about your brother? He already said he doesn't remember him being here."

"Yes, and that corresponds with what the Pinkerton detective said. However, that same detective tracked him here and is certain he arrived at least two years ago. James continued to draw regular payments from the Broderick trust until just over a year ago."

Zeke glanced over in her direction. "He must not have been using his own name. Laird has been our postmaster since I was a child. He would know."

She looked away. "I suppose."

He returned his attention to the trail ahead. Silence fell between them, punctuated only by the sounds of birds overhead and the crunch of the wheels and horses' hooves on the ground below them.

"Zeke, Mr. Anderson knows more than he was willing to tell us."

He slowed the buggy to ease the wheels over a rut in the path and thought back to the postmaster's response when he asked about James Broderick. Had he missed something?

"What makes you think that?" he asked as a chill wind blew past.

"It's more of a feeling than a thought." She swiped a strand of dark hair away from her face. "You being a former sheriff, I'm sure you understand."

His fingers tightened on the reins. "So you know about that."

"Yes," she said slowly as he felt her eyes on him. "Rose told me. I'm sorry about your wife and child. That must have been devastating."

His gut lurched. Devastating did not begin to describe it.

"It wasn't your fault."

Zeke whipped his head around to stare at her. "You don't know that. You weren't there."

Eloise's expression was soft, kind. "No, I wasn't. Please forgive me. My intention was not to add to your pain."

He let out a long breath. Several responses came to mind. He could have told her why she was wrong. Why he shouldn't have gone to Austin without insisting his family stay with the Swensons. Instead, he traded the lives of his wife and son to see justice done.

He'd done what he swore to do when he took his oath as sheriff. And that was why he no longer wore the badge. Because he knew he could never swear to that oath with any sort of honesty.

Never again.

They fell into a companionable silence until he made the turn away from the road that led to the Swenson farm. Eloise gave him a look that showed she was curious, but kept quiet.

So she trusted him. Good.

A few minutes later they arrived at the clearing. Zeke pulled the wagon to a halt and looked over at Eloise.

She was studying the frame and timber structure with some measure of curiosity. "Whose home is this?" she finally asked.

"It belongs to Simon Benton."

Zeke set the wagon in motion again as they headed toward the home he hadn't been in since the day he lost his family. He pushed all thoughts of that day aside and tried to look at the scene as he would have back in his lawman days.

Nothing had changed on the outside since then. Talk around town was that the money that Benton used for upkeep on the place had kept coming even after he disappeared. Though Zeke hadn't cared then, he was beginning to now.

He pulled the buggy to a halt in front of the house and then went around to help Eloise down. Even here in this place he didn't want to be, Zeke found a moment's happiness holding her in his arms.

As soon as he set her feet back on Colorado soil, he stepped back. While he saw to untying his horse from the buggy and securing it at the rail, he watched Eloise. She appeared to be looking at the house with an investigator's eye, studying and not speaking.

Finally, she met his gaze. "Are we allowed in?"

"He's not here to stop us," Zeke said. "And there was a time when I passed freely through those doors. So considering this is part of our investigation, I'd say we are."

"Our investigation," she echoed. "Yes, all right, but I should like to see the outbuildings first."

He took her around to the back where she could see the entirety of the Benton spread. The land here sloped up to the ridge at the back of the property. Several outbuildings dotted the landscape, the barn being the largest of all.

"What are those?" Eloise asked as she shaded her eyes from the sun with the back of her hand.

"The smokehouse is over there," he said. He pointed out the rough wooden building and then told her what each of the other smaller structures were.

"I would like to go into the barn," she said.

Zeke led her across the property toward the big red barn. "He used to have horses when I knew him. And cattle." He glanced back at the empty pasture. "Looks like they're all gone now."

Though he didn't know what to expect, opening the barn doors to find horses was not it. Eloise stepped in to pause beside him.

Sunlight filtered in, showering the center of the barn in speckled gold. The earthy scent of animals and their hay rose, but it was not unpleasant. Someone was taking good care of these animals.

"They're beautiful," she said as she walked past him to stroll down the row of stalls. "I see a half dozen. Good stock, it seems."

"They ought to be," a voice behind them called. "Mr. Benton paid good money for 'em."

Zeke turned around to see Thomas Anderson, the postmaster's grandson, walking toward him. "What're you doing out here, Thomas?" he asked the young man.

The last time he'd seen the fellow, Thomas had been running errands for his grandfather and helping his father around their farm a few miles down the road. It must have been awhile since then, for the gangly youth had added some bulk to his skinny frame. His red hair was still unruly and his face clean shaven.

"I was about to ask you that, Mr. Potter. What happened to your head? Is that where the bear got you? Heard about that in town and. . ." He looked past Zeke to Eloise. "Who's that?"

Before Zeke could answer, Eloise headed their way. "Eloise Broderick, Special Constable, London Metropolitan Police. I wonder if I might ask you a few questions."

Thomas shook his head. "I, well, sure, but I don't know you."

"You do now. I just told you who I am." Eloise inched closer to him as if carrying out an inspection. She pointed to Zeke. "You apparently know him. Who is this, Mr. Potter?"

Mr. Potter. Well, all right. Two could play at that.

"This is Thomas Anderson, Special Constable Broderick. He's the grandson of our postmaster."

She gave Zeke a curt nod and went back to looking at Thomas as if she might arrest him at any moment. It was all he could do not to smile.

"Mr. Anderson, are you here because you take care of these horses?"

"I am," he said before cutting a sideways glance toward Zeke. "I'm paid to take care of this place until Mr. Benton returns. He wanted it kept just as he left it."

"I see," she said. "And who is paying you?"

His attention returned to Eloise. "Well, the man at the bank is the one who gives me my wages. I get paid once a month on the first day, always have."

"Since Benton left?" Zeke said.

"Oh no, sir," Thomas told him. "Mr. Benton, he hired me to help with the horses because he said I had a way with them. I do other odd jobs, but mostly it's the horses that keep me busy now that the cows are gone."

"Where are the cows?" Zeke asked.

A crimson flush climbed up Thomas's neck and into his face. "They were more than I could handle alone, so they got put in another pasture."

"Whose pasture?" When Thomas did not seem inclined to answer, Zeke continued. "Your father's or your grandfather's?"

"Both," he stammered.

That figured. Not that it was his business who divided the spoils of Simon Benton's property. At least not yet.

"And you get paid the same now as you always have?" Eloise asked.

The question seemed to confuse him. "Why wouldn't I?"

"You do have less work," she offered. "Although I suppose Mr. Benton would have no idea of that unless he's been here to see it for himself." She inched closer, making Thomas decidedly uncomfortable. "Has he been here, Thomas?"

"He has not," Thomas said, taking a step backward. "But I'm to keep things just as he left them for when he returns."

Zeke looked to his companion for her response. Rather than speak to Thomas, Eloise met Zeke's gaze for a moment before looking back at the young man.

"Did he tell you that?" she asked.

"In a way, sort of." Thomas shrugged. "No," he amended. "But Mr. Benton wouldn't just go off and leave this place. He loved it more than anyplace else, even his home in England."

"Did he tell you about his home in England?"

"Some," Thomas said. "We'd talk a bit when we were working alongside one another. He loved England and felt bad he wasn't there, that he hadn't gone back. He was considering 'making it right,' whatever that means. I figure that's where he is."

"Yes, right. Thank you, Thomas." Eloise walked briskly past him and out into the sunshine, where she paused and seemed to be staring off toward the house.

"Why all the questions?" Thomas asked. "Has Mr. Benton done something wrong?" He ducked his head. "He's a good man. Always good to me and my family and. . . Well, other than the thing with the fire where. . ."

His voice trailed off. As with most citizens of Benton Springs, Thomas had no idea how to talk about what happened that day.

Zeke clasped his hand on Thomas's shoulder. "It's all right, Thomas."

The young man lifted his gaze. "I'm awful sorry. I shouldn't have mentioned that."

"I understand your family was the first to get there after Mack sounded the alarm, so I owe you a debt of gratitude for your help."

Tears shimmered in his pale eyes, and he quickly swiped at them. "I wish we could've done more."

He shrugged. "Thank you, Thomas. You did all you could. No

sense in reliving it. Let's go see what the special constable wants to do next."

"I would like to go inside the house now," Eloise said when they joined her.

Thomas shrugged. "It's not locked, but I need to let the horses out to pasture now."

She barely spared him a glance as she set off walking. "Yes, go on and carry out your responsibilities. We won't keep you any longer."

Thomas quickly ducked back into the barn, leaving Zeke to catch up to Eloise. As he fell in beside her, he noticed her brows were now furrowed. Just before they reached the broad expanse of front porch, she paused.

"I have a theory," she told him. "But you will likely think I'm mad."

"Mad as in angry or mad as in crazy?" he offered to lighten what had quickly become a somber mood.

Her chuckle was a welcome sound. "Crazy," she said as her fingers traced the length of the stair rail and her attention went to the front door.

"You think Simon Benton and your brother are the same person."

~ Chapter 7 ~

*E*loise jolted at the sound of the words she had been thinking being spoken aloud by Zeke. "Yes," she managed. "Do you think that is possible? The Pinkerton detective didn't, but only because he could find no evidence of it."

"It's possible," the former sheriff said. "Describe your brother for me."

She thought a moment. "He's taller than me by a bit with hair like mine and brown eyes. He is my fraternal twin, so I suppose we also favor each other in some of our facial expressions."

Zeke remained silent, leaving Eloise to wonder what he was thinking. Finally, she added, "I've described Simon Benton, haven't I?"

His gaze collided with her. "Maybe. There's only one way to find out. Let's go in."

She nodded, and yet she hesitated. Zeke must have taken her reluctance as his cue to go first, for he swiftly pressed past her and opened the door then stepped inside.

"Anyone home?" he called. "Zeke Potter and Special Constable Broderick here."

Hearing him call her that made Eloise smile despite the feelings swirling inside her. It also gave her the nudge she needed to follow him across the porch to the threshold of the home. Indeed, she was James Broderick's sister, but she was also a trained policewoman.

She could do this.

Taking a deep breath, Eloise let it out slowly as she stepped inside. Expecting gloom and dust, she was pleasantly surprised to find neither.

Sunlight filtered through white lace curtains, illuminating a modestly furnished parlor with a matching pair of settees made of carved rosewood and covered in pale blue striped silk fabric. A painting of mountains on the wall opposite the rock fireplace echoed the colors of the furnishings.

"Bud painted that," Zeke said. "He told me he was paying back a debt with that one. Likely Simon loaned him money to keep the hotel doors open." He paused as if considering what he would say next. "He was like that with his money. Never would take payment in return."

"A good man, then," she said as she continued her perusal of the room.

A lone chair had been set between the fireplace and the window. Beside it was a small table that held a stack of books, a pair of eyeglasses, and a wooden box inlaid with mother of pearl. Atop the box was a folded newspaper.

Zeke picked it up. "It's a copy of the *Rocky Mountain News* dated two days before the fire. Did James wear spectacles to read?"

"Not the last time I saw him, but he might have since," she said, trying to shake the feeling that the owner of this home would return any moment to take up his eyeglasses and return to his enjoyment of the Denver newspaper.

"How long ago was that?"

"Too long. Gennie is ten years old, and he hasn't yet met her. He never did meet his son."

Zeke shook his head but remained silent. She continued.

"Once Diana announced her pregnancy, James announced that his duty to provide an heir had been carried out and he was free to go back to his life in America. In Colorado," she amended.

"Possibly in Benton Springs," Zeke added.

"Possibly. I never understood how he could do that."

"No, I've seen you with that little girl. I cannot imagine you would abandon her."

She shook her head. "I'm not completely comfortable leaving her at the Swenson farm while I'm away investigating, but I do know she is safe there."

"Because you couldn't keep her brother safe," he supplied.

The statement caused her heart to lurch. "Exactly," she said. She moved out of the parlor and back into the wide center hallway that split the home in half, so he wouldn't see the tears gathering in her eyes.

"Wait," Zeke said. "I didn't mean to. . ." He shook his head. "Look, I'm sorry. It's just that, well, I know how it feels to fail an innocent little one. However your nephew died, you must know you cannot blame yourself."

"But I can," she said. "His mother died in childbirth, leaving me and my mother to raise them. I did my best. Kept them at the family home to be educated as we were, James and I, with Mother overseeing their care while I worked in London. Still, I should have been there supervising the children myself. James knew not to climb on the garden wall, and yet he did. Gennie ran for help, but it was too late." She paused. "He was always such a curious child."

"So was my son," Zeke said.

She looked up at him. "You do understand."

Zeke nodded and gathered Eloise into his arms. She nestled her head against his neck. The tears fell for the first time in a very long time.

"You all need anything?" Thomas called from just outside the door.

Eloise stepped out of his arms and moved away from the hall and back toward the parlor window while Zeke went out to talk to the young man. Her knees shaking, she settled onto the chair by the fireplace and rested her palms in her lap while she gathered her wits.

This was an investigation. As such, she needed to put all emotion aside. If this indeed was James's home, there would be some evidence to prove it. He couldn't have walked away from everything he once was. Something would remain.

Eloise slid the newspaper aside and retrieved the box. Something inside slid as she moved it to her lap. Outside, the sound of the men's voices rose and fell on the breeze that wafted through the open door. Here in the parlor, as she traced the edge of the box with her index finger, all was silent except for the furious beating of her heart.

She opened the box to find it contained a Bible. Her fumbling fingers dropped the book twice before she managed to open the front cover.

"Well?" Zeke said from his place at the door.

"Nothing here," she said. "I had hoped maybe. . ."

He shrugged. "If he took on a new name, James would be more careful than to leave something with the old one it in where it could be found, don't you think?"

"I suppose." She closed the lid and returned the box to the table then rose. "Let's see what else we can find."

The kitchen was as pristine as the rest of the house, with no evidence of the biscuits from the story Rose told. Of course, the kitchen was as clean and tidy as the rest of the house.

Unlike the parlor, this room was more utilitarian. She moved around the kitchen, taking note of the dry goods still in the cupboard and the dishes stacked neatly on the sideboard.

"Did he have someone to cook and keep house for him?"

"I have no idea," Zeke said. "Never gave any thought to that until now. Thomas would probably know. I'll go ask while he's still here."

"All right." She opened the drawer on the sideboard to find it filled with modest eating utensils and a few wooden spoons. The other drawer offered a similar collection of kitchen items and nothing that would indicate the identity of the owner of this home.

She crossed the hall to find a small room with two narrow beds and a larger room next to it. Stepping into the larger room, she knew this must be where the home's owner slept. The wall pegs were devoid of clothing, and the table next to the bed held only an oil lamp. The walls were also bare, and the curtains matched the ones in the parlor, but the bed with its red-and-white quilt folded at the end looked inviting.

Backtracking to the smaller room, she stepped inside, and her knees went weak again. The same empty pegs and parlor curtains met her here. Here the quilts were patterned in blue and white. Just as she'd found in the larger room, it was a space that held no clue to its owner.

If this was truly James's home, she had found no proof here. Disappointment overwhelmed her, and she sank onto the bed nearest her.

Her fingers grazed the edge of the pillow and felt something that did not belong there. She reached for it and pulled out a folded slip of paper. Inside were two words in a very familiar handwriting: "*Welcome, Theodore.*"

Zeke found Eloise in the small bedroom with her head in her hands and a slip of paper at her feet. He picked it up and read the words.

"Who is Theodore?"

Eloise looked up at him with tear-filled eyes. "Gennie's brother."

He sat down beside her. For a while, neither spoke.

Then she leaned against him. "Where do you think James is?"

Thinking on his response, Zeke decided on the truth. "For a long time I thought he had run away after the fire. Now I don't know." He paused to hand her the slip of paper, then watched her tuck it away in her skirt pocket. "Why would he do this? Do you think he was expecting his children to join him here?"

She swiped at a tear. "It certainly looks that way, but it makes no sense."

Zeke stood and offered his hand to help her to her feet. "No, it doesn't, but you've hired me, and I am going to figure it out."

"About that," she said. "We never did agree on a price."

"Keep your money, Eloise," he told her. "I have as much interest in finding this man as you do."

"Yes," she said slowly, "I suppose you do, but I will insist on paying you."

He could have continued to argue. Instead, he decided to allow the stubborn woman to believe what she wanted. For now.

"Thomas said his sister comes weekly to see that the house is always ready for Simon's, or rather, James's, return. She is also paid from the bank, the same as her brother."

Eloise pressed past him and went to retrieve something from beneath the pillow of the second small bed. The slip of paper matched the one he'd picked up from the floor. As she slid it into her pocket, her expression changed.

All evidence of sadness disappeared, and a look of determination met him. "I will be moving in here, Zeke. It is the right thing to do."

"Is it?" he said. "You're safe at the Swensons, and Rose is loving having Gennie there with William. She's said so."

"The Swensons are wonderful. If Rose will have her, I will continue to allow Gennie to learn alongside William as long as I am here." She met his gaze. "I cannot bring Theodore home to his father, but I can see that Gennie is here if he returns. With Thomas and his sister here to help, I will be fine. If we discover he will not return, at least one of his children will be welcomed here as he wished."

Again, he had several responses he might have chosen. "All right," he said instead.

"I won't tell them today. I have notes from the detective to study, and I need to decide the right words to let Gennie know about all of this."

"That makes sense," he told her. "I won't be at the evening meal tonight, but you let me know tomorrow if you need me to help move your trunks in here."

"I will. Thank you." They walked out together and paused on the porch to look across at the mountains in the distance. "He had a lovely view from here."

"He picked this spot to build because of the view."

"I forget you were close."

He shrugged. "Close enough to trust him with what was most important to me."

Eloise reached over to touch his sleeve. "Have you forgiven him?"

An emotion he didn't like washed over him, but Zeke shrugged it off. "I'm working on it."

She looked up into his eyes and smiled. "So am I."

"Eloise, I suggest you don't mention what we've learned here today to anyone other than Mack and Rose."

"Yes," she said on an exhale of breath. "All right."

Zeke was still standing on the porch when she and the buggy disappeared over the ridge. Thomas came around the side of the porch. His timing made Zeke wonder if the young man had waited until she left to make his appearance.

"Am I in trouble, Zeke?"

"Why would you think that?"

He scratched his head. "Because I've never had the law come

all the way from London, England, just to ask me questions. Seems like that's bad."

"She's come all the way from London to find Simon." He paused to look directly at Thomas. "Where is he?"

"I wish I knew, and that's the truth. Last time I saw him, he was talking about how he was waiting for an answer to his letters. Said we ought to prepare to have little ones here soon." He shrugged. "I thought maybe he'd ordered one of those brides who put ads in the newspapers."

"Well, Thomas, there will be a little one here soon. Miss Broderick, that is Special Constable Broderick, will be moving in temporarily along with her niece."

"All right, but she will have to explain to Mr. Benton why she's here when he gets back."

Zeke grinned. "I don't think she will mind. Now, before I leave, I need to ask a few questions about the last time you saw Simon."

"Aw, Zeke, you've already asked me about that day more than once. I wish I could help you, but I just can't. I was at my grandpa's place before sunrise working his cattle and helping out there until we got word of the fire. Then I skedaddled over to your place with the rest of the menfolk."

"Yes, I know. But remind me, were your father and grandfather with you at all during that time?"

"I was helping alongside Pa for about an hour until my grandfather had need of him and called him away." He paused. "Grandpa was working at the post office, as always."

"Was Amelia cleaning here that day?"

Thomas shook his head. "No. It wasn't her day to clean."

So there was no one here to know what went on at the Benton

place. This meant something. He just had to figure out what.

"Thank you, Thomas," he said as he headed for his horse. "I'm counting on you to make Miss Broderick feel welcome."

~ Chapter 8 ~

*A*fter spending the afternoon poring over the books of notes from the Pinkerton detective and the evening playing games with Gennie and the Swensons, Eloise went to sleep having kept the discovery to herself. By the time she came downstairs the next morning, Zeke was already gone, but the sheriff and his wife were at the breakfast table.

"Where's Gennie?" Rose asked. "William is out with Zeke, but I can fetch him soon as she's had her breakfast so they can start their schooling."

"I told her she could sleep a little longer." Eloise paused. "The truth is, I have something to tell you, and I didn't want her to overhear it."

As Eloise expected, Rose put up a fuss about losing her house-guests and extracted a promise that Gennie would continue to do her schoolwork with William at the Swenson ranch.

"I was hoping you would want her to," Eloise said.

The sheriff listened in silence then shook his head. "Just so I understand, Miss Broderick, your brother changed his name to Simon Benton and has lived among us for years. That Pinkerton fellow tracked James Broderick to here but couldn't work out the connection between the two. Then you and Zeke figure it out in a day's time."

"That's right," she said as she pulled the two slips of paper from her skirt pocket and handed them to Sheriff Swenson.

"Oh, my heart," Rose said softly. "It appears the man not only had children, but he also wanted them here with him."

"Yes," she said, returning the paper to her pocket. "I would like to honor that wish."

"Well, of course you would." Rose looked up at her husband. "You'll get Eloise and Gennie situated there, and we will loan her a horse and buggy to use. I'll fetch enough to feed them until she can make a trip into town to fill the cupboard."

"Thank you, Rose, but the barn is full of horses there, and I saw a buggy and a wagon. However, I wouldn't mind a loan of the buggy just once more so I can bring Gennie there first."

"Does she have any idea?" Rose asked.

"No." Eloise rose. "And I have no idea how I am going to tell her."

Later, as she pulled the buggy to a stop in front of her brother's home, she still wasn't certain what she would say. She climbed down and then helped Gennie out.

"This is a lovely home," Gennie said. "Who lives here?"

"We will, temporarily," Eloise said.

As she expected, the little girl looked surprised. "Why?"

"Come in and I'll show you." She opened the door and found

that someone had placed flowers in a vase on the parlor table. Amelia perhaps. Or maybe Thomas.

"It's very pretty," Gennie said as she hurried to the settee and ran her hand over the blue silk cushions. "Not like our homes in England, but pretty all the same."

"Yes, well," Eloise said as she cast an eye toward the chair where her brother had apparently spent a certain amount of his time. "There is a story behind this house, and I need to tell you about it." She paused to take a deep breath and let it out slowly.

"Is this a story you do not want to tell?"

Eloise's brows furrowed. "Why would you think that?"

"Because you look worried."

Eloise smoothed the girl's hair and forced a smile. "Maybe just a bit. See, this is difficult, but, well, this house belongs to your father."

"Papa?" Her face lit up. "Is he here?"

"No," she said carefully, "he isn't, but he left something for you." She retrieved the note from her pocket, having packed away the matching one for Theodore between the pages of her Bible, and handed it to Gennie.

" 'Welcome, Eugenie,' " she read aloud and then scrunched up her nose.

Eloise knelt down on eye level with the girl. "What's wrong?"

"Only Grandmother calls me Eugenie," she said. "I shall have to tell Papa he is to call me Gennie."

"Yes, definitely." Eloise rose. "Now let's see the rest of the house, shall we?"

The little girl skipped happily from room to room, exclaiming over every detail as if she hadn't grown up in an English castle full of priceless antiques. Finally, she stepped into the small bedroom and her chatter fell silent.

"Gennie?" Eloise said softly. "What's the matter?"

"He remembered," Gennie said softly as she hurried to the bed where Eloise had found the girl's name under the pillow. "I told him I wanted a blue quilt ever so much, and he said I should have one when I came to visit." She glanced at the other bed. "And he has given me two."

"Yes, sweetheart," she whispered as she collected her thoughts, "he has."

After a moment, Eloise found her voice. "Gennie, you didn't tell me you had been writing to your papa."

"Theodore and I wrote, and the footman mailed them for us without telling anyone. We used coins from Grandmother's wishing fountain to pay for the postage." She cast her eyes down at the pale blue rug on the floor between the beds. "I'm sorry."

God bless that footman.

Eloise hurried to her side. "There is nothing to be sorry for, Gennie. I'm very glad you wrote to him. And he wrote back?"

"Just once, but then not again," she said. "Once I heard Grandmother Broderick tell the maids to throw his letters into the fire. That's why the footman didn't tell anyone when he went out to post our mail to James Broderick, General Delivery, Benton Springs, Colorado."

"Oh honey," she said. "I wish I'd known. You see, I've been looking for your papa for years."

She smiled. "And now you've found him."

How to respond? She had found evidence of him in this home, but to say she had found James would not be a fair statement.

So she settled for a hug. Later that night, after she and Gennie had made their first dinner in their new temporary home, she tucked the girl into bed beneath the blue quilt with more hugs.

Pausing at the door, her smile was bittersweet. *I did what I could to bring her home, James.*

Returning to the kitchen, she retrieved the stack of notebooks and a pencil from the sideboard where she had stowed them earlier in the day and took them to the table along with the oil lamp. She added notes regarding her conversation with Gennie and then closed the notebook.

What did it all mean?

She was still trying to fit the pieces together the next morning when she delivered Gennie to the Swenson ranch for her lessons. After a hug and a wave, Eloise left a beaming Gennie with Rose and William and set off toward town for supplies. She would need to fill Zeke in on what she'd learned, but first she wanted to make another attempt at speaking to the postmaster.

To her surprise, she was greeted not by the elderly Mr. Anderson but by another Mr. Anderson, with the first name of Howard, who looked to be in the prime of his life. "I'm his son," he said when she inquired.

Now she could see the resemblance to Thomas, and she nodded. "Eloise Broderick. Very nice to meet you."

"Say, I know that name. You're that police lady from London who is staying at the Benton house with her little girl. Thomas told me about you."

"Yes, I am. Your son has been most helpful in getting us settled."

He shrugged. "It's my first time taking over for my father, but he's feeling poorly today, so I can help with any postal needs you might have, Miss Broderick."

"Yes, thank you," she said. "I am here to pick up some letters that my niece may have sent here. It would have been months ago, I'm afraid. Do you keep letters that long?"

"We keep them until they're picked up by the owner. It's the law."

"Wonderful." Eloise upped her smile. "My brother's name is James Broderick. The letters would be from Eugenie Broderick or possibly Theodore Broderick."

A curious expression crossed his face. "I just saw those this morning in a box under my father's desk. I figured they were being collected to send to the Dead Letter Office. Come on back here with me."

He opened the door to allow her to come around to the back of the office and then looked out at those in line. "Sorry, folks. Need to close now. Be back in a few minutes."

He pulled down the shade and then gestured for her to follow him to the back of the building. Only then did she begin to wish that she had informed Zeke of her plan before she set off to town.

The back of the post office was dimly lit and smelled like paper and ink. She made her way carefully down a narrow hallway that ended at a closed door.

Mr. Anderson used a key from his pocket to open the door. "Don't move, Howard," a familiar voice said.

"Zeke?" She pressed past the substitute postmaster to see Zeke sitting at an oversized ornate desk that was strangely immaculate given the mess of boxes and papers that surrounded it. Eloise quickly moved to his side. "How did you know I would be here?"

"What's going on here?" Mr. Anderson demanded. "My father doesn't let anyone in his office."

"And yet you had a key," Zeke said evenly as he lifted his pistol from his lap and pointed it at Howard. "Where are the letters?"

"What happened to your head, Zeke? That where the bear got you?"

Zeke frowned. "Just answer the question. Where are the letters?"

Howard shook his head. "I told her they were in a box under the desk. I saw them this morning and figured they were being collected to go to the Dead Letter Office. I heard tell that was the same bear that tore up my mama's kitchen. She sure wasn't happy about that."

Zeke rose and moved away from the desk then nodded toward Howard, his weapon still pointed at the man who apparently had no idea how much trouble he was in. Or he knew and was trying to stall.

"Get the box," he said evenly.

"Come on, Zeke," Mr. Anderson said, his hands up as if he were being arrested. "You and I go way back. You don't have to treat me like that."

"Just do it," Zeke said again.

Mr. Anderson stepped behind the desk then crouched down. A minute later he rose, a battered wooden box in his hand. "I was looking for the receipts that my father uses because we'd run out up at the front desk. I can't tell you the last time I worked here for him, but I figured they'd be somewhere in this room. Hunted high and low and never did find those receipts, but that's when I found these."

"Set it on the desk." Zeke glanced back at Eloise. "See what's in there."

She reached over to move the box across the desk and then opened the lid to find stacks of letters inside. All were addressed to James. Her heart lurched.

"Why did you do this?" she demanded of Mr. Anderson as angry tears sprang to her eyes. "You kept a father from his children and let them think they were unwanted."

"What the devil?" Howard shook his head. "I don't know what you're talking about, ma'am. Until this morning I had never seen that box or its contents. Who is James Broderick?"

� Chapter 9 ✅

Zeke sighed. "He is telling the truth."

Eloise shook her head. "You're certain?"

From what he knew of Howard Anderson and the facts he'd already determined, he was. Leaning against the edge of the desk, he stared at the man he'd known for decades.

"Howard," he said slowly, "do you have any idea what this box of letters is or what it means?"

"No," he said, his face as red as his hair. "I told you I've never seen it until today. While I'm thinking on it, I figure that James Broderick must be some relation of Miss Broderick here."

"He is my brother. Or was. I'm not certain which."

"Oh," Howard said on a rush of breath. "Well, I do see your point. For some reason, he wasn't picking up his letters."

"Or your father wasn't delivering them."

"But why?" Howard asked. "What purpose would my father have for keeping them in a box under his desk? If the Broderick fellow had moved on, then these should have gone to the Dead Letter Office. That's the law. I do know that much about this job."

Zeke nodded. "But if James Broderick was actually Simon Benton, and he didn't want anyone to know that, then what?"

"Doesn't matter." He paused. "Wait. What?"

"You didn't know?" Zeke asked him.

"No," Howard said. "That's not true. If he had another name, then so be it, long as he didn't admit to it, nobody asked. That's just how it is around here. More men come here to get lost from something somewhere else than they do for any other reason, at least in my estimation."

Indeed, that was the truth.

"Then under the circumstances, Miss Broderick is going to take these letters back to the Benton place so they will be there if Simon returns. You'd consider them delivered then, wouldn't you?"

He scratched his forehead. "Seems fair."

"Where's your father today, Howard?" Zeke said.

"Still abed when I left him this morning. Said he felt poorly and asked me to stand in for him. I did what I could, but I'm not cut out for this indoor work." He gave Eloise a sideways look. "That's why I was glad to shut it all down to help you. Don't figure I'll open again today."

"I'd like you to open again," Zeke said. "At least for a few hours. I'm not sure, but I believe there's a rule about how often this place has to be open, and it doesn't allow for early departure of the substitute postmaster just because he isn't cut out for indoor work."

"You think so?" he asked.

"I do," Zeke responded.

"Well, all right, then, but I'm going to have to lock up back here first."

Zeke nodded toward the door. "We'll just get on our way and let you do that then." He paused long enough to shake hands with Howard. "I appreciate your help," he said. "No hard feelings on pulling a gun on you?"

Howard grinned. "'Course not. It's not like you shot me."

"I wouldn't do that," Zeke told him over his shoulder. "Unless I had a good reason."

They both laughed, but only Howard's held any humor. Zeke escorted Eloise through the post office and waited while Howard unlocked the door and raised the shade. A moment later, Howard had plenty of customers.

He led her down the sidewalk away from the post office. While he had arrived at the post office with a plan, it hadn't included Eloise. Not until she walked into the middle of it.

Zach gave her a sideways look. He had to admit things had turned out better than he'd expected.

"How did you know I would be there?" she asked, the box of letters tucked carefully under her arm.

"I didn't." He paused. "Why didn't you let me know you were going to interview Howard?"

She paused her steps in front of Stillman's Mortuary, and he did the same. "My intention was to ask Mr. Anderson—that is, the elder Mr. Anderson—my questions and then get on with my shopping. I didn't expect his son would be there, but I thought maybe he would know the answers."

"And he did."

Eloise nodded as she clutched the box to her chest. "Yes, but now I have so many more questions."

"I think I can get some of those questions answered, but it's going to require you to put off your shopping for another day."

"I assumed that was why you insisted Mr. Anderson reopen the post office. With him busy here, he couldn't follow us."

"Well done, Special Constable Broderick," he said with a grin.

"You know, Zeke," Eloise said a short time later as they were headed out of Benton Springs with his horse tied to her wagon, "this is the second time in two days that we've left town together like this. People are going to talk."

He looked past her to the sidewalk where a gaggle of matrons were watching them pass by. At the center of their midst was Mrs. Ross.

"I'd say they already are," he told her. "But I never cared much for idle gossip."

"And I never had time for it," she said. "Seems an awful waste of time when you can go to the source and get the story straight."

"Spoken like someone who's done an investigation or two."

Eloise laughed. "A few more than that," she said. "My superiors were reluctant to accept a woman constable, but they certainly were not slow in realizing that certain men will say things in front of a woman that might not be said in front of a man." She shrugged. "I've solved more than one case just by allowing people to underestimate me."

"You have my word that I will never underestimate you, Special Constable Broderick," he told her.

And he meant it. Not only was she beautiful and smart, but she had an innate instinct that brought her right to the heart of a problem that others missed.

"Thank you," she said, and then her expression turned serious. "Do you think my brother and the postmaster colluded in any way to keep his identity secret? I cannot think of another reason why mail addressed to James Broderick could be picked up by Simon Benton without the elder Mr. Anderson knowing about it."

"I cannot figure a scenario where the two of them weren't in collusion in some way. Can you?"

She shook her head. "No, and that's the problem. Was James in a friendly arrangement with Mr. Anderson, or was he being blackmailed?"

"I could make a case for either," Zeke said.

"So could I." She looked away. "Zeke, is that a fire?"

Dark curls of smoke rose on the horizon, and his gut clenched. The only home in that direction was Simon Benton's.

Eloise's home.

Zeke watched the sky for signs of the fire that continued to rise. "Hold on," he told her. "This might get bumpy."

Their speed was limited by the bulky wagon, but still he urged the horses on as he gave thanks that James had invested well in the animals he'd purchased. Though they strained against the load, the pair were surefooted and swift.

Eloise reached to press her hand over his.

"It's James's house, isn't it?"

Her voice was calm, as was her expression. He replied in the same way.

"I believe it is."

When they reached the rise, the house was still standing in the distance. A thin trail of white smoke rose, but there was no evidence of fire. Someone had arrived before them and put it out.

Eloise bounded from the wagon as soon as Zeke pulled it to a halt in front of the house. "I don't see where the fire is. Or was," she said as she ran inside.

"Who's that?" someone called.

Thomas stepped around the edge of the house. Zeke immediately pulled his weapon.

The young man's hands rose. "Don't shoot," he said. "I've got him."

"Who've you got?" Zeke demanded, though he had a pretty good idea who it was. The only man with an interest in chasing Eloise out of Benton Springs was Thomas's own grandfather.

The man who sent his son to work for him today, claiming illness.

Thomas shook his head but kept his hands up. "You better come see, Mr. Potter."

Zeke fell into step beside him, his gun at the ready. As he rounded the corner of the house, he spied a stack of burned kindling piled against the house and a trail of soot climbing the home's exterior.

"I put it out before the fire could spread here, but there's a place over by the back bedroom that's going to need repair. My guess is he started that one first then came over here to make sure the whole place went up."

A thought occurred and the grip on his gun tightened. "Thomas, is today your day to be out here?"

"No," he said, guilt etched across his face. "But I got called home early yesterday and didn't get finished with my work here, so I had to come back this morning and finish up."

That was convenient. Or a godsend. Zeke wasn't yet sure which.

"So you're saying you've caught the man who did this?" he asked the young man.

He nodded. "I didn't want to hurt him, so I locked him in the smokehouse."

"A man was in the process of burning down a house and you

didn't want to hurt him?" Zeke demanded as he spied Eloise on the back porch.

Of course. He wouldn't want to hurt his own grandfather.

Eloise caught up to them. "There's some smoke in the house, but it seems to be concentrated in the larger bedroom." She glanced around to see the scorched wood outside the bedroom window. "Now I see why."

"There's another spot on the other side. Thomas here stopped the culprit before he could finish his work."

She shook her head. "Where is he, then?"

They stopped in front of the smokehouse, and Zeke motioned for them to be quiet. Eloise stepped behind him as he aimed his weapon. On his cue, Thomas opened the door.

There, sitting in a heap on the floor, was Dr. Ross. Though his silver hair was in disarray and his suit was rumpled, he looked otherwise unharmed.

Thomas stepped inside and reached down to help the old man up. "Come on out, sir. Mr. Potter and that English lady are here, and I've told them what I saw you doing."

The physician ran his hand through his hair and straightened his lapels, then stepped out into the morning sunshine. Though his posture was straight, his eyes were downcast. When he looked up, defiance showed on his face.

"I know you're not sheriff anymore, Zeke, but I would like to lodge a complaint against this young man who has held me prisoner with such indignity. I insist you make a citizen's arrest and haul him off to jail immediately."

Zeke looked into the eyes of the man who'd stitched him and placed the bandage on his head. "Why'd you do it, Dr. Ross?"

"I have no idea what you're talking about. I was merely

investigating the smoke I saw while out in my buggy, and this man decided to hold me prisoner."

"For no reason?" Eloise asked. "I find that difficult to believe."

"As did I," he told her. "As you can imagine, I am unused to such treatment. Thomas must be held accountable." The bluster was there, but fear tinged his tone.

"You know that's not true, Dr. Ross. Why would you say that?" Thomas looked at Zeke. "Don't believe him. He's lying."

"Thomas, I believe you," Zeke said as he put his gun back in the holster. "Have you seen your grandfather this morning? I am wondering about his health."

"I have not, but like I already told you, I was called off my duties here to help Pa because he had to go see to Grandfather." Thomas paused. "I didn't pay much attention to what was wrong except that it would be keeping him from his work, and also keeping my pa from his. I ended up having to see to the cattle there instead of the horses here."

"Why don't you go see about him now? I'd wager he will tell you he had cause to visit with the doctor yesterday and is feeling worse today."

"Now?" he asked.

When Zeke nodded, Thomas took off. "If he's able, bring him into town, please," Zeke called. "I will need him to testify against the doctor."

"How dare you?" the old man said. "He is as guilty as I. Do not dare consider Laird Anderson innocent in any of this."

"Any of what, Dr. Ross?" Eloise asked as she gestured toward the scarred wall outside the bedroom. "The arson you committed in order to try to frighten me into giving up my search for James, or is there more?"

"Oh, there is more," Zeke said. "Here's my guess. You figured out the post office was receiving letters for James Broderick, and Simon Benton was picking them up. What I can't figure is how you two were to profit from all this. Thomas and Amelia are still being paid, so the money is still in the bank. All I see missing is the cattle. Is that enough to kill a man over?"

❧ Chapter 10 ❧

$\mathcal{E}$loise gasped, and Zeke instantly regretted his statement. Still, it had the intended effect on the doctor.

"That was an accident! If that wife of yours hadn't been so nosy, none of it would have happened."

Hot temper coiled just beneath the surface. "What're you talking about?"

He sighed and shook his head. "I might as well tell it all," he said.

"Sounds like I'm here just in time for a confession." Mack appeared around the corner of the house with Deputy Wilson following two steps behind. "I saw the smoke then saw whatever was burning had been put out. Made a note to check on my way home for lunch since it looked to be close to the Benton property." He looked at Eloise. "We haven't known you long, but you're family to us."

She offered a smile, but it was shaky at best. "Thank you," she told him.

Mack turned his attention to Zeke. "You want to catch me up on what I've missed?"

He shrugged. "Thomas kept the doctor from burning this place down. He hasn't said why exactly, but I'm sure it will all come out when he confesses, or when Laird Anderson testifies against him."

"I see," Mack said, covering his surprise well. "That all?"

"He says my brother's death was an accident." Eloise straightened her shoulders. "And I believe he was about to tell Zeke how that accident was caused by his wife."

Mack shook his head and then looked at Dr. Ross. "I don't want to believe any of this. You delivered my boy and saved my wife's life in the process. You've been nothing but good for this community."

"That's the point, don't you see?" he said. "Benton or Broderick or whatever his name was, he had no intention to help our community. All he wanted to do was pile up all that money he got from his family in the bank and leave it there so his children would have a legacy. Because of us, he did lots of good. Mack, you know yourself all the things Simon did to help our local citizens. He wouldn't have done any of that without us."

"So you're the hero?" Zeke said. "I don't see that at all when I look at you."

The doctor shook his head. "He talked about those children to me sometimes. No specific details, of course, but said they were back in England growing up in a castle, but he meant to bring them here soon as he could. Meanwhile, there were needs right here. Then one day Laird was away, and his wife filled in for him. Simon came in and got a letter from his little girl saying she would come and live with him. It ruined everything. Laird and I, we just decided to help the community, that's all."

"By killing my brother," Eloise snapped. "How in the world could you possibly find that helpful?" She shook her head. "I see," she said slowly. "Once Theodore and Gennie arrived, he would have had to own up to his real name, so you would have had no power over him anymore."

"Mack," the doctor said. "Could you just take me on to jail now, and please be kind when you tell Dolly what I've done? I don't believe I want to talk about this anymore."

"Not yet," Zeke said. "You mentioned my wife, and I will have you finish that story."

The old man looked tired, even beyond his years. "Mack, do I have to?"

"You can tell it to me at the jailhouse or you can be a man and tell it to Zeke right here. Your choice."

His shoulders sagged. "Zeke, if I could fix all that or take it back, I would. I'm a healer. Hurting someone is not in my nature."

"Apparently it is," Eloise said.

He shook his head. "Simon sent for me to come and see to the both of them. Mrs. Potter had taken to her bed, and the little boy was sick with a stomachache. I gave them both a little something for sleep so neither of them would hear my conversation with Simon. See, he'd claimed he would tell Mack what we were up to, and we couldn't have that."

Anger bloomed into rage. Still, Zeke refused to give in to it. "How did they die?" he demanded through clenched jaw.

"Just like you were told. Fire got your wife and boy. Your wife crawled out, which is how she survived as long as she did."

"A fire that happened because they were unattended." He

glanced at Eloise and wrestled with his next question before finally deciding to ask it. "Where was Simon?"

The doctor looked away. "He got a dose too, only he thought I was just offering him something to help with his aching back. I didn't mean to give him the dose he got though. I was nervous. Angry. I just wanted him to believe we still had leverage. If he thought we would harm him, maybe he would keep using his money for good. My hands were shaking. I mixed it too strong, but I let him drink it anyway."

"How fast did it kill him?" Mack asked.

"Fast," Dr. Ross said. "I didn't know what to do. I took him home. We buried him in the pasture even though it seemed sacrilegious to have cows grazing over him."

"How kind of you," Eloise muttered as she swiped at a tear.

"You didn't put that man in your buggy alone," Mack said. "Who helped you?"

"Laird," he said defiantly. "He was there the whole time. Brought him with me on the house call because I knew Simon would be there. He took his responsibilities seriously, and he took good care of your wife and son, Zeke. It was me and Laird who let you down." He turned to Eloise. "And you. But we meant it all for good."

"I forgive you," she said. "But may God hold you accountable all the same."

"I fear he will," Dr. Ross said. "And I will accept what I deserve."

"Take him now, Mack," Zeke said. "I'll come write up my statement later. I figure you can do without Eloise coming into town to do that too."

Their eyes met. Mack nodded and then looked over to the empty cow pasture. "And I will see to the other issue too."

Long after the sheriff took the doctor away, Eloise remained sitting on the back steps watching the aspens shimmer between the purple, snow-topped Rocky Mountains and the lush green pasture where her brother had rested for more than a year.

She'd been so angry with James for so long, so very disappointed in him for not being the father she thought he ought to be. Regret refused to leave her as she shifted positions.

Zeke had done his best to hide the damage from the fires, but the smoke would take days to dissipate, and new boards would have to be added where the old wood was scarred by the flames. Minor things, but things that needed to be done all the same.

He eased down beside her, settling into a companionable silence. There was nothing to say that would make any of this better for either of them.

So she reached over to take his hand.

Then she rested her head on his shoulder.

And in that moment, Eloise knew everything would turn out just fine.

One year later. . .plus a few days. . .

Eloise sat on the back steps, watching the aspens shimmer between the purple, snow-topped Rocky Mountains and the lush green pasture. Gennie skipped out of the house, twirled three times, and landed beside her with a most unladylike plop.

The days and months had passed so quickly since that awful afternoon when she had to tell this sweet child that her papa wasn't coming back. Since then the town of Benton Springs had adopted both of them, making Eloise and Gennie feel more at home here than they ever felt in England.

Neither Dr. Ross nor Laird Anderson stood trial. Owing to their ages and the fact that Eloise pleaded for leniency, the men agreed to leave Benton Springs and the state of Colorado and never return. Despite that, Howard and Thomas and the remainder of the Anderson family had become close friends.

They, along with others from the town, made sure she had the best of care. The burned places on the back of the house were hidden long ago under new wood cut and planed by Zeke and put up and painted by the men of the town. James's cattle were back in the pasture, and thanks to Stillman's Mortuary, James had been laid to rest in the local cemetery.

At Gennie's insistence and the kind hearts at Stillman's, there was also a memorial stone with Theodore's name on it. And over the fireplace in the parlor was a painting of James done by Bud, the fellow who owned the hotel in town.

She often caught Gennie staring at it. The first time she found her there, Eloise asked what she was doing.

"Memorizing my papa," she said.

"I have something for you." Eloise pulled a letter out of her pocket and handed it to Gennie.

Eyes wide, she grinned. "It's from Cousin Emma." She opened the letter and read both sides of the paper and then smiled. "She loves living at Broderick Park." Gennie made a face. "She even likes that she doesn't have to go to school! Can you imagine?"

Eloise laughed. "Well, not everyone enjoys their lessons like you do."

Gennie feigned a serious expression. "I'm very excited for our science experiment tonight. Mrs. Rose is teaching us about the phases of the moon."

"And it will be full tonight," Eloise supplied. "Yes, you might have mentioned that a time or two."

A cry of, "Gennie," split the silence. "It's William," she said as she handed Eloise the letter and scrambled to her feet. "I have to go."

"Slow down," Eloise said. She hurried to catch up with the girl. Gennie had already crossed the long hall to emerge onto the front porch, and she was headed toward the wagon where William and his father were waiting for her.

"We'll have her home first thing after breakfast," Mack called.

"Tell Rose I appreciate her more than she will know." She turned her attention to Gennie. "Remember your manners, sweetheart."

"I will," Gennie said as she climbed up next to William and waved. "I love you, Mama."

Mama.

Eloise's heart soared. It happened every time. Somewhere between grief and gladness, she had officially become Gennie's mother. Her mama. And Eloise couldn't be happier.

Later, as the shadows began to gather and another buggy appeared on the horizon, Eloise amended that statement. There was another relationship in her life that also made her smile.

"Zeke," she said as she watched him climb down from the buggy a few minutes later. "Give me just a minute. I've left the picnic hamper right there on the porch next to the rocker."

She doused the lamps and grabbed a quilt and her shawl. While the weather was lovely this time of year, the nights could be chilly, especially where they were going. Not that she knew exactly, but Zeke had told her to prepare for a picnic under the stars.

"Good evening, beautiful," Zeke said with a smile as he enveloped her in an embrace and then helped her into the buggy. "I want to show you what I've been doing."

A few minutes later, he pulled the buggy to a stop in front of what appeared to be the beginnings of a building. She recognized neither the land nor this structure, although due to the short drive, it had to be adjacent to her own property.

"What is this?" she asked when he helped her down.

"Funny thing. That bunkhouse just isn't as comfortable as it used to be. I made a deal to sell my property to Mack's deputy, and then I found this place. Beautiful view, but it needs something."

Eloise grinned. "Like a house?"

He shrugged. "That would be a start. I do have a dining room though."

"I think that's wonderful. It is a fresh start for you, and we will be neighbors."

"Until I can convince you to marry me, that is."

He'd started asking about six months ago, and so far Eloise had turned him down every time. However, she suspected he had enlisted Gennie in the effort, for she had certainly been talking about how wonderful Mr. Zeke was more often than usual.

Eloise followed him around to where a beautiful table long enough for a dozen or more diners had been placed under the stars. "Zeke, what is this?"

"My dining room. Hold on and I'll light the chandeliers." He struck a match, and a few minutes later four torches illuminated the table. "Welcome, Miss Broderick. Will you join me?"

"It is lovely," she said, "but I would suggest adding some walls before winter."

He grinned. "Walls, yes, I will put that on the list. I had hoped you would help me with the design of this place, so that gives me hope."

"Zeke Potter, you are incorrigible."

"No," he corrected. "I am in love."

She smiled. "And I am very glad."

"Glad?" He shook his head.

"Glad I love you too. Now let's eat."

Later, after they had consumed their feast, Zeke carried the basket back to the buggy and then returned to the table to remove one of the torches from their makeshift dining room. "Follow me, former Special Constable Eloise Broderick of the London Metropolitan Police. I have one more surprise for you."

"Since you've referred to my former position as a constable, please tell me the surprise is not another pitch to become Mack's newest deputy. The answer is and will always be no."

He laughed. "No, and I tell him the same every time he asks. Now stop being so curious and come with me. It's going to require a little walk, but I promise it will be worth it."

She followed Zeke up the trail, the night air growing fresh as they ascended. Here the trees were thinner and the stars were brighter, even despite the torch and the full moon. After a while, Zeke paused to whistle. A moment later, a whistle of response set them off in that direction.

They emerged into a clearing with a view that took Eloise's breath away. To her surprise, a man was waiting for them. Seated in a chair that would have been at home in any fine dining room, the man had set up an easel and a canvas and was dabbing paints onto a piece of wood.

"Evening, friends," Bud said. "Lovely night, isn't it?"

"Remember when we first met at the hotel?" Zeke said. "I told you Bud likes to paint on the mountain at the full moon."

"It's the best light," Bud said.

"Tonight he is painting us," Zeke said.

"Us?" she said. "Why in the world would he do that?"

Zeke stepped in front of her and took her hand then knelt. "Because I made a promise to Gennie that I would have the moment her mama said yes to marrying me captured forever in a painting."

"Oh," she said as tears threatened.

"Want to know why?" he asked her.

"Because she wants to memorize us?" Eloise managed.

"Yes. Will you marry me, Eloise?"

This time she said yes.

Bestselling author **Kathleen Y'Barbo** is a multiple Carol Award and RITA nominee of more than eighty novels with almost two million copies in print in the United States and abroad. She has been nominated for a Career Achievement Award as well as a Reader's Choice Award, and is the winner of the 2014 Inspirational Romance of the Year by *Romantic Times* magazine. Kathleen is a paralegal, a proud military wife, and a tenth-generation Texan, who recently moved back to cheer on her beloved Texas Aggies. Connect with her through social media at www.kathleenybarbo.com.

Love Conquers Oil

by Annette O'Hare

Lady Bird had Lyndon,
Kemmie Lou had Red Adair,
Barbara had George H. W.,
And I have Dan O'Hare.
To my own Texas oilman
and the love of my life,
Daniel P. O'Hare

❧ *Chapter 1* ❧

1901

*F*ern Fisher left her house before sunrise in fear of being seen in the light of day. Stopping at the corner, she glanced down the alley to make sure no one tarried there before dashing toward the back entrance. Once safely inside the schoolhouse, she allowed herself to breathe.

The empty building creaked and moaned with her every step. Fern flinched at the eerie sounds that went unnoticed when boisterous students filled the hallways. Her classroom was up ahead; she walked faster. Slipping inside the room, she went straightway to her desk, hopeful for some busywork to clear her mind of the horror she'd witnessed the day before.

She reached for a stack of assignments that needed grading and

335

froze. Sensing a presence, her hand trembled and gooseflesh rose on her arms. A large, dark shadow of a man filled the doorway of her classroom. Fern gasped. Her eyes darted around the room. With nowhere to escape, she was trapped.

Fern's heart pounded when he walked into the classroom where her students would soon arrive. The man's face was hidden behind a mask pulled up below his eyes just as it had been the day before, but she knew full well who it was—not by identity, but by his evil deed. She raised her trembling hands toward him. He was alone.

Oh Father God, please don't let the children find my dead body.

He walked to her desk, a gun pointed straight at her. "We need to talk."

Tears burned Fern's eyes. "Please, don't shoot me."

The ominous-looking man stared into her soul. "What did you see, schoolmarm?"

His deep, gravelly voice was a chilling reminder of what the man was capable of. Fern shook her head. "I. . .I didn't see anything, and I don't know who you are, so please just go away and leave me alone!" Tears trickled down her cheeks.

"Good answer, sis. Because there'll be consequences if you do anything stupid."

Fern sucked in a deep breath when he pointed the pistol at Lillian Harper's desk and pulled back on the gun's hammer.

"You do something stupid like go to the police, and. . .*bang!*" He pretended to fire the gun. "Little Johnny won't be home for supper."

"No!" Fern covered her mouth.

"You tell anybody what you saw or that your buddy Mark was with me, and every desk in this classroom will represent a gravestone." He pulled back farther on the hammer, uncocking the gun. "You understand me?"

Fern nodded. More tears poured down as the faces of each one of her students flashed through her mind.

The horrible man aimed the gun at her head. "I don't think you believe what I'm saying, sis."

"Please," Fern begged. "I won't tell anyone! I promise!"

He sneered and cocked the pistol. Fern raised her arms, covering her face. She sucked in her last breath. He pulled the trigger. *Click.*

"*Ha, ha, ha, ha, ha!*"

Fern peeked out from behind shaking arms as the man backed out of her classroom and guffawed at her expense all the way down the hall. How could she possibly teach after such a harrowing experience?

"Lord, please help me," Fern sobbed into her trembling hands. "If that man is brazen enough to track me down at work, then what's keeping him from going to my home and. . ." She gasped, raising her head. "Aunt Matilda! Oh Lord, no."

Fern's mind raced. She had to come up with a way to protect her helpless aunt, but how? Bowing her head, she prayed.

"Heavenly Father, I come before Your throne. I pray You would calm Your child, Lord. I beseech You to show me the way You would have me protect my precious aunt, my students, and myself. And Lord, please make haste with Your answer, as time is of the essence. In Your Son's name I pray. Amen."

The familiar sound of her fellow teachers arriving drew Fern from her prayers to the task at hand—preparing herself to teach the daily lesson. Touching her cheek, she could only imagine how she must look. She removed the small bag of cosmetics she kept in her desk drawer and headed out of the classroom toward the ladies' room.

Fern wanted to make sure she looked her best on what would possibly be the last day she would ever spend with her coworkers and students.

⚜ Chapter 2 ⚜

Fern gazed at her rippled reflection in the train's window, hoping she wasn't making a terrible mistake. Who would have thought a simple schoolmarm from Springfield, Illinois, would be running for her life to a place called Beaumont, Texas?

What kind of idiot robs a bank in broad daylight, doesn't wear a mask, and in his hometown of all places? And that poor bank teller. . .

She squeezed her eyes shut and shook her head, but images of the dreadful crime she had witnessed refused to depart from her mind. If only she hadn't gone to the bank on that particular day, she wouldn't have made eye contact with Mark Stanley, and her life wouldn't be spinning out of control. She willed away the tears rimming her lower lids.

Fern had been confident that Mark would never harm her. His

accomplice, on the other hand, was a cold-blooded murderer—tracking her down at the schoolhouse, threatening to kill her and her students if she went to the law. She had no other choice but to leave the only place she'd ever called home for a part of the country she knew little about. But change wasn't always a bad thing. Perhaps God had a plan in moving her away from Springfield. She had no choice but to wait and find out what her future held.

Her chest shook, dragging in a labored breath. *Oh Mark. What on earth happened to the sweet boy I grew up with?*

Worst of all, Fern was abandoning poor old Aunt Matilda. Dementia took her aunt further and further away with each passing day. How would the poor thing manage without her? Would her cousin Olivia watch over Aunt Matilda as she'd promised? Fern blew out a long breath.

Lord, please take care of Auntie. . . .

Fern had prayed for an answer, and her salvation came in the form of a mail-order bride advertisement she happened upon in the *Illinois State Journal*. Even though the idea of marrying a perfect stranger seemed outlandish, Fern answered the newspaper ad. And upon reading Mr. Jesse Stewart's enticing missive, she decided Texas might be just the spot where a person could disappear.

"What if this man is nothing at all like he's made himself out to be, Fern? Have you even considered that option?"

The words Olivia had challenged her with goaded Fern. But what else could she do? She spent what money she had saved up on the train ticket to Texas. Her only hope was that Mr. Stewart was the decent, upstanding man he proclaimed to be on paper. There was no other option.

Beaumont, Texas. Fern rolled the strange name around in her head. *I wonder if there will be gunfights in the streets and tawdry saloon girls, like in the dime-store westerns.*

A chuckle bounced in her chest at the very thought of a town as overdramatized as those portrayed in her favorite reading material. However, having never ventured outside Illinois her entire life, a touch of excitement might not be such a bad thing. And if what the newspapers claimed was true, Beaumont, Texas, was sure to please. Fern lifted her hand to her chin and tapped her lips with a white-gloved finger, contemplating what lay ahead for her.

News of the Lucas Gusher at Spindletop, south of Beaumont, spread across the country like wildfire. Much like the California Gold Rush of forty-nine, droves of people migrated to the small southeast Texas town expecting to strike it rich. Not Fern—she traveled to Beaumont with the hope of getting lost in the crowd.

The train *clackity-clackity-clack*ed down the track, lulling Fern into a melancholy trance. With her head bent toward the window, she gazed at the most enormous pair of deer she'd ever seen, leaping across a field of amber straw. Thoughts of what she'd left behind and what lay ahead brought forth a hodgepodge of emotions, none of which were settling. Would Mark's partner in crime find out where she'd gone and make good on his threat? She didn't hold much stock in the idea, considering the depth of their criminal skills.

Her mind wandered to the romantic letter Mr. Jesse Stewart wrote and how marvelous his words made her feel inside. Would he make a suitable husband for her?

A quickening in Fern's heart thrust aside her rapturous ideas of matrimony. She sat up straight in her seat. A hand to her heart, she concentrated on slowing her breathing. She'd been so frightened and anxious to get out of town that she hadn't fully considered the consequences of her decision. The thought, the very notion of what she had done, scared the living daylights out of her.

Fern's demanding teaching position and her responsibilities for Aunt Matilda consumed all of her time and energy, leaving no occasion in her life for courting, men, or marriage. The innocent schoolmarm had never even been kissed.

Oh dear Lord, I've agreed to be someone's wife! And as his wife, he's going to expect me to...

"Memaw, why would you do this to me?" Jesse Stewart swiped the Stetson off his head and struck it against his thigh. Extending the wide-brimmed tan hat, he pointed at the old woman sitting on her front porch. "Of all your harebrained schemes, this has got to be the worst."

Jesse pinched the bridge of his nose, remorseful for his harsh words. He lowered his hat and waited for Memaw Stewart to defend herself, but she wouldn't even make eye contact with him. Instead, she reared back in her rocker and reached for her red tin of W. E. Garrett & Sons snuff from the windowsill where she kept it.

Sheriff Levi Woods leaned against a porch column, twisting a toothpick in his mouth and listening to their exchange. Jesse spread his arms wide and looked to his best friend for support.

The sheriff removed the toothpick and flicked it into a bush. "I don't know what you want me to do. She's your memaw." Levi chuckled and nodded toward the old woman. "And furthermore, I tend to agree with Memaw. It's high time you got yourself a wife. There's nothing like a good woman to put some meat on your bones." He patted his midsection. "Look what it's done for me."

Jesse's shoulders sagged. Levi's comments were all the fuel Memaw needed. She leaned forward and pointed at Jesse, the tin of snuff gripped tight in her hand. "You see there. Why don't you listen to your friend, the sheriff? You seem to do everything else he says. Why not now?"

Taken aback, Jesse rested his hand atop his sidearm. "And just what do you mean by that?"

"He talked you into wearing that silver star, didn't he?" Memaw's snuff tin now pointed accusingly at Levi. "You sure don't mind going out there and risking your life like a dern fool. So why won't you listen to some good advice for once?"

Levi raised his hands, deflecting her ire. "Whoa now, don't blame all this on me."

Jesse closed his eyes and scrubbed through the growth of whiskers on his jawline. He'd never won a war of words with Memaw. Why should this time be any different? He softened his tone. "Look, Memaw, there's plenty of pretty girls right here in Beaumont. I don't need you or anyone else writing letters to girls clear across the country on my behalf. What with our whole town in a state of chaos ever since the oil strike, I don't have time for a wife anyway. You of all people should know that—sitting there on your front porch with your shotgun at the ready to defend your land."

He kicked a rock with the tip of his boot. "Besides, what kind of woman wants to marry a man who has to have his memaw do his courtin' for him? It makes me look plumb pitiful."

Memaw relaxed in her rocker, a satisfied grin on her face. "You'll be happy to know she don't know it was me writin' them letters."

Jesse's eyes darted from Memaw to Levi and back again. "What do you mean she don't know it was you?"

"Because I signed your name to them, of course."

"Aw, Memaw." Jesse's head dipped back as he imagined all the embarrassing things his grandmother might have said to the girl.

Levi's laughter galled him. "There you go, Jesse. Memaw's done all the work. She baited the hook and got her to bite. All you gotta do is reel her in and marry her when she gets here."

Memaw pounded the snuff tin against her frail palm, packing tight the powdery tobacco. "From what she said in her letter, she sounds like a real good-lookin' woman. Her name's Fern Fisher, and she's got long yellow hair. Oh, and she's a schoolmarm too. I think you're gonna be real pleased when you see her."

Jesse stared at the woman in disbelief. "Memaw, did it ever occur to you that she might not have been completely honest about her looks? For all you know she could be bald, toothless, humpbacked, and—"

"Aw, come on now," Levi interrupted. "I'm sure she looks fine. Now what you gotta worry about is whether or not she's coming here in hopes of marrying a rich oil man."

A smirk twisted Jesse's face. "Yeah, we got enough of that going on around here. That's for sure."

Memaw lifted the lid off the snuff tin. "Well, you ain't no rich oil man, so you don't got to worry about that." She grabbed a pinch of tobacco and slid the dark wad between her bottom lip and gum. "And as long as that's all she knows, there won't be no problem."

Jesse slid the tan Stetson back on top of his head. "When is this Miss Fern Fisher supposed to arrive?"

Leaning over the side of her rocker, Memaw made a deposit into her coffee can spittoon before speaking. "Her train is due first thing tomorrow morning. And I expect you to be here when she arrives."

"*Ooo-wee!* Come on, Jesse, we gotta get back to town."

Jesse numbly turned to Levi. "Why? What's going on?"

Levi walked over to Jesse and draped an arm around his shoulders. "I gotta get you in for a shave and haircut before the barber closes up shop." He tugged at one of Jesse's overgrown dark locks. "We can't have you looking like a scruffy cowhand when your lady love arrives."

"Oh, good thinking, Sheriff. And make sure he slaps on some of that toilette water in the morning so he smells good too." Memaw wiped spittle off her chin with the bottom of her apron.

Levi answered with a hearty, "Yes, ma'am," tipped his hat to the little woman, and led Jesse toward the post where their horses were hitched. "This is downright exciting, don't you think?"

Jesse untied his horse and mounted up. "If you think watching your best friend get thrown into the lions' den is exciting, then I suppose you're right."

Levi laughed as he climbed onto his horse. "Well. . .what do you plan on doing about all this?"

Jesse bumped the mare's flanks. The horse nickered and turned toward the road to town. "Well, first I need to talk to the Boss and see what He thinks I ought to do. Then I reckon I'll have my answer come morning time."

"Sounds like a good plan to me."

Jesse clicked his tongue and urged his horse on with a gentle nudge. Levi's gold-colored gelding followed behind his ruddy mare, and they took off, leaving a cloud of red dust behind them. And though he would never let on to either Levi or Memaw, Jesse was intrigued with the idea of meeting the schoolmarm with the long yellow hair. Maybe his grandmother's idea of fishing somewhere other than the local pond wasn't as crazy as it seemed.

❧ Chapter 3 ❧

Three disquieting whistle blasts signaled that the train approached the station. When the locomotive jerked to a stop and the train's steel wheels squealed in protest, Fern was thankful she'd decided against breakfast. She was anxious and fearful of what lay ahead, and her stomach roiled like a tempest and would not have tolerated one of the hardboiled eggs or buttermilk biscuits she'd packed for the journey.

Raising the window sash, Fern squinted against the bright sunlight shining through the glass and had her first glimpse of the town. She gasped at the image and covered her mouth as she sank down in her seat. Did her eyes deceive her? What appeared before her made the Wild West towns depicted in her dime-store novels seem tame in comparison.

Fern drew in a deep breath and sat up straight to take another look. The crisscrossed wooden slats of an absurd number of oil der-ricks blurred her eyes and blocked out the horizon. Deep wheel ruts lined the muddy street. Every manner of transportation known to man clogged the main thoroughfare. There were saloons and bawdy houses aplenty. Peddlers paraded about like prideful peacocks hawking everything from local land maps and medicinal tonics to souvenir bottles of a black liquid labeled with three large letters, *OIL.*

Throngs of men, women, and even children tottered about the crowded mucky avenue, flocking to slipshod-built establishments only to stand in long lines waiting to purchase their wares. The town was a veritable den of pandemonium, the likes of which Fern had never seen. So much depravity, and all of it a disappointing result of what the discovery of oil could do. Her desire was to become lost in a crowd, and she had certainly chosen the right place to do so.

Gathering her nerve and her belongings, Fern made her way toward the rear door of the train—and that's when it hit her. An odor permeated the air like nothing she'd ever experienced before. The stench that hit her square in the olfactory senses smelled like a disgusting mixture of sulfur, rancid grease, and horse manure. Her first instinct to cover her nose wasn't possible with both arms loaded with luggage. But even if her destination didn't live up to her expectations, Fern had no desire to spend one more minute on the train. She would have to endure it.

A young man stood on the platform at the bottom of the stairs leading off the train. He wore a smart blue suit, crisply starched and pressed. A black stripe running down the side of his trousers matched the one on the cap sitting atop his head.

"Ma'am," he said, tipping his hat and relieving Fern of her bags. Hefting the luggage onto the ground, he held her hand as she stepped down the short set of stairs.

"Thank you." Fern smoothed out her skirt and opened her reticule. The attendant thrust his palm toward her.

Surely he doesn't think I owe him a tip for moving my luggage two feet. She raised her eyebrows and continued rummaging in her clutch.

"Ah, here it is." Fern produced a folded piece of paper and handed it to the young porter. "Would it be possible to arrange transportation to this address?"

He took the note from her hand and smirked. "Sure, lady." Unfolding the paper, the attendant scoffed when he read what she had written. "Going out to the Stewart place, huh?"

Fern was taken aback, as she hadn't included a name with the address she had given him. "Yes. Are you familiar with the Stewarts?"

"Sure, Mrs. Stewart has lived around these parts longer than most."

Surprised, Fern lowered her chin. "Excuse me, did you say, Mrs. Stewart?"

"Yeah, but most everyone around here just calls her Memaw." He chuckled. "You gotta watch out for Memaw Stewart. She's as wily as a fox and as cunning as a raccoon!"

Fern's mind was a muddle of confusion. "Memaw? Who is Memaw? I. . .I'm here to meet a Mr. Jesse Stewart."

The attendant's lips turned down at the corners. "Oh, is that right?"

"Yes, it is." Fern's brow wrinkled. "Now if you don't mind." She pointed to the note in his hand.

"Oh yeah, right. Well, he's usually in town around this time, but I haven't seen him all day." The young man turned to the bustling roadway, raised his hand, and waved. "Hey, Burton, over here!"

It was a wonder anyone heard him over the cacophony of motorcars, bicycles, and horse carts jamming the street. The carriage driver whose name he called out pulled back on his horse's reins and looked their direction. Giving the attendant a nod, he slowly maneuvered his buggy through the busy thoroughfare toward the railroad platform.

Fern huffed out a deep breath. Everything seemed to move slower in the South—including the people. It wasn't her nature to exercise impatience, but having traveled so far on a bed of frazzled nerves, her tolerance had all but run out.

The carriage pulled up next to the platform. Lifting her bags into the back of the buggy, the station attendant handed the driver the handwritten address. "Here ya go, Burton."

Fern sized up her driver as he looked down through small round spectacles perched at the end of his nose and read the paper he'd been given. Thin as a spindle, slow as a slug, a white beard that hung down to his waist, and smoking a long-stemmed pipe—Fern sensed no imminent threat.

"The lady needs a ride out to the Stewart place," the young porter said.

"Uh-huh." The driver shoved the address in his shirt pocket as thick white smoke flowed from his lips and pooled in a fluffy cloud around his head. He turned his gaze to Fern. "You ready, ma'am?"

Fern forced her gawking eyes away from the peculiar little man long enough to answer. "Um, yes. Of course." She managed a shaky smile and handed the train station attendant a coin from her clutch before allowing him to help her onto the carriage bench.

"Thank you, ma'am." The young man pocketed the coin and tipped his hat to her.

Fern nodded at him and turned to her driver. "Shall we then?"

"Yep."

The slow-moving older gentleman raised the reins and let them fall on the horse's rump. Fern wondered if the animal even felt it. She surmised it had when the sway-backed steed clopped out into the swarm of traffic.

Fern pressed a handkerchief over her nose and mouth, dampening the smell as the carriage sluggishly rolled through downtown Beaumont. The town faded behind them, offering her a far nicer view of Southeast Texas. The acrid odor followed them, but mixed with the sweet country air, it became somewhat tolerable. Soon she was able to breathe without the aid of her hanky.

"Whew. . .the town has quite the awful smell, doesn't it?" Fern chuckled so her driver wouldn't think she was completely rude.

"Yep," he replied without taking his eyes off the road. "Some people says that's the smell of money."

Fern's brows rose. "Is that so?"

"Yep."

Was oil really as profitable a commodity as was touted in the newspaper's business pages? It was no wonder so many flocked to Beaumont in search of it.

Stands of tall, spindly pine trees like those she'd seen on her train ride replaced the wooden oil derricks in town. Offshoots of the Neches River stretched out watery fingers that almost touched the route they followed. Fern watched a large bird swoop down and grab a fish in its talons. Taking in the beautiful countryside, she reckoned she could easily get used to living there.

"Not much farther now."

It startled Fern when her driver spoke, not having said a word for some time. Her hand went to her chest. "Oh?"

"Yep."

Fern attempted to engage the man in conversation. "So, um, Burton, is it?"

"Yep."

"Yes, Burton, what can you tell me about Mr. Stewart?"

Burton took the long-stemmed pipe from between his lips, the tobacco long since extinguished, and held it on his lap. "You talkin' 'bout Jesse? 'Cause this here's the way to Memaw's place."

Fern pursed her lips, perturbed with the man who talked as slow as his horse walked. "Who is this Memaw I keep hearing about? And what—"

"Now Jesse's place is connected to Memaw's. Ain't far at all. You want me to take you there instead?"

She wasn't sure how to answer. Should she allow a man she didn't know to take her somewhere other than where she'd been directed? Considering she had known her driver longer than she had Mr. Stewart, Fern decided to stay on course.

She released a long sigh. "No. . .I suppose we should continue to. . .Memaw's place."

Mr. Slow and Steady let out a deep throaty chuckle. "Now you gotta watch your step around Memaw Stewart. And whatever you do, don't get between Memaw and that shotgun of hers." He laughed again. "Or she might just use it on you."

Despite her driver's laughter, Fern was overcome with dread and gripped her handbag like a vise. "Excuse me? What are you talking about?"

Burton stared straight ahead and jutted out his chin. "Why don't you see for yourself?"

She turned to see what it was Burton gestured toward. The wagon rolled up a long drive, and a beautiful white farmhouse with green trim sprawled before her eyes. And just as Fern had been warned, a little old woman sat in a rocking chair on the front porch, a double-barreled shotgun poised in her hands.

Fern grabbed Burton's arm. She was on the verge of asking him to turn around and leave when the screen door opened and out stepped an honest-to-goodness Texas cowboy. He exchanged words with the one called Memaw, and she leaned the shotgun against the clapboard wall behind her. The tall, muscular man hopped off the porch. He skipped the steps, and Fern's heart skipped a beat.

Burton guided the carriage up to the farmhouse, giving Fern a closer view of the big man. With a sigh, her fears were forgotten. She released her tight grip on Burton's arm and quickly smoothed her windblown hair and wrinkled skirt. Fern regretted not stopping in town to powder her nose and tidy up a bit. She wanted—no, needed—to look her best, because the handsomest man she'd ever seen sauntered straight toward her.

❧ *Chapter 4* ❧

"Put that shotgun down before you scare her away." Jesse let the screen door slam shut behind him.

Memaw's lips curled into a wicked little grin. "You don't want me to scare her away, because you think she's purdy, don't you?"

"Dang it, Memaw. Would it be too much to ask that you mind your own business, just this once?"

The old woman cackled. "I notice you took my advice and wore your Sunday best. That was smart of you."

Jesse scowled at her. "Don't you think you should get in the kitchen? Your beans are going to boil over the pot."

"Now you're just trying to get rid of me," Memaw retorted.

He grimaced. "Pretty clever of you to figure that out."

Jesse clenched his teeth and hopped off the porch. From what he could see through the kitchen window, the woman sitting in

Burton's carriage was mighty good-lookin' indeed. Regardless, Memaw had no right roping him into something he hadn't bargained for.

Tromping toward the carriage, Jesse made it a point not to make eye contact with the woman. He nodded at the driver and handed him cash to cover the fare. "Burton."

"Thank you, Jesse," Burton answered, counting the cash in his palm. "You need to fetch her bags out the back there."

Hoisting her luggage from the buggy made Jesse's nightmare become a reality. Unable to avoid the situation any longer, he removed his hat and looked up at the woman seated on the bench next to Burton. She gazed back at him with eyes the color of a Texas summer sky. He no longer felt the tight grip he had clamped onto the brim of his hat.

"Howdy, ma'am. I'm Jesse Stewart."

The woman touched her brightly colored cheek, a bashful smile on her lips. "It's nice to meet you, Jesse Stewart." She extended a gloved hand. "I'm Fern Fisher."

Fearing he'd drop his hat, Jesse put it back on his head. "Miss Fisher." He gently shook her hand.

"Help her out of the carriage!" Memaw hollered.

Jesse cringed. "Um, here, let me help you down." He put his hands around the young woman's waist and lifted her out of the carriage.

"Thank you," she said, smoothing her skirt.

"Goodness, you're as light as a sack of down feathers." Jesse immediately regretted speaking before thinking and was thankful when she changed the subject.

"I presume the woman on the porch is Memaw." She looked up at him with a smile. "I've heard a lot about her since arriving in town."

He smiled and bowed his head, embarrassed his grandmother's reputation had preceded her. "Yes, ma'am, that's Memaw."

Jesse retrieved her bags. "Come on. I'll introduce you."

"I'm glad you got her to lower the gun." She chuckled and walked beside him.

"What? Oh. . .well, there's a reason she totes that gun around everywhere."

"Oh?"

Miss Fisher's blue eyes fluttered, momentarily distracting him. "Uh, yes, ma'am, ever since they struck oil at Spindletop, she's had many a scoundrel wanting to buy parcels of her land for cheap— and for good reason too. Her property is in a prime location."

"Is that right?"

"Yes, ma'am. Anyway, she carries that shotgun to ward off all the trespassers wanting to drill on her land. That's also why the sheriff deputized me."

"So, you're a deputy?"

Jesse swelled with pride at her immediate interest in his current situation. "Um-hmm. The sheriff needs all the help he can get. The town's not what it used to be. People are crawling out of the woodwork, thinking they're going to strike it rich."

"Yes, I witnessed the crowds firsthand when I arrived."

Jesse stopped at the porch, his arms laden with bags covered in a yellow flowery pattern. He turned to the beauty standing next to him and sighed. "Miss Fisher, I'd like to introduce you to Mrs. Eva-Lynn Stewart, or as she's known by everyone around these parts, Memaw."

Memaw stood and tucked her folded hands beneath her chin. "Oh my goodness. Miss Fisher, you are more beautiful than I, uh, we imagined. Come here to Memaw."

Jesse stared at the old woman speaking with the sugary-sweet voice and wondered what had happened to his grandmother. Miss Fisher took the bait like a hungry perch. She stepped up onto the porch and tumbled into Memaw's outstretched arms.

"You are too kind, Mrs. Stewart."

"No, no, you can call me Memaw like everyone else."

"Well, if you insist. . .Memaw." The young woman giggled.

You've got to be kidding me. Jesse shook his head, exasperated with his grandmother's deception.

Memaw patted the young woman's back and ushered her toward the door. She looked over her shoulder at Jesse. "Leave those bags on the porch. We can take care of them later. And would you please bring my shotgun, honey?" She turned back to her new best friend. "Now let's get you inside. You must be worn out after your long journey."

Honey? You aren't fooling me, old woman.

Fern's mouth watered from the delicious smells in the quaint country kitchen "Oh Mrs. . . .um. . . .Memaw, you shouldn't have gone to all this trouble."

"Oh hush, it ain't no trouble at all." Memaw ushered Fern to the table and pulled out a chair for her. "You sit down and relax and let me and Jesse take care of you."

The woman ladled beans into a serving bowl from a big pot on the stovetop while her grandson carved a roast. When all the food was served, Jesse set a pitcher of water on the table and sat down across from Fern. Memaw gripped the back of a chair, and a smile graced her thin face.

"Jesse?" Memaw said.

He nodded and turned to Fern. "Let's pray."

She bowed her head and listened to Jesse Stewart ask the blessing.

"Heavenly Father, hallowed be Thy name in all the earth. We thank You for delivering this young woman safely to our door. Lord, I pray for those who may need Your divine help in considering the decisions they make and how they may affect those around them. We thank You for this food, Lord. Bless it to our bodies and our bodies to Your service. Amen."

Fern opened her eyes and glanced at Jesse. "That was a lovely prayer, Jesse." She picked up her napkin and placed it on her lap. "Strange, but lovely."

"Thank you, Miss Fisher," he said, staring at Memaw with icy cold eyes.

Memaw took her seat and extended her hand. "Let me serve your plate, Fern."

"Thank you, Memaw."

She handed the woman her dish. Not knowing what to do with her hands, Fern picked up the pitcher and poured water into the blue glasses at each table setting. She stole a glance at the handsome man across from her as he filled his plate. He split apart two corn bread muffins, laid them out flat, and drowned them with pinto beans.

Fern determined that Jesse must be a hardworking man. Otherwise, how could he maintain such a firm, lean body with his hearty appetite? Realizing Jesse saw her ogling his muscles, she snapped her head around and hoped her cheeks weren't turning as red as they felt.

"Here you go, honey." Memaw handed her the plate and chuckled. "I gave you an extra portion of beef. You look like you could afford some meat on your bones."

Fern took it from her, grateful for the distraction. She dug into the fork-tender, melt-in-your-mouth roast beef. It tasted delectable. She didn't even realize she'd made an *mmm* sound chewing the meat. Not until she noticed both Memaw and Jesse staring at her.

Jesse chuckled. "I guess you like Memaw's cooking, huh?"

Embarrassed more than before, Fern covered her mouth and finished her bite. "I'm sorry, but everything tastes so delicious, and I'm starving. I haven't eaten a thing all day."

"No need being sorry. Memaw's a good cook. And it's nice seeing a woman enjoy a meal." Jesse motioned at her with his fork. "Go on and eat."

The remainder of the meal was spent for the most part in silence except for polite conversation about her long train ride and the weather. When Memaw began scraping food scraps into a pile, it was apparent the meal was over. Fern dove in to help her clean up.

Jesse pushed his chair away from the table, and she noticed he was watching her work. Her shoulders tensed under his scrutiny. He had, after all, inquired for a wife. It was logical he would want to know if she was any good at being one.

He crossed his legs and cleared his throat. Fern ceased removing the dishes and gave him a sideways glance. He looked straight at her.

"Miss Fisher, there's a matter we need to talk about."

Fern tipped her head slightly, and a foreboding chill traveled up her spine. "Oh?"

Crash!

Fern jumped at the sound and turned to see what had broken behind her.

"Oh for goodness' sake. Would you just look at what I did?" The shattered remains of one of the pretty blue glasses lay at Memaw's feet. "Fern, honey, would you mind fetching the broom and dustpan from the back porch?"

"Yes, ma'am."

Fern went in the direction Memaw pointed to get the supplies she requested. Once out of the room, she heard a string of hushed questions flying between the two of them. Neither party sounded happy.

What is going on here? Did Memaw break that glass on purpose to get me out of the room?

She found the broom and dustpan hanging on the wall and headed back to the kitchen with them. All conversation ceased when she returned. Memaw smiled, but her ruddy cheeks told a different story. Jesse's expression said but one thing—he was mad.

"Thank you, honey." Memaw took the items.

"You're welcome." Fern shied away and leaned against a row of cabinets.

Jesse huffed out a chest full of air. "I'm sorry, Miss Fisher, but as I was saying before Memaw *accidentally* broke that glass, there's something we need to talk about."

"But we haven't had dessert yet," Memaw exclaimed, practically hollering. "We have some delicious lemon meringue pie waiting for us in the pie safe."

Jesse pounded his fist against the kitchen table. "Memaw, that's enough!"

Fern flinched. Her senses were on high alert. She covered her fiery hot cheeks with her palms. *Oh Lord. . .what have I gotten myself into now? Out of the frying pan and into the fire.*

She looked at Memaw, whose head hung low. Anger welled up inside Fern at the man who'd caused the precious woman's pain.

Fern stared at Jesse, indignation burning in her eyes. He shook his head, looking as though he was the innocent party. But Fern knew better. She marched over to Memaw, glass crunching beneath her shoes, and stood as her champion.

Fern pointed a shaky finger at the offender. "How dare you talk to this sweet, sweet woman like that? Why, I know schoolboys with better manners than you have. Now you listen to me, Mr. Stewart. Whatever it is you need to say can't be more important than this poor dear woman wanting to serve some of the homemade lemon meringue pie she slaved to make for you."

Finished with her rant, Fern dropped her accusing finger to her side. Memaw put an arm around her waist and squeezed tight.

Jesse didn't respond. He didn't even look at them. Instead, he sat there rubbing his jaw like he had been punched.

Fern was quite satisfied with the results of her scolding.

After a minute or two, Jesse looked up at the two women, smiled, and nodded at them. "You know. . .now that you mention it, lemon meringue pie does sound pretty good." The big man stood, filling up his side of the room.

Relieved, Fern released the breath she'd been holding. She smiled at the little woman standing beside her and said, "I'll get the plates."

Jesse leaned against the doorway to the living room and crossed his arms over his chest. "I sure hope that pie is extra sweet."

"Oh, it is." Memaw moved toward the pie safe to fetch the dessert.

"That's good to hear."

Both women stopped what they were doing and turned toward Jesse, who had pushed off the doorframe.

He spoke directly to Fern. "Miss Fisher, you better hope that pie is as sweet as she says it is." He scoffed. "You're gonna need something extra sweet in your mouth to stomach the bitter news that old woman needs to share with you."

Fern turned to Memaw. She didn't understand the weak smile pasted on her face, but she knew for sure that something was terribly wrong.

Memaw pointed to the cabinets behind Fern. "The forks are in that drawer, honey."

Jesse looked at Fern, shook his head, and smiled. "I'll be in the living room waiting for that pie."

Fern's jaw went slack. The huge meal she had eaten felt like it was trying to make an escape. What had Memaw done? What did it have to do with her—and Jesse?

Nothing could be half as bad as the crazy notions her mind was concocting. She took three forks from the drawer and placed them beside the stack of dishes. The last thing she wanted was a big slice of lemon meringue pie. But if Memaw insisted they have dessert before she learned the mysterious secret news, then pie she would have.

❧ Chapter 5 ❧

$\mathcal{M}$emaw Stewart's famous lemon meringue pie had won more than its share of awards over the years. Her lemon filling had just the right sweet-to-tart ratio, and her meringue peaks were so tall the pie barely fit inside the oven.

Jesse set aside his pie when the bite in his mouth went bitter on his tongue. He snuck a glimpse at Miss Fern Fisher on the settee across from him, her untouched pie perched precariously atop her knees. The poor woman looked like she was next in line for the gallows. Jesse wiped his mouth with a napkin and sat back in his chair. "Might as well get this over with."

Memaw dipped her head to the side. Her countenance pleaded for Jesse to remain quiet. He shook his head and blew out a deep breath.

"Miss Fisher, I want to start off by saying you are the bravest woman I've ever met. Anyone who would up and leave everything behind has got to be fearless and confident in my book. And any man would be lucky to have a wife as beautiful and—I'm assuming, since you're a teacher—as smart as you."

The woman's hand shook as she set her pie plate on the coffee table. "Thank you, Mr. Stewart."

Jesse's shoulders drooped. He hated the job he had to do. "You see, ma'am." He spread his hands out before him. "The news I've been beatin' around the bush about. . ." He glared at Memaw. "What my grandmother doesn't want me telling you is this."

Memaw placed her hands between the folds of her skirt and hung her head. Jesse sighed. "I didn't write those letters to you, Miss Fisher—Memaw did." He hooked his thumb toward his embarrassed grandmother.

"I'm sorry, but I didn't know she'd done it, and furthermore, I don't know why she did it in the first place when I'm not even ready to get married."

Jesse watched Miss Fisher's expression change from fear to disbelief in a matter of seconds. Her rosy cheeks bloomed to a fiery crimson red.

Miss Fisher rose from the settee and railed at Jesse. "You mean to tell me I came all the way from Illinois thinking I was going to marry the perfect man and he doesn't even exist?"

Jesse held up his hand to the enraged woman. "Now, ma'am, I can see how mad you are, but let me remind you that it isn't me you should be mad at."

She got the message, because she turned to Memaw, but she no longer yelled. In fact, she whimpered like a whipped dog. "How could you do this to me? Or him, your own grandson?"

Memaw looked up at the fractured woman. Tears ran down

her face. "I'm so sorry, Miss Fisher. It wasn't supposed to turn out this way."

Jesse hated to see women cry, especially when it was Memaw or a beautiful, blond schoolmarm. He stood, aiming to remedy the situation. "Miss Fisher, I'd like to add my apologies to Memaw's. Now, I'd understand completely if you want to get on the next train out of town and go straight back to. . .to. . ."

"Illinois," Memaw informed Jesse.

"Yes, Illinois. And I'd be more than happy to pay for your ticket."

Jesse put his hand on Miss Fisher's petite shoulder and waited for her reply. Her bottom lip quivered, and she looked from his hand to his face before shrinking down onto the settee. The poor girl's chest heaved with her sobbing.

"I can't go back home now. Everyone knows I came here to get married. I'd be the laughingstock of Springfield when folks find out what Memaw did to me." She laid her head on the arm of the settee and bawled.

Her weeping broke Jesse's heart. Memaw had pulled a lot of crazy stunts in her day, but nothing as bad as this. He'd never been so mad at her as he was now.

Memaw left her chair and sat next to her. She rested her wrinkled hand on the girl's knee. "I can't tell you how sorry I am for the way things turned out. But you've got to believe me when I tell you I only did it with the best of intentions for you and that boy over there."

The young woman raised her head. "How can you possibly believe that? You write letters, forging your grandson's name on them. You falsify yourself to me and lure me away from my hometown. If those are your best intentions, I'd hate to see your worst."

"But Fern." Memaw's sad droopy eyes appealed to the young

woman. "I just don't know how that boy will ever find a wife without my help."

"Memaw!" Jesse hollered. "I don't need anyone's help to find a wife—especially not yours." He flopped down onto a chair and huffed at his grandmother.

Memaw rolled her eyes. "Don't listen to him, Fern. He's just too ornery to admit he needs my help."

"Oh come on now!" Jesse threw up his hands, exhausted with the old woman's cantankerous ways.

"Listen to me, Fern. When I read your letter, I knew you were perfect for my Jesse." Memaw patted her knee and smiled warmly. "Bless his heart. . .he's a good boy, but he needs to settle down with a good woman and stop hopping from one crazy scheme to the next."

Jesse wanted to stuff a cork in Memaw's mouth, but he let her continue. Maybe she would say something to make Miss Fisher feel better about what she'd done to her.

Her tears had stopped. Her brow furrowed at Memaw. "What do you mean by that?"

"Honey, just in the past few years that boy has tried his hand at being a rancher, a farmer, and now the crazy fool is playing sheriff's deputy with his best friend, Sheriff Woods. And with all the craziness going on in town, I'm afraid he's going to get himself killed!"

The young woman's jaw dropped. She took Memaw's hand in hers. "Oh my word, you poor dear. Is he not able to keep a steady job?"

Memaw waved off her question. "No, no, it's not that. My Jesse's a good worker. He's just never satisfied." Her eyes grew wide. "You see, that's why I think he needs someone like you. A strong, educated, godly young woman who can help steer him in the right direction."

Jesse drummed his fingers on the chair arm. How had Memaw suddenly won the heart of Miss Fern Fisher, especially after what she'd done to the poor woman?

"Excuse me, ladies, but do you not see me sitting right here? I can hear everything you're saying about me."

"Hush, Jesse," Memaw said. She turned her attention back to Miss Fisher and patted their joined hands. "I just hate seeing the boy all alone. And he's not getting any younger. I'm afraid he's too old to find a suitable bride at twenty-eight."

Jesse stopped listening to the women chattering and started watching the mysterious creature talking to Memaw. He could tell by the empathy in her eyes and how she held Memaw's hand that she had already forgiven her. What kind of woman does that?

Well, Miss Schoolmarm from Springfield, you're a better person than I am.

"You're welcome to stay here with me for as long as you'd like. I have plenty of room for the both of us." Memaw released Fern's hand. "That is, of course, if you can find it in your heart to forgive a silly old woman."

Jesse shook his head at what he referred to as "Memaw's poor little old me" act.

"Oh Memaw, I can't stay angry with you. I know you only did what you had to because you love your grandson and only want what's best for him."

Memaw fanned flushed cheeks with her hand. "Fern Fisher, you are the sweetest thing I've ever met. I think I'm going to cry."

Miss Fisher cooed at the old woman. "Come here, you." And they fell into each other's arms.

You've got to be kidding me. That's all it took. . .and it's over now?

"Would you just look at me? I'm a mess." Fern dabbed at her teary eyes with the back of her hand.

"Come on in the kitchen, and we'll get you freshened up. Then I want you to tell me everything there is to know about Springfield, Illinois."

Memaw stood and waited for Fern. Before the two women left the room, Memaw spoke to Jesse over her shoulder. "Gather up them dishes for me, would ya, hon?"

Jesse didn't reply. Instead, his gaze remained glued to the wall across the way, contemplating the bizarre conversation that had taken place before his eyes. He clasped his hands atop his belly and tapped his thumbs together, deep in thought.

Lord, I may be amiss in my thinking, but what just happened leads me to believe You must have had something to do with it. Otherwise, why would that sweet young woman forgive Memaw after what she did to her? Lord, it probably would have been easier to part the Neches River than accomplish what You did between those two women. . . .

Jesse pinched the bridge of his nose and released a long sigh. God tugged at his heart like He never had before. He suddenly felt sorry for a woman he didn't even know. And for some odd reason, he felt the need to make it up to her. Was he really that lonely, or was Fern Fisher just that comely?

Why do You want to do this to me, Lord? I know I've been praying for the right woman to come along, but not like this. Things are fine just the way they are, right? Right?

Pushing up from the chair, Jesse tromped across the room. He stood in the kitchen doorway, waiting for Memaw and Miss Fisher to notice him. The two women sat at the table. Deep in lively conversation, they didn't notice him.

"*Ahem!*"

They whipped their heads toward him, smiles on their faces.

"Oh Jesse," Memaw said. "Fern and I were about to have a cup of coffee. Would you like to join us?"

"Memaw, that can wait." Jesse stepped into the room, his expression resolute. He puffed out his chest, his fists firmly planted on his hips—as any righteous man would.

"Oh?"

"Yes, ma'am. There's something I need to say. And I'd better say it before I lose my nerve."

Memaw looked at him, fear in her eyes. "Now, Jesse. . ."

He held up his hand, cutting her off. "Just. . .just please. . .listen to what I have to say."

Jesse turned his attention to Fern. "Miss Fisher, now that everything is out in the open, you know it was Memaw and not me who asked you to come down here."

"Yes." She narrowed her eyes.

"I want you to know that I'm a man of my word. And even if the words used to coax you into coming here weren't mine, I'm willing to honor them."

Jesse could tell by the look on the woman's face that he had confused her. He held his hand out and continued, attempting to make his meaning plain.

"What I'm trying to say is. . .Miss Fisher, if you're still willing to get married, I'm obliged to hold up my end of the bargain and go through with it."

Her lips tightened. "Thank you, but I'm going to need some time to make up my mind. Why don't you come back in a week, and I'll let you know my decision." The young woman jumped up from her chair and headed out the back door.

Memaw's hands were poised to clap but instead dropped to her side. She stared at the door Fern exited through and then at Jesse. "What just happened?"

His mouth turned down at the corners, and he pointed toward the door. The troubled look on Memaw's face made him wonder what his own eyes must look like. He had much to say, but none of it being wholesome, he settled on one word, "Women!"

Memaw spread her hands open, her eyes pleading with him. "I–I'm so sorry she done you that way, boy. Let me go outside and talk to her, and I'm sure I can get her to change her mind."

"Oh no you don't!" Jesse tightened his fists and squeezed his eyes shut for a moment. "You've done quite enough already, old woman. Just let her be. I'll honor her wishes and come back next week."

His feisty grandmother looked as timid as a kitten, wringing her hands together. "All right then, son."

He turned and walked out of the kitchen and the house. He needed some fresh air—quick.

Memaw ran after him and called to him through the door. "You know I love you, right?"

Jesse ignored her, mounted his horse, and rode off toward home. Even though the woman had turned the tables on him, he reasoned that Miss Fisher deserved a break after what Memaw had done to her. Nevertheless, he hated himself for allowing it to happen.

What kind of dern fool asks a complete stranger to marry him?

Jesse rolled his eyes when another troubling thought crossed his mind. Once his buddy Levi found out what happened, he would be in for a full week of nonstop heckling.

Lord, can I please stop digging now? I think the hole I'm in is plenty deep enough.

❧ Chapter 6 ☙

*F*ern ran her finger down the page to the verse she'd underlined in the book of Jeremiah and read the encouraging words. " 'For I know the thoughts that I think toward you, saith the Lord, thoughts of peace, and not of evil, to give you an expected end.'"

Hmm, was Your expected end for me to marry a man I have absolutely nothing in common with, Lord? Maybe I should have made him wait one more week.

In her two weeks as a married woman, there was many an occasion when Fern doubted the permanence of their union. She closed the book and set it on the dinner table in Jesse's spacious home. Taking in the adjoined kitchen and family room, she considered what need a bachelor would have for such a large place to live. Was he expecting to sire a big family some day? There were so many bedrooms. One of which Jesse had graciously allowed her to sleep in—alone of course—since becoming husband and wife.

With Jesse off to work in town, Fern gathered the breakfast dishes and carried them to the counter. Opening the kitchen screen door, she cupped a hand round her mouth and hollered outside. "Bass! Here, boy."

The big brown dog galloped across the yard and bolted through the kitchen door. Ignoring his new mistress, he headed to the bowl where Fern had scraped enough overcooked eggs and burned bacon to feed a whole pack of dogs. Bass lapped them up with gusto.

Fern released a long sigh. "At least *you* like my cooking."

She added Bass's licked-clean bowl to those in the sink and finished washing the dishes. The pup nudged her leg and emitted a throaty *ruff*. That surely meant something, and after all he'd eaten, she figured she'd better rush him outside. Bass ran to his favorite spot to do his business while she sat on the porch steps enjoying the warm sunshine.

Pondering what she should cook for their dinner, Fern released a heavy sigh. Her cooking paled in comparison to Memaw's and was one of many points of contention between the newlyweds. Jesse was too polite a gentleman to tell her outright how bad her cooking was. But when he suggested they join together in an evening spiritual fast, it became painfully obvious he was running out of excuses for not wanting to eat anything she prepared. Aunt Matilda had never complained about her kitchen skills. Then again, her aunt never finished a meal, and Fern had come across at least six caches of sweets the old woman had stashed around their home.

The list of recipes Fern knew by heart was exhausted after only one week of marriage. Thankfully, Memaw shared a few of Jesse's favorites with her. Unfortunately, her rendition rarely resembled the original creation. The dear old woman generously brought over meals to help them as they settled in together. The poor thing, she probably feared her grandson might starve to death without her assistance. At least Fern could clean the house and mend his clothes. But most assuredly she didn't do it half as good as Memaw—or so she supposed anyway.

Fern wrinkled her brow. Had Memaw perhaps raised a spoiled brat? She chuckled at her wicked thought about the man she'd married.

Bass trotted up to Fern and bathed her face with sloppy wet doggie kisses. "Aw, you're such a good boy, Bass." She gave his soft brown ears a good scratching. "That's the first kiss I've had since your daddy pecked me on the cheek at our wedding ceremony."

If only establishing a relationship with Jesse came as easily as it had with Bass. It seemed the only two things the couple had in common was their love for Memaw Stewart and sweet old Bass.

Fern baby-talked to the big dog. He listened and wagged his tail. "You poor boy. Mean ol' Daddy named you after a fish just because you tried to eat his catch off the stringer. Doggies don't know any better. Do they?"

Bass tried giving her more kisses, but Fern couldn't take anymore. "All right, all right." She pushed him back and stood. "Ready for our adventure wal?"

Woof, woof.

"Let's go then."

Fern picked up her basket and grabbed the walking stick leaning against the porch railing. She walked toward the back of the property with Bass by her side. Jesse's land connected with Memaw's on the northern boundary. Although, according to Fern's husband, Memaw's property was not within walking distance. When she asked Jesse why he needed so much land, he told her Texans needed a lot of room to stretch out.

Hiking the footpaths with Bass had become a favorite daily routine. With all that hadn't gone right in her marriage, exploring the beauty of Jesse's vast land gave Fern great pleasure. While Bass sniffed and hiked his leg on everything he saw, she basked in the serene countryside and collected huge bouquets of wildflowers. The brilliant red, yellow, blue, orange, and pink flowers she arranged in canning jars added a much-needed feminine touch to their home. If Jesse noticed, he hadn't mentioned it to her.

Up ahead, alongside the path, an enormous patch of flowers caught Fern's eye. She had never seen such vibrant colors. The interesting blooms looked like asters, but the petals were a deep shade of orange with bright yellow tips.

Deciding the beautiful flowers would make a festive centerpiece for their dinner table, and perhaps even give her husband something to smile about, Fern stopped to pick some. With her basket full, she got up to leave, but where was Bass?

"Bass! Bass! Where are you boy?"

Woof, woof. The bark came from some distance.

"Where has he gone off to now?"

The trail took her farther from the house than ever before. Fern hesitated to venture out farther for fear of getting lost. Weighing her options, she determined that if she found Bass she wouldn't be lost, because he could help her get back home. She took off in the direction of the barking.

Woof, woof!

"There you are." Fern cautiously approached the tree Bass sat beneath. "What is it, boy?"

The strong-willed dog jumped and barked and growled like a fierce animal. He had treed something within the leafy boughs. Fern crept closer to see what it was.

"Shhh, be quiet, Bass." He didn't obey. "I don't see anything up there. Now hush."

"Kee-aah!" A piercing scream sliced through the air.

"Good heavens, what was that?"

Fern looked up and saw a large bird swooping down from the tree. It flew straight toward her. She gasped and raised her arms for cover. But she forgot about the basket draped over her arm, and all the pretty flowers she'd picked tumbled down on top of her head. The bird dove in and pecked her several times.

"Ouch! Ouch! Ouch!"

Flailing her arms to shoo the flying menace away, Fern tangled the wickerwork basket in her long hair. The magnificent bird flew off without a scratch.

"Uh! Stupid blue jay!" She painfully removed the basket and flower stems from atop her head. A good amount of her own hair fell victim to the winged nemesis as well. As she pitched the mess to the ground, tears rimmed her eyes, and her bottom lip quivered. Having successfully dispatched the bird, Bass stopped barking and sidled up to her with a doggie smile on his face and wagging his fluffy tail.

Fern hollered at her furry companion, "I guess you think you did a good job, don't you?"

Bass stopped short, his tail tucked between his legs.

"Look at what you've done." Fern gestured to the ground and talked to the dog as though he understood her every word. Bass whined and crouched down on the pile of tattered flowers.

Remorse set in for yelling at a poor animal—two poor animals.

"I'm sorry, boy." She refused to apologize to the blue jay.

Fern wiped the warm liquid running down the side of her face. She looked at her hand and smirked. "And now I'm bleeding."

She gathered a few of the less broken flowers into the basket and rolled her eyes when she noticed strands of her hair woven into the wickerwork. "Come on, boy." Bass obeyed with a little less pep in his step.

After walking a ways down the trail, Fern stopped to get her bearings. Up ahead was an expanse of log and wire fence. She looked past the railing. As far as she could see were fields of fallow ground overgrown with weeds. Among the overgrowth was one volunteer stalk of corn stretching above the brush. Birds made quick work of the shoots. Why hadn't Jesse seeded his fields?

Fern followed Bass as he walked in the direction of the rising sun, hoping the path was leading her home. Along the way, they came upon an enormous barn. Bass ran around hither and yon sniffing where she figured animals had once been. On one side of the barn there were holding pens for cattle or horses or perhaps both. She wanted to venture inside but didn't want to meddle.

Did the barn and land belong to Jesse too, or had she ventured onto someone else's property? Why would he own such a nice barn and pens if the only animals he had were one brown dog and a few horses? Fern's mind swirled with curiosity and questions, then something Memaw said came to mind.

Just in the past few years that boy has tried his hand at being a rancher, a farmer, and now the crazy fool is playing sheriff's deputy.

An unsettling gloom settled in Fern's chest. She had seen the various tools and equipment around the property from Jesse's failed attempts. How could he afford to cast them aside to rust and rot from disuse? That was wasteful. Where had the money come from in the first place? She would talk to him about it.

"Bass," Fern called. The dog padded toward her, and together they continued on the path.

"Oh, thank goodness." Above the trees, Fern saw the top of a windmill. She was close.

Bass ran ahead of her. Not wanting to lose sight of the dog, she picked up the pace. When she caught up to him, Fern halted and covered her nose and mouth with her hand. "Ugh! What is that smell?" It was reminiscent of the horrible odor she'd witnessed when she got off the train in Beaumont, but this was different.

Fern stood at the edge of a great clearing. Bass sniffed the air and then sank his claws in, digging up the smelly dirt. All around him the ground was a barren patch of dry, cracked, gray mud. Off to one side, long pieces of rusty metal pipe lay strewn about the ground. There was a cart filled with even more pipe. Behind it was a number of oak barrels stacked three high like a pyramid.

Fern walked toward the center of the open space where an oil derrick like the ones she'd seen in town lay in a heap. Only this one was burned down to the scorched earth. Beneath where the wooden derrick had stood, a length of pipe extended out of the ground from a hole about three inches across. She stared down into the hole. What had happened here?

Another one of Jesse's projects—failed and abandoned.

She backed away from the place of desolation and neglect, her hand covering her mouth. "Did you really think you were going to hit a gusher like Spindletop?" Fern shook her head. "You clearly don't know what you're doing."

Something niggled at her being. What had Jesse said about Memaw's place?

"Her property is in a prime location. She carries that shotgun to ward off all the trespassers wanting to drill on her land. People thinking they're going to strike it rich."

Fern released a long sigh of defeat. "Oh Jesse. . .not you too."

Jesse walked around the perimeter of the house. "Bass! Bass! Where are you, boy?"

He could understand Fern running away, but not his dog too. On the verge of alarm, he whistled, hoping Bass would hear him.

Woof, woof. Bass ran up the back trail. Cockleburs stuck to his furry legs.

Thank You, Lord.

"Hey, boy." Jesse knelt down and scratched Bass's head. "Now where's that wife of mine?"

Woof!

Bass turned and ran back to the trail. A moment later he emerged, his tail hung low. A bedraggled woman who looked like she'd just been on the losing side of a bar fight trudged along beside him. Having never seen a single hair out of place, Jesse took a closer look.

"Fern?"

The disenchanted glance she gave him confirmed it was his wife who approached. And he didn't quite know how, but the disheveled mess of a woman somehow looked even more attractive to him. His heart went out to her and he wanted to give her a hug but thought better of it. "Are you all right?"

Fern dropped a tattered basket of Indian paintbrushes at his feet. The look on her face did not invite questions, but he was compelled to ask them anyway.

He pointed at his head. "Your hair is—is that *blood* on your face and your dress? What in the—"

She raised her hand, halting his words midsentence, and hollered, "Don't even ask!"

❧ Chapter 7 ❧

Dear Olivia,

    This will be short, as I don't have much time at present to write. Rest assured that I am in a safe place here in Beaumont, Texas. I went through with the marriage, and I am now the wife of Mr. Jesse Stewart. You'll be happy to know I am very protected, as my new husband wears the badge of a deputy sheriff. One thing is for sure though. Married life isn't at all like I thought it would be.

    I pray all is well with you and Aunt Matilda. Has her dementia advanced any further? I worry about your ability to continue caring for her needs and your husband's too. My prayers are lifted for all of you daily. I'm sorry I have put you in this situation, and I thank you so much for what you are doing. I promise I'll take over her care whenever it is safe to come home again. I have enclosed the address where I *may be reached. I look forward to hearing back from you.*

Love,
Fern

Fern sat at the sturdy oak rolltop desk, folded the letter, and sealed it inside the envelope addressed to her cousin back in Springfield. She tapped the note against the desktop and sighed before shoving it into the skirt pocket of her nicest frock. How had her life gone so awry that she had to put her cousin and her dear old aunt in such a predicament?

Woof, woof! Bass barked, signaling that her ride had arrived.

"What is it, boy? Is Memaw here?"

Bass growled at the door and barked some more. Fern loved goading her mighty protector. She closed the cover on the desk, her favorite piece of furniture. Jesse had encouraged her to choose anything in his home she wanted to use in the bedroom he had given her. He told her to "fancy up" the room any way she liked because it was her home too.

Fern picked up her picture hat from the bed and rushed out the door with Bass close behind her. She didn't want to keep Memaw waiting.

"Goodbye, Bass. Be a good boy and protect the property." Bass circled twice before curling up in his favorite sunny spot on the porch.

Memaw held the reins of a big workhorse hooked to her buckboard carriage. "Morning, Fern. Don't you look nice."

"Thank you, and good morning to you." She climbed onto the seat beside Memaw and smoothed her skirt. Pinning her hat atop a mound of curls, Fern noticed Memaw had dressed for the occasion as well. She wore a dark blue dress with matching jacket and bonnet.

"You look lovely too, Memaw. And thank you for inviting me to town with you. I'm excited to get out of the house. Where shall we go first?"

Memaw flopped the reins on the horse's rump, and he moved forward. "You remember we're going to Beaumont, right? Ain't much there to get worked up about."

Fern shrugged. "I know, but for me it's a new adventure."

Memaw chuckled. "I figure we'll take care of the shopping first and then see what kind of trouble we can get into. Then if you'd like, we can have some dinner at the hotel. That sound all right?"

"It sounds wonderful."

Even in her fancy suit and bonnet, the old woman turned her head and spat tobacco onto the road outside of the wagon. Fern cringed at Memaw's nasty habit but would never say anything to offend her, so she silently endured it all the way into town.

Fern's trip to Beaumont hadn't been the roaring good time she'd expected. Thanks to the dreadful incident back in Springfield, she eyed every passerby with heightened suspicion. That anxiety combined with the constant fear of being mugged or knocked into the busy streets only to be trampled by horses utterly marred her shopping enjoyment. She stayed close to Memaw's side for both of their protection. And how could she have forgotten the horrible smell emanating from the town in less than a month's time?

Her arm linked with Memaw's and a handkerchief pressed to her nose, Fern saw the town's most elite hotel come into view. A doorman stood outside the beautiful arched entryway. His dapper uniform was of solid gray wool from top to bottom. The coat hung down past his knees and sported two rows of shiny brass buttons on either breast. From what could be seen of his pants, a dark blue stripe ran down the side of each leg. He looked very professional and yet absolutely out of place among the oil field workers and shady peddlers lining the streets.

Tipping his hat, he said, "Good afternoon, ladies," and opened the huge wooden doors with the gilt handles.

"Thank you, sir." Fern allowed Memaw to enter before her.

Fern gasped at the lavish decor inside the grand foyer. Not even in all of Illinois had she seen such extravagance. Was this the upshot of what Texas oil money afforded? There were vases of fresh flowers set on gilt pedestals and large crystal dishes brimming with potpourri scattered throughout the lobby. The aromas were not only intoxicating to the senses, but they covered the odor of crude oil, which was nowhere present within the hotel walls. Closing her dropped jaw, Fern caught up with Memaw waiting at the hostess stand.

A shapely young woman dressed in a red satin dress accentuating her cleavage returned to her post and greeted Memaw. "Good afternoon, Mrs. Stewart." She picked up two bills of fare. "Will there be anyone else joining you today?"

"No. Just the two of us," Memaw answered curtly and pulled Fern close to her side.

The hostess extended a sideways glare in Fern's direction. "Right this way, Mrs. Stewart."

A chamber group played softly in one corner of the vast room. Each table was adorned with a linen tablecloth, crystal stemware, silver utensils, and a stem vase containing a single red rosebud. The young woman seated them close to the center of the large dining room. "Will this be all right?"

"Yes, it's fine, Helen."

"Wonderful," Helen said, pulling out a chair for Memaw. "Nothing but the best for you, Mrs. Stewart."

Memaw sat in the chair offered to her. Fern noticed a look of annoyance on Memaw's face as she chose a seat across from her.

Helen placed a bill of fare in Memaw's hands. "It's good to see you in town, Mrs. Stewart. Haven't seen you or Jesse lately. How is that handsome grandson of yours anyway?"

Memaw took her focus off the bill of sale and slowly cut her eyes up at the woman. "Jesse is doing just fine. As a matter of fact, my handsome grandson is no longer on the market." She turned her gaze toward Fern. "Helen, I'd like to introduce you to Jesse's new wife, Mrs. Fern Stewart."

Helen the hostess stared at Memaw, her lip quivering as if she might cry. Turning to Fern, her forsaken expression faded to one of anger. She flung the bill of fare onto the table in front of Fern and huffed out a loud breath as she turned and walked away. Memaw raised her menu, covering her face. Fern unfolded her napkin and placed it on her lap and, like Memaw, politely ignored what had taken place as a server filled their glasses with chilled water.

Since arriving in town, Fern had noticed that more than a handful of beautiful women had asked Memaw about Jesse. And each time she shut them up by introducing Fern as his new bride. Like Helen, their reactions to the news of his marriage ranged from disappointed and brokenhearted to even nasty. Was her husband some kind of Casanova?

Fern made eye contact and smiled at the waitress approaching their table. The middle-aged woman spoke to Memaw. "Good afternoon, Mrs. Stewart. How are you ladies doing today?"

"Afternoon, Gladys. We're mighty fine indeed." Memaw

gestured to Fern. "Gladys, I'd like to introduce you to Mrs. Fern Stewart, Jesse's new bride."

The waitress took a step back. Her eyes grew wide, and she put a fist on her ample hip. "You telling me Mr. Jesse finally took himself a wife?"

"That's right," Memaw answered.

"Well, good for him." Gladys nodded, sizing up Fern. "He sho got himself a pretty bride."

Heat rose in Fern's cheeks. "Thank you."

Gladys turned her attention back to Memaw. "Cook's got a good special on for today. Y'all want to order off the menu or have the special?"

Fern followed Memaw's lead and ordered the special of the day. Before long Gladys returned from the kitchen holding two big bowls of seafood gumbo she placed before them along with a heaping basket of corn bread muffins. Fern leaned forward and smelled the delicious aroma. Except for Memaw's generous contributions of meals, she hadn't tasted good food for weeks.

"Y'all enjoy now." Gladys set their ticket on the table before leaving to tend to her other patrons.

Memaw clasped her hands together and bowed her head. Fern waited for her to pray, but when she didn't begin, Fern asked the blessing. "Thank You, Lord, for the beautiful day You have blessed us with and for the time I can spend with Memaw. Bless the hands of those who have prepared this food we are about to receive. In Your Son's name, we pray. Amen."

Fern dug her spoon into the tasty gumbo while Memaw sorted through the muffins until choosing the perfect one. She observed the older woman's technique of pulling apart and slathering butter on the one she'd chosen. Jesse used the exact same method. Had Memaw raised her husband? She didn't know but desired to find out.

"Thank you for taking me to the sheriff's office to see where Jesse works. And I've truly had a wonderful time shopping with you today."

Memaw didn't look up from her corn bread routine. "Glad to hear it. I enjoy your company, but truth be told, I had an ulterior motive for bringing you into town."

"Oh?" Fern's spoon clinked against her bowl, capturing Memaw's attention.

"Yes," she said, her lips curling into a sly smile. "I wanted to show you off to all these local girls so they would know once and for all that my Jesse is no longer available."

Memaw placed her butter knife beside her bowl and picked up a spoon. Fern's curiosity was piqued concerning the "local girls," as Memaw called them. Why weren't any of them good enough for her grandson?

"But never mind all that." Memaw dipped her spoon into the hearty dish. "How are things going between you and Jesse?"

Fern's shoulders drooped, and her hands fell to her lap. She didn't look at the old woman. "Honestly. . .not very well."

Memaw dipped her head to the side, staring at her like she'd said something terribly wrong. "Why ever not?"

"It's hard marrying a man you don't really know." Fern crossed her arms over her middle. "I've tried doing little things I think he might like. But Jesse is so quiet, and he keeps to himself, so I have no way of knowing what he likes and what he doesn't like." A long sigh escaped her lips.

"I know. . .he's always been a quiet one." Memaw shook her head and continued eating her gumbo.

Fern brought her hands up to the table. "I wish I knew how to get through that tough ego and find out who Jesse Stewart really is."

"It takes time, honey."

Fern returned to the wagon after posting the letter to her cousin Olivia. She climbed up and sat beside Memaw. Her fun day in town had come to an end. She would miss the excitement of downtown Beaumont, despite her fears and the putrid odor that hung in the air.

"You get it sent?" Memaw asked.

"Yes, ma'am, I did," Fern said and smiled.

"All right then." Memaw flipped the reins, and the horse pulled away.

Their cart filled with all the goods they would need for the next few weeks, the town passed behind them. Fern missed Springfield and her dear old aunt, but she could get used to living in Texas—especially if she and her husband ever fell in love with each other.

She turned to Memaw with a thought that had plagued her all day. "Memaw, I'm curious. Whatever compelled you to write inquiring about a wife for Jesse when there are so many gorgeous women in Beaumont? It seems to me that any of those girls we ran into in town would love to get their hooks into my husband."

The old woman stared straight ahead. "I have my reasons."

Fern rolled her eyes, sick and tired of the mystery surrounding the man she married. "What reasons, Memaw? Tell me."

When Memaw pulled on the reins, and the horse came to a halt, Fern was afraid she had upset her. The elder woman studied the road in front of them, seemingly in deep thought. Finally, she turned to Fern. "Because. . .all them women back in town know too much about my Jesse."

"Oh, all right." Fern could see in Memaw's eyes that she had touched on something deep and personal to her.

"That's why I sent that advertisement." She pointed at Fern with the reins. "Jesse needs a woman who can fall in love with him for who he is on the inside."

Memaw turned her attention back to the road ahead of them. "Someone just like you, Fern." She slapped the reins against the horse's rump, and he took off with a start.

Fern didn't understand Memaw's meaning, and she had more questions swirling around inside her head than before. But there was no further conversation between the two women the whole way home.

Who was Jesse Stewart—on the inside? Fern had no idea. She was, however, willing to stick around long enough to find out for herself.

❧ *Chapter 8* ❧

*J*esse leaned against one of the support beams on Memaw's porch, waiting for her to put an end to the man's suffering. In less than a minute, a city slicker wearing a Stetson hat, boots, and bolo tie, all of which appeared to be brand-new, stormed out of the house. The screen door slammed shut behind him. He stopped and turned around, pointing at the door.

"I'll be back, Mrs. Stewart," he hollered, red in the face. "And next time you'll accept my offer." He stomped off the porch all the way to his rented carriage.

Jesse crossed his arms over his chest and chuckled behind the carpetbagger's back. He spoke to Memaw through the screen door. "I came out here in search of a hot meal, not some dog and pony show."

Memaw stepped out onto the porch as the city fellow rode off.

"I thought I saw you riding up. You've got a wife at home to cook for you. Why you need to come out here and spoil my fun?"

"Because good cooking is a scarce commodity over at my place." Jesse took a seat in the wooden rocker next to the one Memaw sat in.

His grandmother chuckled. "I tell you what—it's a good thing that girl of ours is a beauty and smart as a whip too. Because, bless her heart, she sure can't cook."

He smiled and crossed his arms over his chest. "Yeah, it's not one of her strong suits, that's for sure."

Jesse's disposition turned sober. He needed to say his piece before she tried changing the subject on him again. "Memaw, how many times do I have to tell you not to deal with those owl hoots coming around here trying to buy plots of your land? And now, here you are letting them come into your house."

"Eh!" Memaw swatted at Jesse and picked up her snuff tin. "He had a good story, and I wanted to see how far he was willing to go with it before I ran him off."

Jesse tightened his lips and shook his head. "If I've told you once, I've told you a thousand times—"

"I know! I can't trust anyone!"

"I'm sorry, Memaw. I just don't want you getting taken in by some con man."

Memaw tucked a dab of snuff between her lip and gums. "I know, son. You've always got my best interest at heart. But believe it or not, I wasn't born yesterday." She patted Jesse's leg and laughed. "Love you, boy."

He gave his grandmother a tender smile. "If you love me, then you'll say you're finally ready to let me drill on your property."

The old woman leaned forward and spit in the coffee can. She sat back in her rocker and folded her hands over her middle. "Well, you know, I've been thinking about just that." She cut her eyes toward him. "And if you'll agree to give up playing sheriff's deputy, I'll let you drill anywhere you please."

Was he hearing her right? Memaw was actually giving him permission to let him do what he'd been asking her for months on end? He sat up straight in the chair. A renewed energy flowed through him. "If you really mean that, I'll head into town and talk to Levi about it today."

Memaw smiled and looked straight at him. "You know that what's mine is yours, son."

He leaned over to his grandmother and kissed her cheek. "Thank you, Memaw. Now, I'll probably have to give the sheriff time to find someone else, but this is great news." Jesse clapped his hands together. "I've been waiting for this day. When I leave here, I'm going to go stake off a plot of land where I know there's oil—guaranteed!"

His enthusiasm was contagious. Memaw released a hearty laugh and nearly lost her chaw. "Just don't go and burn the whole thing down like you did last time. I don't want that mess and mayhem on my property."

Fern rode up to Memaw's place on one of Jesse's horses. She was proud of herself for how quickly she'd picked up riding. Her household chores done for the day, she found herself lonesome and in need of some female conversation. She came up with the excuse of returning some of Memaw's dishes to get out of the house for a while.

The shortest way there was a trail that took her up to the back of Memaw's property. Fern dismounted the horse, allowing him to graze in the back pasture. With the sack of dishes in hand, she went in through the back kitchen door expecting to find Memaw there.

"Memaw?" Fern set the sack of dishes on the counter and went to the living room.

The front door was open. Memaw must be sitting out on the front porch. Fern heard her husband's voice and stopped before reaching the door. What was Jesse doing here? She listened a moment before letting her presence be known.

"Oh come on now! My well burned because I hit a shallow pocket of gas."

Intrigued by what Jesse said, Fern continued listening.

"I don't know, Jesse. On your very first try you burned the whole dern rig, derrick and all, right down to the ground. Sounds to me like you don't know much about drilling for oil."

"You be quiet, old woman. It was a freak accident, and it won't happen again. . . . I hope."

Memaw was laughing at him. He began talking with vigor.

"Now you know as well as I do how oil-rich your land is. We've both seen on the plot maps how close you are to the salt dome. It's the perfect geographic spot!"

"I know, I know," Memaw replied.

"Now don't you even think about changing your mind. You going to let me drill or not?"

Why was Jesse continuing to badger Memaw about drilling on her land when he clearly didn't know what he was doing?

"Well, if that's what you want, I guess I can't stop you."

Jesse had finally succeeded. He'd pressed Memaw so hard the poor thing probably didn't know what else to do but give in to him.

Fern covered her mouth with her palm, and her cheeks burned with the resentment she felt toward her husband.

Oh Jesse, I had no idea you were the kind of man who would force his own grandmother into doing something she's not comfortable with. Is this just another one of your get-rich-quick schemes? How could you?

She couldn't listen anymore. With tears in her eyes, Fern ran out the back door she'd come in through. She marched to the grazing horse, mounted up, and slapped the reins. Disappointment and anger were the only feelings that remained for Mr. Jesse Stewart.

Jesse rode high in his saddle all the way home from town. It felt like his horse trotted on a cloud. He hadn't been in such a good mood in a long time. Memaw was ready to let him drill on her land. When he told Levi the news, the sheriff seemed happy for him. They both agreed Jesse would stay on until another deputy was hired. He hated leaving Levi in the lurch even if his good-for-nothin' best friend teased him that it wouldn't be hard finding a replacement for someone with his skills.

His thoughts turned to Fern. It felt good having someone besides a big brown dog to go home to. And she seemed to be coming around to the idea of being his wife, holding his hand on the porch while watching the sun go down. At least he hoped she was coming around. It was getting awful hard for him to sleep under the same roof and only two doors down from a woman with long blond hair and curves in all the right places.

Bass ran out of the house barking. Even his dog had grown accustomed to having a woman around to love on and protect.

"Hey, Bass." Jesse climbed down from the horse's back and

rubbed the dog's head. He led the mare to the corral next to the house and released her. Her saddle and brushing would have to wait until after dinner. He was starving.

Jesse closed the gate behind his horse and noticed the old roan he let Fern ride was saddled and tied to a post. *Hmm. . .that's strange. She must have been out riding today.*

He headed up the three short steps with Bass on his heels. Excitement coursed through him in anticipation of seeing his wife. Maybe he would try giving her a hello kiss. The thought vanished when he opened the door and saw what awaited him on the other side.

"What's going on here?" Jesse stared at his beautiful wife. She sat in one of the living room chairs, her packed bag lying at her feet.

Fern's chin quivered. "I'm leaving you, that's what."

He walked farther into the room. "Well, I can see that. . . but why?"

Fern held her hand out to him, indicating that he shouldn't come any closer. "Because. . ." She sniffed back tears. "I happened to come by Memaw's house today and overheard you talking to her out on the porch."

Jesse's brows clinched together. "You were there?" He shrugged. "Then why didn't you come outside?"

"What kind of man bullies his own precious memaw into letting him drill for oil on her land when she clearly doesn't want him to?" The woman's cheeks were as red as ripe apples. Tears coursed down her face. "Someone like you, that's who!"

Jesse reached up and scratched the top of his head. "Uh, look, I uh. . ."

Fern stood and marched over to him. She pointed her finger in his face. "Now you listen here. I've been all over this property of yours, and I've seen all your abandoned projects. . .the fallow fields you've failed to plant, the empty barns that should be filled with milk cows at the very least. Oh. . .and I know all about your dry hole oil well too!"

Jesse could have told her he'd fenced off the plot of farmland and offered it to the preacher at the Baptist church to plant crops whenever he needed to supplement his family's income. Or he could have explained why the barn was no longer in use, but instead he set his jaw and let her rant.

"And now you've set your sights on swindling your poor old grandmother out of her oil when you clearly don't even know what you're doing. You disgust me, Jesse Stewart!"

"Are you finished?" He scowled at her, upset at how quickly she jumped to a conclusion about him.

"Humph." Fern retreated and picked up her suitcase. "Yes, I'm quite finished. And I refuse to live under the same roof as a man who would steal from his own kinfolk."

"Then where will you go?"

"I'm moving in with Memaw."

Fern twirled around and headed out the door. He didn't follow her. He was comforted to know that his irrational wife was at least going somewhere she would be taken care of.

Jesse sat in the chair Fern had vacated and rubbed his stubbly jawline. He smiled, pondering how Memaw would react when Fern showed up on her doorstep. Bass sat in front of him and whined, placing his paw on Jesse's knee. "I know, boy. She up and left us."

Woof.

Jesse shrugged and shook his head. "No, I don't think she'll be back anytime soon."

Woof. Bass lowered his paw and twisted his head to the side. "I bet she didn't even fix us any burned dinner."

Woof!

Jesse scratched his friend behind the ear. "Yeah, I know. I'm gonna miss her too."

❧ Chapter 9 ❧

*J*esse pinned the shiny silver star to his shirt and pushed through the sheriff's office door. The wooden chair in front of the sheriff's desk scooted back when he dropped into it. Levi leaned forward and stared at his friend's anxious fingers drumming on the chair's arms.

"Trouble in paradise?"

A heavy breath escaped Jesse's lungs. "That's putting it lightly."

The sheriff chuckled. "Well, it was just a matter of time."

Jesse cut narrowed eyes toward his friend. "And what do you mean by that?"

"*Humph.* You're newlyweds. It happens to everyone, me and Beth included."

Jesse straightened up and brushed dust from his trousers. "Yeah, well I don't know. I made Fern mad as a hornet, and all because she took something I said to Memaw the wrong way." He shook his head and lightly pounded his fist on Levi's desk. "All Fern does is gripe and complain that I don't talk to her enough." He shrugged. "And when I finally do open my mouth, she misinterprets what I say and goes off on me for it." He stared at Levi, his eyes opened wide. "And I wasn't even talking to her."

He struck the sheriff's desk with his fist again, making him flinch.

"I'm so dang tired of it!"

"All right now." Levi held up his hand. "Just settle down and don't worry about it. These things happen all the time. It'll blow over before you know it. Heck, everything will probably be back to normal by the time you get home this evening."

"I don't think so. She up and packed her bag and moved to Memaw's house."

The sheriff's eyes grew wide with surprise. "Oh boy. You must have really made her mad."

"Yeah, she's somehow got it in her head that my plan to drill on Memaw's land is a ploy to cheat my own grandmother out of her money."

Levi chuckled. "Well, for all she knows you might be some kind of lowlife who would steal from a sweet old lady."

"Sweet old lady, huh?" Jesse smiled and shook his head. "Fern ought to know I'd never do anything to hurt Memaw. I love her too much. Heck, I'm too scared of what she would do to me!"

"Aw, come on now, Jesse. Give Fern a break. Y'all just met, and she don't know that much about you. I mean, just look at it from her point of view. She thinks you're so lame you can't even find a suitable wife for yourself." Levi lowered his voice to a sinister tone. "Who knows what kind of person Jesse Stewart really is?"

"Yeah, I can see that." Jesse slid down in the chair and clasped his hands over his middle. "It sure was easier when it was just Bass and me."

The sheriff sat back and relaxed. "Ya know, Jesse, being in a relationship with a woman is a lot like having a dog."

He glanced sideways at his friend. "Oh, is that right? Is this your idea of giving me marital advice?"

"Yes, it is. Now shut up and listen." Levi held out his palm. "Think back to when Bass was a pup. What would he do when a storm came up with thunder and lightning?"

"Well, I guess he'd run to me and jump up in my arms."

"That's right, and it may not be something as simple as bad weather, but like that puppy, a woman needs someone she can run to in times of trouble and feel safe." Levi took a pencil from his desk and twirled it between his fingers. "And how did Bass learn not to do his business inside the house?"

Jesse lowered his brows and smirked. "That hasn't been an issue with Fern."

"Just answer the question."

He thought a moment. "I suppose I consistently made sure he knew what I expected of him."

Levi pointed the pencil at Jesse. "Yes—communication! A woman needs to know what's expected of her, and you need to know what she expects of you. You've got to communicate with her, Jesse!"

He lowered his head. "Yeah, I haven't been too good at that." Jesse looked at his friend. "It's hard trying to strike up a conversation with someone you hardly know, not to mention the way we were thrown together and all."

Levi nodded. "I understand, but if you're going to make this work, you need to hear me out."

Jesse jutted out his chin in acknowledgment.

"Okay, I have one more thing to add. Where is Bass when you get home in the evening and when you get up in the morning?"

"He's right by my side, of course."

"That's right. Bass needs to have you near him." Levi bounced the pencil on the desktop. "A woman needs companionship to be happy, and so do you. Now, you don't see me running off drinking with those owl hoots from the oil rigs after work, do you?" Again he pointed at Jesse with the pencil and didn't give him a chance to answer. "No, I go straight home to my good-lookin' wife. I take her in my arms and kiss her like I ain't seen her in a month."

"I don't need to know that."

"Yes, you do. And you need to know that Beth respects me for it too."

Jesse's head bobbed in a nod. A playful grin curled on his lips. "So what I'm hearing is that all I have to do is treat Fern the same way I do Bass and everything will work out fine."

"Well, yeah, something like that."

"All right then, boss. I appreciate the advice."

Levi spread his hands apart. "It's what I'm here for."

"Oh, and by the way, I promise never to tell Beth how sorry I am about you treating her like a dog."

The sheriff scowled and tossed his pencil at Jesse.

The mare slowed to a walk and stopped when she reached Memaw's house. The old woman sat out front in her rocking chair as she usually did come evening time. Jesse dismounted and tied the horse to a porch rail and stood at the foot of the stairs with fists firmly planted at his waist.

Memaw acknowledged him with, "Well, well, look who's come to call."

"I'm here to get my wife."

"Um-hmm." Memaw thumbed toward the house. "She's in the living room working on making a dress."

"Surely by now you've told Fern I wasn't bullying you into letting me drill on your land. You have, right?"

Memaw's brow wrinkled. "Well no. That would defeat the purpose. If she figures out how much money it takes to drill a dern oil well, then she's going to have a pretty good idea what you've got in the bank. And I don't want her running back to you just because you're well off."

Jesse rolled his eyes and huffed out a deep breath. "I've got to tell her something, Memaw! Thanks to you, she already thinks I can't find a wife on my own, and apparently I quit every project I ever started." He dipped his head to the side. "Let's say Fern does find out what we have in the bank. She doesn't seem like the kind of woman who would care much about being wealthy, so what difference does it make?"

Memaw set her jaw. "It makes a difference to me, that's what. Now, I'm sure you'll be able to come up with something to tell her when you get inside. Just don't tell her that. You hear me?"

"Yes, ma'am." Jesse walked up the stairs onto the porch. He heard Memaw mumble under her breath.

"Sure didn't take long for you to start pining for her."

He cut his eyes toward Memaw as he went inside the house. Fern sat on the floor beside a length of soft green fabric rolled out from a bolt. She lifted the stick of chalk used to mark the material and looked toward the door. Was he the cause of her tear-streaked cheeks? He already knew the answer.

"What are you doing here?" Her words were cutting. "Have you come to do something else terrible to Memaw? The woman who *raised* you."

Jesse tried his best to remain civil, speaking slowly and calmly. "No. I've come to, uh, make you an offer."

"Oh, is that right? What kind of offer?"

Thankfully, an idea popped into his head. "I want you to partner with me in drilling an oil well on a piece of Memaw's land. . .and. . . and don't worry, I've already asked for her permission, and she's given me her blessing."

Fern set her jaw and her eyes grew wide. "There you go again—"

Jesse held up his palms to her and spoke firmly. "Will you please listen to me for just one minute?

She huffed out a breath of air. "All right. Go on."

"Now, if we do strike oil, I'll only take money out for what I've put into the well. All the rest of the profits will go to Memaw."

"You won't take anything more than what you've put into it?"

"Not one red cent."

Fern's eyes narrowed. "How will you afford to drill the well? Will you have to secure a loan?"

"No, I have a little bit set aside I can use to purchase the equipment I'll need."

Fern got up off the floor and swiped her damp cheek with her sleeve. She stood in front of her husband and crossed her arms over her chest. Her cold look of disdain gave Jesse an unwelcome chill.

"All right, I suppose I could agree to your plan. That is, providing you keep your word."

Jesse raised his right hand. "I promise. But there's one more part to this deal."

Fern scowled and lowered her brows. "What is it?"

"You have to come back home and be my wife."

"*Uh!*" Her arms dropped to her side. "I don't know why you want me to come back when you hate my cooking and you don't appreciate any of the little things I've done to brighten the place up."

"Hey." Jesse took her soft hand in his, and she didn't pull away. "That's not true in the least. Okay, so you don't cook like Memaw. Not many do."

"Y'all can come over here and eat whenever you want!" Memaw hollered from the porch.

Jesse took a deep breath and looked heavenward before speaking. "Listen to me. I really appreciate how you've mended all my clothes, and I love all the things you've done to make our place feel like a home."

Fern's cheeks blossomed pink. "I didn't think you even noticed."

"You gotta talk to people, Jesse!" Memaw yelled.

"All right!" Jesse answered before turning his full attention back to his bride. He squeezed her hand. "So, what do you say?"

She looked up into his eyes. "How will you have time to drill an oil well and do your job as deputy too?"

"You don't need to worry about that. I've already talked with Levi, and he's allowing me to take some time off."

Fern shrugged. "Well, I suppose I can agree to it, for a while anyway. Who knows, it may not even work out."

"All right then." Jesse smiled. "Whew, thank goodness you said yes."

Fern's brow furrowed. "Oh, why is that?"

"Because. . .I was talking to Bass just last night, and he told me that if I didn't get you to come back home, he was moving out too."

Jesse noticed a hint of a smile on Fern's face.

"Neither of us wants that to happen," she said softly.

"No, ma'am." Jesse released her hand and offered her his arm. "Shall we, Mrs. Stewart?"

Fern didn't answer or smile back, but she did hook arms with him, and that was good enough for him. They stepped onto Memaw's porch. Jesse winked at his grandmother and headed down the steps.

He lifted Fern onto his horse's saddle and climbed on behind her. He thought of what his buddy Levi had said, and smiled. His wife sat safely between his arms. At least for the time being, he and Fern both knew what was expected of each other. And they were right where they needed to be—together as one.

"You ready to go home, Fern?" He tugged the reins, turning the horse around.

His wife snuggled closer to his chest. "Yes, I suppose."

Jesse nudged the mare's flanks with his boots, and she took off in a trot, taking the newlyweds back where they needed to be. Home.

✎ *Chapter 10* ✎

*I*n the weeks after Fern returned home with Jesse, they had taken the time to get to know one another. When Jesse realized Fern's proficiency at reading and following building plans, he gave her the title of chief engineer. And the wonderful smell of fried bacon seeping into Fern's bedroom most mornings was a testament to Jesse's skills as an accomplished cook.

The couple had taken to sharing the household chores as well as the work on the oil rig. No job was too big for one or too small for the other. The distribution of duties in the home led to a friendship. Dividing work on the rig led to a partnership. It seemed that by doing so, they had found a way that worked for them both. The next step was surely a deeper relationship.

Fern inspected her image in the mirror and hooked her thumbs around the straps of her overalls. Her hair plaited like a schoolgirl in pigtails and red bows looked nice against the denim. She knew to enjoy her fresh clothes early; by day's end, they would be soiled with mud and grease. Grabbing a roll of plans she had studied the night before, Fern followed her nose to the kitchen.

"Good morning, partner."

Fern smiled at the handsome man holding a spatula, standing at the stove. "Morning, partner." She liked the nickname they called each other since becoming associates in the oil drilling business.

Bass ran to her and licked her fingers. "Hello, boy." She patted his head. "You smell that delicious bacon cooking too, don't you?"

Jesse slid the skillet aside and carried a plate of bacon and another of fried eggs to the table. "You hungry?"

"Starved."

Fern sat in the chair she'd claimed as her own and accepted the hand Jesse held out to her and bowed her head. It was a routine they had grown accustomed to, and she loved it. Either he said the prayer, or he squeezed her hand, wanting her to.

"Heavenly Father, we come to You this morning as husband and wife to thank You for this food You have graciously provided. Lord, we pray You would bless the work of our hands and forgive us where we fail You. And thank You, Father, for this woman You sent to be my wife. In Jesus' name, amen."

Fern's eyes opened with a flutter. She smiled at the man holding her hand. He turned away. Beneath the stubble, his cheeks donned a bashful blush of pink. He took a deep breath and picked up the plate of bacon.

"Let's eat."

A homemade sign buried in the ground near the work area bore the name Fern and Jesse had decided on for their partnership: STEWART FISHER OIL. Fern slogged through a muddy trail to a table laden with stacks of instruction sheets for the various components needed to drill for oil. She thumbed through the pile and sighed. If drilling took as long as it had preparing the site, Fern might be as old as Memaw when they struck oil—if they struck oil.

Constructing and erecting the big wooden derrick had taken over a week, and that was with two hired men helping them. And that was only one of a dozen more steps in the drilling process. But now all their hard work had paid off. With pipe and drill bit down the hole, the Stewart Fisher Oil venture was under way.

Fern glanced at her handsome husband. A warm flush crept up her neck at the sight before her. The muscles on his tanned forearms swelled as he twisted an enormous wrench, tightening a loose bolt. She could have stared at him all day, but she had a job to do.

Jesse insisted the grease barrel not be placed near the drilling platform. His past mistakes and the fire made him diligent about safety, especially now that he wasn't alone. Fern removed the metal lid and scooped up the honey-colored goop with a ladle and plopped it into her bucket. She would coat each drilling component, keeping them all well lubricated and in good working order.

Bucket in hand, she started toward the well and noticed her husband no longer used the wrench for its intended purpose. Instead, he rested his hand on it like a cane while ogling her every move.

Fern stopped and placed her hand on her hip, smirking at her man. "Can I help you?"

A bashful smile graced Jesse's lips. "Just making sure you don't need any help."

Fern dipped her chin. "Is that right?"

"Yes, ma'am."

"Always watching over me, aren't you?" The grease bucket gripped in her hand swung back and forth.

"That's right."

Fern batted her lashes. "I appreciate it. I need someone to watch over me, and I'm glad it's you."

"I'm glad it's me too."

She lowered her head. "Well, I'm going over there and. . ." She pointed at the rig and smiled. "You know. . .do my job."

Jesse's chest bobbed up and down as he chuckled. "Okay. Don't you worry, I'll keep an eye on you."

Fern worked with passion. She had never partnered with a man on anything, and now she had a partner in marriage and in business. After every few joints were lubricated, she seized the opportunity to steal a glimpse at her husband. What had she done to be blessed with a man as righteous and honorable as Jesse Stewart? She never imagined that running for her life would end in her falling for a wonderful man.

A loud crack pierced the air. Jesse hollered in pain. Fern jumped to her feet at the sound as terror rose in her heart. She dropped the grease bucket and ran to him. Jesse lay on the ground clutching his bloody left hand to his chest. Chains used to drive the rotary table swung free.

Fern knelt by his side and touched his arm. "Oh no! What happened?"

Jesse's face contorted in pain. "Chain sheared off. Got my hand."

"Wait here." Fern ran to the shed where they stored supplies and returned with a shop rag. "Here, let me see."

"You sure about that?"

She nodded even though she wasn't really sure. He raised his hand from his chest and showed her. A dark red circle had soaked through his overalls. Fern winced and tried to determine the extent of his injury, but it was difficult with so much blood seeping from the wound.

"It looks like a pretty bad cut on your palm." She took the shop rag and wrapped it around the hand. "Keep this tight."

Jesse moved the injured hand back to his chest and pushed off the ground with his other hand, but Fern pushed him down on his backside. "What'd you do that for?"

Fern waved her hands. She wiped sweat from her lip. She couldn't slow her speech. "I'm sorry, but you can't get up yet. You've lost too much blood. I don't want you fainting on me."

"Hey, hey, calm down." Jesse grabbed one of her flailing hands. "I'll be fine. And I'm not a fainter." He chuckled. "Now, sit down here beside me." He patted the ground, and Fern sat next to him. "Take a deep breath and let it all out."

His soothing words eased her fear, and she did as he suggested. He put his arm around her shoulders, and she snuggled close to his side.

"Hey, look here at me," Jesse said.

Fern rolled her eyes up to meet his.

"I'm all right, okay? After we get the rig secured, I'll ride into town and have Doc stitch the wound. It's you I'm worried about. Are you all right?"

Fern nodded, and a tear rolled down her cheek. "It's just. . .I—I don't want to lose you." She looked into his eyes, her expression sober, and her bottom lip quivered. "You're starting to grow on me, Jesse."

"Aw, come on now." He chuckled and pulled her closer. "It's gonna take more than a little cut to finish me off."

She bopped him on the thigh. "It's not funny."

"Hey." Jesse mirrored her dark countenance. "I feel the same way about you."

Another tear escaped Fern's eye, and even though it wasn't the right time, she desired more than anything for Jesse to kiss her. Was this what love felt like? Yes—she was sure of it.

❧ Chapter 11 ❧

Jesse's hand throbbed as he hurried out of the doctor's office. Doc said it was a good thing he came to see him. The cut wouldn't have closed up properly without stitches. Jesse refused Doc's pain tonic. Working on an oil rig was dangerous enough. There was no good reason to abide a tipsy-headed worker.

Mounting the mare with his hand stitched and bandaged proved harder than Jesse had anticipated, but he had to get to Wilkie Hardware and Machinery to pick up a replacement part before they closed for the day. The same chain that split open his palm had wrapped around a pipe down the hole and warped the rig's rotary table. It couldn't be fixed. He had to get a new one. Pulling the reins to the side, he nudged the horse's flanks, urging her toward the store.

The ride into town had given Jesse time to think, and once again his mind lingered on what had transpired between him and Fern at the rig. Her concern for him had surprised him. When had she grown so attached to him? In that moment, he'd desired to kiss her quivering lips and fought to keep himself from it. He wasn't one to take advantage of a woman, especially in a moment of frailty.

Jesse had to admit, he was quite smitten with Fern. Every morning he spoke to the Lord about that very thing before emerging from his sleeping quarters. Sheer willpower and the grace of God kept him out of his wife's bedroom. But something else too—a deep respect and a desire to honor her privacy until they fell in love. That's what kept him chaste—but how long would it take?

It was natural for a man to think about his wife. Good thing too, because her long blond hair and eyes like clear blue water were always on his mind. The view from behind when she wore overalls became a favorite as well. Yes, he wanted her, he desired her, he loved everything about her, but was he *in* love with her? He needed to find out sooner rather than later, because with each passing day it became more and more difficult to live under the same roof as his beautiful wife.

The mare turned toward Wilkie Hardware at Jesse's prompting. He tied the reins to the hitching post and joined the crowd of customers inside. A long line of rig workers waited at the counter, holding all manner of parts they needed to replace. Jesse skipped the line and went straight to the catalog to search for what he needed. He wrote down the information and looked around at the men who worked there.

"Hey, Bud. Got a minute?"

The young man looked up at hearing his name. He left what he was working on and came over to where Jesse stood. A big grin spread across his face as he extended his hand. "Jesse Stewart." They shook hands. "I ain't seen you in a month of Sundays. How you been?"

"Hey, Bud." Jesse smiled and raised his bandaged hand. "Well, not so great, to be honest."

"Oh boy. What happened to you?"

"Yeah, well, I'm drilling a well up at Memaw's place, and a chain sheared off, warped my turntable, and cut my hand open."

"Dang, you got all the luck, don't ya?"

"If you say so, Bud." Jesse chuckled and handed him the slip of paper. "Why don't you make my day and tell me you have one of these in stock."

Bud took the paper from him and scrutinized what he'd written. "Shoot, Jesse." He laughed, making his small belly bounce. "Do you know what kind of demand there is for well parts around here? You ain't gonna find one of these anywhere in Texas, much less Beaumont."

Jesse's shoulders sagged along with his countenance. "What? This is oil field country. You can't drill without a rotary table."

"Yep, and it seems like you and everybody else in town wants one yesterday." Bud shrugged one shoulder. "I'm sorry, but I'll have to order it for you."

Jesse released a distressed breath, drumming his fingers on the counter. "All right then, I guess that's all I can do."

Bud thumped his fist on the counter. "I'll get this ordered and let you know when it comes in."

"Thanks. How long you think it'll take?"

Bud took another look at the paper before answering. "Oh, about two to three weeks."

Jesse's jaw dropped. "You've got to be kidding me."

"Afraid not."

Jesse flinched when a hand gripped his shoulder.

"Hey, stranger." The sheriff offered his hand.

"Howdy, Levi. What brings you in here?" Jesse shook his hand.

"Noticed your horse out front. Thought I'd come in and say hi. Haven't seen you around these parts lately."

"I'll get this ordered for you, Jesse."

"Thanks, Bud." The young man returned to his job.

"What'd you do to your hand?" Levi asked.

"Aw, I cut it open working on the rig. Messed up my turntable. That's why I'm here."

The sheriff shook his head. "Sorry to hear that."

"Yeah. Bud told me it would take two weeks or more to get a new one."

"Well, Jess, that's a shame you're shut down. In the meantime, you can come back to work for me."

Jesse lifted his bandaged hand. "Wouldn't be much help to you with only one arm. Besides, the wife might not like me being away from her for too long."

"Oh, is that right? Sounds like the two of you are getting along better than you had been."

"Yeah." Jesse's lips curled into a smile. "Funny—I did what you said and started treating her like I do Bass, and we're getting along just fine."

They shared a laugh. "Well, it's a shame you can't pull yourself away from her. Crime in town is getting worse by the day. That's why I'm out making rounds. Want everyone to see I'm doing my job."

Jesse shook his head. "How's the search for a new deputy going?"

Levi released a long breath. "It's not as easy replacing you as I thought it would be."

"Yep. I told you it would be hard finding good help like me."

Levi smiled and was about to reply when a woman burst into the hardware store. She panted and clasped the neckline of her dress.

"Is the sheriff in here?"

"Yes, ma'am," Levi answered.

"Come quick! The saloon's been robbed!"

Levi turned to Jesse. "Well, duty calls."

He shook his friend's hand. "Be careful out there."

"Always am."

Jesse followed Levi outside and watched him mount his horse. He was turned toward his own ride when the town mailman approached him.

"Excuse me, Mr. Stewart, but I've got a letter here for Memaw. You mind dropping it off on your way back home?"

"Sure. Give it to me."

He handed Jesse the envelope. "Thanks, Mr. Stewart."

Jesse tipped his head up, acknowledging the man, and tucked the letter inside his saddlebag. Untying his horse, he mounted into his saddle with great difficulty. He was beginning to rethink his decision to forgo Doc's pain tonic.

Leading the mare out of town, Jesse was anxious to get back home. Memaw had promised to bring over a big pot of her chicken and dumplings. And strange enough, it wasn't his favorite dish that enticed him homeward. It was the thought of his lovely wife serving it to him.

❧ Chapter 12 ❧

How could Jesse have forgotten to give her a letter from her family for two whole weeks? Fern was upset, but in Jesse's defense, the mail carrier mistakenly told him the envelope was for Memaw and not Fern, and it was the same day as his accident. Regardless, Jesse should have been more attentive about such things and not shoved an important piece of mail in his saddlebag and forgotten about it.

When Memaw handed Fern the last dinner plate, she dragged the dish towel across it and placed it in the cabinet. With the dishes done, Memaw would head out to the front porch for a snuff break while watching the sunset. Jesse had already taken his leave to the outside rockers. Over the two weeks since ordering a replacement for the broken well part, the couple spent many an evening supping with Memaw. Jesse and his grandmother's after-meal routine was always the same.

"Well, that's done," Memaw said, wiping her hands dry. "I'm going out front. We'll have coffee and some of that chess pie after the sun goes down."

"Yes, ma'am. I'll be out in a bit."

Fern dried her hands and untied the apron from around her waist. She hung it on the rack beside the kitchen door, anxious to read the letter. Deep inside her skirt pocket, the envelope's sharp corners poked her thigh all through dinner, continually reminding Fern of its presence.

The lamp beside the living room sofa offered the best lighting in Memaw's house. Fern took the letter from her pocket and sat. She'd recognized her cousin Olivia's script when Jesse first gave it to her. Unhinged by his adorable sheepish look, she'd slipped it into her pocket without expressing her disappointment.

She unfolded the letter and started reading.

Dearest Fern,

I hope this letter finds you in a timely manner, as I have a bit of troublesome news to share with you.

Fern covered her mouth with her fingers. A vise tightened around her heart. Was this a message regarding her aunt's demise? She sighed with relief when she read Olivia's next line.

First of all, let me assure you, Aunt Matilda is as fine as can be expected considering the poor thing's advancing dementia. My news, however, does involve Auntie. I write to you with utmost regret and embarrassment for my actions and pray you can find it in your heart to forgive me for my ignorance.

Fern blanched, and her stomach churned. "Oh Olivia. . .what have you done?"

The day I received your letter, I was in the company of Jane Archer, my sister-in-law. Since I had previously told Jane all about your story, we were both anxious to hear what you had to say. I read your words aloud in the presence of Jane and Auntie. Better than a week had passed before I found out what Auntie had done. In my defense, it was the woman we hired to sit with Auntie in my absence who let it happen.

A whoosh of air spewed from Fern's lips. "For heaven's sake, Olivia, get on with it."

Anyway, Esmeralda—that's the helper woman—told me Auntie answered the door to two complete strangers. And they were asking for you, Fern. Esmeralda said Auntie spoke to one man like she'd known him his whole life.

Fern's hands trembled. "Mark Stanley. . .how could you?" Her childhood friend used her aunt's frailty to his advantage and gleaned information from her. She kept reading.

She managed to tell the man the exact name of the town where you are living now and that you're married to a lawman, which is incredible to me, considering how most days the poor thing doesn't know who I am or what year it is.

Fern, I don't know who the man was or why he came by asking for you, but with your current situation, I thought I should let you know. Be ever cautious and watchful! I say again

how sorry I am that this happened. Please write back soon so
that I may know how things are with you and that new hus-
band of yours.

> *Love,*
> *Olivia*

Fern's hand fell to her lap, the letter grasped firmly in her grip.
She stared at the wall where a daguerreotype hung of a young beautiful Memaw and her handsome husband, made on their wedding
day. Over time she had learned how Memaw and Papa took Jesse
in after the untimely death of his parents. Papa Stewart remained
unwavering in his faith and his devotion to family until the day he
went on to his reward.

Had Jesse inherited the stalwart character of the man who had
raised him? What would he think of Fern when he found out she'd
brought this trouble on him and Memaw? Would she have to pack
her bags and leave on the next train out of town? The front screen
door opened. She would soon find out.

"Are you all right, Fern? I thought you would join us outside."
Jesse crossed the room and sat beside her. Memaw waited by the
door. He glanced down at the letter in her lap and placed his hand
on her leg. "What does it say? It's not bad news is it?"

Fern looked at her husband. She pleaded for his understanding
through troubled eyes. "Memaw, please come and sit down. There's
something I have to confess. . .to both of you."

Memaw did as she asked and sat in the armchair beside the
sofa. She leaned forward and clasped her hands together atop her
lap. Her concern was apparent in her facial expression. "What is it,
Fern?"

She hated what she had to do but could no longer avoid it. She spoke to Jesse. "It seems that Memaw wasn't the only one who had a secret she was hiding."

Jesse tipped his head to the side, his eyes narrowed in question. Fern recounted the whole story for them. Witnessing the bank robbery and murder, recognizing her old friend, Mark Stanley, being threatened by his accomplice, and answering the letter Memaw falsely wrote on Jesse's behalf. Her secret was no longer hidden. But how would her new family react?

Fern lifted her hands and shrugged. "So that's the story. I'm sorry I put you both in this troublesome situation. I hope you can find it in your hearts to forgive me."

Memaw extended a sad smile to Fern. "Oh, I can't stay mad at you. Of course I forgive you."

"Thank you, Memaw." A tear of relief slid down Fern's cheek.

Jesse sat back on the sofa without looking at her. He rubbed his whiskery chin while she waited for what seemed like a lifetime to answer.

"Do you think these are the kind of men who would harm either you or Memaw?"

Fern's eyes darted from Jesse to Memaw and back again. "I–I'm not sure, but it worries me that Auntie told them where I've moved to *and* that I've married a man with a badge. However, I was an eyewitness to a robbery and murder." Fern looked away. "Surely Mark wouldn't hurt me, but the other man frightens me." She turned her gaze to Jesse. "He already threatened me once, and now he knows where to find me and that I've done a bit more than just go to the law. I married the law."

The words poured from her lips. "And perhaps I'm wrong, but they are more than likely very desperate at this point."

Jesse fiddled with a loose thread on the seam of his trousers.

Without speaking, he stood and crossed the room, stopping at the coatrack beside the door.

Fern stood, pleading, "Jesse, please don't leave."

Memaw grasped the arm of her chair. "Where are you going, son?"

He removed his gun belt from the coatrack and fastened it around his waist. The heavy pistol hung at his side. "The part for the well won't be here for at least another week. There's nothing for me to do here. I might as well pick up my badge from the sheriff and make sure no harm comes to you—and my wife." Jesse shrugged on his coat. "Fern, I want you here with Memaw. Don't go outside, stay away from the windows, and keep Bass with you at all times. Memaw, keep your shotgun loaded and get Papa's gun out and load it too."

"All right, son."

"I'm going to stay at our place tonight. I want to pick up my rifle so I'll be prepared in case they do show up. I'll go into town in the morning and warn Levi. If those men are looking for a lawman, his life is in danger too."

Jesse pushed through the screen door and let it slam shut behind him. Fern sank to her knees. Tears of deep regret fell from her eyes.

"Come to Memaw."

Fern laid her head on Memaw's lap.

"I'm so sorry, Memaw. What are we going to do?"

"Hush now, child. There's no need to be sorry." She stroked Fern's hair. "We've all made mistakes. . .me being the worst. What we can do is pray. God has taken care of many a problem worse than this. And you've got to believe He's still on His throne and He's still in control."

Fern closed her eyes and listened to the sweet, loving grandmother pray a great hedge of protection over their little family. The

Lord comforted her and washed away the overwhelming fear of losing all that had become so dear to her.

"Thank you, Memaw."

Thank You, Father God.

After a restless night, Jesse arrived in town with the morning sun and rode straight to the sheriff's office. Levi looked like a grumpy old man, holding his mug of coffee and staring over the top of the spectacles pinching the bridge of his nose.

"Morning, Sheriff." Jesse took a seat at the desk across from Levi.

"Jesse." The sheriff removed his glasses and laid them on the stack of papers he was poring over when Jesse entered the office. "What brings you to town?"

Leaning back in the chair, Jesse clasped his hands over his middle. "Well, Levi, I never would have guessed in a million years how interesting life would be marrying a schoolmarm."

"Is that right?" Levi chuckled. "You two having more trouble with the rig?"

"Shoot. I wish." Jesse shook his head. "I just found out Fern answered Memaw's marriage proposal to get away from Illinois because she was an eyewitness to a robbery—and murder. She even knew one of the men."

"What?" The sheriff's eyes grew wide, and his chin dipped low. "Did I hear you right?"

"Yep. They threatened to kill her and all her students if she went to the law." Jesse sat upright and scratched at a notch in the wooden desk. "And now she tells me her family back home told the criminals right where she lives and that she married a lawman."

"You're kidding me. Why would they do that?"

"Nope, not kidding, but it wasn't done in malice. Her aunt has senility and didn't know any better."

The sheriff rubbed his chin whiskers. "Mm, mm, mm. For all they know, I might be the lawman Fern married."

"The way my luck's going, they're probably already on their way here. That's why I came to warn you."

Levi looked at his empty jail cells. "What town did you say Fern came from?"

"Springfield. Why?"

"There was something I saw. . ." Levi thumbed through the stack of papers on his desk. "It struck me when I saw it because I recalled you telling me that Fern was from somewhere in Illinois." He stopped at one particular poster and pulled it out. "Here it is." He held it up for his friend to see.

Jesse reached out and took it from his hand. The soulless eyes of a murderer stared back at him.

REWARD—$2000 FOR THE CAPTURE OF TOM PARKS
AND HIS PARTNER, MARK STANLEY. WANTED DEAD OR
ALIVE BY THE STATE OF ILLINOIS FOR BANK ROBBERY IN
PAWNEE AND TAYLORVILLE AND FOR ROBBERY AND
MURDER IN SPRINGFIELD, ILLINOIS.

"Well, I'll be a—" He looked at the sheriff. "This has got to be them. Fern even said her friend's name was Mark. Do you think they might be headed this way?"

The sheriff glanced out the front window. "I've got a feeling they might be here already. A couple of men robbed the saloon, and I haven't been able to track them down."

Jesse nodded. "Yeah, that happened the last time I was in town."

"Could be them." Levi stood and adjusted his gun belt. He took the wanted poster from Jesse. "Let's go over to the saloon and see if anybody's seen this ugly mug."

Jesse followed Levi out the door. The streets were already bustling with morning activity. They walked toward the tavern, and Jesse kept watch for any sign of the face on the wanted poster.

"Mr. Stewart, wait up!"

Jesse stopped to see who called his name. "Hey, Levi, hold up a minute." The sheriff halted and turned.

The mailman who had previously given Jesse the ill-fated letter from Fern's cousin approached him from across the street. The tall, wiry man wearing the official uniform stopped and let out a deep breath. "Whew, glad I caught you."

"Can I help you?" Jesse lowered his eyebrows.

"Yes, I want to apologize to you. A couple of weeks back I gave you a letter thinking it was for Memaw Stewart, but—"

Jesse held up his hand. "No need to apologize. It eventually got to the right Mrs. Stewart."

"Well, good, but I've since found out that you've taken a wife, and I wanted to congratulate you." The mailman thrust his hand out to Jesse.

"Oh, well, thank you." He shook the overeager man's hand. "Um, if that's all, I need to be—"

A big smile spread across the postal worker's face like he deserved a cookie. "I want you to know I won't be making that mistake again. It's like I told those two strangers who stopped me and asked about your wife. It's Fern, right?"

Jesse tightened his grip on the man's hand. His tone turned grim. "What two strangers?"

A stricken look came over the mailman's face. "Why, I don't know who they were, but two men met me going into the post office this morning before sunup. I gave them directions to your place. I–I hope that was okay."

Jesse's face burned with rage. "Why would you do that?"

The man tried jerking his hand from Jesse's grip. "What? Did I do something wrong? I'm sorry, I didn't know any better!"

When Jesse released the mailman's hand, he took off down the road clutching his mailbag in one hand and his cap with the other.

The sheriff put his hand on his revolver. "Do you think it's them?"

"Of course I do. Who else could it be?"

"Where's Fern now?"

"She's at Memaw's."

"Then she's safe."

"For now. Unless that idiot mailman told them how to get to Memaw's house too."

Levi patted Jesse's shoulder. "Come on. Let's mount up and ride out to your place."

Jesse was way ahead of him. He wasn't about to let two hardened criminals rob him of the best thing that had ever happened to him.

❧ *Chapter 13* ❧

Jesse had never experienced such intense rage before. The idea of someone wanting to harm his wife lit a firestorm of righteous indignation he could not quench. And all because she was in the wrong place at the wrong time—saw something she shouldn't have seen. Fern didn't deserve any of this, and he would see to protecting her.

A stiff wind blew in his face as he rode from town. He tried praying, but his anger was a hindrance, blocking the words from coming to mind. It was up to Memaw and Fern to cover him in prayer. He slapped the reins, and his horse galloped faster. Levi kept up, riding close behind. Only one more hill to cross and they would arrive at his property.

Jesse passed the road leading directly to his ranch house and took a back way onto the property. If the two men were there, he didn't want to alert them to his and Levi's presence. He rode up to a pen behind the barn. Levi came up next to him.

"We'll go the rest of the way on foot," Jesse said, trying not to make any unnecessary noise as he climbed down from his saddle and pulled his rifle from the scabbard.

"Good idea," Levi answered. "Don't want them getting the jump on us."

Levi dismounted and removed his Winchester rifle. After Jesse tied their horses outside the pen, both men walked quietly around the side of the house.

The sound of heavy footsteps coming from inside his home stopped Jesse. He turned to the sheriff and raised a finger to his lips and then tapped his ear. They halted and crouched beneath a window and listened. The footfalls were heading away from them. What were they doing inside his home? He heard glass breaking. His lip curled into a snarl.

Jesse felt a hand squeezing his shoulder. "Stay calm," Levi whispered.

"What are you doing in there, Tom?"

Jesse clamped down on his weapon when the man hollered. The voice came from outside, somewhere in front of the house. No one answered.

Tom Parks was inside the house, tearing the place apart. Another man was out front, most likely keeping watch. It had to be Mark Stanley. Jesse crept closer, hoping to get a look at the man who had betrayed Fern. He stooped at the front corner of the house and stole a glance. His eyes narrowed to slits. There he was.

Levi tapped on Jesse's back, interrupting a string of vile thoughts passing through his mind. He turned to his friend, who pointed to a thick stand of bushes on the side yard. "Stay here. I'm going to make my way around to the other side," Levi whispered and started to move.

Both men froze when the front screen door was kicked open and slammed against the house. A bearded man holding a big knife stepped through the doorway. Seeing the antler handle knife he had made with Papa in the hands of the criminal, Jesse seethed with anger.

Tom Parks walked to the edge of the porch. "See anybody coming?" He repeatedly stabbed Jesse's knife into the wood railing.

"No." Mark answered from the hitching post where two road-weary horses drank from the water trough. "Come on, Tom. Let's get out of here. Texas is a big state, and there's plenty of places we can go where nobody will ever know who we are. Fern won't go to the law—she's too scared. You made sure of that with your threats, and besides, I don't want her getting hurt. You already killed one innocent man that I know of. You don't need any more blood on your hands."

"Shut up, boy!" The older man stared at the other as he sank the knife deep into the wooden rail. "You heard what that old woman said. Your friend Fern is married to a lawman."

Levi whispered to Jesse. "That one over by the horses must be Fern's friend, Mark Stanley."

"That's what I figured too. Sounds to me like he still cares about her."

Levi nodded and whispered back, "Yeah, I guess, but a real friend wouldn't help a murderer track you down to kill you."

"You're right about that." Jesse's temper flared at what Fern's so-called friend had done.

"The one on the porch is definitely Tom Parks. I recognize him from the wanted poster," the sheriff said.

"How you want to handle this?" Jesse asked, glad that Bass was with Fern at Memaw's place. He would have been right in the middle of everything trying to help his master.

Levi held up his hand. "I've got an idea. Just stay here and follow my lead. And don't hesitate to shoot if you have to."

"Hey, where are you going?" Jesse asked.

The sheriff went past him and crept swiftly along the ground toward the bushes. He stopped and laid his rifle down while unholstering his pistol.

Jesse hung back and waited. He removed his gun from his belt and watched for Levi to make his move, or give him a signal—whatever that might be. It didn't surprise him when his friend took action without any warning.

"Tom Parks!" Levi spoke the criminal's name with authority. Both men turned to the bushes and the sound of his voice.

Dang it, Levi. . .what are you doing?

"This is Sheriff Levi Woods. I've got six guns trained on you as we speak. Now, I need you and your partner to relieve yourself of your gun belts and step out into the open with your hands up."

Jesse watched the scene unfold from his vantage point at the corner of the house. The nervous younger man began raising his hands.

Tom Parks clamped a meaty fist around Jesse's knife and pulled it from the porch rail. "Put your hands down, fool," he yelled at Mark.

Mark Stanley did as his partner commanded and put a shaky hand on the handle of his holstered gun.

Tom hollered back at Levi. "And just what are you going to do if I don't?"

"Well, your wanted poster said dead or alive. So what do you think I'm gonna do?"

Parks drew his pistol. Two shots rang out, and a cloud of dirt exploded in front of the bushes where Levi was hiding. The sheriff yelped in pain. Jesse couldn't see anything through the spray of earth and leaves. Where was Levi?

"Six guns, huh? That's what I thought."

Jesse turned back as Parks aimed at the bushes. In one quick motion he raised his pistol and fired on Levi's attacker. Tom Parks yelled as he fell over backwards, his revolver flying from his hand.

"Mark Stanley, put your hands up," Levi hollered, his rifle trained on the younger man.

Mark's hands shot toward the sky. "Don't shoot!"

Upon hearing his friend's voice and seeing him standing, Jesse released the breath he'd been holding. He came out from where he'd been hiding.

"One move and you're a dead man, Stanley." Levi limped out from behind the bushes. Blood seeped through a slash in his dungarees. "Jesse, get his gun."

"You all right?" Jesse asked, his pistol aimed at his wife's childhood friend,

"Yeah, I'm fine. He just grazed me." Levi glanced down at his bloody thigh. "Hey, thanks for not hesitating to shoot back there."

Jesse shook his head. "Thanks for not getting yourself killed." He continued on toward Mark Stanley while Levi hobbled over to the porch where the downed criminal lay. Mark's raised arms trembled at his approach.

"How could someone as rotten as you have been friends with my Fern?" Jesse disarmed him, holstered his own weapon, and shoved Stanley's pistol down the back of his trousers. "And then you track her down for that murderer?" He nodded to the man's partner in crime.

Stanley said nothing. "Turn around," Jesse demanded. He jerked the man's arms behind his back. Stanley winced and hollered in pain as Jesse manhandled him, slapping the cuffs on his wrists. "You know, Mark Stanley, you are some kind of lowdown scoundrel."

Stanley hung his head in shame. "Look, I told Tom I didn't want Fern getting hurt!"

"I didn't say you could talk!" Jesse shoved him toward the porch where Levi knelt beside Tom Parks. Blood pooled around the downed man.

"Well? He gonna make it?" Jesse asked.

"Good shot. Went right through his shoulder." The sheriff looked up and shrugged. "Eh, he'll live."

Since Jesse had left the day before, Fern barely had an hour of sleep and only a slice of buttered bread to eat. As the afternoon sun began to fade into evening, she kept vigil on the sofa next to Memaw, waiting and praying. Bass, her constant companion and protector, lay at her feet. Between polishing her shotgun and dipping snuff, Jesse's sweet old grandmother kept herself busy, but Fern was too worried about her husband's welfare to concentrate on much of anything else.

Memaw lowered the polishing cloth to her lap. "You know, Fern, that dress pattern you started is folded up in the front bedroom. Why don't you go get it? It'll give you something to take your mind off things."

She put her hands together. "No, I'm afraid it will just make me more nervous."

Bass emitted a low growl.

Fern strained to listen. She heard hoofbeats coming up to the house. "Do you hear that?"

"Hear what?" Memaw replied.

Bass stood to all fours, ran to the door, and howled. Fern rushed to the front window and looked out, careful not to be seen.

Memaw tossed the cleaning rag onto the lamp table and stood—shotgun in hand. "Fern, don't you open that door!"

She ignored Memaw's demand and relayed what she saw. "It's Jesse. . .and Sheriff Levi. . .and two others." She rushed to the door.

With Memaw trailing close behind, Fern and Bass flew out the door to the porch. Bass barked wildly. Fern's handsome husband, riding atop his mare as proud as a peacock, gave her a smile and a wink. A horse, attached by a rope, trailed behind him. The rider's hands were behind his back. Her eyes grew wide, her palm covering her gaping mouth.

Mark Stanley. . .

She gasped upon seeing Levi, his leg covered in blood and a sash tied around his thigh. Another horse walked side by side with the sheriff's. The man atop the horse was handcuffed as well, his shirt also soaked with bloodstains, his right shoulder wrapped with strips of cloth.

Fern stared at the rider. She recognized the bloodshot eyes of the man who robbed the bank and killed the teller. Those same cruel eyes belonged to the man who threatened to kill her and her precious students. They were the eyes of a cold-blooded murderer.

Memaw appeared at Fern's side. "Levi Woods, what do you think you're doing bringing that riffraff up to my front door?"

Levi chuckled. "Your grandson wanted to show off his catch of the day." He rested one hand on the saddle horn. "What do you say, Fern? You know these two lowlifes?"

Fern nodded and walked toward the horse behind Jesse's. She

squeezed her hands into fists to ease the trembling and looked up at the man. Tears of anger and betrayal streamed down, burning her cheeks.

"How dare you, Mark Stanley. You were my friend." She turned to the criminal on the horse next to Levi and pointed at him. "And you! You murderer! You did this to him. He was a good, decent boy, and you turned him into a monster! I hope you hang for what you've done!"

Tom Parks snarled at her and spat. The disgusting wad landed at Fern's feet.

Levi reared back and elbowed Parks across his face.

The man's head swished to the side and blood sprayed from his nose.

Fern jumped back a step.

Jesse winced. "Hey, be careful, man. You almost got blood all over my wife's dress."

Levi grinned. "Sorry about that, Fern." He pulled up on the reins and his horse gave a loud snort. "All right, Jesse. Let's get these sorry losers back to town."

"And make sure you get in to see Doc about that leg," Memaw hollered.

Fern looked up at her handsome man, tears in her eyes. Parting her lips, she mouthed the words, *Thank you.*

❧ Chapter 14 ❧

The story of the capture and arrest of Tom Parks and Mark Stanley blazed across the front page of newspapers all over Texas and Illinois. Levi and Jesse were heralded as heroes, and the town of Beaumont treated them as such. The two criminals were locked up in Levi's jail, awaiting extradition back to Illinois to stand trial for robbery and murder.

With all the sordid drama behind her, Fern could finally get on with her life. She now had all the time in the world to spend concentrating on the wonderful man God had blessed her with.

A week later, with all the commotion finally dying down, Jesse installed the replacement rotary table, and the maiden well of Stewart Fisher Oil was up and running. Fern never dreamed a partnership in an oil company would be as fulfilling as educating young minds. Perhaps the draw wasn't so much the partnership as it was her handsome partner.

Fern and Jesse soon came to an agreement that they would move Fern's Aunt Matilda down to Texas. If, that is, they were still together at the completion of the well, be it an oil strike or a duster. Memaw even talked about the old woman staying at her place so Fern could go back to teaching if she decided to. But she and Jesse agreed they would cross that bridge when they came to it.

What little time she'd spent in Texas was long enough for Fern to realize what she felt in her heart. The schoolmarm from Springfield, Illinois, was head over heels in love with Jesse Stewart. Surely Jesse felt the same, even if he hadn't professed his love for her. She was ready to become his wife in every sense, but not until he told her he loved her.

Fern barely heard Memaw's buggy arrive at the worksite over the whirring of the engines and rushing water used to force the drill bit down the borehole. Her belly growled—it was dinnertime.

She looked over as Memaw pulled the reins, stopping her horse. Fern took a second glance. Who was that man sitting on the bench next to Jesse's grandmother?

Memaw raised a cupped hand beside her mouth and hollered, "Dinner's here!"

Fern smiled and wrinkled her nose at her overall-clad hero of a husband. She nodded toward the buggy. He looked, shrugged, and joined her as they stepped off the drilling platform together.

Closer to the wagon, Jesse stopped. "Hold up a minute."

Fern stopped. "Who is that man?" She waited as Jesse removed the heavy leather glove from his right hand and reached for her face. "What is it?"

He wiped something off the bridge of her nose and rubbed it on the leg of his overalls. "Just a dab of grease. You looked so cute, I thought about leaving it there."

"Oh Jesse." She smiled and swiped at his arm.

"And to answer your first question, that's ol' Burton Futter."

"What's he doing here? And why is Memaw wearing her Sunday bonnet?"

Jesse scratched his cheek. "Your guess is as good as mine."

"Anybody gonna help out this old woman over here?"

Jesse chuckled. "We're coming, Memaw."

Fern retrieved the old patchwork quilt from the wagon. Not knowing what to do next, she stood with her arms crossed over the bedspread and an awkward smile on her face. Thankfully, Jesse broke the silence.

"Afternoon, Memaw, Burton." He lifted a gray-and-blue-striped pottery urn from the wagon bed and considered the man sitting beside his grandmother. "I'm surprised to see you out in these parts."

"Yep."

At the man's utterance of the single-syllable word, Fern instantly remembered who he was.

"Fern, you remember Burton Futter don't you?" Memaw's tone sounded defensive.

"Yes, ma'am, I do." She turned to the old gentleman. "You were the one who drove me to Memaw's when I first arrived in town."

The old man looked down at Fern through his round spectacles and said, "Yep."

"I have to admit, I didn't recognize you without your long whiskers," she said, remembering the white beard that hung down to his lap.

Burton raised his funny pipe with the long stem to Fern and smiled. "Yep. Had a little accident and had to shear it off."

"Oh my," Fern replied and turned her gaze to Jesse, who again came to her rescue.

"Will you two be joining us for dinner?"

"No, no," Memaw said, waving off his question. "We just brought this out for the two of you. Burton has asked me to join him in town for supper."

Fern and Jesse exchanged glances. She noticed Memaw's cheeks were flushed.

"Oh, is that right?" Jesse said, slowly nodding his head.

"Yep."

It was time for Fern to take her leave and allow Jesse to handle the situation. Holding two corners of the quilt, she unfurled it with a pop of her wrists. The blanket spread open and floated to the ground where they usually ate dinner.

"Hey, Jesse," Burton said.

Fern giggled under her breath, amazed at how slow the old man spoke.

"Yeah, Burton?" Jesse picked up the plates, cups, and utensils, carried them to the quilt, and returned before Burton started speaking again.

"Now, you know. . .you need to fetch the rest of these vittles your memaw made for you and that pretty young wife of yours out the back of this here wagon."

"Yes, sir. I'm taking care of that right now. Fern."

She joined him at the wagon, and he handed her a basket filled with something that smelled delicious.

"Goodness, Memaw, what smells so good?"

Memaw waved off Fern's compliment. "All right, all right. I believe that's everything." She turned to Burton. "You ready?"

"Yep."

"Fern, Jesse, y'all have a nice dinner, and bring them dishes home this evening."

"Yes, ma'am," Fern replied.

Memaw flopped the reins against the horse's rump, and the wagon started to move.

"You two behave yourselves!" Jesse said.

Memaw's head snapped around. The look on her face would have scared the devil himself.

"I love you, Memaw!" Jesse hollered after her, grinning from ear to ear.

"I love you too, Memaw!" Fern added.

"Love you, Fern," she said before begrudgingly turning to her grandson. "And I guess I love you too, Jesse!"

Fern and Jesse waved as the founder of their marriage rolled away with her new beau.

"You hungry?"

Fern raised the basket for her husband to smell. "I'm starved."

Jesse sat beside Fern, who went to task removing goodies from the basket and placing them on the quilt. She found homemade yeast rolls Memaw had cut in half along with a dish of butter. There was a jar of dill pickles and a plate heaped with fresh sliced ham. For their dessert Memaw had packed fried peach pies.

"Mm, mm, mm. My mouth's watering." Jesse rubbed his hands together, ready to dig in. "Think I'll try this ham."

He reached for a slice, but Fern slapped his hand before he could pick it up. "Not before you say the blessing, you're not."

Jesse twisted his mouth to the side. "I thought Memaw had left."

Fern giggled and bowed her head after Jesse had.

"Father, we thank You for this meal and pray You bless the

hands of the precious woman that made it. . .even if she is going out on the town with that slow-talkin' Burton Futter."

"Jesse," Fern scolded. Her eyes remained closed as she waited for Jesse to continue.

"And, Lord, I pray for Your continued protection over Fern and me as we work together drilling this well."

Jesse stopped praying. Fern opened her eyes and saw him staring intently at the well.

"What's the matter?" Fern asked.

"Do you hear that rattling noise?"

She trained her ears to hear what he heard. "Just barely. Let's finish the prayer."

He bowed his head. "Lord, I thank You for sending Fern into my life, and I pray—"

Fern looked at her husband and then at the rig. The noise grew louder.

Jesse didn't take his eyes off of it and quickly ended grace. "In Jesus' name we pray. Amen."

When Fern opened her eyes, he was already getting up from the dinner quilt. "What's happening, Jesse?" Fear coated her words.

He jammed his fists into his waist and shook his head. "What in tarnation is wrong with the dern thing now?"

Fern stood to her feet in panic. "Stay back here, Jesse," she demanded. "I don't want you getting hurt again."

He glanced at her. "I need to go check on something. I think I know what it might be."

Fern inhaled just enough breath to scream, "Jesse, no!"

~ Chapter 15 ~

What started out as a soft rattling noise had turned into a wild clattering that shook the entire wooden platform and derrick. It sounded like the well was about to explode.

"Fern get back. Now!"

She refused to leave his side. Jesse shook off her tight grip on his arm and moved toward the well. Fern cautiously followed. The rattling became stronger and the clanking louder the closer they came to the platform.

"Please, Jesse, don't go any farther!" she begged.

A screeching sound like metal rubbing against metal halted their movement. "What was that?" Fern yelled.

Jesse looked down at her. His face changed in an instant. The concern faded away and his eyes sparkled with wonder. "Come on. We need to get back."

A rumbling like nothing she'd ever heard before shuddered the ground beneath her as they moved to a safer place. Fern buried her face in Jesse's chest.

He held her tight and whispered in her ear, "Wait for it."

What did he mean? Fern sucked in a deep breath and prayed she wasn't about to blow up along with Jesse and their oil rig. The deep rumble culminated in a geyser of oil rising up from the ground. She looked up just in time to see black crude gushing to the top of the hundred foot tall derrick and beyond.

Fern screamed with joyous abandon while Jesse squeezed her tight and lifted her off the ground, spinning her round and round.

"We did it, Fern!"

"Yes! We struck oil!"

In one quick motion, Jesse released her, bowed, and extended his hand. "May I have this dance, madam?"

Fern raised her hand to her chest. "Why yes, of course you may."

The couple danced together beneath the fountain of black gold raining down on them. The music that only she could hear was a song of love overflowing from her heart to his.

Jesse pulled her close and gazed into her eyes. She knew the time had come. Their lips pressed together and he kissed her—firmly and passionately beneath the flow of ebony drops of oil. The kiss ended with Fern feeling flushed and weak in the knees. Her eyes fluttered open to the man of her desire.

"I love you, Fern Stewart."

Her heart was full. He said those three magic words—and she knew he meant them.

"Oh Jesse, I love you too." He pulled her into another long kiss. Anticipation for the coming night sent shivers down her spine.

With all the commotion going on, neither of them noticed

Memaw had returned. "Jesse! Jesse!" she screamed, running toward them. "Are y'all all right?"

Hand in hand the couple stepped out of the geyser. Dirty black crude oil dripped from their smiling faces. Jesse released Fern's hand and rushed to his grandmother. "We did it, Memaw!"

Fern's eyes widened with glee when he scooped the old woman up in a bear hug, covering her in oil.

"Jesse!" Memaw screamed.

He released a hearty laugh and put her back on solid ground.

She looked down at her filthy dress and shook her head. "Yes, yes, you did it all right. Just look at my dress. How am I supposed to go to town looking like this?" She rubbed at the oily stains to no avail. Her face proclaimed annoyance—but a giddy happiness too.

Burton moseyed up and joined the celebration. "Congratulations, Jesse."

"Thank you, Burton." Jesse looked absolutely overjoyed as he shook the man's hand.

"Well, boy," Memaw said, "seems you've got the Midas touch just like your Papa Stewart before you. Everything he touched turned to gold, and now you've got the gift too."

"Don't you mean black gold, Memaw?" He placed his oily black hand on his grandmother's shoulder. He laughed when she gave his arm a swat.

"Would you stop that, boy? Just because you're gonna add another pile of cash to the family fortune don't mean we can waste good money on buying new clothes."

The smile on Fern's face faded. She bent her head to the side and stared at Memaw. "Family fortune. What are you talking about?"

Memaw chuckled and turned her eyes up to her grandson. "Well, I suppose it's time we told her the truth."

"What?" Burton slowly drew out the word. "You mean to tell me she don't know?"

Fern grew perturbed. "What don't I know?"

Memaw put her hand on Fern's oily arm, and with love in her eyes, she said, "Honey, you had no way of knowing, but you married the sole heir to the Stewart Lumber fortune."

Stewart Lumber. . .Stewart Lumber.

Fern rolled the name around in her mind until it dawned on her where she'd seen that name before. Of course. It had been stamped on most every shipment of lumber she'd ever seen passing through her hometown of Springfield.

Jesse. . .my Jesse is the Stewart Lumber heir?

She stared at Memaw in disbelief. "So that's why you didn't want Jesse marrying any of those local women. You wanted to find someone to love Jesse for who he is, not for how much he's worth."

"That's right, child. I wasn't gonna let them gold diggers get their claws into my grandson just because he has money. So I did a little praying and a little letter writing, and God sent you to us."

Fern turned to Jesse. "And you have so many abandoned projects on your land because you have more money than you know what to do with."

Jesse shook his head. "Now, that's not exactly true. There's a good reason why I. . ."

Fern tightened her lips and shook her finger at her husband. "Those days are over, mister. From now on, you and I are partners in the Stewart Fisher Oil Company. Period."

Memaw laughed and clapped her hands. "Yes!"

Jesse grimaced. "Memaw. . .you know good and well it was your idea not to tell Fern anything. Instead of gloating, why don't you tell my wife how those fields have fed Pastor Kenneth's family or about your idea to build a barn to store Papa's original sawmill equipment in?"

"Yep, that's right," Burton agreed.

"Aw, now you hush, boy. Let me have my moment," Memaw said. "I finally got you married off to a woman who really loves you, and you struck oil!"

After the laughter died down, Fern grasped her husband's hand. "Jesse, I know we've had a rocky start." Tears welled in her eyes and her voice cracked. "I've been holding back telling you this for a long time."

His loving eyes implored her. "What is it, Fern?"

"I want you to know that I love you with all my heart, and I truly feel that it was God's answer to Memaw's prayers that brought us together."

"I love you too, Fern. And I agree, God is definitely at the center of what we have together. He sure knew what He was doing when He brought you to me."

"Yep," Burton agreed. "Gotta trust the Lord."

"Yep." Fern looked up at her husband and giggled. "And just like the Lord, Memaw *always* knows best!"

"Yep." Jesse kissed the tip of Fern's oil-stained nose.

"All right, you two, there'll be plenty of time for that later," Memaw said. "It's time to get back to work. We've got a well that needs to be capped before we run out of oil!"

Fern looked into Jesse's eyes and smiled.

"You heard the woman. There's work to be done." He chuckled and winked at her.

As Jesse dove back into his work, Fern pondered all that had taken place to bring them to where they were now. What an odd chain of events the Lord had orchestrated to match a schoolmarm from Illinois with a Texas millionaire. Their partnership in the Stewart Fisher Oil Company turned into a relationship they didn't even know they needed. And together they struck. . .a gusher of love!

Annette O'Hare is an award-winning author living in South Texas with Dan, her husband of thirty-four years. Her love for the history and heritage of her home state shines through in her writing. She is a longtime member of American Christian Fiction Writers, Christian Author Network, and current president of ACFW The Woodlands, Texas Chapter. Annette's desire is to reveal God's love to her readers and hopefully give them a laugh or two. The O'Hares enjoy fishing on the Texas Gulf Coast with family and loving on their rescue fur babies, Max, Jay, and Tris, and a Russian Tortoise named Frankie!